Chameleons

An Untold World War II Story

Marcus A. Nannini

BLACK ROSE
writing™

The final approval for this literary material is granted by the author.

First printing

This is a work of fiction. Names, characters, businesses, places, events and incidents are either the products of the author's imagination or used in a fictitious manner. Any resemblance to actual persons, living or dead, or actual events is purely coincidental.

ISBN: 978-1-61296-889-6
PUBLISHED BY BLACK ROSE WRITING
www.blackrosewriting.com

Printed in the United States of America
Suggested retail price $19.95

Chameleons is printed in Adobe Garamond Pro

A special thank-you to my editors:

Major Robert Bauman (USAF-retired) and
Susanne C. Johnson, M.A.

"Every morning we are born again. What we do today is what matters most. Nothing ever exists entirely alone; everything is in relation to everything else. Every human being is the author of his own health or disease. If you are facing in the right direction, all you need to do is keep on walking."
Gautama Buddha

Chameleons

Based on Actual Events

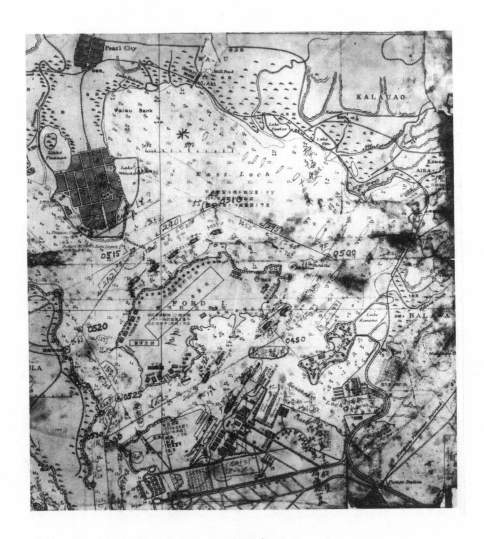

Pearl Harbor

CHAPTER ONE

PEARL HARBOR, OAHU
DECEMBER 7, 1941

Imperial Japanese Navy midget submarine, the *I-16-tou*, hides in the muddy bottom of Pearl Harbor. A few hundred yards ahead seven first-line battleships comprising the nucleus of the United States' power in the Pacific rest quietly at anchor.

The midget sub's commander, Lieutenant, junior grade, Masaharu Yokoyama is stripped to his waist with sweat dripping from every pore of his body in the one-hundred-twenty-five-degree temperature. He sleeps restlessly. The iron hull upon which he is leaning bleeds drops of water. A few feet away the sub's engineer, Sadamu Kamita, stripped to his loin cloth, his forehead resting on a control panel, also sleeps. The only sound in the dimly lighted iron tube is the low humming of the ventilation system.

Yokoyama is considered to be among the brightest of the first class of Imperial Japanese Navy midget submarine commanders. As a result, he has been rewarded the honor of being released from his mother submarine closer to the entrance of Pearl Harbor than the remaining four midget submarines. He is a quick thinker and charismatic. One of his superiors said he has an angelic smile that can immediately disarm otherwise confrontational situations. He is also a first-rate student and has studied every detail of the proposed Pearl Harbor attack along with the geographical features of Pearl Harbor and Oahu. He has memorized the names and contact information of various Japanese sympathizers upon whom he may rely in the event of the need to scuttle his sub.

Their sleep is abruptly ended by the shock waves of the first aerial torpedo and bomb strikes. The surprise Japanese air attack on Pearl Harbor has begun. Yokoyama stands, wipes the sweat from his eyes and shouts:

"Kamita! Quickly, make turns for five knots and bring us to periscope depth."

Kamita, a few years older than Yokoyama and considered one of the finest of the midget sub engineers, picks up his head as he feels the vibrations of the explosions coming through the hull. Before the orders are even spoken he begins to discharge ballast and re-start the electric motor. He does not even glance at Yokoyama as he firmly replies:

"Aye, Sir, five knots, periscope depth."

It's not long when Kamita calls out, "Periscope depth!"

Yokoyama grabs the handles of the periscope as it slides into place and presses his forehead against the moist rubber edges of the viewer. Moving from left to right he takes in the length of battleship row then lowers the periscope and turns towards Kamita.

"Prepare for firing torpedoes!"

"Aye, torpedoes are ready for firing." Kamita's tone is calm and collected.

"The *West Virginia* and *Oklahoma* are directly in our path. I will confirm our firing solution and strike the *West Virginia*, just aft of amidships. We will target the *Oklahoma* second. The effect of firing the first torpedo should place the port bow of the *Oklahoma* nearly dead-center for torpedo two." Yokoyama closes his eyes momentarily as he envisions the path of the second torpedo.

"Sir, if the Emperor could know of our situation he would most certainly be smiling," says Kamita.

Yokoyama does not respond as he has returned to the newly raised periscope. He makes a final calculation of his firing solution, lowers the periscope and turns to Kamita.

"Fire one!"

As Kamita lets the one-thousand-pound torpedo loose he replies, "Firing torpedo one!"

The little submarine violently lurches fore and aft in response to the sudden discharge of the torpedo and corresponding weight loss. After many months of practice they both know firing their second torpedo at this time will veer left of the original target, but in this event, unlike the practice runs, the battleship *Oklahoma* lies in its path. Precious moments pass as the submarine begins to stabilize.

"Raising periscope!" As the periscope slides into position Yokoyama checks the firing solution for his second target, the *Oklahoma* now slightly listing to port. As the periscope lowers he shouts:

"Fire two!"

"Firing torpedo two!" Kamita, no longer able to disguise his excitement, shouts his reply.

Again, the little sub lurches even more violently than upon firing the first torpedo as it is now two thousand pounds lighter. Kamita loses his grip and bangs his head against a control panel, opening a gouge above his right eye. He grabs his uniform shirt hanging nearby and presses it against the wound.

Yokoyama stares at his stop-watch as he times the first torpedo.

"Our venom is in the water. Now we wait." Yokoyama's voice is just above a whisper.

The seconds pass and frowning, he continues: "Our first torpedo malfunctioned! It certainly could not have missed as I witnessed the propeller trail steering directly at the *West Virginia*."

"It cannot be," cries Kamita, his voice full of anguish.

Yokoyama continues to stare at the stop-watch. He raises his free hand and calls out:

"Now, Kamita, it should strike now!"

No sooner are the words spoken than the little sub shudders as the concussion of torpedo number two pushes them fore and aft, up then down, as if they are on a roller coaster. As soon as the sub settles, Yokoyama decides it's time to assess their success.

"Raising periscope." Yokoyama's voice reveals only modest excitement.

As he presses his forehead into the viewer he witnesses the result of his torpedo strike. A thirty-eight-foot hole straight through the protective torpedo belt of the *Oklahoma* has been opened in her port side dramatically increasing the doomed ship's list to port. He observes little white bodies. Some are scrambling to crawl along the hull of the capsizing ship to the relative safety of the ship's bottom while others are jumping into the water. In a matter of moments he is viewing one of the once-mighty *Oklahoma's* propellers jutting from the oil-covered surface of the harbor.

Without saying a word, he lowers the periscope. Both men say nothing as they contemplate the fate of the sailors aboard the battleship they just sunk.

CHAPTER TWO

KAILUA, OAHU
PRESENT DAY

It's a typically beautiful April morning on the Oahu coast. Surfers are riding waves while snorkelers are bobbing on the ocean's blue-green surface, just off a hidden sandbar. A group of young children are busy making sand castles on a pristine beach that stretches out in the form of an arched curve for over a mile. Only a few yards away from the beach, just beyond a stately row of Royal palm trees is the backyard of the locally popular "Auntie" Lee. She is well known for her senbei rice crackers, white pineapple plants and her many papaya, lemon and tropical fruit trees.

Auntie Lee is a diminutive lady, standing only about five feet tall and weighs, maybe, one hundred ten pounds if she's holding her purse and wearing slippers. This morning her shining grey hair is pulled back into a braid which extends to her ankles. If she didn't tuck a piece of the braid into her dress pocket her hair would trail onto the ground behind her.

Auntie Lee is perched on her lanai watching a crew of two well-tanned workers excavating her new back-yard pool. She's also keeping a wary eye on a gathering of neighborhood children lingering near the edge of her yard. The children are watching the construction while also eyeing the tantalizingly ripe papayas hanging just over their heads.

Akoni, a slender, curly-haired Hawaiian standing deep in the excavation is guiding Danny as he operates the back-hoe. Suddenly Akoni throws both his arms up in the air.

"Stop! Stop! Danny, hold it up, brah, there's somethin' down dere!" Danny turns off the tractor and peers around the upright shovel as he strains to see what's the problem.

Akoni's pointing at the ground. "Lookit dat! Lookit dat!" Akoni's hard hat flies off his head as he excitedly motions for Danny to join him.

Akoni's actions also draw the children closer to the excavation, as the papayas no longer seem as important to them. Auntie Lee stands, but remains in the cool shade of the lanai.

Danny, a huge, dark skinned Hawaiian slowly climbs out of the tractor and works his way into the excavation. By the time he reaches Akoni he's down on his knees digging with his gloved hands. At first Danny can't quite see what he's digging, but then he spots the unmistakable outline of a pistol gripped in the bony hands of a partially unearthed skeleton.

"Don't touch dat gun Akoni! It might be loaded." Akoni stops in mid-motion as Danny plops down alongside him and lays a hand on Akoni's shoulder.

"Think anyone's seen da gun?" Danny whispers. They both look over at the children, one of whom is taking photos with her cell phone. Danny shakes his head as he realizes there's no way to keep this secret.

"Akoni, da boss's going ta blow a valve when he hears 'bout dis. We're way behind schedule." Danny pauses as he glances at the kids. "Guess we got no choice. Have ta call in da cops. Crap!" No doubt in Danny's way of thinking the preferred course of action would be to quietly dispose of their discovery and continue excavating.

Danny casts a scarily angry look at the kids, causing them to run off in the direction of the beach. The two men pick their way out of the excavation, leaving their finding intact, and casually walk to the lanai where Auntie Lee is impatiently waiting to learn what's going on.

As they approach, she calls out to them: "Would you like some nice senbei and iced tea?" In Auntie Lee's opinion a chance to put together refreshments for any manner of guest is never to be missed.

Danny and Akoni look at each other and shrug their shoulders. Danny answers, "Danks Auntie, dat sounds like da bomb!"

"Oh, and Auntie, can we borrow your phone? We gotta call da boss." Danny appears sheepish as he explains, "We can't bring our cell phones to work anymore 'cause he says they could make us have an accident. He says da two of us are accidents waitin' ta happen, so no cell phones!"

Auntie Lee is already walking back into her house, but pauses just long enough to respond; "No worries Danny, I shall get you my phone. It cannot cause you to have an accident." She quickly disappears and soon emerges with a plate of freshly made senbei crackers and two glasses of iced tea which she places on the lanai table. Without saying a word she flips around and scoots back into

11

the house. Moments later she reappears and hands him her cordless phone, which resembles a World War II walkie-talkie.

"I don't understand the problem. What did you find out there?"

He gives the phone a quizzical once over. "Sorry Auntie, dere's a skeleton in da pool and dere's a gun too so we need ta call da cops."

"Oh my! Who would do that?" Auntie Lee frowns, shakes her head back and forth and slowly wanders towards the excavation while Danny dials their boss.

"Listen boss, dis is Danny, me and Akoni just dug up a skeleton wid a gun. 'Fraid we gotta stop 'til the cops get it outta dere."

Akoni can hear the entire conversation as he gulps down a handful of senbei. He longingly glances at the excavation as he considers returning for the gun and perhaps selling it at Colonel Nat's surplus store.

"No Boss, we didn't call da cops yet. I'm calling you!" He sounds flustered as his boss is screaming so loudly even Akoni can hear him.

"Yeah boss, I'll call dem now. You want we should wait for 'em?" Obviously upset, he shakes his head back and forth as he disconnects the phone. After a brief pause his frustration turns to happiness with the realization they have the rest of the day off.

"Akoni! Good news! We got da day off! Just gotta call da cops and den we can get outta here real fast."

Akoni greets the news with a huge smile. "Danny, let's cut out ta my boat and see what we can catch for dinnah tonight! Dere's plenty of 'ono fishing time left!"

"What? You're stopping work?" A very stern looking Auntie Lee, standing about half way between the excavation and the lanai is staring at them, hands on her hips. "You know my grandson is graduating high school next month and I need this pool finished! Can't you just dig around that skeleton?" The harsh tone of her voice slightly unsettles the two men.

"Sorry Auntie." Danny feels a bit guilty, but knows there's nothing he can do. "Boss says we can't work till da cops get dat body outta dere. Can't argue with da boss! So we goin' fishin'. We'll bring you some ahi or 'ono filets when we get back. But right now, we got ta do what da boss says we got ta do." Danny shrugs his shoulders. Akoni, who is busy shoveling another senbei into his mouth, can only shake his head in agreement while Danny dutifully reports the incident to the police before returning the phone to a very dejected Auntie Lee.

Phone in hand she watches as they slowly disappear around the side of the house. Now alone, she returns to her kitchen quietly mumbling minor curse words to herself in Japanese.

•   •   •   •   •

Two hours later the police have not yet arrived and curiosity is finally getting the best of her. She's been sitting on her lanai the entire time. Patiently sitting, waiting and fretting.

"That's it! I'm going to see what's causing such a commotion!"

She hurriedly rises from her chair and looks around the yard to be certain nobody is watching. The neighborhood children are long gone, along with some of her papayas. Confident she's alone she quickly walks to the edge of the excavation and navigates her way down the gently sloping work-site to where Danny has placed an orange stake for the police. She notices the head and chest of a skeleton poking through the dirt and spots the pistol, but her attention quickly focuses on a fancy handle that is just barely poking through the ground several inches below the pistol.

Without giving it a thought she rushes the final few feet between her and the skeleton. Despite her long dress and without thinking about the likely red clay stain which will result, she drops to her knees. She begins digging around the handle and soon the blade of a heavily tarnished sword is exposed. Though in poor condition, it reminds her of a sword her grandfather once hung on the wall of his personal Shinto altar.

"I am going to take this into the house and clean it up!" Auntie Lee pauses as she realizes she might have been overheard. Looking around the yard, she confirms she's still alone.

"Nobody here, so nobody to know. Besides, I don't want this sacred sword to get ruined when they come for the body." She verbally rationalizes her theft, takes a final look around before she carefully pulls the sword from the earth and covers it with her dress. She hastily picks her way out of the excavation, scoots across her backyard and bursts into the kitchen.

She's looking around for a good place to clean the sword when the doorbell rings. Alarmed, she drops the sword on the floor and runs to the front door to find two detectives waiting, each holding his badge up for her examination. She partially opens the door and slips into the opening between the door and the frame.

"Good afternoon, Ma'am. I'm Detective Kane," he points toward a second detective, "and this is my partner Ooha. Are you Leilani Yamada?" Ooha, who is always quick to smile, grins widely.

Kane is tall, very well-tanned, has a muscular build and short, dark hair. He is very neatly dressed in a solid, dark blue shirt and black trousers and Auntie Lee finds him to be good looking. She greets Kane with a big smile, but then she looks over at Ooha and frowns. His skin is deeply tanned and his strong physique is clearly visible through his floral-print Hawaiian shirt. She looks over his black pants and decides they are too tight. He is native Hawaiian and sports longish, black hair. He reminds her too much of one of her grandsons who spends all his time surfing rather than attending school and decides she will talk to Kane and angles her body so as to be looking at him and not at Ooha.

"I have been waiting for you young man! There is a nasty skeleton in my swimming pool and I need it out of there right away!" Her voice softens as she notices Kane's pained look. "I know it is not your fault and, please, I prefer to be called Auntie."

The detectives glance at each other as they wonder how a skeleton winds up in the swimming pool of an elderly woman.

"Auntie, why do you think someone would throw a skeleton into your pool?" Kane's voice is calm and assuring.

Auntie Lee bursts into laughter. The sudden outburst from such a diminutive lady takes the detectives by surprise.

"No, no! The pool is not finished." Auntie Lee is laughing so hard she needs to pause and regain her breath. The two detectives quickly glance at each other with the thought that perhaps this little lady is not dealing with a full deck.

"No, the pool is not anywhere close to being finished." She fights back the continuing urge to laugh. "They are only digging the hole. That is where they found the skeleton. It is still in the ground!" She pauses a moment to think, stares at Kane and points her right index finger directly at his face.

"I need my pool finished very soon!" She again pauses, for emphasis. "My favorite grandson is graduating high school next month and I am hosting a big celebration for him, so please, go remove it right away!"

Kane and Ooha shake their heads in acknowledgement. Both of them are a bit relieved as they realize they are dealing with a potential crime scene. Of late, it seems to them that nearly half their calls have proven to be situations that were totally blown out of proportion, if not outright fabrications.

"Okay Auntie, that makes more sense. We'll do what we can to get your pool back under construction." Kane motions to Ooha, "Let's walk around back and take a look."

Auntie Lee breathes a sigh of relief that they didn't ask to cut through her home. A dirt-encrusted sword lying on the kitchen floor would be difficult to explain.

"If you detectives do not mind, I can just wait inside. The work crew marked the spot with a big orange stake. You can't miss it." She abruptly closes the door behind her, rushes through the house and over to the kitchen window to watch. Kane and Ooha look at each other and shrug their shoulders.

"Kind of hasty, don't you think?

"Guess she has something better to do," responds Ooha.

"Ooha, go grab the evidence kit and let's check it out." Kane begins to walk down the front steps, but stops in his tracks as Ooha says to him, jokingly:

"Sure Kimo, I'll grab it."

"Damn Ooha, you know I hate my Hawaiian name. It reminds me of the Lone Ranger."

"Why do you think I call you Kimo? I like to see some emotion from you! You're always too stiff!" Ooha laughs out loud, jogs over to the car, opens the trunk and pulls out a large, black metal case. Kane desperately tries to come up with a smart comeback. As usual, he can't think of one, so he does his best to feign a serious face as Ooha returns with the evidence kit.

"Okay then, do you think we can get on with it now?" Kane's failure to hold back a smile gives him away as Ooha laughs again. With smiles on both their faces they beeline for the backyard. In a few moments the yard lies before them and they instinctively pause to take in the majesty of the ocean view opening before them.

"Wow, Ooha, I never get over how beautiful the Pacific is. What a view!" Kane shades his eyes from the Sun as he stops and takes a long look. On the far side of the yard a row of Royal palm trees sway majestically in the ocean breeze.

"Yeah, it's all good Kimo. What a place for a house!"

Ooha turns his attention from the adjacent beach to the pool excavation where he easily spots a tall, orange stake. "That must be the spot, Kimo."

"Well, let's get on with it," Kane replies.

Both detectives carefully pick their way to the orange stake where they discover only a skull and the partial upper body of the skeleton are visible. Kane edges around the left side of the skeletal remains while Ooha approaches from the right.

Ooha carefully sets the evidence kit nearby, opens it and pulls out two pair of latex gloves. He tosses a pair to Kane who catches them without really looking as he's staring at the skeleton.

"Pull out a brush, Ooha. Let's see what we have peeking out at us there." Kane points to a spot about a foot below the skull where the earth has taken the straight-edged shape of a box. Ooha squints in the mid-day sun as he follows Kane's finger.

"Kimo, that looks like it might be some kind of a box." He removes a brush from the kit, edges as close as he dares to the exposed bones of the chest and meticulously begins to brush away the dirt.

"Take it slow," says Kane as he continues to fixate on the box. He's oblivious to a pistol which is firmly planted in the skeleton's right hand as they are consumed with carefully picking away the dirt and clay concealing the balance of the box. In a matter of moments they find themselves face-to-face with a smallish, rusted metal box.

"What's that painted on the top?" Kane asks.

Kneeling, Ooha carefully pulls the box from the grave and rests it on his knee. A raised, stamped emblem with bits of red and white paint still clinging to it is partially visible.

"It looks to be some sort of emblem," says Ooha who looks puzzled as he lightly brushes away the last stubborn bits of dirt and clay. The faded red and white stripes of the Rising Sun insignia, most often associated with the old Imperial Japanese Navy of World War II, jumps out at them. A series of barely visible painted characters, a combination of numbers and Japanese lettering, are centered just below the emblem.

"Stop right there Ooha!" Kane sits back on his knees with a look on his face that is a combination of complete surprise and deep thought. Ooha pulls out a towel from his kit and wipes the sweat from his forehead.

"Let's have a look at that pistol." Kane points to the gun in the skeleton's hand, half covered in dirt. Ooha retrieves an expandable steel poker from their kit and picks up the gun by running the poker into the barrel. He gives the gun a twist, releasing it from the boney hand and, a little too casually, swings it over to Kane.

"There you go. Anything special?" Ooha asks.

Kane is rightfully upset at Ooha for the manner he handled what could be a loaded gun. He carefully takes it off the poker and gives it a once over before gently returning it to its original position.

"Listen, Ooha." Kane's low and serious tone of voice captures his attention. "We are way overloaded with cases right now and don't need this kind of extra aggravation. This box looks to me to be something out of World War II and this pistol is most definitely not anything we see on the streets. I'm not sure, but I might have seen something like it in a display case at Colonel Nat's surplus store." Kane pauses a moment as he stares at the faint red and white insignia on the top of the box.

"That insignia," Kane points towards the box, "tells me this box may well be related to the Imperial Japanese Navy. At least that's my opinion, and obviously this lettering is not English."

"What are you saying?" Ooha quickly stands and looks down, first at Kane, then the box, then at the pistol, and finally back to Kane.

"What I'm saying is simple. We can call the Shore Patrol over at Pearl and once they're here we can pass this matter off to them and get on with business as usual." Kane is obviously pleased with himself as he has a grin on his face. "Clearly between this odd-looking pistol and the box we can justify calling in the Navy. In a worst case scenario the Navy eventually bounces it back to us, but only after they do all the real work."

Ooha's expression changes from a frown to a wide grin.

"That's da bomb, Kimo. I'm all for it." Ooha repacks the evidence kit while softly whistling a melodic Hawaiian tune. As a thought occurs, he stops abruptly, smiles even more broadly and looks up at Kane.

"Nobody will blame us for calling in the Navy and we can close the file! You're a genius." Ooha slams and locks the lid, snaps off his gloves and sprightly stands, looking to Kane for the next order.

"I'm going back to the car to put the call in." Kane pauses as he suddenly realizes something is missing.

"Wait a minute. What happened to the guys who were working here? I don't see anyone around?" Kane squints as he scans the beach.

"Good point, Kimo. You put the call in and I'll go ask Auntie about them." Kane returns to the car while Ooha takes the evidence kit and carefully makes his way out of the excavation and over to Auntie Lee's lanai.

Auntie Lee's been watching from her kitchen window and the moment she notices Ooha walking towards the house, she hides the sword in her pantry, pours a glass of lemonade and rushes out to meet him. The last thing she wants is for one of the detectives to be in her kitchen.

"Detective, Sir, I have a nice cold glass of fresh squeezed lemonade for you.

I picked the lemons this morning from my own trees." She motions towards her lemon trees with her free hand.

"Why thanks, Auntie." Ooha sports his most charming smile as he accepts the lemonade. "But Auntie, what happened to the work crew?"

"Oh," she's clearly relieved to learn Ooha apparently has no intention of entering her house, "they told me their boss ordered them to leave and not come back until the skeleton is taken away by the police. I'm pretty sure they were going fishing. They go fishing almost every day after they work because they have a boat and they even brought me some very nice ahi just yesterday." Auntie Lee smiles at the memory of the delicious dinner she made for herself and two of her granddaughters.

Ooha takes a long drink. "Wow, Auntie, this is da bomb!" Ooha pauses to take another gulp before continuing. "Could you give me the name and phone number of your contractor please? We might need to question the work crew."

Reaching into one of the over-sized pockets of her dress, Auntie Lee pulls out a business card for 'Swim Time Pools' and offers it to Ooha.

"Hhmm, 'Swim Time Pools.' I've heard of them, pretty big outfit." Ooha finishes the lemonade and hands the empty glass back to her.

"Thanks Auntie. We're goin' to stay here until the Navy shows up so if you need anything, we'll be in the car."

"The Navy? Why the Navy? You promised to take that skeleton away! *Now* how long must I wait? I need that pool finished!" Auntie Lee stares directly into Ooha's eyes, as if he were a little boy caught doing something wrong. Ooha has seen that look far too many times in his life and immediately goes on the defensive.

"Sorry Auntie, but we don't have jurisdiction here. Kimo, I mean Detective Kane, says this skeleton has something to do with the Imperial Japanese Navy of World War II so naturally it's a U. S. Navy matter, not a local matter." Ooha pauses to gauge her reaction, but his hopes she would understand are dashed when he sees she has crossed her arms and is glaring at him. If she had a yardstick in her hands, he'd probably run away.

"Please understand Auntie, I'm sure the Navy will get that skeleton out of there and your pool work can continue in a day or two, at most. In fact, I'd bet the Navy gets it out of there tonight!"

"I see." Auntie Lee continues to stare down Ooha. "So long as they are finished by tomorrow! I must have my pool!" She firmly places both her hands on her hips for emphasis.

"I know they'll do their best. After all, it's the Navy!" He quickly turns and wastes no time jogging back to the car.

Auntie Lee returns to her kitchen, moves a chair over to the window and begins a vigil of waiting for the United States Navy. Glancing at the sword, just visible inside her pantry, she whispers aloud to herself. "You are going to require a great deal of cleaning!"

CHAPTER THREE
"SOMETHING OF PARTICULAR INTEREST"

It's a little after eight in the evening, the sun has set and Auntie Lee is busy in the kitchen as she feverishly puts together a considerable platter of assorted homemade cookies. Two of her twelve-year-old granddaughters, Kanae and Alanna, are thoroughly absorbed in their roles as kitchen assistants.

The staccato sound of a diesel generator penetrates every room in her home, carries across the neighborhood and drifts out over the Pacific. Her backyard is basked in a sea of white light, as if one hundred full moons were overhead. Armed Shore Patrol guards are at each corner of her property while a pair of Navy technicians are busy filling plastic evidence bags. Auntie Lee is very excited at having so many guests she can feed.

Regardless of the pool construction delay, attending to so many people fills her with a renewed sense of purpose. For the moment she's feeling happy and satisfied, especially since she's been assured the Navy people will be gone by sunrise.

Lieutenant, junior grade, Stephanie Ferguson is in command of the excavation. She's wearing a standard-issue working uniform which appears to be a camouflage of dark and light blue and grey blotches. Her sleeves are rolled up in a manner that allows an immediate transition to long sleeves and she's wearing a dark blue mock turtle neck. Finishing the look, her eight-point matching camouflage cap is pulled low on her forehead, just above her eyebrows. People routinely make the mistake of assuming her "jg" status translates into "inexperienced." Not the case here.

Ferguson's father is one of the first Black Americans to serve as chief of a major West Coast police force. She spent two years following in his footsteps after ignoring her mom's advice to go into education as she did; a tenured professor. One particularly boring day Ferguson came to the realization she had not seen much of the USA, let alone the world.

Being a few inches taller than the average American female and with long, sun-streaked brown hair, she has something of a commanding presence. On the advice of her paternal aunt, the widow of a Navy captain, she decided to visit her Navy recruiting station to discuss her options and she soon found herself ushered into the office of the regional commander. With an MS from Stanford she was well received and promptly enlisted.

Ferguson quickly established herself as a person who does not miss any detail and leaves no loose ends. For the first time in her life the color of her skin, a product of her mixed parentage, no longer matters; in fact nobody blinks an eye. All that matters is her performance and she is thriving.

Lieutenant Commander Christopher Pastwa has the lead on this matter and is particularly appreciative of Ferguson's thoroughness. Pastwa is a fan of Ferguson's father who would often lecture her: "When there are no loose ends, there are few surprises…and in my profession, surprises are seldom a good thing."

Ferguson's busy cataloging evidence as young Alanna walks up to her holding a small plate of cookies in one hand and a glass of iced lemonade in the other. Alanna's long, shiny black hair is tied back in a pony tail that reaches her thighs. She's wearing a light pink t-shirt with advertising from a local restaurant emblazoned across the front and cut-off blue jeans. At twelve years old, she's one of the tallest in her class and spends hours watching every manner of forensic evidence television show she can find. Ferguson is fascinating to her for several reasons; she's female, an officer, is tall and working in the same field young Alanna aspires to eventually join.

"Ma'am, I brought you some homemade cookies," she pauses, unsure of how Ferguson will respond. "And I'm kind of wondering if I could watch you work for a little while." Alanna offers Ferguson her best "begging" face.

Ferguson instantly recognizes her sincerity and replies with a smile: "Sure, I'd love to take a short break and you're very welcome to stay around. Just don't touch anything without asking first, ok?" Ferguson smiles even more broadly as she notices Alanna is now sporting a very large grin.

"Thank you, and I promise I won't touch a thing." Alanna immediately assumes a position alongside Ferguson, practically staring at her. Ferguson is amused and politely eats a couple of cookies while extending the plate to Alanna who takes a few herself.

"My name's Alanna." Alanna offers Ferguson her right hand, which Ferguson accepts. "I'm Stephanie, Alanna. Great to have you on board." Ferguson throws Alanna a short salute which Alanna smartly returns, still sporting a huge grin. Ferguson thinks to herself a smile that large must hurt.

Alanna cleans off the plate and idly holds it to her side as she intently watches Ferguson's every move. Ferguson finds Alanna's presence to be a nice break in the routine and thinks to herself: "Who knows? Maybe this little girl will one day be in the Navy." Besides, she reasons, the overwhelming majority of the work here is completed, so Ferguson allows herself to indulge the aspiring young girl.

"Alanna! Alanna!"

Ferguson and Alanna look across the yard and spot her cousin, Kanae, calling to her from the lanai.

"Alanna, your mom's here, you have to go now!"

Even from a distance Ferguson recognizes Kanae is sporting a very self-satisfied grin. The two granddaughters are seemingly always in a race with one another for they are the same age and in the same class, which has effectively created a very real competition between them. Nobody in the family pushes them, but they are under the self-created impression each must outdo the other. The fact Alanna must leave while Kanae can stay has made Kanae a happy camper as now she has Auntie all to herself.

Alanna appears quite downcast. "Sorry Lieutenant, I have to go."

Ferguson notices the disappointment and rips off a blank evidence catalog sheet, signs her name and hands it to her.

"Here, take this as a souvenir. It was a pleasure to work with you."

Alanna takes the sheet and begins to run towards the house. She pauses halfway, turns around and says, "Thanks again Lieutenant!" Alanna then quickly disappears into the house. Ferguson glances at her watch and notices it's already a little after ten pm. As is her habit, she quietly voices her thoughts: "Where the hell is Commander Pastwa?" She is slightly startled as she hears the familiar voice of Lieutenant Commander Christopher Pastwa behind her.

"Hello Lieutenant Ferguson. Tell me, what do you have here?" She quickly whirls around to find Lieutenant Commander Pastwa, who loves to make his appearances, is only a few feet away.

Pastwa is second generation Navy, about six foot two inches tall, not too closely cropped dark hair, clean shaven and is looking magnificent in his white uniform as he is fresh from an event back at Pearl. Everyone is keenly aware he is the right hand man of Rear Admiral Roman Reardon. Consequently, Ferguson was surprised to find him assigned to lead this investigation as only matters of national security or particularly unique circumstances ever merit the attention of Reardon, so Pastwa's presence has genuinely piqued her curiosity.

Ferguson quickly regains her composure. "I'm surprised to see you on such a relatively routine matter Commander. This just doesn't look to be so important as to bring you all the way out to Kailua."

"Well, seems someone whispered in the Admiral's ear there might be something of particular interest with regards to this skeleton. Perhaps, and this is a long shot, but perhaps it involves events dating back to World War II." Pastwa pauses to allow Ferguson time to absorb the information. "So tell me, Lieutenant, *is* there something here of particular interest?"

Ferguson reaches down with her gloved hands and pulls up a rusty black box. Holding the box with both hands she presents it for his scrutiny. "Sir, this is certainly not a run of the mill find, not to mention the other items here."

Pastwa slips on a pair of gloves, takes the box from her and gives it a good once-over.

"Well, this insignia could be *IJN* and that *would* be of interest." He turns the box over a couple of times and gently shakes it, causing the contents to rattle.

"It's locked, Sir and rusted up tight."

Pastwa returns the box to Ferguson. "What else do you have?"

"There are fragments of clothing, but more interesting is this." Ferguson bends down, picks up a sealed baggie and offers it to Pastwa. "This pistol definitely appears to be Japanese and quite old at that. In fact, I've never seen anything like it, not even in my dad's gun collection. And by the way, it's loaded!"

Pastwa carefully accepts the baggie and stares at the pistol. He turns to gaze toward the ocean for a few moments as he creates a little time for some thought before returning the pistol to Ferguson. Since he was a kid playing on the beach in front of his family home on Hanalei Bay he has found the sight of the ocean to be relaxing for he believes he can better focus when he stares out to sea. Realizing Ferguson is patiently waiting, he turns and looks her in the eyes.

"Lieutenant, I've seen this type of hand gun before in the *Smithsonian* and unless I'm seriously mistaken it's a 'Nambu, semi-automatic.' I think it was favored by officers in the old Imperial Japanese Navy, but don't quote me on that, at least not just yet. This makes me even more curious about what's inside that box." Pastwa pauses as he looks around the site and notices Auntie Lee watching them as she stands on her backyard lanai.

Pastwa points over to her. "Is that the owner?"

"Yes Sir, that's Auntie Lee and she's quite concerned her pool construction is going to be delayed. She's telling anyone who comes within earshot she must have it ready for her grandson's high school graduation next month."

Ferguson pauses a moment. "Sir, we're just about finished. In fact, I should be out of here within the next hour. Maybe you'd like to speak with her and appease her fears?"

"I'll do that, but first I want you to ship everything over to Lieutenant Karen Yamura back at Pearl, tonight. I gave her a heads up so she'll be in her lab early tomorrow. Oh, I almost forgot, any word on the crew that dug this up?"

"Yes, Commander, we tracked them down and I understand they were a bit shook up when the Coast Guard pulled them over." Laughing, Ferguson continues, "We have their statements and they'll be on your desk by morning. Nothing unusual there. They basically cut out of here to go fishing as fast as they could."

"Good job, Lieutenant. As usual, you have everything wrapped up water-tight. We all admire that trait and you can be sure the right people have taken notice. I also want you to know you didn't draw this assignment by mere chance."

"Thank you Commander." They exchange quick salutes as Pastwa turns and walks over to Auntie Lee while Ferguson returns to the task of cataloguing the evidence.

Pastwa cannot help but notice Auntie Lee's expression and recognizes she's very concerned. He immediately likes her and is pleased he will be giving her some good news. "Good evening, ma'am, I'm Lieutenant Commander Chris Pastwa and believe me when I say I am truly sorry for all this activity. I know it must be very disrupting, but I assure you we *will* be packing up and leaving within the next hour or so."

"Oh thank you! Thank you!" Her facial expression instantly blooms from deep worry to unadulterated happiness. "You know my oldest grandson is graduating high school in a few weeks and I am having a big party for him. That is why I am putting in the pool."

She quickly reaches over to a nearby table and picks up a small dish filled to overflowing with senbei rice crackers and offers them to Pastwa. "Please try some of my senbei. I just made them this afternoon."

"Why thank you." Smiling, he slips a cracker into his mouth. "My goodness, this is great. Better than any I've ever had!

"I can put some in a bag for you to take home." Auntie Lee is about to turn and rush into the house when Pastwa stops her.

"No need Auntie. I think it best if you save them for your pool workers tomorrow. You know they should be back here first thing in the morning."

"Oh my, that *is* great news!" She exclaims. "I think I better get into the kitchen now. I need to be ready for tomorrow so forgive me, I must get busy, and thank you Sir! Have a good night." She wheels around and scurries into the house while Pastwa, a smile on his face, turns to make a final survey of the scene.

Ferguson is busy directing a pair of investigators as they carry an evidence bag containing the skeleton to a van parked near the excavation site. Over at the generator a sailor is getting ready to begin the process of shutting down the lighting. All in all, Pastwa is feeling satisfied the situation is under control. Glancing at his watch, he notices it's nearly eleven pm.

He motions for Ferguson to join him. "Listen, Steph," his voice is barely above a whisper, "don't speak with anyone about what you found here until I have clearance from Reardon. No need to stir up outside interest. If this stuff really dates back as far as World War II there will be a lot of folks wondering how the hell it wound up in this backyard. Until I can get the loose ends from my perspective all tied up, I strongly prefer this matter stay totally under the radar, understood?"

"Of course, there are no rookies here. You can be sure I'll brief my crew properly so consider it a closed issue."

"I'll leave you to finish up. I need to be at the base for an early start tomorrow." Pastwa pauses for a moment. "Listen, if you come across anything else, or if you need any assistance, call me. Really, I mean anything at all. You have my cell number, right?"

"Yes I do and you'll be the first call I make should I need anything."

"Good night," says Pastwa.

"Good night Sir."

Pastwa quickly disappears towards the front of the house while Ferguson stops and stares at the now empty grave site.

"I have to wonder how this little guy wound up buried way out here." Ferguson catches herself talking out loud and looks around to assure herself nobody is within earshot. Though alone, a slight red tint of embarrassment tones her cheeks.

CHAPTER FOUR
"A PANDORA'S BOX"

Pastwa is sitting behind his expansive, cluttered desk as he stares towards the early sunrise-lighted Pearl Harbor. He's on the phone with his boss, Rear Admiral Roman Reardon.

"Yes Admiral, I'm going over to Lieutenant Yamura's office in a few minutes."

Pastwa continues to patiently listen, but finds it necessary to pull the phone a few inches away from his ear, for the longer Reardon speaks, the louder his voice becomes, a trait peculiar to him and to which Pastwa has become accustomed. "Sir, I'll phone you as soon as I learn anything." Pastwa continues listening. "Yes. I'm going right now. Yes Sir, consider it done!"

"Whew," Pastwa says out loud as he hangs up the phone. He walks to his outer office where his aide, Petty Officer First Class Mike Clarke is sitting at his desk. As usual at this time of day Clarke's eating an over-sized, chocolate covered, fried buttermilk donut and reading a Honolulu daily newspaper. Pastwa stops and stares at him, waiting for an acknowledgment. Clarke, however, continues reading the paper totally oblivious to the fact his boss is standing about four feet away. Finally, Pastwa can't take it anymore.

"Clarke! Damnit! We're heading over to Lieutenant Yamura's right now! Drop the damn donut and grab my file!"

Clarke practically falls out of his chair as he almost drops the donut while jumping to attention. "File, Sir? Which file is that?" Clarke is temporarily confused and flustered as his eyes desperately scan his desk in search of the requested file.

Mike Clarke has been assigned to Pastwa for nearly three years and knows him pretty well. Clarke is slightly pudgy and Pastwa enjoys teasing him that he never misses a meal or a snack. Clarke generally cannot put up a defense to such joking as he makes no bones about the fact he loves to eat. The camouflage pattern of his working uniform is something he appreciates for he is not particularly neat when it comes to eating. If it were not for his high metabolism rate and daily work-outs he likely would have eaten himself out of the navy years ago.

He has grown to genuinely like and admire Pastwa and makes it a point to never let him down. Right now, however, Clarke's in a bit of a panic because he's drawing a blank on the file Pastwa's seeking. In fact he feels as if his head is suddenly cramped up. Pastwa recognizes the confused look on Clarke's face and decides to help him out.

"The Kailua John Doe file from yesterday. I told you to set it up for me about an hour and a half ago." Realizing what Pastwa is talking about he relaxes a bit. "Of course, Sir. It's right here. We're all set." Clarke points to a green file on the top of his desk.

"Fine, now ditch the donut, grab the file and let's get going. Admiral Reardon's made this a priority matter and you know what that means!" Pastwa hurries out the door. Clarke shoves the donut into his mouth, grabs the file and rushes to catch up.

As they walk between the various buildings on the Pearl Harbor Navy Base, Pastwa brings Clarke up to date. "Seems this body they dug up yesterday out in Kailua might be a Japanese sailor because there was a rusted Imperial Japanese Navy officer's pistol in its hands along with a rather mysterious metal box. And to top it all off, Reardon has a hunch it has something to do with the attack on Pearl Harbor back in '41."

"Sir, why would the Admiral think it could possibly have anything to do with the Pearl Harbor raid? Especially, as I know my history, they never recovered the bodies of any Japanese sailors, save for the shipmate of the midget submariner they discovered sleeping on a beach. All the other bodies were those of aviators." Clarke can barely get the words out as he chomps on his donut.

"Listen, I've known Admiral Reardon long enough to respect the fact that he has an absolutely uncanny ability to sense something is amiss before anyone else even has a clue. When it comes to a sixth sense, the Admiral can be outright scary. In fact, sometimes he's beyond scary so I don't ask questions, I just press forward." Pastwa pauses as he sifts through his thoughts.

"I have to admit there was something about that pistol, not to mention the metal box they dug up with it." Pastwa stops for a few moments, Clarke at his side. "Clarke, the whole thing just feels wrong. I don't know why, but I have a feeling we're looking at big trouble here."

With the Forensics building coming into view they pick up their pace.

"I'm really anxious to see what Karen has to say. She's holding off opening that box until we get there."

"Yes Sir." Clarke holds back a smile as he's aware Pastwa and Lieutenant Karen Yamura have a social relationship. He's known Pastwa since before then and is aware his demeanor has noticeably softened. Pastwa is much less on edge these days which usually makes life easier on Clarke.

"I looked at the field notes this morning from Lieutenant Ferguson. It's more than a little odd to find an old Imperial Japanese Navy sidearm like that one. Anyone who had an inkling of what kind of pistol it was would have sold the thing or put it on display in their den. They wouldn't have buried it without damned good reason."

Clarke is growing slightly red in the face as he matches Pastwa's increasingly brisk pace and is relieved as they finally reach their destination. They quickly climb the front stairs to the building and steer straight for Yamura's first floor office. Once inside, they discover the inner door to her lab is closed and Pastwa politely knocks on the door.

"Lieutenant Yamura, its Commander Pastwa and I have Clarke with me. Can we come in?" Both men pause until they hear Yamura respond. "Yes, of course, glad you're here. I've been waiting for you."

They enter and find Yamura's wearing over-sized protective goggles and a black rubber smock over her working uniform. She has twisted her body to face them as she sits on a tall stool alongside her workbench, her hands protected by a pair of black rubberized gloves. A lighted magnifying glass, mounted on a heavy metal base hovers over the heavily rusted metal box sitting before her.

Lieutenant Karen Yamura is, by any standard, a remarkable looking Japanese/Hawaiian with long, jet-black hair. She's about five foot, six inches tall and has a small scar just below her left eye from a run-in with a dog when she was young. The scar adds additional depth to her persona while also serving to make her appear more approachable. She possesses the unique ability to raise half of just her right eyebrow, enabling her to quickly turn a provocative look into a questioning stare so fast as to make a person's head spin. Her dark brown eyes have an intensity which are a reflection of her dogged determination. Clarke usually feels a bit intimidated in her presence while Pastwa finds himself wishing they were off duty.

Pastwa quickly walks over. "Well, Lieutenant, what do you have for me so far? Admiral Reardon's already been on the horn twice this morning."

Without affording Yamura the chance to respond, Pastwa calls out:

"Clarke!"

He turns around and finds Clarke is standing close behind him. Slightly taken aback, he quickly composes himself. "Oh, there you are. I want you to take a few photos of this box before we open it up." He pauses as he realizes Yamura most certainly has taken plenty of photographs and covers himself by rationalizing. "I need to have a back-up set, so let's be doubly redundant on every aspect of this case."

Pastwa glances at Yamura and realizes he'd cut her off, one of his bad habits. She is, however, patiently standing by. She knows he has a bad habit of interrupting and is aware he is cognizant of it, and has been working on it; so far, with limited success.

"Well Commander, I'm ready to open this mysterious black box." Yamura holds the box up with both hands, looks it over and returns it to the exam table with a slight thud, causing a soft metallic rattle from within. "It appears to me as if this little bugger's been buried for a very long time. Most of the corrosion is quite significant making it likely moisture has leached inside so I do have my doubts about the condition of the contents. And, as for how long this has been buried," she pauses and points to the box, "this looks to have been buried for a very long period of time indeed, easily dating back to World War II days."

Pastwa momentarily stares at the box, glances at Clarke and turns to Yamura.

"Okay Karen, go ahead and pry it open. Let's see what this little package holds for us." Pastwa and Clarke put on goggles and gloves while taking up positions on either side of her.

Yamura, utilizing a mini crow-bar, gets just enough of the crow-bar's slanted edge under the lid so as she twists the bar the lid quickly pops open with a rusty clang.

"Open sesame you little Pandora's Box!" Clarke's attempt at humor causes Pastwa to cast him a scolding glance. Yamura doesn't even notice as she's focused on the contents, now also drawing the attention of Pastwa and Clarke.

Newly revealed are a pair of watches, a locket, a stop watch, a compass and a rectangular shaped object resembling a small book which is wrapped in an oil cloth type of material.

"Sir, would you like me to remove them or would you prefer the honor?" Yamura smiles as she speaks.

"You can have the honor." He glances at Clarke. "Take photos as we go." Clarke pulls out his camera and begins snapping away.

"Gentlemen, let's see what we have here." Yamura is mesmerized as she decides what to examine first.

"I think we'll begin by taking a look at these watches." One at a time she retrieves the pocket watches and carefully lays each of them onto separate glass dishes. "I can tell you they did not stop at the same time, which infers there was not a sudden, dramatic trauma involved here." She takes her time examining each one before continuing. "Well, sorry to say they don't present any obvious clues as to ownership. There are no inscriptions, but they are definitely of Japanese origin." She returns her attention to the box.

"Here's a compass." She holds it up for inspection. "Definitely Japanese and it still works." She places the compass onto another glass dish.

"This is interesting. It's a stop watch." She lifts the stopwatch by its corroded chain and holds it about the height of her eyes. "Looks pretty beat up and the lens is cracked." She turns it over and focuses on the back of the case. "Wait a minute. I can make out some inscriptions on the case."

She places the stopwatch under the lighted magnifying lamp for a better view. "This inscription states it's a 'Type One Navy, Number Two Nine Six.' There's even a movement serial number on it."

Yamura glances at Pastwa. "You know, depending upon what kind of records survived the war, assuming this does predate the war, we might be able to trace this to the original owner. In any event, it could yield some useful information."

Pastwa absorbs her comment, briefly looks at the stopwatch again and responds. "I assume you are referring to World War II, so why don't you put that on Lieutenant Ferguson's to-do list? There appears to be a lot going on here and I fear time may become of the essence, so all the more reason to divvy up the work."

Yamura replies, "Yes, I am referring to World War II." She picks up a small, heavily tarnished locket, briefly examines it and places it into another glass dish. As it touches the dish, it pops open and what appear to be finger nail clippings and a lock of hair spill out. "This is amazing. After all these years, still intact. No inscriptions, but I will run tests on these and who knows, maybe something will come of it. It would be nice if the DNA matches the skeleton as it would make for one less mystery." She pauses, the furrows in her forehead deepening. "I find it strange this would be here. If it belonged to a Japanese sailor he would have shipped the locket home to his family for them to honor in the event he perished in a pending battle."

"You're right about that, but let's keep moving as we're not likely to learn the answer to that question anytime soon, if ever," says Pastwa.

Yamura continues, "This last item seems to be wrapped in some type of protective oil cloth." Yamura lays it on the table and carefully pulls the folds of oil cloth away revealing a small and very much worn leather-bound book. All three of them stare at it in silence as they realize the cover is embossed with the still visible lettering, "*I-16.*"

"Does that say *I-16*?" Clarke asks the obvious.

Pastwa takes a magnifying lens from the bench and examines the print. "No doubt in my mind. I can make out *I-16* easily enough, but it looks as if there had been a bit more to it than that. The embossing is too worn to read, but there are definitely letters after *I-16*." He glances at Yamura. "Maybe you can run some tests and pull up the missing letters?"

"Of course! No problem." She writes a note to herself on the matter.

Pastwa takes a little time to examine the cover with the magnifying lens before he sets it on the counter, a little too hard. This draws a severe look from Yamura, a look he chooses to ignore.

"I think we should risk the pages disintegrating and proceed to open this. What do you think?" Pastwa looks over to Yamura for her opinion.

"I agree. Whatever type of cloth this is wrapped in seems to have done a respectable job of preserving the contents."

Yamura pauses, looks carefully at the cover and continues, "Let me see if I can't just pull this open without tearing it." Using two pairs of very long tweezers, one in each hand, she grips the top and bottom of the cover and slowly pulls it open, revealing the first page. The ink is faded and a little water stained, but remains reasonably legible and there is no mistaking the fact the entire page is hand-written in Japanese.

Pastwa, Clarke and Yamura instinctively pull back from the bench at the sight of the Japanese hand writing. "Reardon's right, there's more to this than we thought. Karen, you read Japanese, can you decipher any of this?"

Yamura stares at the writing for a minute then carefully turns a couple of pages, glancing over each page briefly.

After a few minutes of examination she turns to Pastwa. "The paper is in remarkably good condition." She pauses as she further considers the problem. "This is a little more formal style of Japanese writing than I'm accustomed to, but certainly well within my abilities. I'll need at least the rest of the day to translate all of this. You know, it's not as if I can casually flip through the pages." She pauses again as she stares at the open first page. "If you have some time to spare I can take a look at a few of the passages and maybe get a handle on what we're dealing with."

Pastwa shakes his head in the affirmative as he finds himself mesmerized by the Japanese script.

She examines the opening paragraph of the first page while Pastwa and Clarke remove their goggles and wait for her to translate the faded characters. After a few minutes she stops reading and looks over to Pastwa. "Chris, you won't believe it, but this is probably a ship's logbook. My best course of action would be to dictate a complete translation first, then type it all up for you and Reardon."

"A ship's log? But what ship? Does it give a name? Is it the *I-16*?" Pastwa's questions are rapid fire, leaving Yamura to decide how to answer.

Clarke resumes snapping photographs. "Clarke, I think that's enough for now. I need to concentrate please," says Yamura.

"Take all the time you need." Pastwa motions for Clarke to pull back from the counter and as he does so Yamura returns her attention to the first page.

"This page seems to be laying the groundwork for a logbook being written by a '*M. Yokoyama*,' who identifies himself as the skipper of a new type of secret submarine weapon. It also mentions his engineer went by the name of '*Kamita*.'"

Yamura decides to carefully open a page in the middle of the log, looks it over for a minute and continues. "I'm absolutely certain this is a ship's log! The author made entries every day, sometimes multiple entries in a day, always taking care to note the time. Further, all the geographic locations, so far anyway, are in Japan. There is a particularly interesting passage that discusses training for a secret mission. This passage," she points to the logbook, "is about exercises they are conducting at a secret base located within the Inland Sea of Japan. The log, I'm pretty sure, is from a ship called the *I-16-tou*, not the *I-16*. I'm not really positive of the terminology here as it's a little confusing. For example, in one paragraph he refers to the ship as a submarine, in another he refers to it as a tube."

"Well, isn't a submarine pretty much like a tube in basic design?" Pastwa suggests.

"What kind of a ship had a number like that?" Clarke asks. Pastwa is quick to respond.

"Not one of ours! This type of ship identification was used by the Japanese on their large, fleet submarines."

Pastwa pauses as he strains to remember his World War II history. "I think the additional designation, 'tou,' had something to do with midget submarines. I may have some books back in my office that can shed a little light on it; and I know a good website for everything there is to know about the old Imperial Japanese Navy." Pastwa, his mind racing, pauses as he tries to make sense of what they have discovered.

"*I-16* was a long range submarine, not some experimental or secret sub." Pastwa stops as he realizes the scope of the potential problem is suddenly expanding along with the number of loose ends. He glances at the various objects Yamura has neatly lined up on the work bench, then turns to face her.

"Let's regroup and reorganize." He turns to face Clarke. "Make me a set of the pertinent photos from the dig site as well as the photos you took here. Print them on glossy paper and make certain they're in color and leave them loose, not bound, but organized. The Admiral prefers to spread photos across his desk."

He pauses again as he looks at Clarke to make sure he understands his instructions. "Put them all into a folder, label each photo and tell nobody what you are working on; and don't pass off any of this assignment to anyone else because as of right now this is Top Secret, Understood?"

"Roger that! I'm on it." Clarke, camera in hand, almost runs out the door.

Pastwa quickly turns to face Yamura. "Listen Karen, just how up to par are you on your Japanese? Reardon's going to need to know what this says, probably before you can even finish reading it, let alone print up the translation. Patience is not a virtue with him. You know his motto: 'There is no profit in delay.' Do you think we need to go outside and get you some translation help?"

Yamura shakes her head to indicate the negative. "I can read this pretty well, Chris. The writing *is* a bit overly formal in style, but I can handle it. After all, it was my *grandfather* who first taught me to read and write Japanese."

Yamura pauses as she carefully turns another page. "I'll have this ready for you by late morning, tomorrow. Do you mind if I ask Lieutenant Ferguson to examine the skeleton, the hair clippings and run some dating tests so we can save time? Maybe have her look at the pistol and watches to see what she can make of them?"

"Good idea." Pastwa gives her a big smile while also thinking that maybe they'll have time for themselves later tonight. "I'll give her a call and ask her to come over right away," says Pastwa.

"No worries, Chris. I've already started tests on the box. I'll also ask Ferguson to make a preliminary determination of probable cause of death and should we need her for more, she can handle it. We don't want too many people involved at this stage."

"One last thing, Karen." Pastwa stops as he realizes he almost missed something. "Make that more than one. First, what of the clothing found with the skeleton? I know it's not dated yet, but can you make anything of it at all?"

Yamura walks over to a nearby table where two plastic bags contain some very beat up looking rags, if you can describe a few shreds of cloth as rags. "These are in really bad condition. I think they are, perhaps, two separate types of clothing so I have separated them into, roughly, two sets for now. One material may be a little different than the other, but they're in such bad shape I don't know."

"A second issue is about these Yokoyama and Kamita characters. You say Yokoyama is the author? So tell me, is he still writing when the log finishes, and if so, does he mention anything of Kamita?"

"Chris, I'll get those answers for you and I will be as definitive as possible. Count on me." Yamura flashes a smile.

Karen, I know I can count on you, and I know I'm seeking answers before you can reasonably be expected to have them. I'm just anticipating what Reardon's going to be asking me later today and I don't want to give him any information that could prove wrong, so take your time. I'm also going to request he assign you and Ferguson to me and relieve both of you of all other duties for the duration of this investigation. As of now you should consider yourself on this investigation full time."

"That will make my life a great deal easier," says Yamura, "and I will make the translation of this log my first priority, if that's okay with you."

"Of course, and with a little luck Ferguson will have something concrete on that skeleton for us this afternoon. Is there anything else you need right now?"

"Yes, how many copies of this log do you want me to compile?"

"Good point." Pastwa thinks about it for a few seconds before answering.

"Two, exactly two. I'll give one copy to Reardon and we'll keep one for ourselves. Remember to mark it 'TOP SECRET-EYES ONLY.' Please number them as 'One of Two' and 'Two of Two.'" Pastwa pauses, looks over at Karen and fights back the desire to take her in his arms and give her a long embrace.

"Sorry, but this means you'll have to do your own typing and copying."

"No problem, Chris. Anything else?"

"Not that I can think of. You can get back to work, and really excellent work at that!" Pastwa pauses again to make certain he's not overlooking anything. "Karen, I'll touch base with you after Ferguson reports in with her findings. Right now there are just too many loose ends so we need to tighten this up quickly. I have a strong hunch time is not going to prove to be on our side."

Pastwa turns and quickly walks out of the office.

Yamura returns to her examination of the first page of the log. "Hmm. What secrets are you waiting for me to discover?" she whispers aloud.

CHAPTER FIVE
SHOT IN THE BACK

A few hours later Pastwa finds himself in the pristine lab of Lieutenant, junior grade, Stephanie Ferguson. She's wearing goggles, latex gloves and a black rubber smock to cover her working uniform. The skeleton is lying face down on an examination table and a single, expended bullet lies in a glass Petri dish on an adjacent table.

"So, Stephanie, what can you tell me about our boney friend? Pastwa asks.

Ferguson pulls up a stool, takes a seat and slips the goggles to the top of her forehead, revealing red lines in her temples from the elastic grips. She glances at the skeleton a moment and angles the stool so she can more easily face Pastwa. Her hair is pulled back and braided, the natural wave of her hair fighting at the tension of the braiding.

"Well Sir, *he* was about five foot, two inches tall and, based on my computer analysis, I'm quite confident he's of Japanese descent. As per your orders I have designated all my lab tests as 'Extremely Urgent and Top Secret' which should speed up the testing and none of my test samples refer to the Kailua skeleton in any way."

She reaches over and picks up the glass Petri dish containing the bullet.

"I pulled this rifle slug out of his back. From the looks of it somebody tried to pry it out of him, most likely while he was still alive." She hands the dish to Pastwa, who holds it close to his face as he examines it.

"And what of this; what can you tell me about it?"

Ferguson stands and, using tweezers, removes the bullet from the dish before placing it under a nearby magnification lamp for Pastwa to examine. Pastwa leans forward for a better look.

"See? You can clearly tell where someone tried to pry it loose. Notice the small scrapes on the bottom and the sides? There are similar markings on the bones."

Pastwa shakes his head in agreement.

"This man was shot in the back by someone using an old M1 Garand rifle, a model we started using in the 1930's." She returns the bullet to the dish and sets it aside.

"So, in theory Stephanie, this man could've been shot in the back by, for the sake of argument, an Army sentry. It was certainly the correct type of gun for the anticipated time period."

"Anticipated time period?" The tone of Ferguson's voice matches the quizzical look on her face.

"1941." Pastwa's response is met by silence as they both quietly mull over the facts for several long moments.

"Okay Lieutenant. Good work, as usual."

Ferguson smiles. "Thank you Sir. What do you want next?"

"Stephanie, I've asked Admiral Reardon to assign you to Lt. Yamura for the duration of the investigation, if not longer. This matter is absolutely Top Secret and, at least for the near future, needs to stay this way. Don't talk about this investigation to anyone outside of Lt. Yamura, Clarke, myself or the Admiral, and certainly don't give anyone a reason to nose around into your testing either."

Pastwa gazes out the window beyond several swaying palm trees and over to the harbor itself as he takes a few moments to consider the situation.

"Stephanie, I know you're not a medical doctor, but do you think this guy could have lived if he'd been properly treated?"

Ferguson considers the question for a few moments before responding. "Sir, the human body can do a lot of things when the adrenalin's pumping. He may have been running when he was shot and the excitement of the moment allowed him to keep going and escape pursuit. That could explain the attempt to remove the bullet and his unlikely burial place." She pauses a moment before continuing.

"In my estimation his death had to be kept under wraps or, being Japanese, they would most certainly have cremated him. However, if this was around the time of Pearl Harbor and he was shot for being where he wasn't supposed to be, that might offer an explanation as to why he was buried rather than cremated. You see, a cremation would have drawn some attention and attention is exactly what Yokoyama and Kamita needed to avoid, assuming this body is actually one of them." There being so many elements for her to consider she finds it necessary to again pause for a few moments.

"Whether he could have survived with proper care is beyond the scope of what I can do. Based on the bullet's location near the spinal column and the fact it appears someone attempted to remove it, I think it's quite safe to assume he was not immediately killed and someone apparently was of the opinion his life might be saved."

"Thanks Lieutenant, that's the scenario I was pretty much imagining." Pastwa picks up his cap as he prepares to leave.

"Please call over to Lt. Yamura and confirm you've been formally assigned to assist her. She's expecting your call at some point, regardless. And remember, never hesitate to call me no matter how miniscule you think the matter might be. I have a lot of loose ends to tie off so if you get so much as a funny feeling over something, *call* me. I'm a believer in intuition and advise you to never ignore your intuition as the price to be paid might prove disproportionately severe."

"Yes Sir, I'll call Lieutenant Yamura right away and thanks for the advice."

Pastwa quickly strides out the door, a man with a mystery to solve and an Admiral breathing down his neck.

It's about a two city block walk from Ferguson's office to his own building. Pastwa prefers to take walks when he's thinking matters over and the distance is perfect for the way his mind works. When he was a kid he would take long bicycle rides and allow his thoughts to wander. It was his own way of meditating. When his bike gave way to a car, he would take long drives. But when he's on the base, he prefers to walk. Upon his return he finds Clarke eating a chocolate covered donut while juggling some photographs. Clarke doesn't immediately notice him enter. Startled, he drops a handful of photographs onto the desk and floor.

"Clarke, how many times have I told you not to keep food on your desk? Look at the mess!" Pastwa pauses as he surveys the disarray that is Clarke's desk and softens his tone. "Kindly put a call into Lieutenant Yamura for me and ask her if she has time to stop over."

"Now, Sir?

"Well, I think now is better than after you finish that donut," Pastwa points his right index finger in the direction of a donut lying on top of the desk. "Yes, now please."

Pastwa walks into his office, hangs his cap on the coat rack behind his door, sits at his desk and twirls around in his seat to stare across the harbor. His thoughts are racing to a period of time more than seven decades ago as he ponders the ramifications of what they know so far. About half an hour passes when he's interrupted by a knock on the door.

"Lieutenant Yamura is here Sir."

Smiling, Pastwa stands, ready to greet her. "Please come in Lieutenant."

Yamura walks in, closes the door behind her, removes her cap and holds it under her left arm.

"Make yourself comfortable. I need to run something past you." Pastwa takes a seat behind his desk.

She takes a seat across from Pastwa, places her cap on the empty chair to her right, drops her briefcase beside her, crosses her legs and allows her arms to settle on each armrest. Pastwa cannot help but notice just how incredibly appealing she is. He loves intelligent women and knows he's hard pressed to match her as she's smart as hell and is also an amazing athlete. He pulls himself together and continues.

"Karen, I'd like, actually, I rather much *need* your opinion."

Yamura appears mildly flattered. "Of course, Chris, anything I can do to help out."

"There are elements within the academic community here in the islands supporting a theory some of the midget submariners from the Pearl Harbor attack probably survived. Following the Pearl Harbor raid, and given the general confusion that existed at the time, there is a legitimate school of thought that as many as four surviving midget submariners could have melded into the Japanese/Hawaiian population. Of course, there was never any hard proof offered. But what if this skeleton is a plant, some manner of a hoax perpetrated to try and prove such a melding-into-the-population theory?" Pastwa knows he's grasping at a convenient straw, but needs to hear Yamura's opinion.

"A hoax? But why? What would be the point?" Yamura sounds as puzzled as she appears, her right eyebrow bending into an inquisitive furrow while her left eyebrow remains perfectly straight.

"Karen, I'm only speculating, but the burial could be used as a misguided attempt to prove the midget submariners' survival theory. It would also make the Navy look silly because it insists the only midget submariner who didn't die is the one we captured and certainly no midget sub penetrated the harbor that day either." Pastwa stands and momentarily stares towards the harbor before turning to face Yamura.

"We caught Prisoner of War Number One sleeping on a beach following the attack. We captured his submarine and found the body of his engineer floating nearby." Pastwa, clearly concerned, looks Yamura directly in the eyes.

"What if, *just what if* someone buried this guy, say, within the last twenty years or so, hoping he would eventually be dug up and create a fuss?"

"Well, if that's the case, they must have done this prior to the emergence of DNA testing so it would've been longer ago than twenty years. Otherwise there would be no point. From my research I know Auntie Lee has lived in that home for more than forty five years and I doubt someone could have buried anything in her yard without her taking notice. From what Lieutenant Ferguson tells me of Auntie Lee, she's one of the last people imaginable who would be up to pulling off a secret burial."

Pastwa returns to his chair. "Just a thought Karen. Guess I'm fearing the worst, the worst case of course being this really is one of the midget submariners and, as I like to say, when you find one of something it is likely there are more of the same around, somewhere, somehow. Nature is not big on creating one-offs, you know."

"Well then Chris," she raises her right eyebrow halfway, "you are *not* going to like what I have transcribed so far." Yamura pauses to gauge Pastwa's likely reaction.

"Christ, Karen what have you learned?" Pastwa pushes his chair back from the desk, as if opening some distance between them would soften the news. He has seen that expression on her face before and it generally is a harbinger of something he'd rather not experience.

"I haven't typed anything yet, but the dictation is just about complete." Yamura pours herself a glass of water from the pitcher Pastwa keeps on his desk.

"Chris, I don't think this is part of any kind of a hoax. Sure, all of the dating tests are not in yet, but for now I have to believe this log goes back to 1941. It is without a doubt the log of a midget submarine, and here is where it can get pretty wild as the author of this log describes how his engineer was shot in the back by a sentry. He transported him to a sympathetic Japanese doctor who couldn't save his life and they proceeded to bury him at a house he describes as being 'alongside the ocean.'" Karen pauses while she sips some water. "The author of the log apparently had no idea where on Oahu they were. All he knew was that they were next to the ocean." Yamura shifts herself in the chair and re-crosses her legs.

"The log entry identifies the skeleton as that of a man named Kamita. Apparently he was the midget sub's engineer and the author appears to be Lieutenant, junior grade, Masaharu Yokoyama, commander of the midget submarine identified as *I-16-tou*. The log begins in about April of 1941, and describes, sometimes in great detail, their training in midget submarines. Thing is, Chris, the logbook ends with the burial of Kamita. Yokoyama even writes of his intention to bury the log and all their possessions, including his ceremonial sword, with Kamita."

"Hold it, Karen. There was no sword recovered at the site and I cannot imagine why he would have brought it along unless he was considering the possibility of a suicide charge."

"Yes, I know and I can't explain it. Perhaps when it came right down to it he had a change of heart."

"In any event, we have a problem and more loose ends to deal with than a frayed ball of twine that a cat's gotten hold of." Pastwa quickly stands. Yamura follows suit, picking up her hat and briefcase.

"Thanks for taking time out from your translating work to come over here and hold my hand a little. I assume the Admiral's orders assigning both you and Stephanie have formally come through, correct?"

"Yes they have, and I certainly appreciate the help. I think it was very thoughtful and, for your information, I want you to know I really enjoy working with Stephanie and sure could get accustomed to having her with me full-time."

"Good, I'm glad you two get along and I think that 'full-time' thing may be a good idea. Right now it's rather urgent I bring Reardon up to date, and he is *not* going to be a happy sailor when he hears about Yokoyama. You know how he feels about loose ends." Pastwa walks alongside his desk and escorts her to the door, which he holds open.

Clarke looks up from his work as they enter his office and stands, expecting some new orders.

"At ease, Clarke. Lieutenant Yamura is headed back to her office. Please call over to Admiral Reardon and find out what time he can see me today, the earlier the better."

"Yes Sir. Goodbye Lieutenant." Clarke smiles as he watches her exit.

CHAPTER SIX
A HOT TIP

Auntie Lee is sitting on her backyard lanai watching Akoni and Danny hard at work when she gets an idea and reaches over to pull out the front section of the daily newspaper that is spread across her lanai table. She flips to the bottom of page two and finds a phone number for the "News Hotline."

Picking up her phone, she dials the hotline number to discover she can only leave a message. She considers hanging up, but decides against it. After all, she reasons, if they publish her story they will pay her fifty dollars. She waits for the verbal cue to leave a message.

"Hello, my name is Auntie Lee and I live at 5551 Oceanside in Kailua. I am having an in-ground pool installed in my backyard, but yesterday they had to stop work when they found a skeleton. It had a gun with it too. The police came, but then they said it was a Navy skeleton. Then a lot of people from the Navy came and dug it out and took it away. I heard them talking and someone said the skeleton has something to do with World War II because they thought the skeleton was a Japanese navy man." She almost hangs up when she decides to add one more thing. "Oh, I took pictures when nobody was here. I think this is news for you and should be worth fifty dollars!"

She abruptly hangs up and returns her attention to Danny and Akoni, completely unaware she failed to leave a phone number. She notices Danny appears to be in need of a cold lemonade and rushes into the kitchen to prepare one for him.

•   •   •   •   •

James Mori is the long-time Editor-In-Chief of the Daily Honolulu Tribune. He's in his late fifties, a bit husky and has a full head of shocking white hair which he likes to wear just over his ears. He has a corner office on the top floor of the Honolulu newspaper building overlooking Honolulu Harbor and the more than eighty-year-old landmark that is the Aloha Tower.

Sitting across from him is one of his best reporters, Nalani "Lani" Gale. Gale is in her late twenties, about five foot, six inches tall with soft, wavy blonde hair that nearly flows down to her waistline. She likes to work out in the newspaper's gym for about an hour every other day and, as always, she's perfectly dressed, going very light on her makeup. She really doesn't need much in the way of makeup, but considers herself to be undressed without it.

Her family has been on Oahu since before World War I and she is the beneficiary of a very generous family trust. Mori considers her to be his best investigative reporter.

"Well boss, what's up?"

"Looks like we might have something brewing up in Kailua with an historical twist to it. We received a 'Hotline' message from a lady who's installing an in-ground pool and she says they found a skeleton holding a gun." Mori offers Gale a piece of paper with his hand scribbled notes on it.

"The caller forgot to state her phone number, but she did manage to leave her address. She sounds as if she's a little older which, to me, makes her an unlikely candidate to leave a false tip. So I made some inquiries and confirmed the Navy was called out to that site." Mori looks at Gale as he attempts to judge her reaction.

Without taking Mori's notes, Gale vents, "What?" She sounds incredulous. Standing, she continues, "You want me to go on a skeleton hunt? 'Historical twist'? What the hell is an 'historical twist?'" Gale flips her hair behind her head, takes a defiant pose and waits for Mori to give in.

"Listen Lani, you need to trust me on this one. My senses tell me there's something going on out there the Navy strongly prefers nobody knows about. I have a photographer on the way up here now and if you hurry we might still have time to get this onto tomorrow's front page. If not, certainly the next day."

Gale appears much more interested when she hears the words, 'front page.' "Right, 'historical twist' or not, if there *is* something going on out there, I'll dig it out." She considers her choice of words, smiles and says, "Pardon my pun Jim, but if you've got a gut feeling then deal me in!" Gale takes Mori's notes, grabs her purse and starts walking out the door. She pauses in the doorway and looks back at Mori.

"Tell the photographer to meet me in my office. I'm going to gather a few things and get the hell over there." She's out of sight before he can answer.

Mori leans back in his chair and reads the framed front page of the newspaper hanging on the wall dated December 7, 1941, announcing the surprise attack on Pearl Harbor: "WAR! OAHU BOMBED BY JAPANESE PLANES." Mori, talking to himself, says: "I wonder; I just wonder." The phone rings and his mind jumps back into the present day.

●   ●   ●   ●   ●

Lani Gale and her photographer companion, Bobby, soon find themselves sitting in his car parked in front of Auntie Lee's house. Bobby is in his early twenties, sports close-cropped black hair and owes his heritage to a combination of Portuguese, Chinese, and Hawaiian forefathers. Most of his family lives on Oahu, but some are scattered across the other islands. He recently graduated from the University of Hawaii and this is his first real job. He has loved to take pictures since he was very young and as far as he's concerned, he'd be happy in this position for the rest of his life. He also has a crush on Gale and is excited at the prospect of spending time with her.

Gale, on the other hand, has ambitions that would transport her to New York City writing for the *Times*, or better yet, in Washington D.C., writing for the *Post*. To Gale, Bobby is just a means to an end. In this instance, the end is a front-page story. She is trusting in Mori's instincts and her mind is racing over the possibilities as she stares at Auntie Lee's house.

"I checked this out," says Bobby, "a woman named Leilani Yamada is the registered owner and she's been the owner since 1965. From what I could learn, she inherited the house from her parents so she's probably lived here a very long time." Bobby hands a piece of paper with the name Leilani Yamada scrawled on it. Gale gives it a quick look as she memorizes the name, then hands it back to him.

"Bobby, grab your gear and follow me. Don't talk unless I ask you a question, got it?" Gale shoots him a firm look with perhaps a little too much fire in her eyes as Bobby literally pulls away from her.

Bobby, who's already shy around women, replies with a barely audible, "Yes, Ms. Gale."

Gale and Bobby walk to the front door and just as Gale is about to ring the doorbell, Auntie Lee opens it and greets them with a big smile. "Are you from the newspaper?" Her excitement is obvious.

"Yes, my name is Lani Gale and this is Bobby, my photographer. Are you Leilani Yamada?"

Shaking her head as if to be saying no, Auntie Lee replies, "Yes, but nobody calls me that. Please, just call me Auntie." She slips into a pair of slippers she has placed just outside her front door, closes the door behind her and motions to Gale and Bobby.

"Follow me, the pool is in the backyard." Auntie Lee leads them around the side of the house and as they reach the yard she stops and removes a camera from her over-sized, yellow and orange shoulder bag, a bag she made herself.

"In here I have pictures I took yesterday. You can see the skeleton and the pistol too if you want!" She turns on her camera and begins flipping through the pictures as Gale observes.

"Very nice Auntie, you're a good photographer. You might think about applying for a position with the paper." Gale is pleased with the look of embarrassment that flows across Auntie Lee's face. "Flattery will get me everywhere with this little simpleton," she thinks to herself. Quickly turning to face Bobby, she starts barking out commands.

"Bobby, take a couple shots of the excavation site," Gale pauses as she looks around, "and get the ocean in the background too. Watch the lighting here as there's lots of shade from those trees." Gale points to some tall palm trees casting long, narrow shadows across the excavation.

"Will do, Ms. Gale." Bobby quickly goes about following her orders.

"Can I look at your camera please, Auntie?" Gale is being as polite as she knows how to be, which does not come naturally for her.

"Certainly dear, here you are." Auntie Lee offers the camera to Gale. "Would you like some cold lemonade?" She motions to the lemon trees in the back yard. "I made it fresh from my own trees this morning."

Gale immediately begins to back through the photos in Auntie Lee's camera.

"Yes I would, but first Auntie, where did the sword in this one photo come from? And who took this picture of you with it?"

Looking surprised and a little taken aback, Auntie Lee thinks for a moment before deciding to tell her the truth. "I found it in the pool yesterday. It reminded me of my grandfather so I just took it. After all, it was on my property! All I did was set the camera on the tractor and let the timer take my picture. Is it ok?"

"Don't worry Auntie, the picture is fine. If you don't mind can we take a photo of you standing here next to your pool and holding the sword?" Gale displays her most charming smile. "And yes, we would both love some of your lemonade."

"Oh wonderful, right away! I'll bring you the lemonade and then I can bring you the sword." Very excited, she quickly disappears into the house, leaving her camera in Gale's hands, exactly as Gale had hoped. Turning to find where Bobby has gone, she barks out at him.

"Bobby!" Bobby stops snapping photos, looks up and sees Gale is motioning for him to join her. He quickly runs over as she holds Auntie Lee's camera up for his inspection. "Bobby, can you copy the memory disk in this?"

Bobby takes the camera and gives it a quick look. "Easy. Let me take this up to the car, it won't take me more than a minute or two." Gale grabs his arm before he can leave. "Hold it; just take the disk, not the camera. I prefer we keep this between you and me and I don't want Auntie to see you taking her camera." Gale pauses before continuing. "And when you say 'a minute' you better not mean a 'Hawaiian' minute!"

Bobby pops the disk out and hands the camera back to Gale. "No problem, I don't work on Hawaiian time, I work on news time!" Bobby quickly jogs around the side of the house and out of sight. He waits until he rounds the corner before breaking into an all-out run, almost overwhelmed by the excitement of working with Gale.

Gale decides to take a walk around the perimeter of the pool, but doesn't find anything noteworthy. It looks like a hole in the ground to her and nothing more. There are a few surfers just off the beach and about half dozen kids are playing Frisbee in the surf. "It's kind of an idyllic, yet a rather public setting. I wonder why someone chose this spot to bury a body and how is it they weren't noticed?" Gale thinks to herself.

Soon, she hears footsteps coming up from behind her and turns to see Bobby reappearing from the side of the house while at the same time Auntie Lee is carefully coming down the steps of her lanai, a glass of lemonade in each hand.

"Be careful Auntie, I don't want you to trip!" Gale calls out. Her real purpose, however, is not so thoughtful. She needs Auntie Lee to slow down so Bobby can beat her back and return the disk to the camera.

"Thank you dear, I *am* being careful. I don't want to spill your drinks," calls out Auntie Lee.

Gale hands Bobby the camera who deftly re-installs Auntie Lee's disk and returns the camera to Gale.

"She'll never know." He smiles at Gale as Auntie Lee arrives and extends each of them a glass of lemonade.

"Thank you Auntie." Gale takes a sip. "This is great lemonade. Really, Auntie, you should bottle this stuff." Gale isn't exaggerating this time.

Bobby, just a little out of breath, also accepts a glass. "Thanks Auntie," he says with a big smile. As Bobby takes his first sip, he's instantly reminded of the lemonade his maternal grandmother once made using the lemons from the trees that still grow in his mom's backyard.

"Auntie, are you going to go bring us your sword? We'd love to take a picture of you holding it." Gale smiles as Auntie Lee stops to consider the question.

"Yes, yes. I am so excited I almost forgot about it." She pauses momentarily to regain her breath. "I will go get it right now." She turns and hurries back to the house.

"Bobby, the sword she dug up is something the Navy doesn't know about and the scuttlebutt Mori heard indicates the grave site dates to WWII. Add to that the appearance of the sword and I think I have myself a story that will most definitely get the attention of those Navy folks. If I can ruffle some feathers over at Pearl, who knows what kind of leverage I might create, not to mention who might crawl out from under a rock over there with some juicy insights."

Gale quickly finishes her lemonade and hands the empty glass to Bobby. "Let's get a couple of pictures of Auntie and her sword and then get the hell out of here. I have the front page waiting for me!"

Gale and Bobby walk to the edge of the pool excavation and wait for Auntie Lee, who is slowly making her way to them. She's dragging a heavily tarnished sword that is about half of her height.

"Okay Auntie, hold the sword up with both hands across your chest," says Bobby. Gale helps her place the sword as requested. "And don't forget to smile." Bobby lines up the shot, but not fast enough to suit Gale.

"Bobby, take the picture already!"

"Perfect." Bobby snaps several shots of Auntie Lee, who is rapidly growing tired of holding the sword. "Got it! We're good to go Ms. Gale." Bobby lowers his camera, waiting for the next order.

"Great! Thanks Auntie. By the way, you said it was some construction workers who discovered the skeleton?"

"Why, yes," says Auntie Lee as she drops the sword to the ground.

"Would you mind telling me how to get in touch with them?" Gale continues to force herself to be charming. From what Bobby has seen of her around the newspaper, she appears to be quite out of character.

Auntie Lee, bits of perspiration forming around her temples, fishes around for a moment in one of the two huge pockets of her brightly colored, floral dress. Eventually she pulls out a handful of business cards and gives one to Gale. "They gave me all these cards in case my neighbors want to buy pools. You are most certainly welcome to take one. Danny is in charge of my project."

She accepts the card, grabs Bobby by the arm and quickly leads him out of the yard. She turns around and pauses ever so briefly and calls out, "Thanks Auntie," as they waste no time departing.

Auntie Lee momentarily stands still, staring at their backs before shrugging her shoulders. She walks over to pick up the empty lemonade glasses lying in the grass and makes her way back into the house, dragging the sword behind her.

Gale pauses before opening the passenger door and chastises Bobby: "Damnit, I have a story to write. I'll need your photos and all of Auntie's photos right away, understood?" Gale opens the passenger door, gets in and impatiently watches as Bobby stuffs his equipment into the trunk, runs around to the driver's door, slips behind the wheel and starts the car with a roar, beads of sweat streaming down his face.

"Don't forget your seat belt. I don't want you to get stopped by a cop." She fastens her shoulder belt and continues: We have no time to waste!"

"Yes Miss Gale, don't worry. I'll have you in your office with all the photos before you know it."

Gale is staring out the side window thinking of possible headlines for the morning issue and what it might be like to be working for *The Washington Post*. Bobby smiles broadly as they speed towards downtown Honolulu. It's not often he has a woman in his car, let alone someone as physically appealing to him as Gale.

Auntie Lee comes running out her front door, waving at Gale and Bobby as they disappear down the street. "Wait! What about my fifty dollars?" As she watches their car disappear she throws her hands up in the air, turns around and walks back into her house, mumbling aloud to herself, "Maybe they will mail me a check."

CHAPTER SEVEN
ADMIRAL ROMAN REARDON

Pastwa is standing in the inner office of Rear Admiral Roman Reardon impatiently waiting for his appointment when suddenly the door swings open. Rather than Reardon, he's facing an elderly gentleman about six foot two inches tall with a long, chiseled chin, well-wrinkled face and a dark tan which contrasts with his close-cropped grey hair. He's wearing a navy blue patch over his left eye and is gripping a walking cane with Reardon close behind him. Recognizing Pastwa, Reardon grows a broad smile as the two men come to a halt.

"Dad, I'd like you to meet one of my fine young officers." Reardon points to Pastwa. "This is Lieutenant Commander Chris Pastwa. Commander, this is my father, Captain Clint Reardon."

Pastwa accepts the right hand extended to him by the elder Reardon.

"This is truly an honor Captain. The Admiral has spoken of you many times." Pastwa isn't surprised at the strength of the elder Reardon's grip nor at how long he holds it.

After several moments Captain Reardon releases Pastwa's hand. "*Lieutenant* Commander? Well, you need to get on the ball," he points towards Pastwa's jacket sleeve, "and get that full third stripe on there."

"Yes Sir, I'm working on it."

Reardon motions to Pastwa. "I'm going to walk the Captain to his cab so go on in and make yourself comfortable. I'll see you in a few minutes."

Reardon turns towards his aide who is sitting behind a desk a few feet away. "Jones, get the Commander some coffee, and as you know he likes it strong and black."

"Yes Sir." Jones salutes and quickly disappears down the hall.

Senior Chief Petty Officer Keona Jones has a Caucasian American father and a native Hawaiian mother. His father was discharged from the Navy while on Oahu and decided he liked it enough to stay. He subsequently bought a small bar/restaurant with a killer ocean view on Kauai and has been running it ever since with his wife and three of his sons. Jones is the oldest of four boys and the only one with no interest in the family business. For as long as he can remember, he wanted to be in the Navy.

After enlisting it eventually came to pass that Jones found himself on a patrol boat venturing up a jungle river somewhere in Central America. Reardon was in command of the clandestine mission when all hell broke loose. Out of the jungle darkness streaked the discomforting tracers of heavy machine gun fire. Rocket propelled grenades suddenly exploded on either side of the bow, but before they could zero in, Jones, without waiting for orders, floored the throttle and made a hard turn to starboard temporarily exposing the entire port side of the patrol boat to potential disaster. However, the risk paid off as two explosions marked the place their little boat had just vacated. As fast as they got into trouble, they were out of it. Reardon admired Jones' quick thinking and has retained Jones's services for more than twenty years subsequent.

Pastwa makes himself comfortable while waiting for Reardon to return. Being a corner office, two walls are all windows but the remaining walls are full of shelves hosting an assortment of over fifty scale model ships and submarines from WWII. Pastwa notices one in particular and gets up to take a closer look. It's the *I-16* and strapped on the aft deck is a midget submarine. He picks it up and gives it a good once-over before he returns the model to the shelf.

In a few minutes Jones brings his piping hot, black coffee in a large, navy blue mug with a depiction of the *U.S.S. Arizona* emblazed on it. Pastwa smiles as he lays his folder of photographs on the Admiral's desk alongside a model of the *U.S.S. Arizona,* leaving a free hand for the mug. Reardon returns just as his mind begins to wander.

"No need to get up Chris." Reardon settles into his overstuffed, Hawaiian mahogany and leather chair while simultaneously swiveling to face Pastwa.

"Tell me, what do you have for me?"

Pastwa passes him the file. "This is a complete photo record with notations of the physical evidence we have collected from the pool excavation."

Reardon takes the file without commenting. After flipping through the pages, he closes the cover and looks Pastwa directly in the eyes. Reardon's about six foot tall with short, thinning hair, though still mostly dark brown. His weathered face reflects the years he's spent at sea and his frame is carrying a few pounds more than it once did. His deep blue eyes sparkle, but when angered they expand so much as to be intimidating. His scarred, deeply tanned hands are lying flat on his desktop, almost as if he's ready to pounce.

"So tell me, Commander, what's the significance of this find? Is there anything special about the skeleton, or for that matter, any of the items you discovered with it?" He points to a photo depicting the contents of the rusted box.

Pastwa squirms a bit in his chair as he very much dislikes it when the Reardon barrages him with questions. He never knows for sure if Reardon expects him to answer each question in order or if he's looking for a broad response. He doesn't realize he is guilty of doing the same to his subordinates.

"Well Sir, we found a book we have concluded to be a ship's logbook. It was wrapped in oil cloth inside the metal box you see in the photos." Pastwa pauses as Reardon again flips through the photos, appearing to pay more attention to the box and the logbook.

"Sir, the logbook's written in Japanese." Pastwa pauses as he notices Reardon is looking out one of the windows, almost giving the appearance he's not listening, except Pastwa knows better.

"I directed Lieutenant Yamura to translate the log and type a copy for us. You likely remember her work on the incident out at Kaneohe a couple of years ago when her Japanese language skills proved invaluable." Reardon smiles as he puts a face to the name.

"Right, she's a top notch officer and I'm fully aware of her capabilities. In fact when you requested Yamura and that young Lieutenant Ferguson be temporarily assigned to our unit it made me think you were reading my mind. Of course you couldn't have known I've been considering the possibility of permanently adding the two of them to our special unit; especially as we are short-handed. We'll table that until this matter's been resolved."

Turning his attention to the folder, Reardon picks up one of the photos, briefly looks it over and puts it back down. "Did you brief Yamura and Ferguson relative to the Top Secret status, not just of the photos but of the entire case?"

"Yes Sir, they're taking all the requisite precautions. As for the logbook, we've discovered it purports to be the ship's log from a vessel that was likely part of the Imperial Japanese Navy's submarine fleet. The author sometimes refers to it as '*I-16's boat*,' sometimes as a 'tube' and sometimes as '*I-16-tou.*'"

Reardon suddenly pushes his chair away from his desk and abruptly stands, taking Pastwa by surprise.

"What?" He exclaims. "Do you have any idea what the hell '*I-16's* boat' really was?" Reardon remains standing, as if frozen by the news, waiting for

Pastwa's response.

"Yes Sir. It was probably the midget sub launched just outside Pearl Harbor by the Japanese fleet submarine, *I-16,* in the early hours of December 7th. In fact, from what I've learned so far it looks like we only recently discovered the remains of *I-16-tou* entangled with debris we dredged from West Loch.

"Correct, Commander, but the torpedoes were not there and I believe the sub was empty, to boot! Empty, as in nobody home in there. Abandoned and left to sink in West Loch." Reardon allows his words to penetrate before continuing.

"So what else does Lieutenant Yamura have to say?" Reardon, relaxing a bit, sits back in his chair and pours himself a glass of water from the ever-present pitcher on his credenza. Pastwa somewhat relaxes at the site of Reardon returning to his chair. He always feels particularly exposed when Reardon stands to make a point for as often as not, Reardon will then begin pacing around the office, Pastwa's head twirling around to keep up with him. He considers it to be a good sign Reardon has returned to his chair as it likely means he's calming down and Pastwa will again be able to speak freely.

"Sir, on my way over Lieutenant Yamura phoned with her latest information. She's translated all of the log entries and positively identified the skeleton. It's a Japanese sailor named 'Kamita' and the man who wrote the log is a Lieutenant, junior grade, by the name of 'Yokoyama,' as we already surmised. She'll have a typed translation of the complete log tomorrow sometime, likely early afternoon."

Pastwa braces himself for an eruption, but the Admiral remains seated, listening carefully while staring out the windows towards the harbor.

"Yamura says the writing is a little smeared, but she thinks the burial took place on or about December 10, 1941. Apparently some of the pages are difficult to read due to water damage, but she's certain the two midget submariners made contact with a number of people whose names probably had been given to them by Imperial Japanese Navy intelligence. According to our research the midget submariners were equipped with various maps and hide-out locations in addition to safe contacts. According to the log entries, swimming ashore and making contact with local Japanese was one of the planned escape options."

Reardon reaches for a glass of water, but just as he's about to touch it, he suddenly pulls his arm back.

"Commander, as you well know, I'm a bit of an expert on the Pearl Harbor bushwhack." Pastwa shakes his head in agreement. "But did you know this Yokoyama fellow was credited by the Imperial Japanese Navy with single-handedly sinking the *Arizona*?"

"No Sir." Pastwa sounds puzzled. "How can that be? Everyone knows she was sunk by a perfectly placed aerial bomb strike. In fact, I think it was actually a converted fourteen-inch shell from the battleship *Nagato*."

"You're right about that, however it seems Yokoyama made a few radio transmissions late on the 7th and into the 8th. He was quite the chatterbox and I have always thought it to be unfortunate our boys failed to jump on those transmissions, especially since they appear to have been sourced from within Pearl Harbor itself. So chew on that fact a bit!"

Reardon pauses while Pastwa digests the information. "No Sir, this is news to me."

Reardon smiles as he's pleased to discover he knows more about Yokoyama, at least for now, than does Pastwa.

"Yes Commander, and among his transmissions, some of which were undecipherable, he told his pals back on the *I-16* the attack was a success." Reardon shakes his head in disbelief. "Really, did Yokoyama think the entire Japanese Navy didn't already know the attack had succeeded beyond their wildest dreams?"

Reardon picks up his glass of water and takes a long, deep drink. He gazes out towards the harbor as he considers the situation and mulls over various options. After what to Pastwa seems to be an eternity, Reardon swivels to face him.

"Chris, it gets even better. The Jap Navy had its own version of Nazi Germany's Propaganda Minister Herr Goebbels so when they decided to credit Yokoyama with the sinking of the *Arizona*, their propaganda ministry took that story and ran with it in a big way. They transformed the nine midget submariners, who they presumed were all killed in action, into Demi-Gods. In the Japanese scheme of life that status put them just one notch below their own Emperor, but they paid particular attention to Mr. Yokoyama."

Reardon pauses to again drink some water. Pastwa has noticed in the past the more upset he is, the more water, or coffee, he consumes. He has often mused that perhaps Reardon does so in order to give his thoughts time to unfold.

"They made a full-blown motion picture about Yokoyama and his exploits which I believe was titled, '*Navy*.' That movie would have done Frank Capra proud as thousands of young Japanese men joined the Imperial Navy after watching it. Civilians would write poems about him and the newspapers published stories about his exploits. Hell, the Emperor's wife baked Yokoyama's mom a cake and gave it to her at his official funeral at the Yasukuni Shrine. The Jap media turned this little guy into something of a Japanese World War II super hero, kind of a Captain Japan." Reardon laughs at his comparison to a modern comic book series. However, Pastwa notices he's pressing a finger under his twitching right eye, which is a bad sign.

"So, Chris, if Yokoyama penetrated the harbor, survived the attack, then came ashore and successfully made contact with Japanese nationals, and even had the time to bury his pal, then just what the *hell* became of him?"

Reardon cuts him off before he can get a word out.

"The Japanese Navy stationed a few subs around the islands for quite some time hoping to pick up their midget submariners, except none of them showed up. Well, at least not that we know of. We did manage to pluck more than a dozen Jap bodies out of the ocean in the following weeks, but none of them, with the exception of Prisoner of War Number One's engineer, was a Japanese sailor. They were all pilots. So again, that brings me to the question: what happened to Yokoyama?" Reardon doesn't wait for a reply.

"We certainly can't assume he failed to survive the war. And as far as the war goes, he couldn't even reveal himself after the war. Let's face it, he was a Demi-God so if he was still alive how could he go back to Japan? When he adopted a new identity, which I assume he did, it meant he was basically stuck with it forever. He was dead to his family and to his country, putting him in a difficult situation the likes of which I cannot even imagine." Reardon takes another gulp of water.

Pastwa is staring directly into Reardon's eyes, who's obviously expecting a response.

"Sir, Lieutenant Yamura is going to compile two sets of the translated logbook and will type the translation herself. They'll be marked 'Top Secret-Eyes Only' and numbered. I'll deliver copy number one to you and Yamura and I will work from the second copy. We'll lock the original logbook into our vault along with her dictation. Once we have digested the contents we can formulate a definitive course of action. Naturally, I'll keep you advised each step of the way."

Pastwa pauses as he realizes he may have overstepped, so to cover himself he quickly adds:

"Of course, if all this meets with your approval."

Reardon continues to silently stare at him. After what seems to Pastwa to be an hour, but in actuality is closer to thirty seconds, he breaks his silence.

"Yes, sounds like a sensible plan." Reardon leans forward in his chair. "Listen, Chris, there have already been calls from some local reporters who heard about the discovery of a skeleton that might date back to WWII. One of those queries came from your old girlfriend Lani Gale. She's pretty clever you know, so be certain there are no leaks and warn Clarke to be on the alert."

Pastwa winces at the mention of her name and the memory of their rather noisy breakup a couple years earlier.

"I don't want any leaks on this Commander, understand me? I *do not* want to read about this in a newspaper without first hearing from you." Reardon points his right index finger directly at Pastwa.

"This matter stays right here, with the Navy, until all of the facts are complete. I want no leaks, none! And tie up these God-damned loose ends. I hate loose ends and what you've presented me with is a tanker full of them!" His voice grows louder the longer he speaks. Pastwa, for his part, feels an urgency building within him to get on with the investigation. He knows, however, Reardon must run his course.

He takes a long, deep drink of water and slowly calms down.

"Unless you have any questions you can get on with it." He looks at Pastwa, who quickly stands and responds: "No Sir, no questions."

Reardon watches him leave and turns to gaze through the window. He finds the tranquil waters of Pearl Harbor have no calming effect on his severely twitching right eye. "Damn this twitch," he says out loud, though nobody's within earshot.

CHAPTER EIGHT
A SUBMARINER'S LOGBOOK

Yamura and Pastwa are each reading one of her translations of the ship's log. Clarke is making himself busy by refilling their coffee cups for the fourth time, though it is only nine in the morning. He briefly considers whether he should interrupt them and ask if they would like some donuts, but thinks the better of it and decides to keep a low profile. Experience tells him when Pastwa is deep into a case it's best to leave him alone as much as possible. Pastwa slowly lays what will be Reardon's copy onto his desk and sits back, tilting his chair almost to the tipping point. Yamura sets copy number two on her lap while taking a sip of coffee.

"This is really hard to swallow Karen. Have you received results from the dating tests on the log, or on anything?"

Yamura takes another sip before she responds.

"Preliminarily, the man we believe is Kamita has been dead a good seventy years, though the complete array of tests are not in. I *can* tell you the DNA of items in the locket are a match for Kamita. I can also tell you the materials used in the log, even the inks, match up with what was commonly available in Japan during the 1941 time period. There is some variation in the quality of the inks and that may have been due to material shortages that were starting to become common in Japan as the result of our embargo. It was not just gasoline they were running low on."

Yamura finishes her coffee before continuing.

"The stopwatch is obviously Imperial Japanese Navy issue. The watches were of a brand common in Japan back then and favored by members of the navy. If this is a hoax, it was conceived a very long time ago. The extent of corrosion and rust on the metal box is consistent with having been buried for seventy-odd years. You can't easily fake corrosion of this extent, but I'm not saying it can't be done. As for the clothing, Stephanie has not concluded much from that other than to say they are likely two separate uniforms. One of them

56

has evidence of blood on it so it may have been Kamita's."

Yamura pauses to let Pastwa take it all in before continuing.

"Even the oil cloth appears bona-fide. Frankly, Chris, as far as I can determine everything appears to be legit. Let me add, again, until the final test results are complete there is always the outside chance we could be wrong. And by 'outside chance,' I mean we're talking just about out of the ballpark type odds."

Pastwa swivels around and gazes towards the harbor. Both of them sit silently for about a minute before Pastwa swivels back to face her.

"Reardon's expecting me over at the Officer's Club for lunch, but I think I'll call and suggest he and I meet in his office instead because when he hears what I have to report, he's not going to be pleased." Pastwa pauses as he thinks about his pending meeting with Reardon.

"Reardon's likely to go absolutely over the top when he reads Yokoyama's description of torpedoing the *Oklahoma*. And when he learns how they slipped ashore to meld into the Japanese/Hawaiian population," he pauses and lets out a long sigh before continuing.

"I think his eyes might just burst out of his head. He really has a hard-on for anything regarding the Pearl Harbor attack."

Pastwa has a pained expression on his face while Yamura is thankful she's not the one breaking the news to Reardon.

"Shit! Reardon's going to just shit! All I can do is hope I'm not sitting underneath him when he does!" Pastwa exclaims.

Yamura shakes her head, feeling sorry for him and doubly relieved reporting to Reardon is not her job.

"I don't envy you Chris, but I don't understand Reardon's keen interest in the Pearl Harbor attack after all these years. He wasn't even alive back then."

Yamura smiles as she rises to leave. "Why don't you stop over at my place later for a drink? I'll be up pretty late and can put together some sushi. We can enjoy some wine, rehash things and by then I'll likely have more test results back. Besides, it's been a tough week already and we need a little down time."

Pastwa considers her invitation, smiles and replies: "I'll most definitely see you later, Karen. You can count on it."

Yamura slowly walks to the door, which appears to open on its own. She smiles as she discovers Clarke's about to bring in a tray with a pot of coffee and several donuts.

"Oh, Ma'am, sorry, I was just about to knock."

Yamura smiles. "Thanks Clarke. I'm fairly certain the Commander could use a little sugar and caffeine rush before he sees the Admiral." She slips around Clarke and disappears through the doorway as he continues into Pastwa's office.

"Sir, how about some fresh Kauai coffee and a couple of donuts?" Pastwa smiles and thinks to himself Clarke is right this time.

"You must've read my mind as it's definitely time for a break. Please leave everything on my desk then call over to Admiral Reardon's office and ask if I can see him. Let him know I have the document we discussed yesterday."

"Yes Sir, consider it taken care of. Enjoy the donuts." Clarke quickly returns to his desk. He glances at the few donuts remaining under the glass cake holder he keeps on top of one of his file cabinets and says to himself: "Donut now, or donut after I call the Admiral?" Staring at the donuts, he decides he better phone the Admiral first.

CHAPTER NINE
A LONG FUSE BURNING

Pastwa's been nervously sitting across from Reardon for nearly thirty minutes while he reviews the translated logbook. From time to time he pauses, glances in the direction of the harbor and frowns. Pastwa has been here before and he fears Reardon's painfully long fuse may be burning down.

Finally, after to what Pastwa seems to be a short lifetime, Reardon lightly tosses the translated logbook onto the desk. He takes a slow drink of water before turning his attention to Pastwa.

"Commander, this is easily the most astonishing thing I've ever read." Reardon pauses for effect, as is his habit.

"You say Lieutenant Yamura tentatively dates this log to be accurate for the December 1941, time period?"

Pastwa is quick to respond.

"Yes Sir. She and Lieutenant Ferguson haven't completed all the dating tests yet. It's too soon for some of the more complicated testing, but it's their joint opinion that everything is looking pretty darned authentic. Let me add there's still a remote possibility this is an enormously elaborate hoax. However, that particular likelihood appears to be a more than a long shot and I believe we must move forward on the assumption this is definitely not bogus. If later we find out otherwise, then no real harm done."

Reardon stands and walks over to one of the shelves on the wall where he picks up a model of a World War II Japanese submarine, sets it onto the middle of his desk then sits on the edge of his chair.

"See this model?" He points with his right index finger. "This is the *I-16* and she's set up the way it was configured when she delivered her cargo outside Pearl that day. Her cargo, of course, was the midget submarine skippered by our new friend, Lieutenant Yokoyama."

Reardon takes a deep breath and slowly lets it out, almost as if a sigh.

"Listen to me carefully Chris. There are a lot of folks out there who've made a pretty good case that Lieutenant Yokoyama was clever enough to navigate into Pearl in the dark and under the anti-torpedo nets we had serving double duty as anti-sub nets. They make a solid case to the effect he fired two torpedoes. One torpedo likely bounced off the *West Virginia* while the second torpedo struck and no doubt caused the capsizing of the *Oklahoma*, precisely as described in this logbook." Reardon pounds his fist onto the translated log, which significantly raises Pastwa's anxiety level.

Before continuing, he takes a large gulp of water.

"There's been some solid evidence to collaborate that story and there's been much ado made of a photo many people claim depicts a midget sub shortly after releasing two torpedoes. One torpedo's heading at the *West Virginia* and one is tracking directly at the *Oklahoma,* exactly as Yokoyama describes.

A lot of folks want to disbelieve that photo, but tell me, what's the best way to spot a submarine in shallow water? From an airplane of course! That photo is focused on the midget submarine and not on battleship row. That damn Jap photographer snapped the photo for the sole reason he had spotted the sub. Too bad his notes, if he made any, were lost at Midway where many of the Pearl Harbor pilots bought their lunch when we sunk four of their big flat tops." Reardon pauses to allow time for Pastwa to consider the facts.

"Realistically, the reason for taking the photo had to be because the pilot spotted one of their midget subs. Sometimes the obvious is too painful for historians to admit, but like it or not, this photo serves as excellent evidence of our midget man's success. I could go on about that photo and efforts to disprove the existence of the submarine, but now it's all beside the point." He picks up the *I-16* model and looks it over a few moments before carefully placing it back on the desk.

"The *Oklahoma* would never have rolled over, but for an intervening act. You know your history so you know all our battlewagons had their watertight doors open that day as the result of weekend inspections. She did have a bit of a list to port and, like the *West Virginia* and *California*, she was settling to the bottom. But when that 'Long Lance' torpedo struck her, it ripped a hole about 38 feet wide right through her armored torpedo belt and below the water line. With that much water rushing in, representing scores of tons of weight, there was no chance to counter-flood and over she went." He shakes his head as he contemplates the crewmen of the *Oklahoma* who were trapped below decks when she rolled over.

"To top it off, Admiral Nimitz himself reported the discovery of an unexploded 'Long Lance' torpedo near the *West Virginia*. We just chose the easy route which was to stuff our heads up our collective butts and pretend no submarines could have penetrated Pearl, let alone successfully launch any torpedoes. Really, that they penetrated should not have been a complete surprise. The prior year a German U-boat slipped into the British fleet's main base at Scapa Flow and sunk one of their battlewagons. There was precedent, just as there was precedence for an aerial torpedo attack at Pearl. It was a matter that we fooled ourselves into believing no submarine could penetrate the harbor."

Reardon abruptly pushes his chair away from the desk.

"This is like another kick in the gut only this time it's more than seventy years after the fact!"

Reardon picks up his glass and nervously swishes the water around while Pastwa remains quiet, his own mind racing ahead as he plans a course of action. At this point Pastwa is also growing anxious to get back to work, but Reardon's not finished and Pastwa knows it.

"Frankly, this logbook should be no big shock. That two of those midget submariners made it into the population should also be no dramatic revelation. Hell, there are two other midget submariners who could have made it ashore."

"Damned, for all I know this could even be nothing more than a truly elaborate hoax put together many years ago by some fanatics trying to prove the Japanese midget subs were successful. The burial site is not exactly in an out-of-the-way location and if someone wanted to pull off a hoax they would have chosen a place that would likely be developed in some manner at some future point in time. A site exactly like this one."

Reardon takes a few moments to consider the situation. He takes another drink of water, finding little solace in the knowledge that later this evening he'll be replacing the water with some Johnny Walker Blue and a prodigious quantity of ice.

"No, Commander, I know this is just wishful thinking on my part. We must proceed on the basis the log is the real McCoy. The hoax theory is a long shot and should be tabled just as you said. So here are your orders."

Pastwa immediately tenses up and appears as if he's standing at attention while still sitting.

"First, make absolutely certain this entire business remains Top Secret. This is a Navy matter, plain and simple and I want to keep it that way for at least the near term."

"I'd like you to inform Lieutenants Yamura and Ferguson *in no uncertain terms* they are to guard their work on this project as if their next promotion and *every promotion following* depend on it."

"Second, I want you to do everything possible to find out what became of Lieutenant Commander Yokoyama."

Reardon notices a puzzled look on Pastwa's face at the mention of 'Lieutenant Commander.'

"Oh, I see you aren't aware the Imperial Japanese Navy made this man, and eight other midget submariners, not just Demi-Gods, but gave them all double promotions in rank for good measure. Likely the Japanese High Command assumed they would never need to make good on the pay raises is my guess. If Yokoyama survived they owe him a submarine load of back pay!" Reardon laughs at his own joke, before again growing serious.

"Hell, Commander, as I recall there were Buddhist monks in Japan who raised money for the war effort by manufacturing prayer coins with the likeness of Yokoyama on them. They really promoted the guy, pretty much the way we promoted our own heroes during the war. What the hell, we captured one of the midget subs the next day and sent it across the country on a war bond sale. I'm pretty sure it's still on display over in Fredericksburg, Texas. Back in '42 we cut holes in the sides so that the crowds could peek in and have a look-see. So you really can't blame the Japanese for trying to capitalize on Yokohama as much as possible." Reardon pauses to allow Pastwa a few moments respite.

"Here is something else you likely didn't know. A few years back one of the Jap midget subs was found just offshore in only about sixty or so feet of water. It was not the *I-16-tou* either and the hatch was open. Those hatches opened up, not down, and there was nobody home inside, though we did discover they left their uniforms behind which lends credence to the possibility they swam ashore." Reardon again pauses, this time more to get his breath than for effect.

"So it should come as no surprise that some pretty well respected people here on Oahu believe those two midget submariners popped the cork on their sub, swam ashore and disappeared into the population. Back then the Japanese presence here was in the neighborhood of one third of the total island population. Many of them didn't even speak English or spoke very poor English."

"Speaking of English, if any of the midget submariners chosen for the Pearl Harbor mission didn't already speak it, they were given a crash course. Some of them knew English better than a lot of the Japanese population here. It was always part of the Japanese battle plan that, if necessary, the crews would scuttle their little subs and swim ashore to seek out friendly Japanese. Each crew was provided a detailed map of Oahu and a list of safe houses. In fact, my bet is the house where you found the remains was associated in some way with the one of those lists."

"Bear in mind, Yokoyama, as it happens, was the most likely candidate to have been able to pull off a successful harbor defense penetration and attack. He came from a military background, was multi linguistic and was considered by his superior officers to be the cream of the men chosen for the mission. He was also considered to be charismatic, a trait that likely served him well when he came ashore here. One of his commanding officers once said that when Yokoyama smiled, he looked as if he were an angelic child. That, Commander, is a trait which would come in handy in a big way if he found himself needing to meld into an unfriendly environment."

"I see you noticed I used the word "chosen" earlier. That's right, those Japanese midget submariners were hand-picked by the Imperial Japanese Navy. Everyone knew the mission was highly dangerous, but it was not the intention of the Japanese Navy that they be suicidal. In fact, my recollection is Admiral Yamamoto himself sought assurances there were reasonable precautions taken to make survival a distinct possibility. And think of the importance a debriefing of the crews afterwards would have been. It would have provided invaluable information the Japanese could have used for future attacks."

"Considering Yokoyama, we are dealing with an individual who was under orders to return to the fleet to report on his efforts and who had the requisite background and resolve to do just that. So whatever you do, don't discount this man in any way. Assume he was a natural survivor and fully capable of pulling this off!"

Reardon takes another drink of water before continuing. He's on a roll and is unloading everything he knows on Pastwa in the sound belief Pastwa will need every bit of knowledge he can obtain, from every source available, and as soon as possible.

"We have to assume at least one midget submariner blended himself into the population and that man is Yokoyama. So, again, my advice to you is simple. *Do not sell him short.* In my opinion he was, hands down, the best of the midget sub commanders."

Reardon reaches into one of the lower right hand drawers of his massive desk and pulls out four books. He offers one to Pastwa. It's a small book with an orange cover and is titled, "*I attacked Pearl Harbor.*"

"Treat this one carefully as it's quite rare." Pastwa accepts the book and gives it a quick once- over.

"This was written by the midget submariner we captured asleep on a beach the day after the December 7th bushwhack. Frankly, I think he was an idiot and the skipper of his mother sub was a bigger idiot and should have been brought up on charges. The damn gyroscope on his sub was out of whack so they should never have launched as he couldn't navigate without either staying on the surface or continuously using his periscope. They truly risked ruining the surprise attack by sending this guy in." Reardon chuckles and sighs; "Sometimes people get lucky and it was pure luck this particular sub was not detected and the attack foiled as a result."

"The title is a little silly too, '*I attacked Pearl Harbor.*' It should've been titled, '*I tried to Attack Pearl Harbor, but Never Stood a Chance.*'" Reardon laughs aloud at his joke. Then, using both of his large hands, he picks up three more books and offers them to Pastwa. "Here are some excellent books on the Japanese midget sub efforts. They each contain solid information on the Pearl Harbor episode." Pastwa stands to accept them.

"There are plenty of good photos in these books, including some of Yokoyama. I'm sure Yamura can put together something of what he might look like today based on his 1941 photos and there's also some good background information on him. You know, Chris, I believe it's always best to learn as much as possible about your subject."

Reardon looks Pastwa directly in the eye. I believe you are going to conclude if you had to pick one man out of the five commanders sent to attack us that day, Yokoyama was easily the most likely to succeed. Chris, you have your work cut out for you."

Pastwa quickly glances over the titles of the books before slipping them under his left arm.

"Thank you Sir, I'll review these and very much appreciate the briefing." Before Pastwa can continue, Reardon cuts in.

"Learn your man, Commander, and get me some answers, fast! I need to know what happened to him and I prefer to learn about what became him before any word of this leaks out. So get going and keep me up to date!"

"Yes Sir!" Pastwa turns and quickly exits.

Reardon swivels in his chair and looks across the harbor. Closing his eyes, he imagines what it may have looked like back on the evening of December 6, 1941.

CHAPTER TEN
THE FRONT PAGE

Pastwa is stretched across a sofa in Yamura's living room thirty floors above Honolulu Harbor. A set of double sliding glass doors provides them with a great view of the Waikiki strip. Further in the distance the famous Honolulu landmark, Diamond Head, is outlined in the mid-evening moonlight.

The sun set about an hour earlier and the daily fireworks display has just commenced. The aroma of the Pacific Ocean is mixing with the telltale odor of expended gunpowder, which is a sensual combination Pastwa finds relaxing. He's barefoot, his shirt's slightly unbuttoned, there's a glass of his favorite red wine in his right hand and a California roll in his left. An appetizing arrangement of sushi, California rolls, crackers and Fontinella cheese beckon from the nearby cocktail table.

Yamura, dressed in a brightly colored and very short dress is sitting beside him. It's been a long day for them both and they are enjoying some down-time. Yamura is savoring a glass of her favorite Sauvignon Blanc she stores in a small refrigerator, just a few degrees above freezing. Their wine tastes are a contrast, but as for the balance of their passions, they are in perfect sync with each other.

"Chris, maybe you could fill me in on why Reardon's so zealous about this case?"

Pastwa accepts a chunk of sushi she fairly well pushes into his mouth, so he can't immediately answer. After swallowing he takes a sip of his wine, first gently swishing the wine in his mouth so as to amplify the taste.

"I've worked on quite a number of projects with Reardon and one thing I learned early on, in fact the first time I stepped into his office, is when it comes to the Pearl Harbor surprise attack, he has very strong opinions. He gets a little bent out of shape over it, for sure. I imagine with all of his clandestine intelligence background he still can't understand how our intelligence back in '41 could fail so miserably."

Yamura slips a cracker with a slice of Fontinella into Pastwa's mouth, picks

65

up her own wine glass and inhales a mouthful. She sits back and settles into a mound of pillows.

"Chris, I know he has a fixation about the Pearl Harbor attack, but he wasn't even alive at the time."

Pastwa swallows, picks up his glass and takes another sip. He swirls the wine around in his glass as he considers Reardon.

"Reardon's dad was on one of the battlewagons that day. He was a spanking new, freshly minted ensign so how else would he have drawn OD duty on a Sunday morning in a peacetime navy?"

Pastwa pauses for a moment as he gathers his thoughts. "I don't remember for sure Karen, but I think he was on the *Maryland*."

"So, what happened? Obviously he wasn't killed." Yamura very slowly sips her wine as she settles a little more deeply into the couch, exposing almost all of her shapely legs.

"Obviously he didn't die, but he lost an eye and wound up spending the bulk of the war behind a desk. Despite that he eventually finished his career with the rank of Captain." Pastwa accepts another piece of sushi from Yamura, who leans across the couch to offer it to him, intentionally providing him with a very clear view of her cleavage.

"From what I gather, his dad has told him the story of losing his eye over and over since he was a kid; constantly telling him how he caught some shrapnel in his face from a bomb explosion during the second wave of the attack while he was directing an anti-aircraft gun crew. No wonder the senior Reardon has a grudge and passed it along to the Admiral. You might've noticed his dad around the base from time to time, he wears a blue patch over his left eye. I've met him and he's pretty sprite for a man in his 90's. In my opinion he has the appearance of a man who must have been someone to deal with in his youth."

"That helps me understand Reardon a little better." Yamura warmly smiles as she casts a playful glance at Pastwa.

She slowly slips off the couch, stands, and with a shrug of her shoulders allows her dress to fall onto the floor, revealing she's not wearing any undergarments.

"You *are* going to stay the night, right?" She asks, as if that's necessary.

Pastwa smiles broadly, places his glass on the table and takes her in his arms. As he pulls her close to him he gives her a long and very passionate kiss.

"Karen, I never intended to leave," his voice is barely above a whisper.

It's a little after six the following morning and Pastwa is sitting on Yamura's lanai, enjoying his coffee. Waikiki beach, stretched out in the distance, is beginning to fill with bathers, surfers, and sail boats. They find it relaxing to start their day this way and it sure beats Pastwa's bachelor officers' housing on the base. The somewhat acrid smell of fireworks' gunpowder has long since been replaced with the fresh, sweet and salty air of the Pacific Ocean.

Yamura walks out to join him, holding the morning edition of a Honolulu newspaper in her hands. She pulls out the sports section, hands it to Pastwa and takes a seat opposite him. Pulling open the front page she lets out a loud, "Holy shit!" Startled, Pastwa drops the sports pages. Puzzled, he looks at Yamura, her mouth wide open and staring at the paper.

"What the hell, Karen? What's happened?"

Karen pulls open the front page and turns it around to face Pastwa who reads the headline aloud:

"WW II JAPANESE SAILOR FOUND BURIED IN KAILUA"

"Holy Crap Karen, look at this picture, even we don't have this shot. What the hell's going on?"

They find themselves looking at a picture of Auntie Lee holding a sword with the caption, "Property owner Auntie Lee displays the WWII Japanese ceremonial sword unearthed in her backyard." A photo of the skeleton with the pistol peeking out from the ground is also on the front page.

"Damn it all to hell, Karen. You know the Admiral's probably reading this as I speak." Pastwa quickly skims through the story before handing the paper back to her.

"Seems to me they don't know much of anything. The only real surprise is the appearance of the sword, which is no big issue. But we must be on our guard. This is written by Lani Gale who knows her way around the base in a big way and certainly appears to have connections there."

Yamura finishes reading the story as she shakes her head in disbelief. She's keenly aware Lani Gale is Pastwa's ex-fiancé and no doubt has connections at the base as a result.

Listen Chris, as far as this story goes there's really nothing new here. It looks to me as if all they know is what the work crew or the property owner would know. Any connection they're making to the Pearl Harbor attack is purely speculative on their part and I sincerely doubt Gale actually knows if she's correct, at least not yet." Yamura refolds the paper and stands. "We need to get to the base, regardless. I'll be ready in ten minutes; will you wait for me?"

"Of course, I'm going to call Clarke and Ferguson and get them both down there, pronto!" Yamura slips between the balcony and the table and gives Pastwa a kiss.

She does her best to smile and just before she disappears in the direction of the bedroom, she calls out: "Ready in Ten!"

CHAPTER ELEVEN
UNSETTLING NEWS

About the same time Pastwa and Yamura are reading the front-page headlines, an over ninety year old Ken Kida, a Japanese/American, is doing the same while sitting on the front lanai of his North Shore of Oahu home. From where he is sitting he can see the Pacific, about a quarter mile distant.

Ken loves to begin his day with a pot of hot tea infused with lemon from one of the trees in his orchard-like backyard. Today has begun no differently than most of his mornings since he finally retired, for good, about ten years ago. His once jet-black hair is heavily streaked with grey and, unlike when he was young, he now wears it long and pulled back into a Samurai style chonmage, or topknot. He sports a pure grey, triangular shaped beard which juts about eight inches below his chin and he's wearing a loose fitting, darkly colored Hawaiian style shirt and equally loose fitting solid black trousers. The sparkle in his black eyes gives no indication he is well over ninety years old.

His wife of over fifty years, Sun, is sitting on the opposite side of the table. Ken is reading the story describing the discovery of a skeleton in Kailua and after he's read the entire story, twice, he turns the front page around towards Sun and lays it on the table.

"Sun, this is not good news." Realizing her husband's voice sounds unusually serious she immediately looks up from her magazine. Her eyes open wide as she reads the headline.

"Oh, my!" She exclaims. "Oh, my! I always assumed this day would never come. What should we do?" Sun's voice gives away the fact she is genuinely scared.

"Sun, I know it has been a long time since we last spoke about this." Ken folds the paper and places it on the center of the table with the headline facing up. Sun slowly pushes herself from the table, stands and walks over to Ken and once beside him, gently pulls his head into her chest.

"Ken, what should we do? Should we leave? Where can we go? Where could we go?" Tears begin to slip down Sun's deeply tanned and wrinkled face.

Ken very lightly pushes her away and slowly rises to his feet. He looks at her sparkling gray hair which trails behind her and thinks to himself how much he has enjoyed all the times he would run his hands through her hair. He momentarily finds himself back in a field hospital in South Korea where they first met.

"Sun, no need to cry and certainly no need to run." Ken pulls her hands into his own and looks into her tearfully gleaming black eyes.

"Clearly the newspaper has no idea how much more there is to their story. I imagine, however, the U.S. Navy is aware that I, as Lt. Yokoyama, wrote the ship's logbook, but even that is questionable. There is a very realistic possibility that little of substance survived after all these years and the navy may have nothing more than a skeleton and some artifacts."

Sun stops crying and, wiping her eyes, responds quietly. "You are just saying that. I have known you so long," Sun pauses as she struggles to regain her composure, "so long now that I have come to know better! You are a meticulous man and you insist on always doing the job right. How could I now hope you did not properly protect the logbook as well as the other items you buried? It would be contrary to your essence. No! We must believe the Navy has been able to read every word you wrote. We must be practical my husband and assume the Navy knows you were still alive a week after the attack and perhaps longer."

Sun slips her hands from Ken's grip, sits down, takes a sip of her tea while Ken gazes at their expansive front yard, focusing on the blossoms of his many cherry trees. They remain silent for several minutes when, finally, Ken speaks.

"Sun, if it is to be that I must fall, as the cherry blossoms must also fall, then so be it. At best, the Navy knows I survived for a few days after the attack, but it is unlikely they could know any more than that. We are talking about a time in island history when so much was happening records could not always be perfectly maintained. My very identity is evidence of that." Ken pauses to allow himself a moment to consider the matter as he seeks to calm his wife.

"What will come of this discovery remains to be seen. As for us, nothing has changed and nothing will change. The odds of us ever meeting, the odds of us, a Japanese man and a Korean woman, falling in love, the odds of being capable of putting ourselves into a position where we actually could be wed, all those odds were nearly impossible to calculate, yet here we are! We must move forward on the belief we will overcome any new adversities that may befall us." Ken's words prove reassuring and Sun's breathing slowly returns to normal as they sit in silence, each of them considering what may lie before them.

The silence is interrupted by the sound of a car pulling into their driveway. Gary, one of their grandsons, drives his bright blue Beetle convertible all the way to the front walk. With the top down, he looks over at the lanai, spots his grandparents and waves hello with his left hand as he shifts the car into park with his right. He quickly jumps out, climbs the four steps to the lanai, beelines for his Kapuna and reaches down to gently kiss his grandmother on her left cheek.

"Good morning Kapuna, how are you today?" Gary smiles and looks over at his grandfather, Ken.

"And grandfather, how are you this morning?" He chooses a rice cookie from a plate on the table and makes himself comfortable in one of the padded wicker chairs surrounding the table.

"We are fine, Gary. Let me bring you a nice hot tea and a few more cookies" replies Sun as she rises from her chair and slips into the house.

Gary's about to graduate high school and has been accepted into Annapolis, which has made Ken immensely proud. Gary wears his jet-black hair in a crew cut and his physique reflects his work-out regimen. Upon learning the news of Gary's acceptance Ken picked up the newspaper, chose a bright blue convertible that was featured in a full color display ad and bought it for Gary as a combination graduation/acceptance present. He is one of seven grandsons and particularly reminds Ken of himself. The fact he is headed to Annapolis is additional verification for him that Gary has inherited quite a few of his genes.

"Gary, what are your plans today?" Ken raises an eyebrow as he lightly runs his left hand through his beard.

Gary knows when his grandfather raises an eyebrow while stroking his beard, then he must have something on his mind and responds:

"Nothing at all, today's a school holiday so I thought I'd stop by and see what you're up to. After all, I never know if you'll be out surfing!"

Ken laughs as he hasn't been surfing in more than twenty years, though it is true that once upon a time he enjoyed the sport very much. One of the concessions he has made to the march of time is the retirement of his old surf board which is now displayed on a wall in his pristine garage.

"I was thinking maybe you would like to take this old man for a ride this morning," Ken smiles and winks.

"Let me guess, you want to head over to the *Arizona* memorial, right?" Gary feigns being tired of taking him there, but the fact is, he enjoys his time with his grandfather and loves listening to his stories.

"No, not today Gary. Today I would like us to pack some snacks and a couple of folding chairs. We can go to the *Utah* Memorial and I just happen to have my military pass here in my shirt pocket." Ken places his right hand on his left shirt pocket, the edge of the pass poking over the top.

"Okay, but that means I'm expecting some pretty good story telling. I'll go ask Kapuna to pack some goodies for us," says Gary.

"Yes, that is a good idea and please ask her to include a bottle or two of my favorite flavored water. She has me hooked on flavored water!"

"Consider it done." Gary quickly disappears into the house as Ken slowly pushes himself from his chair, glances at his blossoming cherry trees, makes his way down the four steps of the lanai and over to the car.

Ken seats himself into the passenger seat and buckles in. Gary returns from the house holding a large basket in one hand and two folding canvas chairs in the other. He stores them in the trunk and jumps behind the steering wheel.

"Windows down or the A/C today?" Gary asks.

"Please, leave the windows down. Maybe on the way back I might prefer the A/C, but for now, I feel rested and it is a beautiful morning." Ken adjusts his cap, his chonmage poking through an opening in the back. Printed across the front is the name of the company he founded, "KEN'S CLIMATE CONTROL-ALL ISLANDS," superimposed over an outline of the Hawaiian Islands.

It proves to be about a forty-five-minute drive to the base. After passing through security they park as near to the *Utah* as possible and walk to their usual spot where Gary sets up the chairs in the little bit of shade available at this time of the morning. As they settle in they hear someone calling them.

"Morning there, Captain. I see you brought your first mate with you again."

They look around and spot their friend, Captain Clint Reardon. He's sitting on a lawn chair about fifty feet away, has an earphone in one ear, is sporting a worn golf hat which shades his good eye and is holding a bottle of *Kona Big Wave* in his right hand.

"Good morning yourself, Captain." Ken throws the senior Reardon a casual salute. "Your Dodgers winning?" Ken smiles as he waits for a reply.

"Not yet, it's only the pregame. They're playing one of those damned stupid inter-league games with the Yankees. Damned stupidest idea I ever heard. Inter-league play! Christ, next thing you know they'll be playing the all-star game in England!" Captain Reardon takes a deep drink, pulls his cap down over his good eye, and settles a little more deeply into his chair.

"Sorry to hear that, but good luck to your Dodgers!" Ken smiles as Gary pulls out a bottle of flavored water and hands it to him.

"Thank you, now go ahead and make yourself comfortable," says Ken as he opens the bottle, takes a drink, screws the cap back on and places it into the built-in cup holder. Gary pulls out a bottle of his favorite island soda, *Waialua Root Beer*, and settles in. He's anticipating a good story about how his grandfather started the air conditioning business, or perhaps how Ken and Sun first met. Gary, however, is in for a shock today.

"First," says Ken in a near whisper, "let us take a few moments of silence to honor the fifty four sailors who lie entombed within the *Utah*."

They always begin their visits to any of the military memorials with a silent prayer. Gary's favorite site is the *National Memorial Cemetery of the Pacific*, often called the "Punchbowl." However, he loves any opportunity to go to Pearl and is just happy to have time together with his grandfather. They spend several minutes in silence, Ken, with his eyes closed, and Gary staring at the rusting hull of the battleship *Utah* jutting from the still waters of Pearl Harbor.

"Gary," Ken's voice is just above a whisper, "today is different than most for today it has become apparent to me and your Kapuna things could be changing very soon and not likely for the good." Gary appears to be both puzzled and concerned.

"Are either of you sick?" Gary leans forward, anxious for the answer.

"No, Gary, it is nothing like that. We are both fine."

"I'm just glad you're both okay." Gary, visibly relieved, is keenly aware of their advancing years and makes a deliberate effort not to think about it and visits them as often as possible.

"Your Kapuna and I always believed we would take the story I am about to tell you to our graves. Unfortunately, an event we read about in today's newspaper may change everything as one of the things I have learned over the years is good news reporters do not let go of good stories and I fear I am a good news story, perhaps a very good news story." His gaze switches back and forth between Gary and the still waters of the harbor as he searches for the right words.

"Grandfather, I didn't see the paper today. Is there a problem with the company?"

Ken smiles, "If only that were the case, then it could be fixed. No, I fear the problem lies with me and with who I really am." Gary stares at his grandfather while trying to comprehend, but fear of the unknown rules the moment.

"I don't get it. What kind of story could possibly be in the paper about you and what do you mean it has to do with *who* you are? You're my father's, father! I've known you my whole life. Everyone knows who you are!" Ken passes him the front page of the paper and points to the headline. Gary quickly glances through the story before handing it back.

"Fine, someone digs up a skeleton. Obviously it wasn't you they dug up, so what's the problem?" Ken opens his water, takes another drink, returns it to the cup holder and continues.

"Let me begin with the fact my name is *not* Ken Kida." Gary interrupts, "Oh, I get it now. I was expecting a story, so you *are really giving me a story!*" Gary laughs, but only half-heartedly. The serious look on Ken's face quickly washes away his grin and he turns serious himself.

"Grandpa, I *am* trying to understand. You are serious, so please continue. I won't interrupt anymore." Knowing he now has Gary's full attention, Ken re-settles himself into his chair.

"You do not know anything of my parents, really, besides the fact they both passed away and did not live here. There is a good reason for that. My father, your great grandfather, was an officer in the Japanese Imperial Guards Cavalry and was killed in an incident in China while fighting the Russians when I was only eight years old. In fact, it was the reason I studied Chinese as I felt I might someday find myself fighting in China. The point I am trying to make is simple, I was not born here, or even in the United States. I was born and raised in Japan."

Confusion washes across Gary's face as he reaches over and picks up the newspaper again. Ken waits as he reads the entire article, but when he finishes, he still looks as if he has no idea how the story could impact them.

"I'm sorry, grandpa, but I still don't understand what this story has to do with you."

"The body they found over in Kailua was my shipmate, Sadamu Kamita, of the Imperial Japanese Navy secret weapon, the *I-16-tou*." Ken recalls the memory of his departed friend and smiles. "Kamita liked to call it, *Yokoyama's Boat.*"

"Wait please," Gary interrupts. He's half confused and half ready to cry. What he's being told is about as foreign to him as anything imaginable.

"Who is Yokoyama and what kind of boat are you talking about?"

Ken sighs, unconsciously begins stroking his beard and takes a deep breath before continuing.

"Gary, I was an officer in the Imperial Japanese Navy having graduated from Eta Jima, which is the Japanese equivalent of Annapolis, in 1939. My birth name is Masaharu Yokoyama, not Ken Kida. I only assumed the name Ken Kida once I was on Oahu. You see, the name was provided to me by associates I met here," Ken pauses a moment, "though you might consider them to have been spies, or perhaps worse."

"When you say 'here,' you mean Oahu?" Gary is desperately trying to come to grips with what his grandfather is telling him while also feeling a little sick to his stomach. He reasons to himself, on the one hand this is his grandfather, a man he has known all of his life and on the other, well, suddenly his grandfather is a stranger, a stranger from another world.

"Please continue and I'll hold my questions for later. My stomach's churning so it's better if I don't talk."

Ken takes another sip of water as his ninety-plus year old body combats the eighty degree weather.

"I understand." Ken is quite cognizant of the anxiety in Gary's voice. "To answer your question, by 'here,' I mean Oahu. I am what you might call an 'illegal alien' for I did not come to Oahu as a friend of the United States. The saga of how I came to find myself on Oahu began in April, 1941, while I was in my home country of Japan.

I was about two years removed from the Academy when I received reassignment orders transferring me to a top secret 'Special Unit' being formed within the Imperial Japanese Navy. The other members being called to the 'Special Unit' were as uninformed as I. All we knew was we were reporting aboard a mystery ship, and once there we would engage in 'special training.' That's all my orders said: 'special training.' I found it to be incredibly exciting."

Though Ken appears to be staring at Gary, he's no longer sees him. His mind is speeding back in time and though his eyes are open, he no longer recognizes the present. The past is quickly streaming into focus and Ken's voice takes on a younger and more energetic tone as his memories from 1941 usurp the present.

•　•　•　•　•

Ken is a handsome young naval officer as he finds himself aboard the *I.J.N. CHIYODA*. He's sitting in the ship's wardroom with about three dozen men. It's a mix of academy graduates and engineering petty officers. A hastily constructed stage dominates the front of the wardroom.

Suddenly, from the back of the room a sailor calls out: "Attention!"

Every person in the audience jumps to attention as the ship's commander, Captain Kaku Harada, makes his way to the stage, climbs the steps and walks behind the podium. Glancing around the room he finds himself facing some of the cream of the Japanese Navy, all of whom are staring at him, waiting for his words.

Harada, only about five foot, five inches tall has a very broad chest, developed from years of weight training. Combined with his deep-set eyes and even deeper voice, everyone present cannot help but respect him. The fact the Navy has placed him in charge of this training is an indication to the men of the admiration Harada obviously commands with his superiors. He is resplendent in his dark blue dress uniform adorned with numerous medals and ribbons. He tends to wear his hat ever so slightly tilted back as he wants to be certain everyone in the audience can clearly see his eyes. He motions for the assembly to sit.

"I am honored to have been appointed by the Commander-in-Chief of the Combined Fleet, Admiral Isoroku Yamamoto, to train you for a most secret and potentially glorious mission. Admiral Yamamoto and the Emperor are asking each of you to accept a very special task, a task which marks a landmark event for our great Navy," says Harada in a deep, booming voice.

"This ship is not merely a seaplane carrier. No, not any longer; this vessel has been converted to serve as a figurative 'nest' for an innovative type of warfare. The Imperial Navy has a new secret weapon and you will see to its delivery directly into the heart of the enemy fleet!"

With the last comment Harada finds he must pause as polite applause sweeps across the room. Once the audience quiets down he continues.

"What we have devised and for which you will be the instruments of delivery is, indeed, a true 'Oke-Hazama' strategy! Over the next few months you will learn how to perfectly execute a massive underwater surprise attack in the honorable tradition of the great Admiral Nobunaga Oda himself!"

Most the officers instinctively rise from their seats in response to the mention of Admiral Oda. Smiling, Harada motions for the group to resume sitting.

"We plan to educate you thoroughly in the use of this new secret weapon and to deploy it against a numerically superior fleet, likely that of the United States, though it could prove to be Great Britain." Harada pauses while making eye contact with various officers. He looks directly into the eyes of Ken, who tenses up in response, before Harada continues.

"In what will prove to be a lightening underwater attack, you will torpedo the enemy's capital ships long before they are even within range of our own surface taskforce. While they are foolishly focused on the superior battleships of the Imperial Japanese Navy you will swiftly, and at unheard of submerged speeds, move in on them as if underwater Samurai. You will strike them telling blows from below the surface which shall be a complete surprise to the enemy in the true tradition of 'Oke-Hazama!'"

Harada always calculates his moves so as to maintain his audiences' attention. He pulls the podium out of the way, pushes an armchair to the center of the stage, and seats himself. Leaning forward, his elbows on his knees, he continues, though in a lower and much softer tone of voice.

"Each of you has been carefully chosen for your respective assignment and even the Emperor has been involved in the selection process, along with Admiral Yamamoto and his staff. They have full confidence in your ability to fulfill this mission." He is interrupted by a murmuring that rolls across the room at the mention of the Emperor and Admiral Yamamoto in the same sentence. He abruptly sits upright, allowing his arms to rest on either armrest.

"Having said this, should any of you prefer posting to another task, for any reason at all, please speak now or visit my aide later today. It is essential each of you be entirely dedicated to this plan if it is to succeed! Should you elect not to participate, no shame will follow you; of that I can promise. Nobody will ever know you had even been here. If your heart and soul are not fully dedicated to the mission at hand, and trust me when I say it is a glorious mission, then please, it is your duty to withdraw."

Harada pauses to allow his audience an opportunity to respond. After waiting about thirty seconds, as he makes eye contact with most of the officers in the audience, he concludes nobody desires a transfer and continues.

"For now, this is all I can state. Tomorrow, however, we will commence your training and you will be shown our new secret weapon. I urge all of you to eat full and satisfying dinners and sleep well tonight for tomorrow is the beginning of a series of great and wondrous challenges."

A sailor in the rear of the room calls out: "Attention!"

Everyone jumps to attention as Harada quickly exits. Once he is out of sight the same sailor calls out: "Dismissed!"

Ken sits down and stares at the stage as most of the officers begin to shuffle out. He does not know what the nature of the mission is and has conflicting feelings. On the one hand, he should be honored to be among the chosen few for a special mission. On the other hand, he cannot help but feel nearly overcome by a stinging sensation of impending dread.

●   ●   ●   ●   ●

Ken blinks his eyes several times as he becomes aware of his physical surroundings and his conscious mind chases his recollections back into the past. His quick return to the present coupled with the reality he is over ninety years old and sitting within a peacetime Pearl Harbor floods him with a tidal wave of fatigue. Gary notices his face appears to be turning slightly grey.

"Grandfather!" Gary reaches into the cooler and pulls out a cold bottle of flavored water. He twists off the cap and offers it to him. "You don't look so good. Have some water."

Ken smiles, accepts the bottle and takes several small sips while glancing towards the harbor. The upper mastheads of several ships anchored side-by-side in Middle Loch help bring him the remainder of the way back from his first day on the *I. J. N. Chiyoda*.

"Gary, I think it better for us to continue later this afternoon as fatigue sets in much more easily these days. Especially when it is this hot."

"I think some rest is a good idea, grandfather. Don't worry, I'll carry everything back to the car. You just take care of yourself and we'll be home before you know it!"

Gary stands, closes the cooler and folds his chair. Ken also rises, but before he can begin to fold his chair, Gary grabs it from him and pops it closed with a metallic clank.

"Have no fear Gary; I am fine and we will continue our talk later this afternoon. I have a great deal of my history to cover."

"I think I'm looking forward to it, but my concerns for you have now risen above and beyond any potential health issues." Gary leaves one hand free as he assists Ken to the car.

CHAPTER TWELVE
IT'S ALL A MATTER OF MAKING A RECORD

Pastwa's sitting behind his desk surrounded by stacks of old files, leaving him with precious little workspace. Yamura is a few feet away, rummaging through one of several boxes bursting with severely yellowing files. Her hair, which a few hours ago was neatly pulled back, is starting to loosen and several strands are wildly askew. They have not taken a break for hours as the vision of Reardon walking in, unannounced, motivates them to press forward. Clarke enters with additional boxes, a donut wedged between his right hand and the boxes.

"Where would you like these, Sir?" Clarke looks around the cluttered office while waiting for Pastwa's response.

"Just anywhere there's a space or anywhere you can make a space." Pastwa pauses, looks over at Yamura and realizes they have worked through lunch.

"Clarke, we really need you to run out and bring us some sandwiches. Oh, and please put on some fresh coffee." Pastwa realizes he's overlooked Clarke's own lunch. "Make sure you get something good for yourself while you're at it." Pastwa returns his attention to the dusty file he was reading. Yamura thinks to herself that Chris just read her mind as she's starving.

"Right away Sir! Be back before you know it!" Clarke turns to Yamura.

"Any special requests Ma'am?" Yamura looks up at Clarke, who's still holding a donut.

"Whatever you get is fine with me, but please be double quick about it. I'm starving." She smiles at Clarke who appreciates being allowed to make his own lunch choice for her. He has attended to their food tastes on dozens of occasions and prefers to believe he knows their culinary dispositions better than they do. Clarke takes a bite from his donut as he runs through the doorway, stopping in the vestibule just long enough to put on another pot of coffee before rushing to the PX.

The PX at Pearl Harbor is a wondrous collection of food and goods and also has several better-than-average fast food options. Clarke has several venues from which to choose at low PX prices and has the menus memorized. He rehearses the orders as he jogs to the PX.

Back at the office Pastwa suddenly stands upright and lightly hits the side of his forehead with his right palm. "I have an idea."

Yamura plops onto a chair and throws the file she's holding on top of a nearby box. She's hungry, tired and a little frustrated as they've been working for hours on end with no finish line yet in sight.

"I was thinking, if I was Yokoyama the first thing I'd do once the burial was over would be to try and get myself to one of the recovery points where the Jap Navy had "*I*" boats waiting."

"Fine," responds Yamura, "but if Yokoyama had done so, we'd know about it as history would have confirmed the fact and we'd have no problem."

"Maybe, Karen. From what I've read, no fishing boats would have dared to do anything out of the ordinary after the Japanese attack. Hell, our fly boys shot up quite a few fishing boats and killed more than one unlucky fisherman those first few days after the attack. But there's still an outside chance he tried to get to one of the pickup points and managed to get himself drowned. Who would know? It would certainly make a nice clean ending to our problem, and, as I recall, one of the Jap submarines did manage to get itself sunk. He *could* have been aboard her."

"If he was on the Jap sub we sank, I would expect the Captain would have transmitted the fact they picked up a midget sub survivor to the fleet as soon as it happened. But I'm unaware of any such transmission and from what I've read, we plucked a number of Japanese bodies out of the waters around Oahu over the weeks following the attack and none were in naval uniforms. We had patrol boats scouring throughout the islands so it's just not likely they would have missed his body; if there was a body to be missed. And remember, we thought the Japanese intended an invasion so we were vigilantly patrolling all of the beaches. And let's face it, if we anticipated an invasion was in the offing, Yokoyama would probably have been of the same opinion and would have been lying low, waiting for his countrymen to arrive."

Pastwa momentarily turns to gaze towards the harbor when another thought strikes him.

"In fact, if you consider it, there just might be a clue there."

"How so?" Yamura asks.

"Assuming Yokoyama decided to stick around he needed a new identity and he would have needed one pretty damn quick. It was essential he assimilate into island life, sooner or later, and without a new identity it couldn't happen. He was a living body in need of a dead body, or at least the dead body's identification."

"Right. He had to come up with something, or *someone*, fast," adds Yamura.

"So," she pauses as she puts together her thoughts, "we know he made contact with some Japanese sympathizers, for example; the doctor who operated on Kamita and maybe some German Nationals. They could easily have supplied him with clothing, a job, a place to live, but just how would they have gone about getting Yokoyama a new identity?"

They turn silent while they jointly consider the problem. Pastwa, as is his style, is looking out towards the harbor. Yamura prefers to concentrate her gaze on a fixed object and let her mind go to work and she has chosen their copy of the logbook as the object of her focus. After a few minutes Pastwa raises his right hand, signaling an idea, and swings around to face Yamura.

"You know, Karen, any identity they arranged for Yokoyama would need to closely match his age. My guess is in order for a new identity to work, they needed to be certain he was a Nisei because as a Nisei he'd have been born in Hawaii, which would make him an American; and he'd stand out from the crowd a lot less if he was Nisei. In fact, if I was looking to get someone a new identity *that* would have been a critical requirement. It's just a guess, but with locals involved and maybe the German folks I think it's more likely than not they made him Nisei which would have been absolutely perfect for their purposes."

Yamura, her right eyebrow raised, replies, "So he needed an identity from someone very real, yet very dead. As for Nisei, no doubt they would have sought just such an identity. And where better to get that new identity than from a medical doctor who would, of course, have access to both birth and death records for a large segment of the population back then. Yes, a doctor could very possibly do it, but only if he was Japanese. In fact, according to the logbook we know they sought out a Japanese doctor to attend to Kamita and he likely was the person who helped create a new identification for Yokoyama." Yamura slaps the top of the desk with the palm of her left hand to amplify her point.

"You're right Karen; we should be looking at death records. It's all a matter of making a record!" Pastwa picks up the phone.

"I'm calling down to the *other* Honolulu paper to see if we can't get into their obituary records from, say, early '38 to maybe as late as January, '42. There's no use wasting any time at County as they had that devastating fire back in the late forties."

Yamura perks up as she realizes there just may be a light at the end of the proverbial tunnel. "Right! We compile a list of all male Nisei who died in that time frame and who were about twenty-two years old, give or take, say, five or six years." Yamura pauses, "But what then?"

Pastwa is dialing the newspaper and stops to answer.

"Then we simply cross-reference the list with the rolls of all interred Japanese/Americans from Oahu. Hopefully the resulting list of matching names will be a short one, or at least manageable. From there we hunt down each and every one of the deceased Nisei and figure out if any of them is our man. If it turns out he's still not accounted for, we'll try some other approach; however, I have a good feeling this will bring us the result we want and a final resolution with no loose ends."

Just then Clarke walks in carrying a sack of sandwiches and some coffees. Yamura looks at Clarke while Pastwa phones the newspaper.

"Good timing Clarke! Please go and pull us a car from the pool" She pauses a moment before continuing. "And bring three blank notebooks, pens, your camera and mini-tripod, along with the food because you're coming with us!"

"Yes, Ma'am. Maybe I should put together a couple of 'stay hot' pitchers of coffee too; and some donuts for energy." Clarke can hear Pastwa is talking to someone at the paper, so he looks to Yamura for an answer.

"Hell yes sailor! This could turn into a long afternoon and an even longer night. For once I *will* take you up on the donut idea. Now let's get moving! The sooner we get there, the sooner we can finish. And I really want to finish this before Lani Gale or somebody else beats us to it." Yamura turns to look for a file as Clarke hurries out of the office.

"The paper says they have someone down in records on a twenty-four-seven basis and we're welcome to stay all night if we like. They even have a coffee machine down there so we're in good shape." He notices Clarke is not around and looks over to Yamura. "We just have to be careful not to speak too loudly or leave a paper trail of our research. We don't need to hand anyone there another story." He again looks around for Clarke.

"Karen, where'd Clarke go?"

"He's out getting us a car, coffee, donuts, extra notebooks and pens and I told him he should bring his camera in the event we need to photograph any records. He has our food too, which we can eat in the car. I believe we should be all set in about ten minutes." Yamura smiles as she is suddenly experiencing the type of goose bumps she gets when she knows she's onto something.

"Excellent. By tomorrow morning I trust we'll have some definitive answers." Pastwa grabs his briefcase but momentarily sets it on Clarke's desk as turns to face Yamura.

"Karen, are you getting the same goose bumps I have right now?"

CHAPTER THIRTEEN
LIVE AND LEARN

Sun and one of her granddaughters are clearing the dining table following a late lunch. Gary and Ken are sitting on the rear lanai, the banana leaf-shaped blades of a large fan slowly revolving overhead. Most of the backyard is now in shade from a mix of palms, lemon, lime, cherry and papaya trees. The fusion of fragrances from the collection of mature trees Ken has planted over the years engulfs the entire yard.

The backyard provides Ken with a semblance of what he recalls of his family's home in Japan. Years earlier he attempted to build a koi pond, but discovered the hard way he didn't have a knack for raising koi so he repurposed it into a garden, complete with bonsai trees. The site of dead fish floating on the pond had sent several grandchildren running into the house engulfed in tears, and every once in a while they still remind him of the gruesome sight.

"Gary, whenever I consider my first life I always conclude it was overly sheltered and extremely regimented. I possessed an extremely narrow view of the world, a view carefully constructed by the Japanese government, which was basically controlled by the Army. My second life has been more of an awakening, as if I found myself emerging from a suffocating chemical fog." Ken pauses to enjoy a few sips of Sun's cherry iced tea.

"Growing up I had no choice but to adhere to unbending expectations and rules. Everything I would do was the result of what was demanded of me, including my enlistment in the naval academy. All things seemed to be as simple as black and white and I was a believer in the dogma which propounded that we, as Japanese, owed a protective responsibility to the balance of the people living in the Far East and the Pacific Rim, extending all the way to Hawaii. I was taught we were a superior race and should view Japan as a benevolent guardian. I did not know any other way, nor did it ever occur to me my government was, in reality, seeking the virtual enslavement of the peoples we were sworn to protect." Ken slowly shakes his head. "I lived a carefully sheltered life, a life sheltered from the truth, along with the overwhelming majority of my countrymen."

Ken pauses as he looks at his grandson with the love and pride of a grandfather. He lightly slaps his right hand on his right thigh and continues.

"But I am digressing! Certainly you want to hear about the rest of my first life, correct?"

"I really don't know what to say. I don't doubt you grandfather, but this is amazing and hard for me to grasp. I always wondered why you seldom spoke about your life prior to the time you met Kapuna and out of respect, I never asked."

Gary squirms in his chair as he attempts to achieve a modicum of physical comfort, as he finds it impossible to be emotionally comfortable.

"I know some pretty nasty stuff happens in war and I always believed if you wanted to talk about it, then you would have. For me, it's always been enough to see the medals on your wall, those medals tell me everything I need to know about your past."

"Gary, I appreciate that and I tell you all of this not to confuse you, but to ease the blow. If I am found out, I fear bad things will happen to me, even at my advanced age. But for now," Ken smiles and puts some enthusiasm into his voice, "it is just you and me. You will be staying for dinner tonight, correct?"

"Of course."

"Excellent, then I can continue where we left off after dinner. Right now, however, it is time for my daily afternoon meditation followed by a nice nap."

CHAPTER FOURTEEN
THE *PLANK* BAR

It may only be mid-afternoon, but it's quite dark inside the *Plank* Bar. The place has been a Pearl City fixture since before World War II and the windows still adorn traces of the blackout paint required back in the first few years of the war. The majority of the lighting consists of cheap tiki lights, strings of miniature Italian lights around the bar and a few light fixtures tenuously hanging over the several pool tables scattered around the low-ceilinged premises. The terms "dark" and "dingy" pretty much describe the place. If a person breathes a little too deeply the tell-tale aroma of mold greets the nostrils. The *Plank's* clientele prefers it stay dark and a little moldy and dingy, just as it was in 1941.

Lani Gale walks in the front door which momentarily hangs open behind her. The rush of sunlight causes several patrons to bark out complaints, but one patron in particular is enjoying the silhouette of Gale's body outlined by the bright Sun. She's wearing a short, low cut and brightly colored Hawaiian print dress which hugs her shapely derriere. Her deep yellow high heels exaggerate her height and she's sporting a very cute, albeit small, red purse. The yellow trim of the purse matches her heels and is casually slung over her right shoulder.

Petty Officer Paul Young is off duty, not in uniform and immediately recognizes her. He stands and motions with his left hand beckoning her to his booth. Gale spots him and slowly walks over, though she's clearly unhappy with the lack of cleanliness surrounding her.

It's not Gale's first visit to the *Plank* as it's her favorite venue when she wants to meet with an informer for it's not too far from the naval base and is dimly lighted. The *Plank* is seldom crowded and people who treasure their privacy while eschewing pretense are the primary clientele. If a person's seeking good food and chilled mugs they'd be well advised to keep driving. The *Plank* is not a tourist spot and harbors no aspirations to become one.

Gale walks up to Young's booth and slips onto the opposite, well-worn wood bench. Young resumes his seat and motions to the bartender. The bartender acknowledges him, but doesn't exactly drop everything he's doing to rush over.

"So, Paul, it's been a long time without hearing from you. Why the drought?" Gale slips her purse from her shoulder and sets it on the bench to her right. She presses it against the booth's wall to prevent any insect, or worse, from crawling behind it. She makes certain it's zipped closed just in the event something might sneak into it when she's not looking; these are precautions she has adopted due to prior experiences here.

"There hasn't been much excitement down on my end of the totem pole." He pauses as he breaks into a sly grin. "That is, until this week." He takes a sloppy gulp from his bottle of *Budweiser* and is about to continue when the bartender finally appears alongside the booth.

"Hello little missy what might you be liken' to drink today?" He makes no effort to disguise the fact he's staring directly down her cleavage.

Gale notices, of course. If he wasn't straining his neck trying to determine whether she's wearing a bra then she would have chosen the wrong dress. She looks at him and sits a little further back in the bench which has the effect of drawing her dress up to her neck; the result reveals much less skin than before. The bartender is disappointed the show is over and certainly looks it.

"I'll have whatever Kona Brew comes in a sealed bottle and is as cold as you can make it. Don't open it, I can do that myself." Her business with the bartender over, she turns to Paul.

"So," she pauses as the bartender has not left to fill her order, which draws her attention.

"That's all! Please bring me my beer." She chastises the bartender.

The bartender realizes he'd been staring and lets out a short laugh before returning to the bar.

"So, Paul, what's cooking?" She folds her arms in front of her, places them on the table and leans forward while smiling and staring him directly in the eyes.

Young is a little intimidated by her physical beauty. He's divorced and generally dates girls he meets at the *Plank* and similar places of questionable taste and unsavory patrons. Though he sports a crew-cut, the rest of him appears a bit sloppy, from his day-old beard to his worn Hawaiian t-shirt and loose fitting pants. Even his sandals appear to have been bought second-hand.

Young's out of his league and he knows it, but intends to capitalize on the situation regardless. He has information Gale is going to really want and money is on his mind. He is as yet unaware Gale disdains using money to buy information for in her opinion such use of money leads to mistakes and money can often be traced. Gale does not make many mistakes and most definitely does not leave trails behind her either.

"You know that article you wrote about the body up in Kailua?"

Gale raises an eyebrow and doesn't even glance at the bartender who has just placed a bottle of *Kona Longboard* in front of her. She looks at the bottle and is pleased to find beads of sweat coating the bottle, confirming for her the contents will be cold. She picks it up and twists the top off, though it is not a twist top; cleans it with a napkin and takes a sip. Satisfied, she returns her attention to Young.

"Of course I do, I wrote the damn thing. So what of it?" Her tone is admonishing and the effect on Young is as she intends. He moves to the defensive.

"I didn't mean anything by it. It's just that I know a lot more about what you printed; and I mean a *whole lot more*." He pulls out an oversized manila envelope from the bench beside him and lays it on the table.

"Are you nuts? Get that damned thing off the table!" Gale scolds him as if he were a child while she looks around the room to confirm nobody appears to have been paying attention to them.

Young is obviously flustered and embarrassed. He immediately pulls the envelope off the table and places it back on the bench. He's feeling more than a little intimidated and his confidence level has sunk to depths that make the *Plank* appear upscale.

"Sorry Lani, I just thought you'd like to see I did bring with me exactly what I inferred to you on the phone." Young's also worried as he's beginning to think he literally made the wrong call here and is panicking he might be getting himself into trouble.

"Listen carefully, Paul. You never know who might be watching. Discretion is always my key word." Gale leans back and pushes herself away from the table. Her intention is to create a little distance between her and Paul so he might relax a little. She wants to keep him on edge, but not over the edge.

"So, Paul, tell me what *exactly* is in the envelope and how did you get it?" Gale sweetens her tone. In response she notices he appears a little more relaxed.

"Sometimes I work in the same department as Lieutenant Ferguson in forensics and I got a good look at the skeleton they dug up along with the bullet they pulled out of its back too."

Gale's eyes open a little wider. "Bullet? What kind of bullet?" She instinctively leans forward which again affords him a view of her cleavage. Though he's clearly looking below her face, he continues.

"The bullet came from an M-1 which is the rifle we used back at the time of the Pearl Harbor attack. But there's a lot more." Young downs the last of his beer, holds the empty bottle up and motions to the bartender for another.

Gale takes a sip from her bottle as the bartender walks over and replaces Young's empty bottle with a fresh one. Thus restocked, Young continues.

"That's just the tip of it." Young takes a long drink.

"There was a box buried with the body and in it they found some personal items, but most important they found a logbook from a Japanese submarine." Young pauses as he takes another deep drink.

"A logbook from a Japanese sub? This is kind of far-fetched Paul, how can you know it's true?" She leans back again, intentionally drawing her dress closer to her neck and temporarily ending the subtle peep show.

Young smiles as he guesses from Gale's tone and facial expression she's going to buy his product today. He finishes off the beer with a few long gulps and motions for another. Feeling more confident, he makes Gale wait until the bartender has replaced his empty bottle before continuing.

"Your old friend Lieutenant Commander Pastwa is assigned to this case. In fact, that's what caught my attention in the first place because if this was a routine matter he'd never be involved."

Gale smiles at the mention of Pastwa. She's aware he's part of some type of special investigative unit that's headed up by Admiral Reardon, a man she has found to be a rather secretive individual and correctly reasons if Pastwa is on the case then there really must be something significant going on.

"You are exactly right about that! They don't assign Pastwa unless Reardon is involved. And if Reardon is involved then I *need* to be involved too. So tell me Paul," she lowers her voice to a whisper, "what do you have for me in that envelope?"

After downing several beers in short order Young is feeling much more comfortable and confident.

"Lani, you don't mind if I call you Lani, do you?

"No, that's my name, feel free to use it." Gale smiles at him and takes a careful sip of beer, making certain not to smudge her lipstick.

"Well, Lani, Pastwa called in Lieutenant Yamura who can read Japanese and he needs that skill pretty bad because the logbook's in Japanese. It's from a midget sub that attacked Pearl Harbor on December 7th and it covers the months leading up to the attack, details the attack and describes how the two midget submariners scuttled their vessel over in West Loch and came ashore."

Young takes another gulp of beer. Gale is amazed at what she's just heard and is working hard to conceal her excitement. Visions of yet another front page story are flying through her head as she fully appreciates the fact Young is all that sits between her, the envelope, a front page and maybe even a Pulitzer Prize.

"So, Yamura believes there's only the original and one copy of her translation. Except she apparently was pressed for time and filled out a project slip to have the original copied and guess who got the job?" Young smiles broadly.

"I did! As soon as I saw the words 'TOP SECRET-EYES ONLY' I decided to make two copies, not one." He motions to the envelope on the bench beside him.

"This is my copy and it could be yours."

"You mean to tell me this logbook is authentic and describes in detail how they trained for the Pearl Harbor attack?" Gale intentionally sounds skeptical.

"Yes, and it details the attack itself and how they fired two torpedoes and that the second torpedo turtled the old *Oklahoma*!" Young smiles and takes another gulp.

Gale leans forward and motions for Young to do the same.

"Listen," her voice is barely audible, "just who else knows you have this copy?"

Young laughs and whispers his response.

"You think I'm crazy? I could land in Fort Leavenworth for a long time, or worse; find myself assigned to the Antarctic for an extended tour if this got out."

Young pauses so he can take a good look around the bar and satisfy himself there's no one out of the ordinary milling around. He frequents the *Plank* enough to recognize any out of place 'face'.

"Lani, you and I are the only two outsiders who know about this. I figured you might be interested in compensating me for my efforts and in exchange you can have it all to yourself." Young smiles, sits back and takes another gulp.

Gale also leans back and pauses for a few moments as she certainly doesn't want to appear overly anxious. Nor she does want to pay him for the logbook. After all, she reasons to herself, the front page is one thing, but it's not something she cares to buy with her own cash.

"First, how do *I* know this is the only copy you made? You could just have easily set the machine to make ten copies!"

Young does his best to appear genuinely offended.

"Lani, this sucker is more than two hundred pages long, double spaced so I couldn't hang around making more than one extra copy. As it was, Lieutenant Yamura showed up and grabbed everything less than a minute after I finished. I just barely pulled it off."

Gale looks him over and decides it's more likely than not he's telling her the truth. She takes a couple sips of her beer, finishing the bottle.

"Well Paul, I believe you. But what are we talking here? What is it you want?"

Young starts to motion to the bartender, but Gale interrupts.

"No thanks, I don't need another one, not just now that is. I only want to know your price before we go any further. It's as simple as that."

Young looks at her, waives off the bartender and continues.

"Ok. Simple. I want Two Thousand Dollars. It's a nice even number. Get me that, in cash of course and then you can have the log." Young sits back smiling broadly and obviously quite pleased with himself.

Gale's mind is racing as she mulls over his demand. She has today's front page story and if she delays writing the follow-up story for one day while stringing Paul out it might have a greater impact on readership. She's repulsed at using her money to pay Young and knows the paper won't pay him, so what should she do? An idea strikes her and she can't disguise her smile.

"Sure you wouldn't like another beer?" Young asks.

"I do, but not here." She lets slip a semblance of a sexy smile.

Young looks a little puzzled as he can't figure out what she means.

"Okay, so you want to go to another bar, or maybe a restaurant?" Young says.

Gale smiles a little more broadly as she picks up her purse and slips it over her shoulder.

"No Paul, you're going to come over to my place. I have a twelve pack of *Big Wave* in my fridge, plenty of food and, besides, there's not a chance in hell we're going to finish our business in this dive. I want you to come over and bring the copy of the log with you. We'll be much more comfortable and it's a hell of a lot more private, not to mention cleaner!"

Gale reaches into her purse and pulls out a business card. She writes an address on the back and hands it to Young. He picks it up, looks it over and recognizes the location.

"Do you know where this is?"

"Sure I do. Pretty nice up around there. No worries." He starts to stand.

"Hold it!" You stay here another twenty or thirty minutes. Have another beer if you like; then you can leave. I don't want it to look as if you're leaving with me." She pauses a moment and looks around in disdain. "Listen, better make it more like forty-five minutes. I'm going to need a shower and you might want to bring a change of clean clothes with you because this place stinks to high heaven." She stares him straight in the eyes, allowing herself only a faint hint of a smile.

"So, Paul, can I assume this plan meets with your approval?" She lowers her voice and changes her tone to something she thinks he will consider to be sexy.

Young's smile is so large Gale can't help but notice he could use some serious orthodontic work and a good teeth cleaning. She thinks to herself: "I thought the Navy covered stuff like that."

"Absolutely Lani! I'll see you then." As she turns to walk out Young calls over to the bartender.

"Hey Mick, bring me another one!"

CHAPTER FIFTEEN
A NATURAL BLONDE

Relieved to be out of the *Plank* she drives away in her midnight blue Jetta as if fleeing a hell-hole, the staccato clattering of the turbo diesel seemingly matching her excitement. She opens the moon roof and drops down all the windows in a losing effort to air the smoke and grime out of her hair and clothing while considering Young's demand for two thousand dollars. Gale can't help but think about how many pedicures she could buy, rather than hand the money over to that silly sailor. "His teeth aren't *that* bad and at least they're a little white," she reasons out loud, "and this story may prove to be my ticket to D.C."

The forty-five-minute drive to her home is just long enough for her to formulate a plan of action. Upon arrival she immediately goes to her bedroom where a large walk-in closet bursting to the edges with clothing, purses and shoes awaits. She quickly looks through the racks and picks out a red dress followed by a bright blue dress, but just as she's about to choose between the two an ultra-low-cut black dress, sporting frilly ruffles on the sleeves and along the bottom edge with three large, black buttons up the front of the dress screams out to her. She tosses the red and blue dresses back into the closet and takes out the black one.

"He'll forget about the money when he sees me in this, or at least when he sees this fall off me!" Again, she is talking out loud with nobody to hear. She likes to listen to herself talk. For that matter, she also likes to read her own writing.

She quickly slips out of her clothes and decides to remove her panties, which is the only undergarment she's wearing. After all, she reasons, it would only get in the way, so may as well get rid of it now and increase the effect when her dress falls to the floor. After pausing to admire her tanned and toned naked body in a full-length wall mirror she rushes into the bathroom and sits in front of the vanity to touch-up her makeup.

Afterwards she examines her face from several angles and satisfied all is good, pulls out a brush and strokes her hair. She slips into her dress and fastens only the upper two of the three front buttons. Then it's back to the mirror so she can brush her hair one final time, making certain it softly flows down her upper body. At that moment, the doorbell rings.

"Perfect timing," she says aloud.

On the way to the front door she stops at the thermostat just long enough to set it down a few degrees. "That should have the effect I'm looking for." She smiles a self-satisfied grin and walks over to the entry. She takes a deep breath and slowly pulls the door open, backing up a step in the process so as to afford Young a good look at her.

As the door swings open, Young is pretty much overcome with a combination of lust and intimidation at the sight of Gale. While she is, to him, incredibly sexy and a first class "looker," as he likes to say, she has an air of sophistication that truly intimidates him. Bolstered by several beers he holds his own, at least for now.

"Why hello again, Paul, so good of you to come and see me." She motions to the large manila envelope in his right hand and says, "And you brought me a present too. That's great! Come on in." Gale pulls the door fully open and gestures him inside.

"Thanks Lani." He quickly makes his way into her living room before coming to a stop.

"Please, take a seat while I go get us a couple of cold beers." Gale points to a sofa, smiles and disappears around the corner into the kitchen. Young seats himself on the far end of the sofa while dropping the envelope onto the glass-topped end table to his left.

The sofa is straight-backed with wood trim and arms and he quickly realizes if he leans too far back his head strikes the wood trim. Trying to find a comfortable position he crosses his legs, but his shoe bangs against the glass of the end table, rattling it so severely the lamp nearly falls off. So he changes his mind, uncrosses his legs, swings his left arm onto the armrest and lays his right arm on his right leg. He still feels uncomfortable, since the armrest is wood, but it's the best he can do. He very badly desires to appear calm and is doing his best.

Gale walks in carrying two frozen mugs, each sporting a frothy head of beer. She walks over and extends one to Young, which he takes with a smile. As he does so he notices her nipples are extremely erect and his hand quivers as he accepts the mug. It's only momentary, but long enough to satisfy Gale she's having the desired effect on him as it's her intention to keep him off balance.

"Why thanks Lani, I don't see frozen mugs in the bars I frequent. This is nice." He takes a gulp, wipes the froth from his lips with his hand, then looks around desperately for somewhere to wipe it. Gale, of course, notices.

"Here's a napkin." She picks up a napkin from a nearby end table and hands it to him. Setting her glass on a coaster she notices he's having a hard time keeping his eyes from staring at her breasts. She smiles as she sits down next to him and leans over to pick up her glass. Looking at Young, she takes a small sip before returning the glass to the table.

"So, how about letting me take a look at your merchandise?"

Young smiles, picks up the envelope and offers it to Gale.

"Thanks." She opens the envelope, pulls out the pilfered copy of the logbook and tosses the envelope away. The words "TOP SECRET-EYES ONLY" stand out as if they were lit up in neon. Goose bumps run down her arms, all the way to her toes. Young takes a gulp of beer and settles a little more deeply into the couch.

"Mind if I read a little of it, you know, just to make sure it's something I can truly use?"

"Not at all, Lani, help yourself. I have plenty of time." He takes another gulp, almost draining the glass.

Gale smiles and begins reading. She finds the first few pages to be a bit boring and skips forward a number of pages. She can't believe her eyes as she recognizes that if what she's reading is true, then not only will she have the front page again, but she's going to have an ongoing series of eye popping articles. She skips still further into the log and jumps to the final pages where she learns about Yokoyama burying his shipmate, the very skeleton found buried in Auntie Lee's backyard.

Now she understands this is more than a matter of a successful infiltration into Pearl by a Japanese midget sub. This is a story of one of those submariners actually coming ashore and blending into the population. Gale wants this manuscript and she wants it bad. Already she's considering asking the paper to post a substantial monetary reward for anyone who can prove what became of Lieutenant Yokoyama.

Young stands and saunters into the kitchen to find himself another beer. He glances at his watch and realizes he's been there over half an hour.

"Say Lani?"

Gale pauses and looks up.

"You can read that to your heart's content once you own it. So tell me, do you want to buy it?" Young resumes his seat and this time, buoyed by quite a few beers, he stares directly into her eyes. She slips the logbook onto the coffee table, picks up her beer, chugs it down, sets the empty mug back onto the coaster and returns Young's stare.

"You know darn well I want this log. And I want you to know I'm truly grateful you thought of me first. Truly." She pauses a moment.

"Tell you what, not only do I want it, but I'll need you to continue nosing around on your end. Think you can do that and maybe keep me up to date on any changes or new discoveries as they happen?"

"Not a problem. I know Pastwa's aide Mike Clarke pretty well and if I stop in there with a box of donuts he'll shoot the breeze for an hour."

"Great!" Gale stands and motions for Young to do the same. She steps closer to him until she's less than six inches away when she lays her right hand on the uppermost button on her dress. "This is really bothering me, Paul, I can barely breathe. Think you can help me out?" Her tone is soft yet taunting and inviting at the same time.

Young visibly gulps, but responds to her request, opens the button and realizes there's no bra beneath her dress. He's keenly aware there is now only one button constraining the physical barrier between him and potential euphoria. What he fails to realize is Gale counts on him to feel exactly as he does.

"Money is so impersonal, don't you think?" Gale's not really seeking an answer.

"I like to keep things on a personal basis, Paul. What about you?" Young is breathing more heavily and he's starting to think money is not necessarily everything. His eyes are fixated on Gale's enticing cleavage and the remaining black button which is barely holding the two halves of her dress together.

"Could you do me a favor and take care of this?" Gale glances down at the sole surviving button.

Young slowly slips the button through its hole, leaving the entire front of her dress open. Gale breathes a little more heavily and lets out a sigh when he slips his hands beneath her dress and pushes it to her sides.

"Paul, I truly admire your courage in making this copy and having the very good sense to call me first. In my opinion it takes a true man to do that." Gale pauses just long enough to increase Young's sexual tensions. "Don't you think we'd be more comfortable in my bedroom?"

Without hesitating, Young slides his hands down her hips, taking her dress with them. As the dress falls to the floor he takes a half step back, without removing his hands, so he can get a good look at her exposed body in the light of day. "She's a natural blonde," he thinks to himself.

"Show me the way, Lani." Gale picks up the pilfered log with her right hand while in the same motion taking his right hand into her left and slowly leads him to her bedroom. Once there, she slips the logbook into a drawer before tumbling into bed with Young, bad teeth and all.

CHAPTER SIXTEEN
INLAND SEA OF JAPAN

Sun Kida is being eagerly assisted by two of her granddaughters as they clear away the remains of dinner from their twelve foot long, koa wood dining table. Other grandchildren have found their way into the backyard while two of her children, Ken, Jr. and Lea are busy cleaning the kitchen and loading the dishwasher. Ken and Gary are the only remaining diners at the table and are enjoying Sun's homemade cherry-flavored iced tea.

"Gary are you still interested in learning about the remainder of my first life?" Ken smiles wryly as he slowly strokes his beard, "Or perhaps you might prefer to wait until another time?" The expression on Gary's face twists from enjoyment of the tea to outright alarm.

"No, no! Let's continue. Please grandfather!"

"Good, then let us retire to my study where we can close the doors and not be disturbed." Ken motions towards the nearby pitcher of iced tea.

"You take the pitcher and I will bring my glass."

Ken slowly rises and walks the short distance to his den, enters through the French doors and proceeds make himself comfortable in his favorite over-stuffed leather reading chair. Ken almost resembles a large doll as the size of the chair overwhelms his slender frame.

Ken's mementos and awards are centered on the wall to the left side of the entry, while shelves crammed with books of every possible topic fill the other walls. Directly overhead is a large, five-bladed ceiling fan featuring four frosted cut-glass light fixtures. Recessed ceiling lighting lines the entire room.

In a few moments Gary enters and places the pitcher, along with his glass, on a small table to Ken's left. He quickly retreats to the doors and pulls them closed before taking a seat across from Ken. He patiently waits for his grandfather to speak.

Gary watches him as he closes his eyes, begins to unconsciously stroke his beard and allows his mind to drift through the fog of decades past. Suddenly, as if someone turned on a fan, the fog clears and Ken is, once again, IJN Lieutenant, junior grade, Masaharu Yokoyama and is reliving the summer of 1941. He finds himself at a secret Imperial Japanese Navy training base tucked away within the Inland Sea of Japan and is standing on the aft deck of the *IJN Chiyoda*.

"What followed that first day aboard the *Chiyoda* was an extended period of technical training, sometimes going aboard our respective midget submarines, but mostly in classrooms." Ken's voice tapers off as he begins to relive the experience.

• • • • •

The *IJN Chiyoda*, constructed as a seaplane tender, has been modified to better suit our training. The stern has been reconstructed and resembles an over-size pair of French doors which will allow the aft deck, upon which will sit one of our midget submarines, to be lowered into the ocean, providing a swift launch for each little vessel. Captain Harada likens the procedure to 'a wasp laying eggs' and it will prove to be safe, fast and efficient; much better than employing cranes to hoist the very heavy little submarines into and out of the water.

The *Chiyoda* can only launch a single, two-man midget submarine at a time and each midget submarine requires a commander, which is my role. Each midget sub also has an engineer and Sadamu Kamita has been assigned to me. Following many months of training we have grown to be good friends and are very excited at the prospect of finally starting sea trials.

All the crews are gathered on the aft deck to observe the first crew climb the conning tower's ladder and proceed to enter their midget sub. Once the hatch closes behind them there can be no more communication, the reason being the radios have not yet arrived; nor is there a phone communication link with the ship. It is a true trial and error process and certainly fraught with unknown perils.

I find myself unconsciously holding my breath as the stern opens for the first time and the midget sub slips into the gently rolling waves. It bobbles from side to side, as if a toy, before slowly leveling off. In less than a minute it begins to deliberately slip below the surface, under its own power.

We instinctively run to the railing in an attempt to catch a glimpse of the sub. For a time only the bluish/green waves of the ocean are visible when suddenly, maybe two hundred yards distance, a periscope pops through the surface and we let out a boisterous cheer.

In the distance our practice target ship plows ahead at about fourteen knots, simulating a real-life situation. The practice torpedoes mounted to each midget sub weigh about one thousand pounds each, simulating the weight of our 'Long-Lance' torpedoes and will float once the propellant is expended, allowing them to be recovered and used again. There are shortages of so many things throughout Japan and torpedoes are in especially short supply; for that reason we never use live torpedoes in any of the practice runs. In retrospect, had we used live torpedoes we may well have discovered a flaw in the firing mechanism which did, in fact, exist. However, the flaw was not discovered; thus we unknowingly trained with an imperfect weapon.

I look through my binoculars to seek evidence of the submerged midget sub, but not until the first torpedo is released does she prove easy to locate. Simultaneously with firing the torpedo, the submarine's stern breaches the surface and the rapidly spinning propellers send feverishly swirling fountains of salt water high into the air, clearly visible to the sailors aboard the target ship. They, and any nearby destroyer, would most certainly be able to pinpoint the source of the torpedo. Moments later the second torpedo's wake is visible and again the submarine breaches the water, only more so. Unfortunately, both practice shots miss the target.

Kamita appears dejected, but I am more concerned with the propeller's large spray pattern than whether the first practice shots struck their target as I am keenly aware that had it been an actual battle, enemy destroyers would have quickly been upon them with their deadly depth-charges bringing certain death.

When the first submarine is retrieved, I believe we make a tactical mistake by not taking the time to de-brief the crew before launching the next midget submarine. In my opinion we could learn more quickly if we knew what measures the prior crew took in preparing to fire before proceeding ourselves, especially as we are next in line.

It is difficult to convey my feeling of utter helplessness as my boat slips from the ramp and immediately begins to list heavily to starboard. We are barely into our maiden voyage and are in danger of rolling upside down! This is not an aircraft where we would be strapped into our seats; it is a submarine and there are no safety restraints. I order Kamita to transfer ballast to port, but he is already doing so. He is proving to be a self-starter and not prone to sitting on his hands while awaiting orders.

Ken suddenly coughs several times, bringing him back to the present day. He takes a long drink from his iced tea. "Sorry, but suddenly my throat went dry."

Gary tops off Ken's glass and refills his own. He really can't think of anything to say as he stares at his grandfather and tries to imagine him as a young lieutenant in the Imperial Japanese Navy. He almost says aloud: "My God, the Imperial Japanese Navy," but catches himself. He's unconsciously shaking his head as he simply can't formulate such a picture. He makes a mental note to learn about the Japanese midget subs because their history has suddenly become important to him.

Ken resettles himself, closes his eyes, and continues. Gary notices it's as if his grandfather is no longer in the room and is mentally and physically returning to 1941.

•　•　•　•　•

Once we level off I set our speed at five knots, proceed to periscope depth and begin maneuvering into firing position. I need to be aware of the battery reserves as our speed, especially when submerged, impacts our potential cruising range. While we are capable of submerged speeds up to twenty knots, proceeding at high speeds seriously reduces our useable battery life. Conversely, at low speeds we can confidently travel at least one hundred miles before running out of charge. Truly our little boat is a technological marvel!

•　•　•　•　•

I manage to maneuver us into an excellent angle for the attack and am faced with firing torpedoes for the first time in my life. I have only a technical concept of what to expect, but find comfort in knowing the crew before me survived.

I hold my breath as I give Kamita the order: 'Fire one!' Suddenly it is as if we have been struck by a tsunami. The boat lurches backwards and up, then forwards and down. Both of us helplessly fly about the cabin as our little submarine ferociously reacts to the violent expulsion of a one-thousand-pound torpedo. To complicate matters we discover one of the valves is not fully closed and it springs an unsettling leak, which is a lesson best learned in practice.

Kamita quickly tightens the valve, but the issue of firing the second torpedo remains to be addressed. I do two things differently; I lower the periscope in the belief it will make the boat more stable, and I order Kamita to hold on tightly.

We fire the second torpedo and while the first shot veered wide right, the second shot veers wide left. In fact, of the ten torpedoes fired by our five submarines on the initial day of sea trials, not even one strikes the target. Despite the failures none of us are discouraged.

We are considered an elite service, thus we eat as if Royalty and enjoy exceptional accommodations. Following dinner we all meet in the Officer's ward room where the excitement level is high as the thrill of our experiences that day remain fresh in our consciousness. We are drinking sake with several of the officers from the *Chiyoda* when Captain Harada calls for everyone's attention.

"Good evening, Gentlemen." Captain Harada raises a cup of warm sake in his right hand.

"I toast to all of you for a very entertaining and enlightening initial day of training in your tubes." Harada waves his right hand in the direction of Kamita who is sporting a large bandage across the middle of the forehead.

"I see you are all still alive, though some the worse for wear." Harada allows himself a brief a brief laugh before downing his sake. Kamita, only slightly embarrassed, smiles broadly at the attention Harada has brought upon him.

"We have compiled a synopsis of everyone's mission briefs from today's exercise and you will find them on the rear table." Harada motions to a table at the back of the room with a large stack of reports neatly set upon it. He picks up a fresh cup of sake before continuing.

"Study the reports and tomorrow morning we will review them together. Later, you will attend to your boats and access any damage. I remind you, we have a full staff of experts here, many of whom actually designed or partook in the building of your boats and they are at your complete disposal. Take advantage of their experience and call upon them, no matter how miniscule you might believe an issue to be."

Harada raises his cup, an indication for everyone else to do the same.

"To the Emperor!" Harada enthusiastically exclaims.

The men stand and repeat his toast before swigging down their sake.

"Sleep well tonight, gentlemen."

•　•　•　•　•

Ken blinks hard, pauses and looks directly at Gary. "A number of years ago I attempted to determine what became of Captain Harada." Ken pauses as he fights back a tear. "I learned he had been promoted to vice-admiral and placed in charge of our midget submarine base at Cebu, which is in the Philippines. Unfortunately, I could find no mention of his name by the Allies after their conquest of Cebu, so I assume he died there, probably on land. He was a good officer and a good man. That said, it is time for me to continue." He closes his eyes, gently strokes his beard and settles more deeply into his over-stuffed chair.

• • • • •

Time moves quickly and soon it is early October 1941. Most of us are achieving a high degree of competency and of the five commanders, three of us always hit the target with our first torpedo. Two of the other commanders are still experiencing great difficulties, but we sit down as a group each night and talk through various issues. The accuracy of the second torpedo strike continues to plague all of us.

On this particular day we are the last to be launched. By now we have our boat so well balanced that once we are free of our mother ship, we begin maneuvering almost immediately. Though we do not yet know it, this will prove to be the last day we fail to put both torpedoes onto the target.

The firing solution for the second torpedo is simple and yet complex. Once we release the first torpedo our boat will breach the water as if it is a whale. By the time we can level off and gain suitable control to re-acquire our target, it has continued on its course and traveled well beyond its original position, consistently leaving our second shot in her wake. Therefore, quickly firing both torpedoes is essential, but has proven to be stubbornly difficult.

• • • • •

Ken raises his right hand with his fist closed, save for his middle three fingers. Pointing his hand at Gary, he stares him directly in the eyes.

"There are three reasons it is essential to quickly fire both torpedoes. First, we are in the optimum firing position. Second, the longer we delay firing, the further our target sails. And the third reason is the risk of discovery. Discovery is a vexing issue for no matter how Kamita and I align the ballast, each time we fire a torpedo our stern breaches the surface which results in a series of towering waterfalls that are easily spotted by the enemy. The longer we find it necessary to linger in the area so we may deliver our weapons the more likely it is a destroyer will locate us and depth charge our small boat into oblivion."

"We also have an issue with the periscope. It is only ten feet high which forces us to be too close to the surface when we fire. There is nothing we can do about it at this point. If only it were a few feet longer our stern would likely remain below the surface and not give away our position. Gary, you do not want to experience being depth charged as there are no words I can use to adequately describe what it is like." Ken seems to catch himself going off on a tangent.

"Please forgive me as I fear I have digressed yet again. Where was I? Oh yes, I recall now." Ken closes his eyes and resumes his story as if he was looking into the past as an observer.

•   •   •   •   •

Following dinner most of us are in the officer's lounge. It is about eight in the evening and we are still enjoying excellent weather so several portholes are open. I remember it to be a Thursday. We have one day of training to complete before we embark on a full forty-eight hours of freedom, the entire weekend to do as we please.

Kamita and I notice Shigemi Foruno and Shigenori Yokoyama, his engineer, are sitting and chatting. We each pick up two cups of sake and approach them for I have decided we need to have a discussion. Shigenori Yokoyama is easily the most experienced torpedo man in the group and I desire to gain access to his experience.

"You two look deep in thought. Do you mind if we intrude?" I ask. Foruno and Yokoyama immediately recognize us, smile and stand to greet us.

"Aye! You are most welcome, especially if you are bringing us sake!" Foruno exclaims.

Kamita and I hand each of them a full cup as we all take seats around a small table.

"So tell me, Masaharu, how have your trials been coming?" Foruno asks.

"Not to my complete satisfaction," I reply.

"Do not feel badly for we are not experiencing the best results either. Let us share our issues and determine what we might be able to conclude." Foruno sits back, his arms on his thighs as he prepares to listen.

"We are experiencing great difficulty successfully targeting the second torpedo. If we wait for the boat to cease rocking after we launch the first torpedo then we find there is no time remaining for us to re-acquire the target. And if we fire the second shot too quickly, it goes wildly off course." The frustration in my voice is obvious.

We grow silent as we each consider the problem.

"If it helps you feel better, we are having the same issue and I have been working with torpedoes for years," says Shigenori Yokoyama, who proceeds to offer his thoughts.

"We have experimented with changing the ballast and have moved some ballast forward thinking the loss of the torpedo's weight would have less effect. We have also tried increasing the ballast, both port and starboard, at the sacrifice of range, but nothing has produced a satisfactory result. If only we had radios and could communicate our efforts during the maneuvers!" Shigenori slowly shakes his head back and forth.

"Personally, I believe our boats are too light for the weight of the torpedoes. Perhaps if there could be room for additional battery trays to add additional weight, not to mention greater operational range," Foruno's furrowed forehead conveys his deep concern.

I stand and walk over to pick up a small tray with four cups of sake. Returning to the table, I distribute them, receiving thanks from each man.

"Let's try this idea tomorrow," Shigenori Yokoyama's voice sounds encouraging.

"First, each crew will take a signal lantern with them. Second, and this is the difficult aspect, when we release the first shot," he glances at Kamita, "this will be hard, but after the first shot, hold tight with your left hand and put your right hand on the firing switch for torpedo two. The boat will dip backwards, then forwards very quickly. The third time the bow starts to swing up, and timing here is critical, fire the second torpedo, on the upswing! If you fire too soon or too late it will either drive itself too deep to recover or it will break the surface as if a flying fish and likely veer off course. I do believe this is worth trying."

"So why the signal lanterns?" Kamita asks.

"Aye!" Foruno shouts, "I understand your concept. Once we fire our torpedoes we will surface and signal to the *Chiyoda* the actions we took to accomplish whatever result was realized. Then the following boat can make adjustments!"

"Excellent idea!" I exclaim. "We shall take this to Captain Harada and seek his endorsement; a toast to our success."

"Kamita, bring us a final round of sake before we seek an audience with the Captain!"

Foruno and I have been standing outside the Captain's door for several moments without announcing our presence. After some hesitation, I take a deep breath and knock on the door. It immediately opens and we find the Captain's aide standing before us. He immediately recognizes us and breaks into a broad smile.

"Yes Lieutenants, can I be of assistance to you?"

"We would very much like to speak with the Captain." My tone of voice conveys more anxiety than I intend, which is only mildly abated by the aide's friendly disposition.

"One moment please, Lieutenant Iwasa is with him."

Lieutenant Iwasa is well known to us and is considered to be the father of our midget submarine program. We have not engaged in any casual conversations with him for each time he has approached us it has been over some manner of technical issue.

Not more than a minute passes before the Captain's aide returns.

"Gentlemen, follow me, the Captain will see you both." He directs us through an outer quarters to a large, carved wood door where he pauses and gently knocks twice before opening it.

"Lieutenants Yokoyama and Foruno," he announces.

The aide makes his exit and closes the door behind us while we stand at attention, finding ourselves in the Captain's private study. The walls are paneled with walnut and the furnishings are of mahogany and leather. All four portholes are open, allowing both fresh air and the relaxing sound of waves splashing against the steel hull to drift across the room. Two ceiling fans slowly revolve overhead.

Harada is sitting behind a massive cherry wood desk. Seated at one of four chairs strategically placed in a semi-circle in front of the desk is Lieutenant Naoji Iwasa. Both men are drinking sake and appear quite relaxed.

"Good evening, gentlemen," says Harada. "You know Lieutenant Iwasa." Iwasa smiles while remaining seated.

"Please, relax, sit down. We do not need to worry about formalities here." Harada motions to the empty chairs.

"Lieutenants, I have been following both of you with great interest," says

Iwasa. "I must admit I am not surprised to see you here together."

"So, gentlemen, I presume you have something on your minds?" Harada asks.

"Captain, Lieutenant, we apologize for barging in, but we have been discussing a common problem and would like to propose a somewhat different plan of action for tomorrow's exercises." My voice again betrays too much anxiety.

"I like my officers to show initiative for I believe it is important you keep yourselves sharply honed and always ready to quickly address changing battle conditions. If you cannot adapt then only disaster will result; thus, in my opinion, ideas are not only needed, they are welcomed."

"So, Yokoyama, what is on your mind?" Harada asks.

"But first, I have not been a good host." Harada motions to a small pitcher and several hand-painted china cups sitting on an ornate china tray bearing a depiction of the great Japanese naval victory over the Russian fleet.

"Please, pour yourselves some sake and have a drink. I shall grant you all the time you might need."

I reach across the desk and pour two cups of warm sake. Foruno decides to speak next and stands to address the Captain and Lieutenant.

"Sirs, as you know we have all experienced difficulty striking our targets with both torpedoes."

"Yes, and we have noticed that you two are the only men who consistently strike the target with your initial attack. And we are aware your second shots have produced somewhat less satisfactory results," replies Harada.

"These torpedoes are expensive and hard to come by. It is essential they not go to waste," adds Iwasa.

"I speak for both of us when I say we are pleased the two of you are also concerned about the issue." Iwasa takes a sip of sake and returns his gaze to Foruno. As if on cue, Foruno continues.

"Lieutenant Yokoyama and I have been discussing the need to more quickly communicate our experiences to the crews awaiting their turn."

"Yes," interrupts Harada, "we are keenly aware of the problem. So, Lieutenant Foruno, do you have a proposal?"

"Yes Sir," says Foruno, "it is our thought each crew shall carry a signal lantern with them. Our concept is that once a crew has fired its torpedoes, they will surface and signal the steps they took in attempting to put their second shot on target. Having such additional knowledge will allow the next crew to adjust accordingly and thereby not duplicate a failed effort. We think we can save significant training time in this manner." Foruno sits down, feeling satisfied he has properly plead their case.

We nervously scan Harada's face for any reaction, completely unaware he is a veteran of having played many card games with Admiral Yamamoto and has learned to remain stoic at all times. Several minutes pass as Harada and Iwasa each sip some sake while they consider every aspect of the proposal. Finally, Iwasa gives a nod to Harada who breaks the silence.

"I believe Lieutenant Iwasa would like to comment first." Iwasa stands.

"I am pleased to see you are thinking independently, for yourselves and for the greater good of the Empire and the Emperor. I congratulate you," says a broadly smiling Iwasa.

We grow noticeably relaxed at hearing Iwasa's praise.

"While this proposal will require a somewhat greater interval between launches, I believe it presents us with the very real possibility of actually saving time; time which is becoming ever more valuable. Gentlemen, we shall adopt your plan immediately and incorporate the results into our daily debriefing summaries." Iwasa picks up his cup of sake.

"I propose a toast," he says.

We all stand in response.

"To a successful mission and to further glory in the name of the Emperor!"

We all enjoy the sake.

"Lieutenants Yokoyama and Foruno," says Harada, "I congratulate you. You must always feel free to approach either of us should you ever feel the need to communicate an idea or observation. You may return to your quarters now and I trust you both will enjoy a good night's sleep."

• • • • •

Ken opens his eyes and blinks a couple of times as he returns to the present day.

"We left the Captain's quarters but it was hours before I fell asleep that night. I was quite excited and kept reviewing everything we had tried in our efforts to put both of our torpedoes on target."

"The next day we incorporated our plans which did speed up each crew's experimentation with ballast and firing angles resulting in more successful torpedo strikes. In a couple of weeks the wireless radio sets finally arrived and we were able to incorporate them into the exercises and discontinue the signal lamps. Unfortunately, the radios proved to be plagued with all manner of technical issues. The radios were, among other things, too delicate and not well suited for duty on a midget submarine. However, after much trial and error we steadily worked out many, but not all, of the radio issues while gaining confidence in ourselves and in our equipment. While our subs proved to be remarkably durable we were saddled with radio sets which were simply too easily damaged by any convulsions, even choppy seas could render them useless."

•   •   •   •   •

Ken suddenly lifts his right arm and points his right index finger directly at Gary.

"Did you know that throughout the entire training regimen we did not lose even a single man or submarine? A few of us had our bumps and bruises, but the small subs were so well constructed we never had a serious mishap. I pushed us very hard as I felt an urgent need to know my boat's limitations, for my intuition told me there was precious little time remaining before we would find ourselves in battle conditions." He pauses to take a breath.

"In early November events began to accelerate quickly. Indeed, very quickly."

"You mean the war with China or negotiations with the United States?" Gary asks.

"Gary, imagine what it was like to be in Japan at the time. The United States placed an export embargo on Japan which was forcing us to make do without most of our supplies of oil, rubber, tin and many other essential imports. Shortages of materials were affecting everyday life throughout the country and even the military was not immune. As shortages in basic materials became increasingly widespread, finding a solution to the embargo became ever more pressing. Unfortunately, the Army was in defacto control of our government and its belief in brute force would plunge us into a devastating conflict."

"Despite the random shortages of so many products we did enjoy elite treatment. However, we were short of war items; for example it was months before the wireless sets were installed in our boats nor did we train with live torpedoes, which was most unfortunate." Ken pauses to take a sip of tea.

"Gary, it was a time of many pressures and it appeared to us our nation's eyes were on the navy to find a solution. Japan was, and still is, an island nation which relies on the maritime trade to import most of its needs and the security of our maritime routes was the province of the navy."

"One day we were both shocked and pleased to discover we were being invited by Admiral Yamamoto to join him on the battleship *Nagato* for a luncheon. The invitation proved we had, indeed, been handpicked." Ken pauses as he experiences a slight chill at the memory.

"The *Nagato* was the flagship of the Japanese Navy Combined Fleet. I had once been aboard the battleship *Iso*, which was more of a grand old lady; however, the *Nagato* made a much stronger impression upon me. Once aboard we are directed into the officer's dining room where an amazing display of food and drink line an entire wall. It is only the ten of us and a handful of our supporting officers along with Captain Harada and Lieutenant Iwasa, but there is enough food for one hundred people."

"A small stage is situated at the head of the room and we are told to make ourselves comfortable. After only a few moments we are called to attention as Admiral Yamamoto enters the stage. I remember his words almost as if it were yesterday…"

•　　•　　•　　•　　•

"Gentlemen, it will be my honor to lead you into battle, a battle which appears to be a foregone conclusion. Only the time and place of such battle and the identification of our ultimate enemy is still to be determined. I sincerely believe Japan is truly blessed to have such dedicated and efficient servants to the Emperor and the Empire as you are proving to be." Yamamoto pauses for effect.

"You have been training very hard and I have a reward for you. When you are finished here you are all being sent home on ten days' leave. Go and see your families and enjoy their company!"

Yamamoto pauses as we congratulate each other on such good fortune. After a few moments he raises his hands and we refocus our attention on him.

"Dangerous operations such as you are about to embark upon may well prove to yield far greater success than we might expect from conventional surface-to-surface actions. Your exploits may even outshine the actions of officers much senior to yourselves. This is a significant opportunity for you, both individually and for the greater good and glory of the Empire." He briefly pauses.

"I must emphasize the fact I fully expect to see each and every one of you again, right here, upon the successful completion of your mission; and I assure you even the Emperor is intently following your actions in anticipation of your success. Now let us partake in the feast which awaits us." The recipient of much applause, Yamamoto exits the stage and assumes a seat at one of the dining tables.

Ken suddenly sits upright, squirms a little as me makes himself more comfortable, and looks Gary directly in the eyes.

"I take advantage of the ten days' leave and return to my mother's home where our family takes turns visiting with me. They are completely unaware it will be the last time they see me, though we are all cognizant Japan is on a course towards an expanded war. I harbor strong feelings of dread and discover maintaining a confident façade is tiring, but I do so for their benefit. I must, however, deal with a singularly difficult problem before returning to my fleet; the problem of what to do regarding Shiori."

"Who is Shiori, grandfather?" Gary asks.

"Shiori was my fiancé. Our marriage had been arranged by our families when we were very young. However, I decided to delay our marriage until such time as I attained a higher rank and could better afford to maintain a household."

"But I could not bring myself to keep her bound to me for the reason I harbored a belief I would never see Japan again. In fact there were moments the feeling was so strong as to almost overwhelm me. Several times I went to the grave of the great Admiral Heihachiro Togo, a hero from the Russian conflict, where I spent many hours in meditation during that final visit home."

"You obviously are not aware I am from the same town as Admiral Togo. Besides being a great naval tactician, he was a natural role model for me and his legacy was well preserved in my home town. I prayed for the strength and courage Admiral Togo had displayed throughout his career. More than once I would find myself calling upon him to guide me through difficult moments and it had always been my intention to model my career based on his life and beliefs. But I digress again."

"I met Shiori for the last time on my second day of leave. We were sitting on an ornately carved wood bench in her parent's garden. It was a picture perfect setting, as they say. There was a waterfall in the background, a koi pond, bonsai trees, orchids; it was simply an amazing and peaceful place."

"Shiori was beautiful and it hurt me a great deal to break off our engagement. I took time to explain to her that I, in all good conscious could not bind her to me when I was about to embark on extremely hazardous assignments."

"She plead for us to marry immediately and for me to leave her with my child, but I refused. For years I was haunted by the memory of leaving her on that bench crying uncontrollably. I did not feel very honorable at the moment, but to me it was the only course of action I could take and be fair to her. Believe me, I was very tempted to marry her and consummate the marriage. Very tempted, but it would have been wrong."

"Did you ever make any inquiries as to what became of her?"

"There was no point. I am certain my family offered her comfort and likely assured her I would one day return. Of course, I did not return and I can only hope she married, had a large family and was happy. And remember, it was not long afterwards the Japanese Navy declared me to have been killed in the battle at Pearl Harbor."

"When I returned from my ten days' leave I discovered events would quickly escalate. The *Chiyoda* was anchored at Kure, which was the main base for the Combined Fleet and everyone was on edge. There was activity in every direction. Yes, I remember that first day back from leave very well." Ken closes his eyes as he slips back into the year 1941.

. . . . .

On November fifteenth we are suddenly called for an urgent meeting and upon arriving I am surprised to find Vice Admiral Mitsumi Shimizu is awaiting us. First Yamamoto and now Shimizu. This conveys to me we are, indeed, training for something important. I quickly discover Shimizu does not beat around the bush as he pulls a piece of paper from his shirt pocket and reads to us:

"These are orders directly from the Headquarters of the General Staff of the Imperial Navy."

I feel a lump in my throat for I feel something critical to my life is about to transpire.

"You are each being directed to take readiness positions for war with the United States. For now, forget about each of the possible target missions you have been studying, save one: Pearl Harbor. These are your official orders." Shimizu hands envelopes to an ensign for distribution; each envelope bearing the name of one of the ten midget submariners.

"Gentlemen, we will deliver you and your midget submarines as close to the mouth of Pearl Harbor as proves feasible. This will occur during the night prior to our surprise air attack, a night where there is little or no moonlight. Listen carefully to my words, for should any one of you encounter a problem with your equipment which makes an undetected entry into the harbor problematic, it is your absolute duty to reverse course and return to the prearranged pick-up point without hesitation or delay."

"Under no circumstances may any of you place the absolutely essential element of surprise at risk. I cannot over-emphasize the need for complete stealth. Should one of you be discovered, the resulting alarm could bring disaster to Sixth Fleet. It is far better, and strongly preferred, to return and fight another day than to risk early detection. I trust each of you understands me! If you are not clear on this, please raise your questions now."

Shimizu pauses and looks around at his quiet audience.

"Very well. The battle plan is to penetrate the harbor in darkness, locate the battleships and aircraft carriers, then slip to the bottom of the harbor and hide. Following the air attack there will be much confusion, but you are to stay on the bottom and wait for nightfall. Then, and only then, do you move in and seek out the best targets of opportunity."

"Excuse me Sir," Lieutenant Naoji Iwasa stands and awaits recognition.

"Yes, Iwasa, you have a question?"

"Indeed Sir, we run a greater risk if we do not strike immediately. To lie in the harbor all day while unharmed ships proceed and escape to the open sea would be to miss the best opportunities. I think it much better if once the air attack has commenced our submarines rise from their hidden positions and fire their torpedoes. They can then return to the harbor floor to await darkness and the best chance to escape that darkness brings with it."

"That is not the plan. We absolutely cannot risk early detection," replies Admiral Shimizu.

"Sir, pardon me, please, but I believe I speak for all ten of the submarine crewmen when I state that maximum results are more important than escaping the harbor."

Admiral Shimizu makes eye contact with each midget sub crew member and is met by stoic faces which convinces him to change his mind.

"Very well, Iwasa, I relent. However, one mistake by any of your crews could prove fatal, not just to them, but to hundreds of pilots and thousands of sailors. I trust you and your men fully comprehend the potentially disastrous implications a premature discovery of our midget submarines could have. It is a heavy responsibility!"

"Sir, we thoroughly comprehend our responsibilities to the fleet and I thank you for your confidence," replies Iwasa.

"Now I invite all of you to meet me in the club for lunch!" Shimizu smiles and quickly leaves the room.

•   •   •   •   •

Ken looks at Gary, smiles and takes a sip of tea.

"We proceeded to enjoy a truly lavish lunch. There were many toasts, most of them to a complete victory. It would prove to be my last visit to that, or any other Officer's club as a member of the Imperial Japanese Navy. I still remember the club was named 'Suikosha.' To loosely translate, it means 'Officer's Friendship Association.' Our spirits that day were very high and nobody spoke of the dangers we faced. However, it was not much longer before we found ourselves setting sail and looking at Japan for what proved for many of us to be the last time."

"It was during the voyage to Pearl Harbor, aboard the submarine *I-16*, where I found time to contemplate the enormous task of engaging in a war with the United States"

Ken suddenly rises from his chair, as quickly as you might expect a ninety or so year old man can rise. "Gary, I am late for my evening meditation. Come back tomorrow and I will continue my story; assuming you still desire to hear more. However, at present I find myself fighting off the need for sleep and I must still make time to meditate. Meditation keeps me sharp!" Ken chuckles.

"Of course Grandfather, but I must tell you I'm frightened for you and Kapuna. I'm also kind of mad because there's nothing I can do so I feel helpless; and I assume you don't want me to share this with my dad, right?"

"That is a good point Gary. This is between you, me and Kapuna until such time as events might dictate otherwise. But now I am very tired and the thought of my comfortable bed is strong on my mind."

"I'll see you both tomorrow and will come straight here from school!" Gary watches his grandfather until the bedroom door slowly closes behind him. He finishes off his iced tea, picks up their glasses and pitcher and deposits them in the kitchen. As he walks to his car he is thinks about how everything seems so normal, but also so very different.

CHAPTER SEVENTEEN
A GAME PLAN

Though it's only eight in the morning Clarke is already offering a second pot of coffee. Yamura pauses long enough to acknowledge his effort. "Thanks Clarke, I appreciate it." Clarke smiles and motions towards Pastwa's cup.

Pastwa casually drops a small stack of death certificates onto his desk and accepts Clarke's offer.

"I was not expecting so many names on the death rolls." Pastwa pauses in mid-sentence. "Clarke, remember that portable chalk board we used to demonstrate Navy ranks to the Kaneohe first grade class last year?"

"Yes Sir, do you want me to get it?"

"Absolutely, and grab some donuts for all of us while you're at it. We'll take a short break when you return."

At the mention of 'donuts' Clarke's face lights up. "Yes Sir! I'll be back in less than fifteen minutes!" Clarke rushes through the doorway.

"What's the plan, Chris?"

"We'll write the name, birth and death dates of each candidate on the board. Then we'll divide the names between you, me and Clarke to speed the background research. That way we all work together to narrow the list of potential candidates. We must plow through this today and get ourselves down to the absolute bare minimum of potential impersonators. Reardon is probably fighting the urge to come down here and look over our shoulders so we need to get some results before he shows up."

"Agreed," replies Yamura, "here's the first one. His name is 'Mitsuo Tanaka who died December 3, 1941, and was born September 6, 1920. Tanaka's spelled the same as our favorite restaurant."

"Good. As soon as we get the chalkboard he'll be candidate number One!" Pastwa takes a sip of his hot coffee.

"Chris, I've been dealing with a funny feeling ever since I saw the ship's log. I'm really worried we're lunging headlong into what may prove to be a much larger problem than any of us has imagined. I don't know why, but I'm getting the chills again."

Pastwa gazes through the windows for a few moments. "I have to agree with you Karen. There's something about this case that just seems to be screaming out to me that it doesn't want to be discovered, perhaps shouldn't be discovered; but discover we shall, as we simply don't have the luxury of having any other choice. We're navy, not a bunch of civilians on a treasure hunt. If he's alive, we'll deliver him to Reardon and if not..." He doesn't finish the thought.

Clarke walks in, a folded chalkboard under his left arm and a box of donuts under his right. He places the donuts on the edge of Pastwa's desk and walks to the far side of the office, between the window and the back wall.

"Sir, would this be a good spot for the chalkboard?"

"Perfect, Clarke. "We have a name for you to put up there as candidate number one. Ready?"

CHAPTER EIGHTEEN
A ONE HUNDRED THOUSAND DOLLAR REWARD

Jim Mori is fidgeting with a pen and pencil set on his desk top as he stares at Lani Gale. The look on her face usually means she's about to hit him up for a raise and the fact she appears to be in a good mood is, to him, additional cause for concern. Gale's patiently waiting for Mori to open the conversation, coffee cup in her right hand and a file folder in her left. She loves it when she can put Mori on edge and especially loves to keep him dangling.

"So, what's the 'blockbuster' information you have for me that can't wait?" Mori asks.

Gale casually slips her cup onto a coaster and opens the folder. She's playing Mori a bit and he knows it. After spending a few moments viewing her file, she decides it's time to move forward.

"Boss, I guarantee you've never read anything like this!" Gale hands the file to Mori who places it flat on his desk, cover open. "This is straight out of 1941!" Gale allows herself a broad and obviously self-satisfied smile.

Mori is staring at the first page of the report and she can't figure out if he's in shock or angry.

"Lani, this is marked 'Top Secret-Eyes Only.' Where in the hell did you get this? I'm not sure I even want to read whatever's in here!" Mori's upset, but Gale is not about to be put off, especially after what she has gone through to obtain the contents.

"Boss, as for where I got this, I have my sources and they *are* confidential and they *are* completely trustworthy, not to mention accurate! As for whether you want to read it, well, I can just take it back and call the AP." Gale feigns a motion to pull it back. Mori, in response, puts both his hands on top of the file.

"Alright, alright already. This material is pretty thick so you better give me a couple of hours to read it through. Why don't you go get yourself some early lunch and on the way out please ask Jimmy to bring me a fresh pot of coffee." Mori does his best to sound as if he's aggravated, but the fact is he strongly suspects whatever is in the file is likely to make his day.

"No problem Boss, take all the time you need." Gale smiles, grabs her cup and heads out the door. As she passes through the outer office she slows down just enough to bark some orders: "Hey, Jimmy! The boss needs a fresh pot of coffee and I suggest you make it extra strong." She throws Jimmy one of her patented smiles that gets her what she wants most every time as she quickly struts through the doorway.

"Yes, Miss Gale. I'm on it, good to see you Miss Gale." Jimmy briefly stares at the now empty doorway before jumping from his desk, grabbing the coffee pot and running down the hall to the kitchen.

Mori alternately stares at his empty coffee cup and the cover page of the pilfered logbook. He strongly desires to read the contents, but at the same time he's worried about what manner of shenanigans Gale pulled to get it to him. He looks out the window for a few minutes as he considers the consequences of publishing what looks to be a stolen secret document. Just as Mori's pondering what job opportunities he might find in Sweden, he's brought back to reality as the door bursts open with a flourish and Jimmy comes charging in.

"Sir, your coffee!" Jimmy's voice is almost a shout, holding a pitcher of hot coffee in front of him as if it were a bomb.

"Thanks Jimmy. Please pour me a cup and leave the pitcher. And be so good as to close the door behind you." Mori pulls the file cover over the report so Jimmy can't see it as he pours his boss's coffee.

"Anything else Boss?"

"Not for now." Mori pauses, "Oh, Jimmy," Jimmy's half way through the door, but stops in response, "hold all my calls, and cancel my appointments for the rest of the day. You can tell them anything you want, but I'm only available to Lani Gale. Understood?" Mori gives Jimmy one of his classic stern stares that sends goosebumps down Jimmy's back every time Mori looks at him that way.

"No problem Mr. Mori." Jimmy quietly closes the door behind him.

Mori takes a sip of his hot, black coffee and smiles. Only Jimmy makes it exactly as he loves it and knows Mori well enough to keep a good supply of his favorite on hand at all times. Returning the cup to his desk-top he again opens the cover of the report. He slips off his shoes, takes the report into his hands, pushes his chair back from the desk just enough so he can rest his feet on the top and turns to the first page.

"Lani, this better be good," he says out loud as he begins to read the logbook of Imperial Japanese Navy Lieutenant, junior grade, Masaharu

Yokoyama.

Mori carefully reads the first few pages, but as his excitement increases he begins to skim through the bulk of the log. When he reaches the page dated December 7, 1941, he realizes Yokoyama is on Japan time. He immediately skips to December 8th, which consumes a full four pages of the log. He considers the numerous occasions he's studied the surprise attack on that fateful day and cannot even count the number of times he's re-read the framed Front Page of the December 7, 1941, 1st Extra Edition of the Honolulu newspaper hanging on his wall. Now he's actually reading about the attack from a point of view never before known and he's more excited than any time in recent memory. Mori notices his hands are shaking as he turns the pages. He carefully reads right through the final log entry before he carefully lays the file on his desk, simultaneously releasing a deep sigh.

He picks up his coffee and is repulsed as he realizes it is now room temperature. He pulls a spare cup from the lower right drawer of his desk, where he also stores a bottle of *Johnny Walker Black*. Just as he's closing the drawer there's a knock on his door, which brings his mind back into the present.

"Yes?"

"Miss Gale is here to see you," says Jimmy.

Mori stands and tucks in his shirt as he gathers his composure.

"Show her in, Jimmy."

Gale confidently strides to a chair as Jimmy quietly closes the door behind her.

Gale is smiling broadly as she takes a seat across from Mori. Her hair is neatly pulled back from her face and she's sporting a conservative, solid black dress with matching black, low-heeled shoes. She is purposely presenting a more conservative look today for she believes her product needs no icing. The Front Page is coming her way and she knows it.

"So boss, would you like to see the story I wrote based on what you've just read?" Gale sounds confident, not an inkling of doubt anywhere in evidence.

"Yes, but first let's talk about this for a bit," Mori's voice is barely above a whisper, though his office door is closed.

"How can we be sure this is the real thing?" Mori asks.

"I promise you," Gale replies in a subdued voice, "my source is impeccable and will be feeding me follow-up information as we move forward. The source is close to the people investigating this matter and knows to reach me whenever something happens, large or small, any time of day. I have every reason to believe this is an absolutely authentic copy of the actual logbook the navy dug up. No doubt it's the real McCoy." Gale sits a little further back, crosses her legs and continues.

"I saw the sword buried with the skeleton. The Navy doesn't know about the sword because Auntie Lee grabbed it for herself before they arrived. However it's clearly Japanese and most certainly matches with the type of sword a Japanese Navy officer would have owned back in 1941. I did some research on those swords just to be sure." Gale leans a little forward and points to the log.

"This is the real deal, Jim. And I have an idea about how to shortcut discovering what became of this Yokoyama fellow. I suggest we offer a fifty-thousand-dollar reward for anyone who can present evidence that directly and conclusively leads us to where Yokoyama is today, or to his gravestone or death certificate." Gale leans back in her chair, obviously extremely satisfied with herself.

Mori has been gazing at her without expression, but now he allows himself a hint of a grin.

"Fifty thousand dollars?" Mori breaks into an open smile.

"Let's be serious here, Lani. Radio stations in town offer fifty thousand dollar prizes all the time. No, we can do much better than that! We'll make it *one hundred thousand dollars*, so put *that* into your story!"

Mori pushes back from his desk and stands as he cannot contain his excitement.

"I want you to set up a separate hotline number and lay out complete instructions for supplying tips which we'll run on page two. Make it easy for people to comply and be sure to give them a webmail address, a text address, along with twitter and the rest of 'em. And set up web-based social network sites while you're at it. I want you to go full tilt and grab attention on a world-wide basis and cause my head to spin with your efficiency!"

Mori returns to his chair and pauses a moment, his face flush with excitement.

"Pull out all the stops in seeking what became of this fellow. Would you like a couple of hours to revise your story and get everything set for tomorrow morning's edition?"

"I could use a couple of hours, sure." Gale quickly rises from her chair and begins to leave, but suddenly stops and turns to face Mori.

"Can I borrow Jimmy to help me with the hotline details?" Gale's voice rises above conversational level as she can barely contain her excitement.

"Consider it done!" Mori replies with conviction. "I want to keep the momentum going so we can follow this up on the Front Page every day until it's resolved!" Mori walks around his desk, picks up the log and hands it to Gale.

"Take this and get a copy made and sent up to me as soon as you can. I want to re-read it, a little more slowly this time. Let's plan on publishing this treasure book a little each day, keeping the readers hooked." Mori raises his right index finger, almost as if he has forgotten something. "Oh, and Lani, this is really good work! I am quite pleased with you today." Mori returns to his chair, a broad smile on his face.

Gale's impressed as Mori dishes out kudos as if it physically hurts him to do so. Not only has Mori complimented her, but he appeared to express a genuine smile while doing so.

"Thanks, Boss. You'll have your own copy before you know it!" Gale whirls around and practically runs out of his office.

"Jimmy!" Mori shouts more loudly than he intended.

Jimmy comes running, looking as if a deer caught in the proverbial headlights.

"Yes Sir!"

"Go help Lani with whatever she needs, no matter what it is, and for as long as she needs you!"

Jimmy stands in place not knowing if he's kidding or if his dream assignment is real.

"What are you waiting for? Get moving!"

"Yes Sir! I'm outta here!" Jimmy quickly turns around and slams Mori's door behind him, shaking the glass in the door so hard Mori fears it might break.

Mori pours himself a fresh cup of coffee and again returns to his chair. He swivels around as he sips his coffee and stares out towards Honolulu Harbor and says to himself: "This story's a long way from finished."

CHAPTER NINETEEN
DEATH CREEPS FORWARD

One of Ken's granddaughters is clearing the last evidence of dinner from the dining room table. Gary and Ken are the only two diners remaining while Sun is busy supervising the clean-up and planning the next days' meals.

"Let's go to my study and I will continue my prior life's story, actually you might call it life number one." Ken slowly rises from his chair.

"I'll grab a pitcher of Kapuna's iced tea and a couple of glasses and meet you there," replies Gary.

Ken slowly walks into the den and opens the blinds which lets him watch two of his granddaughters playing in the backyard. The sun has moved along and the entire back yard is well into the shade. This is Ken's favorite time of day.

He makes himself comfortable in his large, over-stuffed leather chair and waits for Gary who arrives in a couple of minutes. He pours each of them a glass of iced tea before settling into a wide, comfy seat with padded leather arms over which he swings one of his legs. Gary quietly waits for Ken to resume.

"Let me think for a moment, just where should I pick up?" Ken is not really asking a question as much as he is talking aloud to himself, slowly stroking his beard as if it helps him remember. "Yes, this would be a good point to continue."

"I have orders to report aboard the fleet submarine, *I-16*, at a secret base near Kure. Upon arriving I am surprised to discover my midget submarine is strapped to the aft deck of *I-16*, held in place by metal straps. You see, until now all of our training involved being slipped off the stern of the *Chiyoda*, not released from the deck of a submerged submarine. We had not practiced such a maneuver even once!"

"A telephone line between the control room of *I-16* and my midget submarine, which has been assigned the designation *I-16-tou*, will allow us instant communications with the captain of *I-16* until the release point. Once we break away the cord will detach and communications cease; until we eventually surface and can employ our radio transmitter."

"We are provided a thorough briefing of the battle plan, along with several maps of Oahu, which, among other things, provide me with numerous navigation landmarks. I will need to recognize them if I am to successfully steer an underwater course into the harbor."

"We are also advised our intelligence is uncertain as to the exact depth of the entry channel into the harbor. The depth of the anti-torpedo and submarine nets at the channel entrance is also unknown. The nets present a serious deterrent to our successful harbor penetration, for even if the net cutter on our bow cuts them, an alarm would most certainly be raised and the element of surprise lost. Regardless, I am assured there will be enough clearance for me to steer my boat safely under the nets."

Ken pauses a moment. "Kamita and I determined in the event should we find it impossible to safely penetrate the harbor, we would slowly make our way to the pick-up point. It was our hope perhaps a fleeing warship would present itself as a target so our sacred mission would not be a complete failure. All the commanders harbored similar plans as sinking enemy ships was our objective. But I digress again. Back to the story!"

"A week passes and it is time to begin the three-week journey to Oahu. Kamita and I are on the bridge of the *I-16* and are staring at the empty horizon. Japan is already starting to feel like a distant memory when the Captain approaches and extends a dinner invitation. As we turn to follow him below deck Kamita makes a final observation: 'the next time we see our homeland, we will be veterans.'"

"During the long voyage to Oahu we spend as much time as possible in our midget sub, checking and re-checking. As we creep closer to the patrol zones where we might make accidental contact with the Americans, or with commercial shipping, we begin to operate submerged during the days and run on the surface only at night. This reduces the time we can spend in our boat."

"After a week at sea we find ourselves in very rough weather. If the much larger *I-16* could be violently tossed to the extent we are experiencing, what damage might be happening to my little midget? There is nothing to do except wait and with the submarine being battered as if it is a sampan, we dare not go on deck, let alone venture into our little boat. However, the inclement weather does provide me with more time to memorize charts of the harbor, lists of safe contacts should we need to abandon ship and swim ashore, maps of Oahu and additional time for meditation."

"I meet with the captain of *I-16* several times a day and we come to know each other very well. More than once he makes it very clear he will be waiting for us after the attack and will remain at the pick-up point as long as he possibly can. He, like Admiral Yamamoto, does not consider our mission to be suicidal."

"Shortly before we departed Kure we were advised the mission would be canceled if a diplomatic solution could be achieved. On one hand, I prayed for such a solution but on the other, we were being sent on a mission of war, not diplomacy. Diplomatic failure would result in our full commitment to action."

"We have been at sea for about two weeks when the Captain hands me a radio message from Admiral Yamamoto which states: 'Climb Mount Nittaka.' This is the code term which confirms we are to proceed with the attack and, at this point, we have only a few days remaining before the opening battle. The message from Admiral Yamamoto brings with it a decidedly more somber atmosphere as war is now inevitable. Casual banter and joking all but disappear among the crew as we are all distinctly aware death now awaits, not just the enemy, but perhaps us as well."

"The day prior to the attack we load food, water, juice, sake, maps, charts, equipment, various tools, my pistol and a few other items we believe could be of use into our midget submarine. I save our orders, our list of safe houses, local maps and the like for the last minute. We are careful to properly secure everything we bring aboard should our departure from *I-16* prove to be rough."

"Finally, the moment arrives. We surface shortly after midnight on Sunday morning, December 7th, Hawaiian time. As I clamber aboard our sub, I look at the cherry blossoms Kamita painted on the conning tower and am surprised how well they have survived the trip. We salute the Captain before each of us descends into our sub and secure the hatch behind us. We take our positions and I establish communications with the Captain using the hard-wired telephone. He advises me we are within seven miles of the harbor entrance and unless I state to the contrary, he is ready to commence diving."

"I agree and soon Kamita and I sense the angle of our little sub is starting to tilt as the *I-16* slips beneath the waves. The Captain calls for a final status check and, yet again, assures me he will be waiting at the rendezvous point. The phone cable snaps away and we are released to our own power."

"We hold our breaths as the steel retraining straps scrape along our hull and set us free from the *I-16*. We begin maneuvering to periscope depth and our mission officially begins! I congratulate Kamita on his fine job of so perfectly arranging the ballast."

• • • • •

Ken makes a moment for himself to enjoy another sip of iced tea. "Any questions for me?"

"No grandfather, but I do wish I had recorded all of this so someday I could play it for my own grandson. Please continue."

Ken settles deeply into his chair and closes his eyes. Gary considers how much younger his grandfather appears; almost as if he were a young lieutenant, junior grade, all over again. Indeed, Ken is reliving history while Gary listens, as if mesmerized.

• • • • •

When we achieve periscope depth and check our location through the viewer I am pleased to discover our luck is good and we are, thanks in large part to the maneuvering of *I-16's* captain, perfectly aligned with the landmarks which signal the location of the harbor entrance. It is now barely after one in the morning and I have all the time I need.

"Kamita, we are commencing our approach to the harbor entrance. Make five knots. Lowering periscope!"

"Aye, five knots, lowering periscope," he replies.

"We shall proceed for one hour on this course, at which time we will check our position."

Kamita is already sweating from every pore in his body as the temperature inside our iron tube steadily rises to more than one hundred twenty degrees Fahrenheit. He continuously checks each of the gauges while listening to the quiet hum of the electric motor, wary of any sound or reading that might be the least out of sync.

I make good use this time to again review the charts of the harbor and the expected mooring positions of the battleships and aircraft carriers. I, too, am immersed in sweat as stripping our uniforms affords only minimal relief. While waiting the next opportunity to plot our location I discreetly observe Kamita as he diligently checks and re-checks every dial, gauge and valve. He has proven to be an excellent engineer and I thank the Emperor for blessing me with him.

"Kamita, it has been one hour, raising periscope."

"Aye, raising periscope."

I strain my eyes as I attempt to pierce the darkness and congratulate myself for I discover we are almost perfectly aligned with the harbor entrance.

"We are about one mile away and there are lights on shore everywhere," I cannot hide the excitement in my voice. "Clearly the Americans suspect nothing."

I slowly sweep the periscope almost three hundred sixty degrees, but before I can complete my search I come to an abrupt stop.

"Kamita, a destroyer is approaching. Lowering periscope, stop engine! We shall wait and see what he is up to."

"Aye, lowering periscope, engine stopped," whispers Kamita.

"Let her slowly drop to fifty feet." My voice is also a whisper.

"Aye, fifty feet," he whispers back.

The whir of the air circulation system ceases, along with the hum of the electric propulsion motor. We are drenched in sweat while we sit and listen in the semi darkness of our metal tube. Suddenly we hear the faint sound of propellers and I wonder whether the sound will grow louder, meaning the destroyer is steering towards our position, or will it fade away? There is nothing we can do except wait. It is possible a particularly astute lookout aboard the destroyer spotted our periscope and should that prove to be the event, I must abort and quickly move away from the harbor."

Several minutes pass when the sound of the propellers begins to fade. We have not been spotted and can proceed on our mission.

"Make five knots and bring us to periscope depth."

"Aye, five knots and periscope depth," Kamita replies.

After a few minutes, Kamita announces: "Periscope depth."

"Raising periscope." I peer into the viewer and sweep the horizon. No ships in sight. Perfect!

"We are not more than five hundred meters from the torpedo nets," my voice gives away my excitement.

I have studied reports which state the nets are only thirty five feet deep with about a sixty five foot channel depth and yet other reports state the nets penetrate to forty five feet deep and the channel has a seventy foot depth. After studying the practices of my own Navy, as well as the English, I have concluded the nets likely are forty five feet deep and decide to act on that assumption.

"Lowering periscope! Make depth sixty feet and proceed at two knots!" I turn to Kamita and observe him as he swings into action.

"Aye, lowering periscope; setting depth for sixty feet and making two knots!"

"We shall slip beneath the American nets as a venomous snake slips between the rocks." I am watching the hands of my stop watch as I calculate the remaining distance to the nets.

"Sir, passing fifty five feet." Kamita's eyes are glued to the depth gauge. "Leveling at sixty feet," Kamita's voice is an excited whisper.

"Good, now hold tight. If we do not clear the nets, or should we strike the bottom of the channel, it could become a rocky ride!"

"We will *not* fail the Emperor and we *will* slip below the nets!" Kamita cannot hide his excitement.

I smile at his enthusiasm as I firmly grip the wheel, holding the sub steady on the course I anticipate will take us under the nets and into the main channel of Pearl Harbor itself. From time to time I glance at my stop watch and make a mental calculation as to our distance traveled and the distance needed to reach, and then clear, the nets. I soon realize we must be very close and decide to slow the pace in the event we find ourselves too close to the bottom of the harbor channel or strike the metal netting.

"Slow to one knot!" I find myself whispering, though there is no need to.

"Aye, one knot." Kamita wipes his hands and arms of sweat. I realize I am gripping the wheel so hard my hands are beginning to ache, so I loosen them and take several deep breaths. I make a mental note to watch for such behavior in the future, lest it be picked up by my shipmate and interpreted as fear, for fear can be contagious. Time appears to have slowed to a crawl as I repeatedly glance at my stopwatch and perform the calculation of time and distance. I am aware that should we strike the nets they may well contain an alarm system which would signal our presence to the Americans and ruin the surprise attack.

"The nets should be above us about now," I whisper.

We instinctively look up, as if our vision could penetrate the iron hull. Will we collide with the nets and perhaps become ensnared? Are we too deep, or perhaps not deep enough? The next few minutes will reveal the answers.

The constant and reassuring hum of the electric engine and air filtration system are the only clues available to the Americans as our little submarine quietly slips beneath the Pearl Harbor anti-submarine defense, undetected. It is not yet four in the morning and I liken us to a venomous snake intruding deep into Pearl Harbor where thousands of sailors are sound asleep aboard the largest single gathering of warships, submarines and support ships in the Pacific Ocean. We have achieved the first half of our goal. Death is now creeping forward at one knot and closing on the Pacific Fleet of the United States.

"Periscope depth, increase speed to three knots," I quietly order.

"Aye, periscope depth, increasing speed to three knots," whispers Kamita.

I pull open the handles of the periscope, peer into the viewfinder and find myself smiling.

"Maintain three knots as I steer closer to the battleships. There are lights everywhere, my friend; clearly the Americans do not expect us. This is good, Kamita, this is very good!"

"Lowering periscope, stop engine. Settle us to the bottom where we will await our attack at daylight." I am satisfied with our location, the only trick now is how well we will settle when we reach the harbor floor.

"Aye, stopping engine, taking on ballast. Depth, forty feet and slipping, Sir!" Kamita, though whispering, is clearly excited.

"Fine, hold tightly, the bottom must be close at hand."

Both of us experience a mild shudder as the sub reaches the muddy bottom of the channel and lists ever so slightly to starboard.

"I believe it is time for some sandwiches and juice."

"Aye!" Kamita retrieves a package, pulls out a sandwich and hands it to me. I pull a bottle of apple juice from a clever little cubicle Kamita crafted for exactly that purpose. The two of us temporarily forget the heat, even as it now approaches one hundred thirty degrees and consume our little feast. Between the heat, having just eaten and the stress, we soon fall asleep.

●　●　●　●　●

Ken moves forward in his chair, blinks his eyes a few times, pulls a tissue from his pocket and wipes away a few small tears. He's sweating profusely, despite the air conditioning.

"Gary, this next part is most difficult as it still causes me very unsettling nightmares." Ken is unconsciously wringing his hands.

"Do you need to stop? I don't want to cause you grief, you know." Gary has never heard such anguish in his grandfather's voice.

Ken shakes his head side-to-side.

"Bear with me a moment while I pull myself together," he says.

"No problem, grandfather. Can I bring you something from the kitchen?"

"Not necessary." Ken waives his hand to the negative and decides to continue.

"We were awakened from our nap by the repercussions of bombs and torpedoes. In fact, once we were underway we were almost hit by one of our own torpedo bombers. When I next looked through the periscope I observed towering black clouds of smoke rising from several battleships, as well as from Ford Island. I immediately targeted the *West Virginia*, but the torpedo malfunctioned. The *Oklahoma* was the recipient of my second torpedo which exploded with catastrophic results." Ken closes his eyes as he struggles with his emotions. Gary notices tears and discovers his own eyes are swelling up.

"She almost immediately began to capsize to port. Forever scorched into my memory is the sight of small, white-clad bodies scampering over the rails and crawling along the hull as the ship was rolling over. In only a matter of moments the *Oklahoma* was completely upside-down, one of her mighty propellers glistening in the sunlight."

Ken, wiping tears from his eyes with a tissue, stands and walks over to the French doors leading to the backyard with Gary close behind.

CHAPTER TWENTY
NO ESCAPE

Ken and Gary are facing each other as they sit in a pair of lounge chairs on the backyard lanai. Ken appears to be staring into space as he slowly strokes his beard and Gary is without words. As his eyes close, Ken picks up the story from where he left off.

· · · · ·

Following the sinking of the *Oklahoma* I found it necessary to spend a few moments meditating, but the continued vibrations coming through the hull as other ships were bombed and torpedoed quickly snapped me out of it. I mustered all the strength I could and began searching for an escape route.

"Lowering periscope," I notice my voice is very subdued as is Kamita's reply:

"Aye, lowering periscope."

"Executing a hard turn to port." I strongly desire to take the two of us out of the harbor and believe it a good time to escape, while confusion is our friend.

"Reduce speed to two knots."

"Aye, Sir, two knots."

We remain silent as I begin to steer a course into the main harbor channel which will lead us to the open ocean and escape. Suddenly our little sub shudders as a loud explosion shakes us to the bone. We look at each other in alarm, wondering what just happened.

"Was that a depth charge?" Kamita sounds anxious.

"I do not believe so, but perhaps I should take a look."

I grab the view finder's handles as the periscope rises into place and anxiously sweep in all directions. I breathe a sigh of relief as, for the moment anyway, the channel ahead is clear. But when I sweep to our port side I witness a tremendous ball of fire and smoke rising further into the sky than my viewer allows and appears to be originating where the *Arizona* should be moored.

"Kamita, the explosion came from the *Arizona*. She is ablaze as if a volcano!" Kamita stares at his feet as the thought of the sailors aboard the burning ship is very sobering. Neither of us take joy in the destruction of an enemy, for it is strictly a matter of duty, and one day it could just as easily be us under attack.

I swing the periscope around to scan the channel leading to the sea only to experience every nerve ending in my body suddenly on fire; a destroyer is rapidly bearing down on our position, clouds of black smoke billowing from her funnels and depth charges starting to explode in her wake!

"Lowering periscope, set us on the bottom and be quick, we are going to be depth-charged!" I am almost paralyzed by fear but manage not to allow emotion to sneak into my voice.

"Aye Sir" The words are barely out of Kamita's mouth when the churning sound of propellers passing directly overhead sends chills up our spines.

"Hold tight Kamita, we are about to feel the wrath of the Americans!" Almost before I finish the words a vicious depth-charge explosion throws our little submarine into the bottom of the channel with such force we both lose our grips and are tossed against the iron hull as our submarine literally bounces off the channel bottom. We are lucky and do not pop to the surface where certain death would await. Instead, our submarine rights itself, allowing Kamita to quickly settle us onto the bottom. I believe surviving the attack is a sign from above.

"Kamita," I whisper, "engine off, blowers off. I doubt the Americans can detect us if we are completely silent, especially with so many explosions rocking the harbor."

"Aye, engine off, blowers off." Kamita's voice is barely audible.

In a few moments we hear, and feel, a sequence of four depth charge explosions, each one a little further away than the one before leading me to conclude the destroyer is hunting a different target. I speculate it may not even have seen us, but is actually in pursuit of a sister submarine for the destroyer does not return to finish us off.

To be safe we remain on the bottom and wait for the excitement up top to subside. I consider the situation of the Americans and decide they likely will open the submarine nets, allowing surviving warships to escape the harbor and am anxious to take advantage of the situation, but believe I must also exercise caution, and patience.

"Kamita, we shall remain on the bottom for a little while longer, just to be certain the destroyer does not return."

"Aye," he whispers.

Pointing to a gash on his forehead I say: "Can I bandage that for you?"

"Yes, thank you. I forgot about it," is his almost sheepish response.

I carefully bandage his forehead and once finished we do our best to get comfortable. Between the stress of the day's action and the suffocating heat, we are soon fast asleep. Only the sound of the ventilation system is audible.

When I finally wake and check my watch I am startled to discover it is well after eight in the evening. I also detect faint, acrid fumes originating from the batteries, a clear signal they have suffered damage as a result of the depth charge attack.

"Time to get our bearings!" I force myself to whisper and rub my face with a towel to clear the sweat from my eyes. At this point we have been submerged many hours and with the strong scent of the acid leak burning our eyes and lungs we urgently need to re-circulate our air supply, which means we must surface soon. But we cannot surface while in the open harbor.

"Three knots and periscope depth," I whisper.

"Aye, three knots, periscope depth," replies Kamita.

Our little submarine slowly rises from the harbor floor and soon reaches a depth of ten feet. I raise the periscope and seek to establish my bearings as I execute a three hundred sixty degree visual survey of the harbor, but there is nothing to observe, save for some distant fires. I begin to navigate but immediately discover the helm is not responding as it should. I can barely turn the wheel, no matter how much effort I exert.

"Something is jamming the rudder. I can barely steer!" I keep my voice calm though my heart is pounding.

"Sir," responds Kamita, "it may have happened when we struck bottom. What do you propose?" Kamita's voice is also calm though I notice blood oozing through the makeshift bandage I had applied to his forehead.

"We will activate my alternate plan and slip into West Loch. According to our intelligence it is only used to demagnetize ships so we should be able to safely surface and refresh our air. Matters could be worse, but we are fortunate as the rudder is forcing us to starboard and directly into West Loch"

I take a few moments to consider our situation and formulate a plan.

"Once we are safely on the surface in West Loch we can determine the extent of the damage. For the time being, however, we cannot expect to break out tonight with our rudder such as it is and we must also ascertain the condition of our batteries. In all events, we will remain in West Loch until after sunset tomorrow for we cannot risk a daylight escape. Fortunately, we loaded extra provisions."

Kamita absorbs the information and considers which tools may prove most useful in repairing the rudder. "Aye, Sir. Maintain three knots?"

"No, reduce to two knots. At that speed it is more likely I can safely guide us into West Loch."

"Lowering periscope," my voice is just above a whisper, not for the reason I intended it, but because it is the most I can muster.

"Aye, two knots, lowering periscope," confirms Kamita, also in a whisper.

"In the event we fail to repair the rudder then we must consider my emergency plan. I am going to refresh my memory of our local agents, friendly farmers and maps, as swimming ashore and making contact with them may prove to be our only chance to return home. The experience we have gained today will prove extremely valuable for future combat operations."

"Aye. Sir, I have considered the rudder problem and believe I can repair it." Kamita sounds confident, but I do not share his confidence as my instincts are telling me we will not be sailing out of here anytime soon.

"Of course, if it can be repaired I know you are the man who can do so," I reply.

We slowly edge towards West Loch. Occasionally I risk raising the periscope to verify our course and review events that might be taking place in the harbor. When we finally arrive at the center of West Loch, it is after two in the morning which leaves us with precious little time to re-circulate our air and for Kamita to repair the rudder mechanism before daylight. I decide to waste no time and immediately surface.

"Stop engine."

"Aye, engine stopped"

"Release ballast, but not too quickly as we cannot create a fuss when we break the surface, just in the event someone is patrolling the shoreline."

"Aye, releasing ballast!" Kamita makes no attempt to disguise his nervous anticipation of what might await our emergence onto the surface.

Quietly our midget sub rises and meets the still surface waters of West Loch as the small conning tower slowly breaks through what proves to be a glass-like surface. I crank open the hatch and am greeted by a shower of cool water as I push it fully open with a dismayingly loud squeak.

"Ah, that feels good!" I quickly climb the ladder to the very small bridge and, realizing I must acclimate my eyes, call down to Kamita in as hushed a voice as possible: "Extinguish all the lighting. Use the candle and allow your eyes to adapt to the dark before joining me!"

It appears we are floating just about in the middle of the Loch. A light wind is gently pushing us to starboard, which suits me. There is some floating debris in the area and the nearest shoreline is overgrown with tall weeds, making shore patrols most unlikely. I smile as I realize our intelligence is, again, correct. This truly is an over-looked location, right in Pearl Harbor itself. Kamita squeezes up beside me, taking deep breaths of the cool air.

"I will allow us to drift closer to shore. Between the darkness and the debris floating nearby I plan to remain surfaced as long as possible. At the first indication of sunlight we will maneuver a little further out and proceed to spend the day on the bottom. We will remain submerged, hidden in the mud, and will bide our time until nightfall. If the rudder is repaired, we will seek to escape after sunset."

"Aye, Sir."

I remain on the bridge and observe Kamita as he carefully picks his way to the aft deck.

In a few moments he slips over the side and disappears. The upper half of the rudder is above the waterline and does not appear damaged. Unfortunately the damage lies below, where rendering repairs in the darkness is problematic.

It is a nearly pitch black, moonless night and Kamita experiences a great deal of difficulty locating the lower rudder on his first attempt. He can only hold his breath for about one minute, or so, at a time, severely limiting his effectiveness. He never claimed to be a good swimmer.

Time and again Kamita works his way underwater to the damaged rudder. After two exhausting hours he drags himself onto the deck, makes his way to the conning tower, hands me his tools and slowly climbs the ladder.

There is not room for us both on the conning tower, so he remains on the ladder, his hands bleeding and out of breath.

"Sir, I had much difficulty. It appears the depth charge caused a deep bend in the rudder housing, or perhaps it happened when we hit the bottom. In any event, I cannot repair it in the dark nor may I prove able to successfully repair it in daylight. My apologies." His head droops and his breathing is heavy.

We stand for a few minutes, hunched together, me on the conning tower and Kamita grasping the uppermost rungs of the ladder. The orange glow of raging fires is visible over the horizon and I can only imagine the efforts going on at that very moment to fight them, while here in West Loch it is calm and quiet. But the problem facing me is to discover a way to return enough steering control so we can reach our rendezvous point with *I-16*. I make my way into the control room, followed by Kamita who lights two candles as the hatch remains open.

"I shall examine the batteries and make whatever repairs I can." Kamita appears to be disappointed in himself. I watch him take a few swigs of apple juice and crawl towards the battery compartment. In an hour he has stopped the acid leaks and we take a few moments to assess our situation.

"Do you think you could repair the rudder if we risked remaining on the surface for an hour after sunrise?" I ask.

"Not likely," Kamita slowly shakes his head side-to-side. "The lower rudder is damaged and I cannot free it from the housing. True, it is difficult to work in the dark, but twice I was able to place both my hands on it and exert all my strength, but met with no success. I believe both the rudder and the housing are damaged beyond repair." Kamita pauses a moment.

"I have one possible solution. If we were to venture further out into the Loch, we could try reversing the engine and the reverse force might free the rudder enough for maneuvering." Kamita sounds reasonably hopeful.

"We shall do precisely that! There is still an hour to first light, so let's not waste time. Make ready for diving, but first I will attempt to radio *I-16* our plan." My voice conveys more confidence than I feel in my heart.

I begin to transmit a report, but discover there is something wrong with the transmitter. I frown as I examine the radio and can see it has been damaged. I am having much difficulty keying the transmission, but feel confident the *I-16* will at least learn we are alive and well. Now it is only for us to exit this place and return to our fleet so we might report on our experiences.

While Kamita readies himself for the coming maneuver I begin to transmit, as well as I can, one last message for the night. Once I am satisfied the message is sent and the *I-16* is aware our mission has been a success, I quietly give the order to get under way.

"Make two knots."

"Aye, two knots!" Kamita's voice is instilled with a newfound confidence.

I carefully time the hands on my stop watch, just as I practiced so many times back in the Inland Sea of Japan.

"Stop engine!"

"Aye, stop engine," Kamita replies.

"Take us to thirty feet."

"Aye, opening valves." Kamita begins taking on ballast, his bloody hands sometimes slipping as he opens the valves allowing seawater to flood into the ballast tanks.

"Approaching twenty feet; twenty five feet; leveling at thirty feet."

I take a deep breath. "This is it then. Full reverse!"

"Aye, full reverse!" Kamita does not seem to realize he has shouted his response which I consider a natural reaction under our circumstances.

We begin moving in reverse, but it is immediately evident something is seriously wrong as the submarine begins shaking, mildly at first, but more violently as we gain reverse speed. Suddenly we begin to list hard to port and I realize we are moments away from flipping over.

"Stop engine!" I shout.

"Aye, engine stopped," replies Kamita with some trepidation apparent in his voice.

The submarine immediately rights itself and I am thankful for the recovery, but decide to chance one final maneuver.

"Make five knots, Kamita, forward motion!"

"Aye, five knots, forward motion." In only a few moments the submarine begins to vigorously shake from stern to bow and I painfully conclude one of the propellers is seriously out of balance, making the situation even more critical than I anticipated. I fear the propeller noise can easily be picked up by any listening devices the Americans likely have, at least by now, placed at the harbor entrance, which is further reason to abandon any plans for escape.

"Stop engine and let her sink to the bottom. We will need to await nightfall." I fail to disguise my frustration as I slip into my seat and let out an inadvertent sigh.

"Aye." Kamita, without acknowledging my obvious frustration, stops the engine and slowly opens the ballast valves. We slip to the bottom of West Loch where we settle on an almost even keel.

"Sir, if only I had thought to bring additional tools, perhaps I could have repaired the damage." Kamita stares at his feet, shoulders slouched.

"My friend, Buddha once said: 'Do not dwell in the past, do not dream of the future, concentrate the mind on the present moment.' I strongly suggest you concentrate on the present for the present builds the future, and the future will take care of itself. But now let us enjoy some sandwiches and sake, for it is time to consider our options." While I sound optimistic I am fully aware a return to the *I-16* is going to be difficult, perhaps impossible, and in all events we will not be returning in our little iron tube.

We wipe the sweat from our faces and make ourselves as comfortable as we can. "Keep the lights on as I need to study the maps of Oahu and enter these events into the log. It is becoming apparent we will not be escaping in our boat so there is no longer a concern for battery life." I notice his hands are still bleeding. "And take care of your hands as you are going to need them."

Kamita signals an acknowledgement by dipping his head. As he produces a bottle of sake, some fruit and two sandwiches, I reach into a canvas bag, retrieve two cups and offer one to him.

"I will pour and we shall toast the Emperor and Admiral Yamamoto!"

•　•　•　•　•

Ken suddenly opens his eyes and blinks, hard, several times. "Gary! This is taking much more strength than I have for one day. Please forgive me, but I truly need some rest now." He reaches over and takes a long drink of his iced tea. "Breakfast would be good time to continue. Why not come back then and I can finish my life history, such as it is."

Gary rises, walks over to his grandfather, leans forward and gently kisses him on the forehead. "It would be a true honor, grandfather. Would 7:30 be about right for you and Kapuna?"

"That would be perfect," replies Ken.

CHAPTER TWENTY ONE
THE TWITCH

The remnants of lunch are strewn about Pastwa's office. Yamura's sipping coffee as she tosses aside another death certificate. Clarke is munching a donut while Pastwa is reviewing a list of fifteen names and dates of death listed on the chalkboard.

"This is the last death certificate, so that, as they say, is that!" States Yamura with a sigh of relief as she plops into an armchair.

Pastwa pours himself a fresh cup of coffee, sets it on his desk, settles into his chair and swivels to face Yamura as they take a short break. He realizes she appears tired as they have been working hard, fast and without respite the entire day. Clarke is leaning against Pastwa's credenza, likely hoping the next order will not include dragging in any more file boxes. Pastwa smiles, for he knows as long as there's a donut available Clarke will work indefinitely. He considers donuts to be small price to pay in exchange for Clarke's excellent work and loyalty.

"Okay, it's time to break these names down. Karen, you take the first five names, I'll take the second five and Clarke, you take the last five. Cozy up in your favorite research nook, wherever that may be and I want us all to meet back here at," he glances at his watch, "around eighteen hundred hours. That should be more than enough time to determine if any of these names is going to be Yokoyama."

"Fine with me." Yamura picks herself up and slowly walks over to a side credenza where she retrieves her hat and purse. Adjusting the hat just slightly off center, as she likes it, she takes the first five files. "I'll see you both later."

She quickly exits and Clarke looks over to his boss. "Sir, I'd like to take my five files over to the research library where I have a little cubicle nobody else will use. I've rigged the keyboard on that particular computer so it only works for me." Clarke smiles at his resourcefulness.

"That's fine, wherever you are most productive is the place you need to be.

I'll be right here so if you finish early get yourself a bite to eat before returning."

Clarke grabs his set of five files, a small bag of donuts and his hat. He rushes out of Pastwa's office and dead-heads for his research cubicle. Pastwa remains seated at his desk and spreads the first file across his desk top. "Crunch time," he says out loud.

•   •   •   •   •

In about three hours Pastwa has managed to eliminate four of the five names on his share of the list. An unfortunate young man by the name of Tanaka, killed by a stray anti-aircraft shell remains to be vetted out. He can't eliminate him until he receives confirmation from a friend at Langley. The time difference between Virginia and Hawaii, six hours at this time of year, is a killer when it comes to coordinating research efforts, but he has little choice as he has consumed every possible resource available to him. He glances at the clock for what feels like the tenth time and sighs when he realizes it's only half past five. There's a knock on the door and in walks Yamura.

"Karen, didn't expect to see you so soon. Good news?"

"Maybe, I have two names that are open-ended. One is a young man by the name of Kida and the other is named Ito. Both are actually good candidates, but I need to hear back from a friend of mine, an aide to the Army Chief of Staff in D.C. because the files require a higher security clearance than I have."

"Seems to me we are both waiting out the time difference. I've left a message with a friend at Langley regarding the only name I couldn't conclusively rule out and can't reach a conclusion until I hear back from her. But you say these names are promising?"

"Only in as much as I could not eliminate them. But this Kida fellow does appear to match up with dates and places well beyond December 1941, when he was supposedly killed. I get a solid case of the goose bumps on this one. The name also appears in numerous Army references, but really, the balance of my research on Kida has yielded dead-ends or requires files I cannot access on my own."

"Good afternoon, Sirs." Clark enters, looking a bit depressed. "Sorry, but all five of my characters are definitely not our man, no doubt about it. I was able to put every file to rest with absolutely no margin for error. Sorry for the pun." Clarke lightly drops the files on Pastwa's desk.

"That's fine, Clarke." Pastwa smiles at Clarke's play on words. "We have three names still to be played out, so I think this is a good time for me to bring the Admiral up to date. Clarke, please call over to his aide, Jones, and ask whether Reardon can still see me today."

"I'm on it." Clarke quickly slips out of Pastwa's office. Within a minute Clarke is again standing before them.

"The Admiral can see you right away."

Pastwa takes Yamura's files and adds them to his own. "Karen, don't wait for me. Clarke, go get yourself dinner and check back with me by phone when you're finished."

Clarke responds, "Yes, Sir, and thank you." He quickly disappears, whistling the *Popeye the Sailor* song, one of his favorites.

Pastwa turns his attention to Yamura. "Karen, why not go home and get yourself refreshed. I'll swing by after I've met with Reardon and we can go to *Tanaka's of Tokyo* for dinner. How's that sound to you?" Yamura smiles. "Perfect! Call me when you're on the way over!"

She grabs her purse and starts to walk out. Reaching the doorway, she pauses and turns to Pastwa, smiles slyly and says, "I trust you'll approve of my outfit tonight, and it *won't* be dress whites!" She quickly spins around and disappears through the doorway. Pastwa smiles and decides he'll be sure to clean up as he is suddenly feeling quite energetic. But first, the Admiral awaits, so he grabs his hat and darts out the door, the files firmly tucked under his left arm.

•　•　•　•　•

Fifteen minutes later Pastwa finds himself in Reardon's outer office. Reardon's aide, Keona Jones, immediately stands and salutes. "Good evening Commander." Pastwa returns the salute just as smartly as was delivered by Jones. "I'll advise the Admiral you're here." Jones picks up the phone and rings the Admiral to announce Pastwa's arrival. "Please, Commander, follow me."

Pastwa is lead into Reardon's office where he finds Reardon is seated behind his desk. "Good evening, Sir."

"I've been looking forward to your report Chris," replies Reardon.

"I've brought some files and would like to bring you up to date on our research efforts."

"Fine, have a seat and let me take a look at what you have." Pastwa sits directly across from Reardon, reaches over the desk and hands him the three files.

"Sir, these are three individuals we have not been able to eliminate. One of them may prove to be Yokoyama, but until we have responses from queries we have placed on the mainland, we're at a standstill." Reardon opens the first file and spends about sixty seconds scanning it. He does the same with the second file, then opens the third one. Something in the file catches his attention and Pastwa notices Reardon's right eye begin to twitch. Several minutes pass before he lightly drops the file onto his desktop.

"Hmmm, I assume you are waiting on Langley and D.C., correct?" Pastwa shakes his head in the affirmative.

"Would you like me to light some fires for you?" Reardon has never before offered to pull any strings on an investigation, so the offer takes Pastwa by surprise.

"Sir, that shouldn't prove necessary as we'll have our answers very early tomorrow."

"Chris, this Kida fellow is catching my attention and looks to be the most viable candidate." Reardon pauses as he picks up a picture of the deceased Ken Kida.

"So you say he was listed as killed just after the attack on Pearl Harbor? It certainly would have been the easiest solution for their problem of a new identification for Yokoyama. He's about the right age and Nisei. The poor young man's demise rather much fell into their lap." Reardon pauses as he spends a few moments gazing through the window towards the harbor. The early evening sun is casting shadows across the waters and lights from a pair of warships resting at anchor are just becoming visible.

"Commander, my right eye is twitching out of control!" Reardon firmly presses his right index finger into the skin just below his twitching eye.

"This Kida fellow is setting off all my internal alarms and as far as I am concerned you can discount the other two for Kida will prove to be your man." Reardon stands, walks over to the window, starts to look out towards the harbor, but catches himself and instead turns to face Pastwa.

"I assume you will have your answers early tomorrow, given the time difference. But mark my words, this is the file that will prove to be the focus of your investigation!" Reardon walks back to his desk, picks up the three files and returns them to Pastwa.

"Good work Chris. I expect you to keep me advised on every move you make, but mark my words, tomorrow's going to be decisive." Reardon pauses a moment. "Now, take the evening off and clear your head because I have a hunch the heat is going to be turned up several notches come morning."

"Yes Sir, I'll do exactly that." Just as Pastwa reaches the doorway, the files under his left arm, Reardon calls out to him.

"Almost forgot something, Chris. I'm conducting some inspections tomorrow and don't anticipate I'll be back until at least fifteen hundred hours."

"Roger that, Sir. I'll phone Jones when I have something to report."

As he watches Pastwa disappear into the outer office, he again presses a finger deep into the annoying twitch, but to no avail.

CHAPTER TWENTY TWO
MONEY SPEAKS

Once outside Reardon's office Pastwa stops and opens the third file. He quickly flips through it while memorizing the most pertinent facts. "If the Admiral thinks this is you, I wouldn't bet against it." He hurries across the grounds to his office where he locks all three files into a desk drawer and deadbolts both sets of office doors on his way out. He stops in an adjacent locker room where he shaves, freshens up and carefully steams his dress uniform. He gives himself a once-over in front of a wall mirror, picks up his cell phone and speed dials Yamura.

"Hello, Chris?"

"Hi Karen, can you be ready in twenty minutes?"

"I'm almost ready now and I'm starving! Look for me out front, okay?" Yamura smiles as she continues to brush her hair with her free hand while holding her cell phone with the other.

"Excellent, I'll see you then." Pastwa disconnects the call and jogs to his vintage, brilliant red with cream leather interior, 325i cabrio. Clarke has made some under-the-hood improvements for him, but on Oahu there is scant opportunity to use them. Nevertheless, he loves putting the top down and cranking up the Alpine stereo.

As he slides into the Recaro bucket seat he decides to keep the top up, on the wise assumption Yamura won't want her hair to get all tangled before dinner. He can't help but smile as he imagines how her hair is going to appear a couple hours *after* dinner.

As he pulls up to the security gate at the edge of the base, the SP on duty salutes him smartly. Pastwa smiles as he returns the salute and immediately points his car towards the Nimitz Highway. He's not in the habit of keeping Karen waiting and has no intention of making an exception today.

Ryota, a Japanese/American is the maître d' at *Tanaka's* in downtown

Honolulu. He is a veteran of twenty years' service and has rotated three month educational residences at the main restaurant in Tokyo several times. He works long hours to ensure the dining experience in Honolulu is as good as what a customer would experience in Tokyo, which is where he first met Pastwa nearly eight years earlier. They've become good friends and Pastwa has attended numerous birthday parties at Ryota's home.

As Pastwa and Yamura walk into the restaurant they notice Ryota is animatedly speaking to one of the waiters. Upon recognizing Pastwa he immediately sends the waiter on his way and rushes over to greet his friends.

"Commander! Lieutenant! So wonderful to see you both this evening. It has been too long. Please let me take your hat." Smiling, Pastwa removes his hat and offers it to Ryota. "Thank you my friend. On our last visit it was one of those rare occasions when you were off duty. However, you'll be pleased to know the staff performed admirably in your absence," says Pastwa.

"Good evening, Ryota," Yamura says in Japanese. Ryota breaks into an ear to ear grin and responds, also in Japanese. "You are most beautiful tonight and I am honored you have chosen to grace our premises."

Pastwa has a working knowledge of Japanese, though he's not too comfortable speaking it. He understands the upshot of what Ryota said and responds in English: "My friend, if I didn't know for a fact you are very happily married, with a beautiful wife and six wonderful children, I would suspect you are trying to undermine my position." Pastwa laughs when he sees a momentary concern cross Ryota's face. Yamura also has a little laugh at Ryota's expense, but he is soon smiling and leads them to a teppan where two couples are already seated.

"Chef Shiro will be out momentarily. Your timing, Commander, is perfect!" He pulls out a chair for Yamura and seats the commander next to one of the men. As Pastwa takes his seat Ryota pulls out a small pad of paper, writes something on it and discreetly slips it into Pastwa's hand, which Pastwa slides into his side pocket.

"Noriko shall be your server this evening. Again, I thank you for choosing to dine with us." Ryota bows and makes his exit.

"Did I see Ryota slip something to you?"

"You don't miss a thing, do you?" Pastwa glances around the dining room searching for any familiar faces and concludes they are in a room of strangers. "Let me take a look." He pulls out the note, reads it over and can't hide a frown as two names jump out at him.

"Chris, what's it say?" Yamura whispers.

"Damn, Karen, you won't believe who had lunch together in here today; Lani Gale and a seaman by the name of 'P. Young.'" Yamura appears shocked. "I know who that is, it's Paul Young, a seaman who performs copying and pretty much office boy type stuff. Chris, I've got a bad feeling about this. Gale's a bit too up market for the likes of Young."

"Nothing we can do at this moment except enjoy our dinner. We'll follow up on this matter later." Pastwa puts the thought of Gale nosing around the base out of his mind and shoots a sly grin at Yamura. She, in turn, picks up his left hand and gives it a gentle kiss. "I agree, let's indulge ourselves and then retire to my place for dessert."

"Karen, you know how I do love my desserts!" Pastwa gently kisses the top of her right hand, as the waitress approaches to take their order.

* * * * *

Very early the following morning Pastwa is drinking coffee while relaxing on Yamura's lanai, taking in the first faint signs of sunrise. He's mentally preparing for what he expects to be a challenging day. A light breeze carries the aroma of salt water, the smell of which is what initially attracted Pastwa to boating and, ultimately, the Navy. He's convinced the only way his life at this moment could be better would be if he and Karen were on his boat, sailing between the islands.

Pastwa's contentment doesn't last very long. Yamura rushes out, dressed only in a sheer negligee and throws the front page of the newspaper onto the table in front of him.

"Now we know why those two were having a cozy lunch yesterday!" Her voice is both excited and aggravated.

Startled, though not fully distracted from Yamura's figure, Pastwa picks up the newspaper. "Damn her! She's obviously been busy snooping around the base!" Pastwa reads the full-page headlines aloud: *"Second Bombing of Pearl Harbor! Captured Documents Prove Jap Midget Subs Sunk Our Battleships! Jap Midget Submariners May Be Your Neighbors! One Hundred Thousand Dollar Reward to Anyone Who Can Prove Their Whereabouts...or Their Gravesites!"*

"That reward offer may well prove more effective than our own research!" Pastwa tosses the newspaper onto the table. "We absolutely must beat Gale and that newspaper of hers to the punch!" Standing, he takes Yamura's hands into his own. "We will not be beaten on this. If Yokoyama's to be found, you and I are the ones who'll find him, guaranteed. And if he's alive, we're the ones who'll bring him in." Pastwa isn't shouting, as he is restraining himself, but his anger is clear. At the same time he's worried about Reardon's reaction.

Yamura notices his face turned a pale gray for a few moments, as if a dark cloud was moving across his psyche. She has seen this look only once before, during an incident a number of years earlier at Kaneohoe when a child turned up dead from a drug overdose. He busted the entire ring, though not until there had been significant bloodshed.

"I agree Chris." Yamura gives him a light kiss on the lips. "I can be ready in ten minutes. Maybe you should call Clarke and Ferguson and get them over to the base?"

"Right!" Go ahead and finish getting dressed, I'll clean up out here and call them." Yamura smiles and disappears into the condo. He grabs everything from the table and heads to the kitchen where he quickly puts the food away and stuffs their plates and glasses into the dishwasher. He pulls his phone from a pocket and starts making the calls as he intends to leave the moment Yamura is ready.

CHAPTER TWENTY THREE
"VISION, SPIRIT, PATIENCE and HONESTY"

Gary races up the stairs to the front lanai of his grandparents' home only to find it empty. The newspaper is in his left hand, his heart's racing and his imagination is running wild. He's worried they've already left town. Breathing heavily he tries the front door, finds it open and quickly enters. Alarm bells are ringing in his head as there's nobody in sight so he runs to the kitchen and calls out "Kapuna! Grandfather!" No response. He notices the rice cooker is in 'cook' mode and the tea pot on the stove top is still steaming. Calming down a little, he walks onto the back lanai and spots both his grandparents sitting in their gazebo, maybe twenty feet from the house. "No wonder they didn't hear me." He thinks to himself.

Gary bounds to the gazebo and excitedly blurts out: "There you are! I was worried you both left town!" Ken and Sun are a little surprised and both smile at their grandson's alarm.

"Gary, my boy, relax. What would you have us do, run away and hide?"

"Please calm down and have a seat. We are enjoying the beautiful morning," says Sun.

"How can you be so calm? Didn't you see the newspaper?" Gary is amazed his grandparents can be so at ease while he's the exact opposite and wonders if they know something he doesn't.

"My boy, if I reacted with emotion to every problem and crisis I have faced in my life, I would have worn myself out decades ago. I must remind you of what Buddha might say: 'The whole secret of existence is to have no fear. Never fear what will become of you, depend on no one. Only the moment you reject all help are you freed.'" Ken pauses to allow Gary to digest the wisdom.

"Gary, you must learn to approach each hurdle that comes your way with a combination of calm, intelligence and resourcefulness. If you let your heart rate dictate your actions, surely the results will prove most unsatisfactory more often than not. Today we are faced with a problem, but it is a problem of unknown urgency and unknown depth. To respond with urgency or fear would likely produce an unfavorable result. Thus, it is time for meditation."

Gary's face contorts into a look of total disbelief. "I don't understand; this looks pretty darn urgent to me!"

Ken smiles and gently takes Sun's right hand. "We have decided there is no action we can take that might change the course of our destiny. If it is deemed I am to be discovered, then so be it. We read the story and there are very few facts for anyone to work with. Maybe they will find me and maybe they will not. We are prepared for either event."

"But grandfather, the U. S. Navy has great resources, won't *they* find you?"

Ken sighs and releases Sun's hand. He turns his chair slightly so he can more directly face Gary.

"Gary, the Navy may have more resources, but if they find me what would there be for me to do? Buy a gun and have a shootout?" Ken laughs.

Gary is frowning as he doesn't find his grandfather to be funny. "Seriously, you plan to do nothing?"

"Quite the contrary Gary, I plan to relate the rest of my first life's history. After all, it is worth One Hundred Thousand Dollars!" Ken smiles, but Gary doesn't appreciate the humor.

"Grandfather, there's nothing I can do to help if you don't let me, so I can at least learn the rest of your past directly from you, rather than eventually read about it in the newspaper."

"Gary, we appreciate your concern, but trust in our judgment. After all, we have made it this far and have fared well for our family." Ken says.

"Yes, Gary, please trust in your grandfather." Sun smiles at her grandson as she certainly understands his concerns. She agrees with her husband's analysis of the situation and recites a line from an American song she liked very much, maybe fifty years earlier: "What will be, will be."

The three of them spend the next several minutes in silence. Finally, Gary speaks.

"Since we're going to take no action, then I think we should make the most of our time." Gary stands and fills each of his grandparent's cups with more tea, pours a cup for himself and takes a seat. "There! Now we're ready. Grandfather, please tell me all about your first life, while we are still relatively safe."

Ken smiles and glances at Sun, who returns his smile. "Allow me a moment to slip myself from the present into the very distant past. The events you are to learn of took place so long ago." Ken begins to slowly stroke his beard as he closes his eyes.

. . . . .

"We are lying on the bottom of West Loch for a second day. It is stifling hot, even with the ventilators running. We know the battery level is no longer a concern as we cannot escape so we make ourselves as comfortable as possible. We eat and drink most of our food supplies this day, leaving just enough so we can easily carry a little food to shore with us after nightfall. While we have many potential safe contacts, we also have no knowledge how close to our location any of them might truly prove to be. So we eat well, all things considered, and we rest."

"When we laid in provisions I decided we might need as much as three full days of food and drink as I had planned for three potential exit avenues: The first was we slipped out of the harbor immediately after firing our warheads. The second exit avenue was my plan to lie low in West Loch and sneak out the following night. The third avenue proved to be the route we would follow."

"You see, I possess a set of maps depicting in detail both the harbor and the island of Oahu along with a list of safe houses and their addresses. The safe houses belong to Japanese living on Oahu and who are known to be trustworthy. I committed their names and locations to memory in advance, just as I memorized the harbor and the island."

"Remember, the passage from Kure to Oahu was very long and I had many hours to study and meditate. I filled myself with a determination to return and personally report to Admiral Yamamoto and, of course, accept his offer to have luncheon with him again. I must consider Kamita and I are Samurai on a mission and the mission includes returning to our Navy to fight again. And I also feel it is imperative I report of the torpedo, radio, periscope, propeller and rudder issues, which should be corrected prior to future operations."

"I am also very much attached to Kamita, as he had proven on many occasions to be an indispensable engineer. This last day in our little submarine I find time to meditate and imagine the two of us standing before Admiral Yamamoto, smiling with pride as he looks at us. The image is so vivid I convince myself it is nothing less than a spiritual glimpse into our future."

"Years later I will read a book written by Kazuo Sakamaki, the midget submariner the Americans captured and labeled 'Prisoner of War Number One.' My opinion of him is not positive; not now and not then for he placed the entire mission at risk due to his improper decision making. But I digress."

"As I said, we waited on the bottom of West Loch until it was near ten at night. There was no moonlight to deal with, which would have been a problem. Judging it is time to proceed, I begin to give the necessary orders…"

•   •   •   •   •

"Kamita, it is time for us to make ready. Put on your uniform and gather the food in the canvas sack."
But Sir, our orders were to go ashore naked and seek civilian clothing," says Kamita.

"Good point, but I remember seeing photos of pineapple plantation workers. You see, I had a cousin return from a long stay on Oahu and his pictures depicted bare-chested men working in the fields. So we will remove our shirts, wrap our supplies and lock box within them and, once we reach shore, roll around in the mud to disguise our trousers."

"Aye that sounds like an excellent plan," Kamita's voice reflects confidence.

"I must make appropriate entries into the log as from this point forward it will be a record of our successful efforts to return to our Navy. I will wrap it in oil cloth for protection during our swim. Please hand me the water resistant box."

Kamita fumbles around a little, locates the box and offers it.

"Good!" I take the box and quickly place some useful items, along with the logbook and Kamita's pendant into it.

With the box slung over my shoulder and my pistol in one of my pockets, I look at Kamita, who is ready for our next endeavor.

"Bring us to the surface very slowly as we need a very quiet emergence."

"Aye, we will barely cause a ripple," Kamita responds.

He slowly turns several valves and in a few moments I feel us break free from the bottom and begin to rise. He does an excellent job as it requires nearly two minutes to reach the surface. Once on the surface I give my final orders as Commander of the *I-16 tou.*

"When I open the hatch, you set fire to our orders and harbor maps, and remember the four words that have brought us this far and which will guide us home: *Vision, Spirit, Patience* and *Honesty.*" I reach up, twist the locking mechanism on the hatch and, using my shoulder, force it open, revealing a starlit night sky while Kamita sets fire to the sensitive documents.

"Kamita, once ashore we must act as if chameleons and disappear into the landscape. Remember, speak only English from this point forward, only English! Now open the flood valves and be ready for a quick swim."

"Should I set the scuttle charges?" Kamita asks.

"No, the explosion would risk bringing undue attention upon us. It is best the Americans never discover we were here."

"Aye, opening the flood valves!" As Kamita opens the valves I scamper through the conning tower, out the hatch and down to the foredeck. Soon he joins me and we slip over the side and into the cool water. We are pleased to discover we are only about twenty meters from the shoreline and we make quick work of the swim. As we crawl through the thick, tall weeds lining the shore we both instinctively turn and look behind us. At that moment the conning tower is slipping below the surface for the last time. We pause for several moments, watching the bubbles escape from our submarine. Soon, there are only the faintest of ripples in the water.

"Let's climb to the top of the berm and take our bearings." I discover I am slightly out of breath, not so much from the swim, but from excitement. Every nerve ending in my body is alive and I feel as if I am attuned to everything around me as we climb to the top of the berm. Once there we have a good view of West Loch which proves much larger than it appeared on the map and is totally deserted. I feel quite safe, at least for the moment.

"Remember, only English now," I whisper.

"Aye, in which direction is the safe house?" Kamita asks.

I glance at the sky in search of the North Star. My compass is useless in the dark and we have no flashlights. The bulbs in both flashlights we had brought with us were shattered during the depth charge attack. Here is where the hours I expended memorizing the map of Oahu and the locations of safe houses come into play. I point towards a mountain range.

"That way, my friend. We must skirt to the left of the mountain and about four to six kilometers beyond is a sugar cane plantation owned by a trusted Japanese family. With luck, we might be there around daybreak."

"Aye, I am ready."

"Wait, you brought my sword! I told you to leave it behind. It can do us no good whatsoever!" Kamita appears offended.

"You carried this sword with you for years, it has brought you this far and I felt it my duty to carry it for you."

"Perhaps you are right, but at the first sign of trouble you must throw it as hard as you can, out of sight. Understood?"

"Aye." Kamita slips the sword under his belt and throws the canvas bag with their provisions over his left shoulder. I point to a spot off to our left where there appears to be a trail.

"Follow close behind me and stay alert. We must hurry." The trail is very crude and soon brings us to a road. There is no traffic and no patrol in sight so we quickly cross and return to the path which leads us in the general direction we must travel. In about one hour we reach another road, only this time we can hear the sound of trucks coming our way. We hide in the undergrowth and patiently wait as four U. S. Army trucks rumble past at low speed, with small slits as their headlights. Once the sound of the trucks has completely faded away we quickly scurry across the road and continue forward to an uncertain welcome.

As the sky begins to reveal the first signs of the coming day we stop to rest. Kamita brings out the last of the sandwiches and an apple juice for each of us.

"We will rest here for a little while. I do not think we can be far away and it makes sense to eat and rest now, just in the event I am wrong about the location of the plantation." With a sandwich in my left hand and a bottle of apple juice in my right, I make myself comfortable under a banyan tree.

"I can use the sword to dig a hole for burying our empty bottles," Kamita says with a smile. "See, it is a handy item to have with us!" He laughs.

I can only smile slightly as I believe it is a bad idea to carry a sword with us and it worries me we might run into trouble so quickly we cannot dispose of it. Despite my apprehension, I allow him to keep it.

After the rest break we soon reach the crest of a small volcanic outcropping. Stretching before us are acres of sugar cane and maybe three hundred meters beyond the edge of the nearest cane field is a small house. "Kamita, this is it!"

Kamita smiles broadly. "Of course it is. I have complete confidence in you," he replies.

We work our way into the cane fields when suddenly we come upon an elderly Japanese man who is startled to see us. I speak Japanese as I address him. "Sir, we are with the Imperial Japanese Navy and require your assistance, please." The man looks us over very carefully before responding, also in Japanese.

"I can see that much from the looks of you, but there has been no invasion that I am aware of. What are you doing here?"

"We were in a submarine that was too damaged to continue and were forced to swim ashore. We very much need clothing and a safe place to rest for a day or two." The old man looks at me almost as if I am some manner of carnival oddity. Finally, he says, this time in English, "For your best interests I trust you can speak some English?"

We smile with relief. "Yes, Sir. We both can speak a little English and have been doing so since we swam ashore. I thought you might not speak it yourself. So, will you assist us?"

"Both of you stay here, out of sight. I will finish my routine morning rounds and return to the house. No need for me to risk doing anything out of the ordinary, for one cannot tell who might be watching!"

I look around and notice a spot about halfway up a small hill, where there is a stand of trees.

"We will go up there where we will sit under the cover of the trees and wait. From that position we can observe your home and in the event we see anyone approaching we will withdraw further into the fields. Will that suit your desires?"

"Yes, yes, go up there and wait for me. When I am ready I will come out the front door and wave my arms. Then come to my house." The old man turns and continues to complete his early morning routine. We watch him disappear into the cane fields before we make our way up the side of the hill, at the crest of which we find the shade under the trees to be quite satisfactory, not to mention, relaxing.

"We might be here half the day so I suggest you sleep now and I will wake you in two hours. If the old man has not come out yet, then it will be my turn to sleep."

Kamita slips the canvas sack from his shoulder and uses it as a makeshift pillow. He is asleep before I can say another word.

The waterproof box is bulky and I am relieved to temporarily be rid of it. I find a comfortable place where I can sit with my back to a tree and watch the road. Everything is so green! There is only the occasional cloud and a very pleasant breeze. The air is light, fresh and feels very good in my lungs. A far cry from the acrid air in our little submarine.

From our hilltop position we seem to be in another world. I momentarily close my eyes and imagine Kamita and I are as if Samurai, lost in a tropical paradise. I am roused from my melancholy by the sight of the old man standing in front of his little shack of a home, waving his arms.

I shake Kamita by the shoulders. "Wake up! We must be moving." He slowly sits up, places his canvas sack over his shoulder and rises. "Look, he is signaling us to come down." I point towards the house. Kamita's gaze follows my finger. "I see him, but what if this is a trap?" Kamita asks.

"I have not seen anyone come or go, only the old man. I believe he is not our enemy, and in any event, we have no choice. We must trust in him and in our luck." I pick up the box, swing its leather strap over my shoulder and begin to quickly jog towards the old man with Kamita on my heels.

It takes about ten minutes to cover the distance and as we approach the front porch, the old man backs up to the entry door, props it open and motions for us to enter. We do not hesitate and upon entering we find a table set for four people, with rice, vegetables, fruits and a steaming pot of boiled fish. What a sight to behold! Standing next to the table is an older Japanese woman. The man closes and locks the door behind him.

"Gentlemen, this is my wife, Sayuri and my name is Nobuo. Please be our guests and honor us by sharing a meal." He smiles broadly as his wife gestures for us to sit.

"Thank you very much. Your hospitality is most appreciated and you can be certain we will convey your generosity to the Emperor. My name is Yokoyama and this is my engineer, Kamita. We are both of the Imperial Japanese Navy and have endured the misfortune of losing our means of transportation as the result of an action with the Americans." Both Sayuri and Nobuo shake their heads in understanding as we take our seats, except for Sayuri. She insists on serving each of us and proceeds to do so. Once we are all served we wait for her to take care of her own plate, at which time Nobuo offers a prayer:

"The Rays of the Sun, Moon and Stars, which nourish our bodies…and the five grains of our Earth which nurture our spirits…are all gifts of the Eternal Buddha. Even a mere drop of water or a single grain of rice are nothing…save the result of meritorious work and difficult labor. May this meal assist us to maintain health in body and mind and to uphold the teachings of Buddha as repayment for the Four Favors, and to perform the pure conduct of service to others, such as these two honorable Samurai who honor us with their presence this day." Nobuo becomes quiet, his head bowed and his eyes closed for several more moments.

"Now we may eat," he says.

After concluding an excellent meal, Nobuo, Kamita and I walk out to the back of the house. We find a comfortable location in the shade where the three of us sit on the ground to discuss our situation.

Nobuo begins the conversation. "I visited Japan just last year. There was much apprehension among my family over the prospects of a broader war than the never-ending conflict with the Chinese. Several of my relatives are in the army and all of them are fighting in China. On the trip back to Oahu there was much talk among us about the prospect of war with the Western Powers, so when we learned of the attack upon Pearl Harbor, it was not a complete surprise."

"I am grateful my brother and sister were able to return to Japan only last month. I was happy to supply each of them with two new Singer sewing machines. Of course we did not expect the war to be on our doorstep so quickly, but still, it appears to have been an inescapable event for in my most humble opinion the Army has been in control of our country for some time now, and the Army is always preaching war. Regardless, my loyalty to the Emperor is not diminished so it is my solemn duty to assist the two of you in any manner of which I am capable." Nobuo pauses as he appears undecided whether to continue.

"May I respectably ask, are you intended as part of the invasion force? The newspaper writes an invasion is expected."

"Sir," I reply," we actually do not have knowledge of any invasion plans. We can assume the newspaper would not be foolishly alarming the citizens, thus we must conduct ourselves on the belief an invasion is, indeed, imminent. So it appears we may need to remain undercover for only a short period of time."

"Then is it your intentions to remain with me for the near future?"

"No Sir, we have the name of a person we are to contact. I think it best, however, to travel as much as possible by night. These work clothes you have been very considerate to provide for us will make it much easier to disappear into the population while we are here. We are most grateful to you."

"By night?" Nobuo shakes his head vigorously, indicating his disapproval. "Don't you know? The United States Army has taken control of the entire island and anyone discovered outside after dark may be shot on sight, no questions asked! To travel at night is very dangerous, especially if you are Japanese."

"I did not know that, but it is better to travel by night regardless. We will rely upon our senses to avoid detection. If we are not seen, we cannot be questioned! One thing we were not provided with in advance is any manner of traveling papers or identification. However, the person we are to make contact with should be able to help us. After all, we cannot count on an invasion. For now, we must follow orders and making contact with our liaison is our first priority." Nobuo slowly shakes his head in polite disagreement.

"Gentlemen, I understand you must follow your orders, however it is my humble opinion you should consider remaining with us. In the event an invasion does not come to this island in the next few weeks, then we can consider alternatives."

"Nobuo, my friend, we truly appreciate your concern. If you could only grant us a provision of water and perhaps some fruit, we would seek to depart shortly after dusk."

"I am also moved at your interest in our safety," says Kamita, "but my Commander is correct. We must move on. I will remember you and your wife in my prayers each day."

"So be it, my brave Samurai. Rest here the remainder of the day and after Sayuri feeds you a good dinner you can be off on your journey." There is sadness in Nobuo's voice as he clearly would have preferred retaining our company.

Following a wonderful dinner we start out for a residence located roughly twenty kilometers distant. Kamita has wrapped the sword with burlap and has tied our canvas sack to it. Our uniforms and some food are in the sack as we did not risk leaving anything behind that might be inadvertently discovered.
"Kamita, if we maintain this pace we can be at our destination before sunrise!"

"Aye, after two fulfilling meals today I feel I can walk one hundred kilometers tonight," he replies.

•　•　•　•　•

Ken suddenly turns to face Gary and Sun. "When I returned to Oahu after the war, I attempted to determine what became of Nobuo and Sayuri. I discovered Nobuo passed away while in an internment camp on the mainland but I was unable to trace Sayuri. Given current events, it is probably a good thing I was not able to make contact with them again.

"Allow me to continue for I have digressed long enough." Ken takes a sip of iced tea, makes himself a little more comfortable and continues relating the story of his first life.

•   •   •   •   •

Kamita and I establish a good pace as we walk in single file, staying to the left side of a single lane dirt road so we can quickly jump into the cane fields in the event of danger. We have been walking for hours when suddenly we hear a command from behind us:

"Halt! I say halt right now!"

Surprised, we whirl around and discover a soldier is standing in the middle of the road, roughly a hundred meters away. We stop, but only momentarily, for the soldier begins to jog towards us.

"Kamita," I whisper with an urgency in my voice, "run!" We turn and run as hard as we can.

"Halt or I'll shoot!" Screams the soldier. But we keep running.

The soldier is not bluffing and soon enough we hear gunfire. I surmise he must be running as he fires, for there is a span of several seconds between the shots. I count six shots when I see a dense area of overgrowth approaching on our right. "Follow me," I call out as I charge into the dense growth.

"Aye" I can hear Kamita gasping for air.

As Kamita overtakes me, there is another gunshot and he falls heavily to the ground. I help him stand, but discover he has been shot in the back. "Can you keep going?" I ask.

"Yes, but there is a burning sensation in my back." He winces as he reaches behind him and feels the wound. "With your help I can still run."

We continue to work our way through what proves to be very thick undergrowth as bullets pass nearby. After some time, I really do not know how long, the rifle shots stop. Apparently he has finally lost track of us or given up.

"My friend, I fear we must keep moving until I am certain we are not being followed." Kamita is breathing too heavily to reply. It takes everything he has to keep moving for he knows there is no other choice.

We continue to press forward for another two hours. Finally, lying before us at the bottom of a small valley is a farm house with outbuildings. Everything is dark and I assume whoever might be inside is asleep. Do I risk going to the door? I look at Kamita's face and decide he cannot go any further so I decide to run the risk. Glancing at the eastern horizon, I notice early signs of the approaching dawn. We make our way to the front porch where I help Kamita lie down. This is the first time I notice a large, dark red area on the back of his shirt and realize he is bleeding profusely.

I knock on the door and wait. Shortly, I hear footsteps. My breathing stops as the door slowly opens. What luck! I am looking directly into the eyes of a traditionally dressed older Japanese woman in a silk kimono who appears shocked to see me.

"Forgive me, ma'am," I whisper in Japanese, "I am an officer in the Emperor's Navy. My engineer has been shot by a sentry." Her eyes follow my hand as I point to Kamita, lying quietly on her weather worn wood plank porch. She stares at Kamita, then back at me, bows and opens the door fully.

Speaking Japanese, she replies, "Please, bring your engineer inside where I have a cot he can rest on." I lift him over my right shoulder and carry him into the house. We find ourselves in an open room with a cooking area off to the left where there is a large table and maybe ten chairs around it. The woman points to my right where I notice two cots along the wall. I carry Kamita to the nearest cot and gently lower him, face down.

I look at the woman and say, "If you speak English, I would prefer it please."

"Please, you sit. Have some pineapple juice," she says in English, while motioning to a pitcher on the table. "My name is Azumi. My husband Kuro is at another plantation until morning helping with some mechanical repairs." She looks over at Kamita. "May I tend to your friend's injury?"

"Thank you. Anything you can do is much appreciated." Azumi smiles slightly, walks over to a cabinet and retrieves a first aid kit along with a stack of white cloths. "If you would not mind too much, could you fill that bowl over there with some water?"

"Of course." I immediately take the bowl over to a sink and pump it full of delightfully cold water. I bring the bowl to her and set it on the floor next to Kamita. Azumi is carefully cutting open the back of Kamita's shirt, revealing a hole in his back that is oozing a steady stream of blood. She soaks one of the cloths in the water, lightly squeezes it and places it upon the wound. Kamita groans in response.

"I believe he very much requires a doctor." She replaces the first cloth, already soaked through with blood, with a fresh one. "As soon as my husband returns he can drive you to a Japanese doctor we trust. You will be safe with him but first I must attempt to stop this bleeding." She presses another fresh cloth onto the wound, however Kamita has passed out and utters no sound at all.

"Azumi, what if your husband is stopped by the Army with us in his truck? I do not want to place the two of you in danger." Azumi shakes her head from side to side.

"No, no, my husband's old truck is seen all over the island as he performs equipment repairs on many plantations and processing plants. He even has occasion to work for the army. I assure you, he will draw no attention." She looks at Kamita, as blood is beginning to drip onto the floor.

"In any event, your companion cannot afford any delays. I truly fear for him." She stands and motions towards the kitchen table. "Please, take a seat and let me fix you some breakfast. The rice should be nearly cooked by now as I have been planning to feed my husband upon his return."

I stare at Kamita until I discern he is, indeed, still breathing then take a seat at the table. Azumi is busy mixing vegetables, eggs and making some manner of a rice flour batter. She pours all the elements together and places them in her oven. It soon begins to smell very good and the aroma amplifies my hunger. I am also very tired as it has proven to be a very long and difficult night. As Azumi removes the pan from the oven I hear what sounds like a small truck approaching the house. She looks out the window and smiles.

"That is Kuro."

In a few minutes there is the unmistakable sound of footsteps approaching the front door. Kuro steps inside and immediately notices me sitting at the table, frowns and stops in his tracks. Then he notices Kamita lying on the cot and an even larger frown crosses his face. Azumi runs up to him motioning in my direction.

"My husband," she explains in Japanese, "these are two Samurai of the Empire in need of assistance. I am afraid one of them has been shot and requires a doctor." She motions towards Kamita. Kuro walks over to him and shakes his head at the sight of so much blood. Slowly, he walks over to me. I stand in response but before I can say a word he raises his right hand to silence me.

"No need to speak. I can put two and two together, as they say. You both must have participated in the attack on the harbor. Where is your airplane?" He speaks in Japanese.

I reply in English: "Sir, on behalf of the Emperor, I thank you for your hospitality. We are members of the Imperial Japanese Navy and our vessel was disabled when we were attacked by the Americans." I pause long enough to allow him to digest my words.

"We have an immediate need and do not have the luxury of waiting for an invasion. My engineer urgently requires the attention of a surgeon." I motion towards Kamita.

"What are your names?" Kuro asks.

"Sir, for your own benefit it is best you do not learn our names or our ranks. We do not desire for any harm to come upon you as a result of assisting us. There are people on this island who anticipate they will be called upon to help persons such as ourselves and we were on our way to meet with precisely such a person when my friend was shot." I notice Kuro keeps staring at the blood dripping on the floor.

"Your wife has been extremely kind to us and I am afraid I must ask you to please transport me and my friend to a surgeon today. I do not believe he can survive the day without professional assistance."

Kuro remains silent as his gaze switches from me to Kamita and back to me. He notices his wife appears to be silently pleading our cause. Finally, Kuro responds:

"Azumi has prepared us breakfast. It would be a dishonor to her and rude on my part not to invite you to join us so it is my suggestion we eat and then you go to sleep. I will wake you when it is time to leave. I have reason to believe Doctor Ito, who is a relative of mine, will be receptive to your situation, but he is getting up in years and does not open his doors before noon. So, sit and eat!" Kuro takes a seat and motions for me to do the same. Azumi begins to fill our plates, after first placing a pot of hot tea into the center of the table.

"These are very sensitive times in Hawaii. Since your attack the Americans have banned all Japanese language publications and they look upon every person of Japanese descent on the island as if we personally had a role in your handiwork! There is talk of an invasion, but I put little credence in such talk. I am a pragmatist. I base my life on what I can see and what I can control and do not believe our country can possibly move the necessary number of soldiers, tanks, equipment and supplies from Japan, thousands of miles across the Pacific, to here. I have seen how little one passenger ship can hold. It would take a thousand such ships for an undertaking of that magnitude and I do not believe there are one thousand such ships in the world." He pauses and sighs deeply before continuing.

"No, there is no invasion force over the horizon. I have made the ocean voyage back and forth from Japan maybe five times in the last twenty five years. Unless you have personal knowledge of such a force, I would be planning on some other manner of transport to return to your friends at sea."

"Sir, before my companion was wounded, a return to our rendezvous point was our first priority. But now, medical attention for his wound is the priority.

Make no mistake, I do honor your opinion but I am very anxious to return to my fleet once my engineer is in safe hands."

With each of us having said what is on our minds we turn our attention to the meal that Azumi has spread across the table before us.

"Azumi, this is a wonderful meal. I cannot express enough gratitude." The smile on my face transmits more than my words.

Azumi breaks into a large grin and bows her head in modest embarrassment. "Thank you. It is truly an honor to cook for you." Azumi returns to eating her breakfast and tries not to stare at me. I am of the opinion she considers us to be some manner of heroes of the Empire, not simply sailors seeking a way home.

I make quick work of the food and enjoy some marvelous mango juice. Though I am very tired, I feel good.

"Friend, time for you to get some rest. I will stand watch in the event someone might stop by," says Kuro who points to an empty cot near Kamita. "Please, use this cot. It is simple, but comfortable."

"Thank you. I am quite tired and the prospect of a rest is most welcome." I fall asleep the moment my head hits the cot.

●　●　●　●　●

"Wake up! Wake up!" Kuro says as he shakes my shoulder. Instantly I jump up and look around. Kamita is still passed out though it appears Kuro has changed Kamita's clothes and generally cleaned him up. As I come fully awake I realize Kuro has placed his hands on my shoulders.

"Time to take your friend to Doctor Ito. You hold him by one shoulder, I'll take the other and we shall lay him in the back of my truck where Azumi will watch over him. You will ride up front with me." Kuro helps me pick up Kamita and I am alarmed when the movement does not wake my friend or elicit even so much as a groan.

"Gently now," says Kuro, as he and I place Kamita into the back of his old panel truck, the faded words "Kuro Ito Mechanical" printed on the side panels. Clearly he has had this truck a long time, so it is, indeed, a common sight on the island. I feel a renewal of confidence that he will safely deliver us to the surgeon.

I close the doors to the truck and join Kuro in the front seat. "We have about a ninety-minute drive ahead of us, my Samurai friend. Should we be stopped by the authorities just appear to be unconcerned and allow me to respond to any inquiries, understood?"

"Yes I do." He immediately starts the truck and points us towards the road. The first part of the trip takes us through many pineapple plantations, but the plantations soon give way to scattered houses. Within an hour we find ourselves in Honolulu maneuvering at only a few miles per hour through an extensive outdoor market.

I notice many Chinese among the Japanese, along with occasional Caucasians, but hardly a police officer or soldier in sight, which I take to be a good omen. Suddenly I see two faces I recognize and without thinking I blurt out, "Foruno! Yokoyama!" Both men look up, but fail to recognize from which direction my voice was coming. I think better of further trying to gain their attention and watch them disappear behind us.

"You know someone here?" Kuro asks.

"No, I found myself imagining I was back in Japan and thought two of my friends were in the crowd.

"You apparently need more sleep," replies Kuro. I am relieved he failed to realize I noticed familiar faces in the crowd. It is much better for him that he does not know there are more here like me. Though I do wonder where they may be going and find myself hopeful we will see each other again, soon.

Eventually we reach our destination which proves to be a large, older home with a side drive. Kuro makes no hesitation and pulls into the driveway which winds around to the back of the house. He fights with the steering wheel as he forces the truck into a position which will allow exiting the rear doors without being visible from the street.

"Stay here and I will seek the doctor." Kuro quickly makes his way to the back door, knocks twice and, after a brief pause, is allowed in. I exit the cab, walk to the back of the truck and open both doors.

Azumi's voice conveys her concern. "He has not regained consciousness the entire drive." I look at a pool of blood on the floor and wonder how much blood my unfortunate friend might still have remaining. I also note that the floorboards in the rear of the truck must be washed before we venture out again.

"Your husband went inside and advised we are to wait here." Azumi affirmatively shakes her head as she changes the cloth on Kamita's wound.

Finally, Kuro and two Japanese men carrying a stretcher emerge from the house. Without saying a word they gently place Kamita onto the stretcher and lower him from the truck.

Azumi exits, but does not come into the house with us as Kuro leads the two men carrying Kamita and I follow close behind. We are taken to a treatment room where, with the help of yet another assistant and a female Japanese nurse in a bright white uniform transfer Kamita to an examination table. He quietly moans in response to the movement, the first sounds I have heard from him all day.

Kuro tugs on my sleeve, pulls me to the side and whispers. "Only Doctor Ito knows who the two of you really are. All the staff are under the impression you both work for me and your friend had the misfortune to run afoul of the curfew. Understood?" "Yes, of course," I reply.

The nurse cuts away the remains of Kamita's shirt, removes the makeshift bandages and cleanses the wound. As if on cue Ito enters, wearing rubber gloves and a magnifying lens over his eyeglasses. He immediately begins to probe the wound which causes Kamita to moan softly. Ito requests a series of instruments from the nurse and is cursing under his breath, in Japanese, of a need for more light.

When we first entered the house clock on the wall read two in the afternoon. At half past three Ito suddenly drops his instrument onto a nearby metal tray with a resounding 'clank!' He peels off his rubber gloves, removes the magnifiers from his eyeglasses and motions for me and Kuro to join him in the hallway. "Regretfully, I am unable to retrieve the bullet; perhaps when I was younger, but I seldom perform surgery these days. In any event your friend has lost so much blood I fear his passing has become inescapable."

He allows me a few moments to absorb the information. "We cannot cremate this young Samurai as it would draw too much attention and involve too many people. Instead, I will arrange a burial and will send a messenger to the appropriate person. In the event he passes today, which is to be anticipated, I would suggest it would be best to bury him during the night. The sooner the better!" Ito is interrupted by his nurse who has appeared from the exam room.

"Doctor," she says quietly, "the patient has passed." She takes one step back, awaiting directions.

Ito shakes his head. "Please clean him and close the wound to prevent leaking as he will be transported soon. The nurse quickly disappears into the exam room.

"Doctor Ito, there is quite a bit of blood in the back of the truck. I suggest it be cleaned to avoid unnecessary questions." I attempt to disguise my distress at Kamita's passing.

"You make an excellent point and we will attend to it. I must tell you how much I regret your friend's life could not be preserved. Considering where the bullet managed to lodge itself I doubt anyone could have saved him and you did well to keep him alive as long as you did." Turning to Kuro, Ito continues: "I will need both the body and our mutual friend delivered to this address today." He hands a small piece of paper to Kuro who only needs to glance at it.

"I know where this is, near the ocean in Kailua. We can leave as soon as the truck is cleaned."

"Excellent!" Ito, who appears pleased with himself, replies. "You!" Ito points directly at me. "You should ride in the back of the truck and stay out of sight. I will join you this evening and sometime after dinner we will bury your friend. I suggest you bury all of your possessions at the same time. From this point forward the future is your sole concern and all remnants of the past should be, quite literally, buried."

The advice is hard to swallow, but correct. "Of course, Doctor. I will bury my friend along with the links to our past. I appreciate your assistance very much and assure you the Emperor will learn of the risks you have undertaken on our behalf."

"Merely a common courtesy to fellow countrymen. But we still have much to do so please excuse me while I make the necessary contacts." Ito turns and disappears up the hallway.

"Follow me and we will advise Azumi as to the developments," says Kuro. Before we can begin to leave the nurse intervenes and ushers me into an ante room, where I take a seat. She quietly exits and I realize I am alone and consider whether I should attempt to find my friends from the marketplace. However, I decide against following that path. The first priority is to discreetly bury Kamita and once accomplished I must then consider the best manner available to me for reaching the rendezvous point with *I-16*.

I wait almost an hour before the nurse returns and guides me to the truck. I make myself comfortable in the back cabin, alongside Kamita's corpse, while Kuro and Azumi drive us to a safe house. It seems to take a long time before we arrive at our destination and park in the backyard of an oceanfront home. Several Japanese men assist me as we carry Kamita's lifeless body into the house where Kuro advises me Doctor Ito will join us shortly before sunset. I am to wait, of course.

* * * * *

Doctor Ito determined it was best to delay the burial until a little beyond midnight. We work in near total darkness for what had been a mere sliver of a moon is now almost set. Three men have excavated a grave in the backyard and are standing nearby, shovels in hand. My understanding is the home is owned by an acquaintance of Doctor Ito who is standing beside him and from what I can decipher of her accent, as I stand near the grave, she may be German or perhaps Austrian.

I completed my final log entries before dinner, wrapped the logbook in oil cloth and have locked it, along with my stopwatch, our watches, Kamita's locket and my compass into the watertight box. I retrieve the key from my pocket, throw it as hard as I can in the direction of the ocean and watch it disappear into the darkness. After spending a few moments gazing at the Rising Sun embossed and painted on its lid the realization I may never see home again serves to increase my melancholy. I place the box on Kamita's stomach and my pistol into his hands, clasped across his chest. I lay the sword at his side, drop our two uniforms into the grave and with the assistance of the gravediggers we lower Kamita's body.

I stand before his open grave and bid my friend farewell with the assistance a gravedigger who holds a candle alongside the prayer book from which I read:

"Oh Compassionate Ones, you who possess the wisdom of understanding, the love of compassion, the power of doing divine deeds, and of protecting in incomprehensible measure.

Sadamu Kamita is passing from this world to the next.

He is taking a great leap, as the light of this world has faded for him and he has entered solitude with their karmic forces.

He has gone into a vast silence and is borne away by the great ocean of birth and death."

I lower the book to my side, accept a cup of sake from one of Ito's assistants and take a final look at my shipmate.

"Kamita, I ask forgiveness for circumstances dictate your cremation is impossible, but I am certain Buddha will understand. I bury you with my sword and pistol as physical symbols of you, the Samurai warrior and sworn servant to the Emperor. In life you brought glory to the Empire and in death you bring it honor. I drink this as my final salute to you, my dear friend." I quickly drink a small cup of sake and step back. The three men silently begin to fill the grave.

Standing about twenty feet away are Doctor Ito and the woman, whose name I later discover is Frieda. They are quietly watching the progress of the burial.

"Doctor, we will need to place this man with a family here on the island and we very much need to procure him a new identity as quickly as possible." Frieda is whispering, though we are safe from outsiders. Ito silently shakes his head in agreement.

"Frieda, I have arranged for him to live and work on a pineapple plantation. The plantation owners only know he is a person of significant importance seeking a return to Japan, but are unaware he is an officer in the Imperial Japanese Navy. He will be known only by his new name, Ken Kida." Frieda appears puzzled.

"Ken Kida?" She asks.

"Yes, a young Nisei recently passed away and nearly the same age as our friend. It is perfect. As Nisei he will be a United States citizen and far less likely to be discovered, but I need your expert assistance with the forgery work." Frieda smiles in response to Ito's praise.

"Yes, I am very good at that. Provide me the details and in a day or two he will have more identification and background than the deceased Mr. Kida would have had! It will only be a matter of transporting the documents to him in secret and allowing time for us to review them with him."

"I was certain I could depend on you. And you, my dear Frieda, can depend on me to address all of your needs. Time is critical and I prefer we deliver everything to him in not more than three days, though I would prefer two."

"Agreed! I will have everything you need the day after tomorrow, by noon in fact. Will you be able to take me to him at that time?"

"I will make the arrangements tomorrow and you can expect to depart here, possibly without me, the day after tomorrow precisely at noon. In fact it is possible neither of us will make the trip as we might draw unwanted attention. The less we are involved, the better." Ito notices the grave has been covered. "Let's bring our friend in for some drinks. From the looks of his complexion some warm sake is in order. He will be staying here tonight."

CHAPTER TWENTY FOUR
SUSANNAH C. JOHANSSON, M.D.

The penthouse office of Susannah C. Johansson, M.D. and Board Certified Psychiatrist, is conservatively furnished in warm woods and earthy colored wall and window coverings. Oil paintings of Paris and Florence decorate the walls. The floor-to-ceiling windows are presently protected by dark green plantation shutters, allowing only minimal sunlight to intrude upon the session-in-progress.

Dr. Johansson, her curly dark brown hair falling to the top of her shoulders is wearing a conservative black dress with a grey sweater, though it is not buttoned for it would otherwise be too warm. Her deep brown eyes are framed by a rectangular shaped pair of navy blue eyeglasses, which she does not need, but prefers to wear when she is with a patient. Her face is sensually oval-shaped and there is evidence of an old injury above her right eye. Her forehead is furrowed as she sits in a lounge chair, legs crossed, supporting a thick notepad while twirling a pen in her right hand and listening to Lani Gale.

Gale, her hair pulled back into a tight bun, is wearing a long, black dress. She is sitting sideways on an adjacent sofa, her torso propped up by two large pillows. Her bare feet dangle over the edge of the seat cushion. After seeing Dr. Johansson for more than a year she has no trouble making herself comfortable.

"Doc, I'm still suffering the same haunting nightmare about my father."

"Lani, just last week you said the nightmares had subsided." Johansson resumes taking notes.

"I know. It had been a few months without the nightmare but the last few nights it has returned with a vengeance. It started at the same time I began working on a new story."

"Would that be the Japanese sailor story?"

"Exactly! This story could be what finally catapults me from this out-of-the way city in the middle of nowhere and right into New York or D.C. It just seems to me that every time I've been close to writing something really important, everything that can go wrong, not only goes wrong but basically explodes in my face. Time is moving along and I can't stand dealing with the fact I'm being left behind and the feeling of desperation has become almost overwhelming."

Gale glances at the clock and realizes the session is near its end.

"These damned dreams about my father! His positive attentions always going to my two younger twin brothers and delegating me to some kind of lower class status. I worked hard to earn straight A's and they barely got out of high school. But they were good at sports and my dad jumped all over that. I was in drama club and was awarded the lead in '*Kiss Me Kate.*' Do you think he would show up? Of course not. He chose to watch a *practice* baseball game my brothers were playing. Imagine that! A *practice* baseball game!"

"After graduating high school in the top three of my class I was accepted into the University of Hawaii. This is what he said to me when I presented him with my acceptance letter: 'Nalani, I was unaware they offered a major in home economics.' "

"He knew full well I was going into journalism and that's what he says to me!" She pauses to wipe a trace of a tear from her left eye. "In these nightmares I relive every demeaning moment I endured with him. And my mom was no help at all. She cow-towed to him and never came to my defense, though she did attend all of my performances."

"Now, just when I am on the verge of success, these nightmares return. They erode my confidence because when I awake, I feel as if the nightmare was real and I had just endured every miserable, undermining moment all over again. I feel unimportant and stupid. It's as if from the grave my father is telling me I'm a loser and should be married and having babies because that's all I might be good at. I can't take this. Will he ever stop haunting me?"

"Lani, you've come a long way this past year and you'll overcome the harm he has done you. Unfortunately we have run overtime and I have a client waiting. But I promise, we can continue next week from where we are leaving off today. How's your prescription? Do you need a new refill?"

Gale sits upright and reaches for her bottle of water sitting on the end table. She takes a few sips, tosses the empty bottle into a nearby trash can and wipes her eyes again.

"No Doc, I'm good for another two months. I know you're right and I *will* overcome this and I *will* get over him. I understand I have value as a human being, but each time I look in the mirror I still see the little girl who in her father's eyes could never amount to anything worthwhile." Lani stands and starts for the door. Pausing, with one hand on the handle, she turns and says: "I don't know where I'd be without you."

"Lani, you'll be alright. Take care of yourself and I'll see you next week." Johansson notices the brief smile Lani flashes as she exits.

CHAPTER TWENTY FIVE
SUBTERFUGE

Lani Gale, naked, is lying on her back. The bed sheets are strewn about the floor and Paul Young is asleep beside her. She's awake, staring at the ceiling, lost in contemplation as she reviews everything he related to her when they met at Tanaka's for lunch earlier.

She silently reviews all the facts. What were Yamura and Ferguson meeting about and why did Yamura go to Ferguson's office three times? Young says Ferguson's only assignment has to do with dating what the Navy is referring to as 'artifacts' that were buried with the skeleton. So what's the significance of so many meetings? He also says Yamura almost never goes to Ferguson, it's always the other way around. Gale is uncomfortable as she has a nagging feeling something she needs to know is transpiring. Perhaps the test results proved none of the stuff they uncovered dated back to 1941? Maybe it's the opposite and they know for certain the dating tests back up the logbook's authenticity. Not knowing the details is driving her crazy.

Gale glances at the clock, notices it is almost four pm and decides it's about time to wake up her sleeping informant.

"Paul, you need to get going!" She kneels besides him and pushes down on his shoulders several times. Paul slips to his back, opens his eyes and finds he is looking directly at her breasts. His first instinct is to take one of her nipples into his mouth, but he thinks the better of it. "Why risk damaging what is easily the best arrangement I've ever had?" he asks himself.

"Right! Time I got back." As he rolls off the side of the bed Gale tosses his pants at him.

"Listen Paul, I absolutely need to know why Yamura was meeting with Ferguson. It's bugging the absolute hell out of me! You're supposed to keep me up to date but right now I feel as if you're not keeping up your end of the deal." She motions to his groin and continues. "If you expect to get *that* end up again, then you better get me some answers!"

Young takes his time buttoning his shirt and cuffs before sitting on the side of the bed so he can pull on his socks. He bends over to tie his shoes, the top of his head lightly touching her knees as she stands directly in front of him, hands on her hips.

Finally, he finishes dressing and stands, almost touching Gale who is expecting a suitable answer. "You can't possibly think that I can actually get inside Ferguson's office and look around, but you know I'll do everything I can to learn what they're up to. Leave it to me, I always find a way to get what I need."

Gale takes hold of the sides of his collar and lightly pulls him into her. "You are as cunning as I could have hoped, but you need to be smart too so whatever you do, don't get caught!"

"Right, so relax, I'll handle it and call you when I learn something worthwhile," replies Young.

"Good, I can get a story into tomorrow's paper as late as eleven tonight so if you learn something let me know."

"Obviously," replies Young.

"Now get your sorry ass out of here. You have work to do for me sailor boy!"

CHAPTER TWENTY SIX
SEEKING CONFIRMATION

Pastwa is relaxing in his office, feet up on his desk as he reads through old personnel records. The high-noon sun has forced him to reluctantly close the window blinds which block his view of the harbor. Clarke lightly taps on the open door as he walks in carrying a pot of coffee, donuts and a file. Clarke's been trying to keep a little distance between himself and Pastwa as a result of the recent headlines that have made Pastwa a bit difficult to be around. He also knows the contents of the file he's carrying will not be well received.

"Sir, I have some fresh coffee and donuts."

Pastwa lifts his feet off the desk and turns to Clarke. "You do realize that by the time this matter is over, I'll have put on about five pounds, don't you?"

"Sir, it would be five hard-earned pounds and therefore I'd consider them worth it."

Pastwa laughs. "Right! The weight would be very well worth it."

Yamura knocks on the open door. Clarke, not realizing she's walked in behind him, jumps back about a foot. "Pardon me, Ma'am, you caught me by surprise."

"Sorry Clarke, I only half intended to scare you." She can't hide a smile as she takes a seat in front of Pastwa's desk.

"I have my final report on the Yokoyama file for you." Clarke's words immediately gain their attention.

"I followed up on the information you received this morning and made use of the Admiral's contact as you suggested." Clarke carefully places the coffee pot onto Pastwa's desk. Yamura takes a seat as Clark grips the file with both hands as if the contents might escape.

"Sir, I have reviewed my findings three times and have found no errors. I've also incorporated the information provided to us by your friends at Langley and the Pentagon."

Clarke pauses as if he expects an interruption. Pastwa motions for him to continue.

"I believe you will concur with my conclusion that we have now determined what became of our friend Masaharu Yokoyama." Clarke hands the file to Pastwa while taking a couple of steps back, almost as if he anticipates an explosion. "Oh, and it appears the Admiral's instincts are right on, yet again Sir."

Yamura and Pastwa perk up with that last statement. Yamura slips around Pastwa's desk so she can look over his shoulder as he opens Clarke's report. Pastwa quickly reads through the nine pages, lays it down, returns to the first page and begins to read it a second time. Pastwa flips to the attached documents sent from the mainland earlier in the day and realizes they further confirm Clarke's conclusion.

"Damn, Clarke, this really can't be right. Or maybe we have the wrong name in the first place?" Pastwa hands it to Yamura, who flips directly to the attachments. She appears astonished while Pastwa looks to be getting sick to his stomach.

"Holy shit! I pray this isn't really our guy!" Yamura slowly shakes her head back and forth. "Damn, I really hope this isn't our guy or we may have problems we never anticipated, not in a thousand years!" Yamura's voice gives away the fact she's feeling trepidation over the potential ramifications.

"Listen Chris, let me have an hour or so to re-confirm all this. I promise to return quickly so you can take it to Reardon." Yamura picks up the report and pauses long enough to look to Pastwa for an answer.

Pastwa appears as if his dog just passed away. He briefly glances towards the harbor, but the closed blinds block his view.

"Alright Karen, you have the keener eye so take it to your office and I'll see you in about an hour." Yamura wastes no time and literally runs out of the office. Pastwa turns his attention to Clarke.

"Have a seat." Clarke takes a seat and awaits his orders.

"Your summary is direct and I appreciate the manner you arranged and identified the supporting documentation. I congratulate you as it makes my life a little easier when you do research work like this." Pastwa leans slightly forward and lowers his voice.

"You know this is extremely sensitive material and if a seaman by the name of Paul Young comes around, be careful. I think he may be working with Lani Gale, so watch what you say and if he does come around, I want to know about it, understood?"

"Yes Sir. Anything else you need from me?"

"Not just now, but good work! We'll just wait for Lieutenant Yamura to return."

Clarke disappears into the outer office.

Sighing, Pastwa realizes it is time to phone Reardon.

"This is Lieutenant Commander Pastwa," he pauses while Jones acknowledges him, "any word on when the Admiral will be back in today? I do need to see him as soon as possible."

"Sorry Sir, I have not heard from the Admiral yet. Based on the last time he was out on inspection I expect it could be another couple of hours. Would you like me to call you when he arrives?"

"Yes, that would be fine. I really need to see him. Thank you, Jones."

CHAPTER TWENTY SEVEN
MASAHARU YOKOYAMA

A beet red Admiral Reardon is shouting into his phone, "Get me Lieutenant Commander Pastwa right now! No! Not on the phone damn it! I want him right here, in front of me, and I mean right now! Do you understand me Jones?" Reardon slams the phone into its cradle and stares out across the harbor. His right eye is twitching out of control.

After a few moments he turns and looks at the front page of the newspaper spread across the top of his desk and reads the headline to himself for about the fifth time this late afternoon. In a few minutes there's a knock on the door.

"Enter, Goddammit!"

Pastwa enters, stands at attention and salutes. Reardon forces him to hold the salute while he glares at Pastwa for a good ten seconds before he returns the salute and takes a seat behind his desk. Pastwa goes 'at ease' but does not sit down.

"Stand at attention! This is not going to be easy for you, Lieutenant Commander! And I advise you not to test me, either. I can't even leave my office for a routine inspection tour without some manner of chaos ensuing." Reardon points to the newspaper as Pastwa's body stiffens to attention.

"Can you explain to me just how in the hell this newspaper got hold of our 'Top Secret' logbook?" The sarcasm in his pronunciation of the words 'Top Secret' is intentionally exaggerated.

"They are reprinting the log, word for word, a little bit each day! That ought to assure them a continuing bump in readership and they even have a contest that pays out One Hundred Thousand U.S. Dollars to anyone who knows what became of Yokoyama! Hell, they even have computer enhanced photos of what he might look like today. Do you have photos like that?"

Before Pastwa can respond. "Don't even answer that! Jesus! What the hell kind of security are you running!?"

"Sir…"

"I'm not finished *lieutenant* commander! Don't even think about cutting me short!"

"Yes, Sir. Sorry, Sir." Pastwa appears to be every bit as distraught as he feels.

"Where does your investigation stand?" Pastwa is hesitant to respond.

"Spit it out! Just what in the hell have you found out!" Reardon pounds the newspaper on his desk with his right fist causing his home-built model of the *Arizona* to bounce precariously.

Pastwa shifts his weight from his left foot to his right, and back again.

"Sir I don't really know yet if the man we are focused on is still alive or if he truly is Yokoyama, for that matter. But if he is Yokoyama, well, Sir, we might have some problems with that."

"What the hell do you mean 'We'? *You,* commander, *you* will have some problems adjusting to life on an ice breaker in the Arctic Circle. After all, haven't you mentioned you might like a command again someday? Right now I am very close to granting you that wish."

"Sir if the man we are concentrating on is Yokoyama, then he holds two Purple Hearts, a Medal of Commendation from Generalissimo Chiang Kia-shek's Nationalist Chinese Army and a Bronze Star from our own Army." Pastwa takes a deep breath as he awaits Reardon's response.

Reardon pushes his chair back from his desk. His face is so red Pastwa half expects him to literally explode.

"Just what are you trying to say?" Reardon's voice is so low as to be barely audible.

"Sir, it appears that Yokoyama got himself a new name. Blended himself right into the culture here, with help, of course. Eventually he was shipped out to an internment camp in California," Pastwa hesitates before finishing, "where it appears he volunteered and was accepted into a Nisei Division and then was transferred into Intelligence."

Reardon cuts him off. "Hold it right there. I'm not sure I heard you right. You say he was a Japanese Naval officer, a product of Eta Jima; and we transferred him into intelligence?"

Reardon holds his left hand up to keep Pastwa from replying, while he takes a long drink of water.

"Please tell me he was not transferred into Navy intelligence."

"No Sir, it was the Army. And it gets worse."

Reardon abruptly stands, walks around his desk and points his right index finger straight into Pastwa's face. Pastwa leans slightly backwards in response.

"That's all I want to hear from you until you find this man and bring him to me or take me to his grave marker. If it turns out Yokoyama's still alive I'll ship him back to Japan where I strongly doubt his resurrection will be well received. Until then I don't want to see you or hear you; hell I don't even want to think about you!" Reardon is standing only inches from Pastwa, who cannot help but notice the Admiral's twitch is out of control.

"I thought I made it perfectly clear I didn't want any loose ends! Instead, you're creating more loose ends then we had in the first place. What the hell's taking you so long to solve this…this…this monumental fuck up of a mess! Don't even consider answering that! Just Go! Get it done, and get it done before this pilfering reporter and her hundred-thousand-dollar reward beat you to it!" Pastwa has never seen Reardon completely lose it before and is praying he can wrap this matter up and save his career.

"So get going already!"

Pastwa salutes and holds it while waiting for Reardon to return the salute. However, Reardon has already walked over to the window and is staring at the harbor. Catching Pastwa's reflection in the glass, Reardon turns to face him yet again.

"And send me everything you have on Yokoyama today. I want to read it for myself!" Reardon finally returns the salute.

"Yes Sir!" Pastwa can't escape Reardon's office quickly enough to suit him, or Reardon, for that matter.

CHAPTER TWENTY EIGHT
INTERNMENT

Ken closes his eyes as he leans back in his oversized leather chair. Sun is sitting nearby, knitting a pair of baby booties, while Gary is perched on the edge of his seat anxiously waiting for his grandfather to continue. The laughter of several of their grandchildren playing in the backyard provides a pleasant, though slightly surreal background. Ken, now slowly stroking his beard, continues to disclose his first life.

•   •   •   •   •

With Kamita buried it is time for me to assimilate into the island population, just as a chameleon, except now I face an unknown future alone. I spend the night in the house by the ocean rather than risk again running afoul of the curfew restrictions. Shortly after sunrise Doctor Ito bids me farewell and good luck. Two of the men who buried Kamita are assigned to escort me to a pineapple plantation on the other side of the island. We travel via bicycle, something I have not done in quite a few years. The ride takes us several hours, but we arrive without incident. While we observe many soldiers along the way we incur no difficulties with them, though there was no shortage of staring on their part. Shortly after our arrival the two men bid me farewell and I am left with the somewhat elderly owner of the plantation, Taro, and his wife, Umeko.

Taro's hair is completely gray and somewhat sparse. He keeps his hair very short, is clean shaven and wears black, round-rimmed eyeglasses, a white shirt and black pants. Umeko is probably not even five foot tall. Her black hair is streaked with strands of bright grey and is wearing it in a braid which trails behind her knees. It appears to me she is likely a good ten years younger than her husband. She is wearing a simple red and black floral dress with large pockets at each hip and sandals which appear to be made from a combination of leather and brightly colored cloth.

With a pleasant grin on his face, Taro looks me over, top to bottom, almost as if I was a prize. "You are welcome here for as long as you need," he says in English. Umeko smiles and vigorously shakes her head in agreement.

"Thank you sir. With luck our invasion force will be here soon and you will be relieved of me."

"The invasion force! I have read of such a possibility in the newspaper, but no such force has materialized. Regardless, you will be our guest for as long as it pleases you and it is an honor to be your hosts. I have been informed there is a submarine waiting to pluck you from the waters and though I have made several very discreet inquiries, I have found no fisherman who will risk the voyage. They tell me there are air and naval patrols everywhere and to risk such a trip would be suicide. So my advice to you is be patient and put away any thoughts of sailing off into the sunset." Taro lets out a brief laugh.

"I am deeply grateful to you and will, I trust, one day be able to report your efforts on my behalf to the Emperor."

Taro and Umeko smile broadly at my words and lead me into their surprisingly large, single-story home where I discover an excellent luncheon has been prepared. We take seats at an old dining table as their servants stand at the ready. Taro offers prayer after which we feast.

"Tomorrow," says Taro, "there will be people coming to meet with you. They will have identification papers and information you will need to memorize. The following day we will introduce you to your role here on the plantation. We are in need of an assistant to our accountant and she will instruct you as to your duties. In such a role your contact with the other workers here will be minimal."

"I understand. However, what is it you would like for me to do in the interim?" I ask.

"Until I know more details of your proposed new identity, I cannot risk you come in contact with anyone other than the two of us and our very trusted household help." Taro pauses just long enough to sip some tea. "After you meet with our friends from Honolulu we can plan your formal entry into our plantation family. During these first few weeks, however, I am certain it will be best that you keep to yourself as much as possible. Everyone here has relatives throughout the islands and I do not desire to raise any suspicions as to where you have been living prior to joining us."

"That is acceptable to me. Tomorrow I will have a new identity and we will proceed from there. For today, I will stay in the house and out of sight, so long as that suits you and Umeko."

Umeko smiles and replies: "We have a guest room for you. Come with me." I follow Umeko to a modestly furnished, but fairly large guest room. There is even a desk with writing utensils and an oil reading lamp. The room is much more spacious than the accommodations I experienced while aboard the *I-16*, which seems to have been many years in my past. I throw myself onto the cot, immediately falling into a deep sleep.

"Sir, it is time for breakfast. You slept right through the afternoon *and* the night. I tried to wake you for dinner, but you seemed to be sleeping very deeply and decided to allow you to sleep."

Umeko's words are slow to sink in. I was experiencing a vivid dream and was on the conning tower of the *I-16* as she docks in Kure upon my successful return. Apparently I look confused.

"You are on our pineapple plantation, remember? We have guests arriving today who will review your new identity with you. Do you remember now?"

I blink a few times and shake my head. "Yes, Umeko. I understand. Thank you. Where might I prepare myself?"

Umeko leads me through a side door and to an outdoor shower which is situated alongside a large water tank. I plunge myself directly into a refreshing stream of cold water and soon I am both reinvigorated and very hungry. Umeko's breakfast is simple; steamed rice, boiled eggs, steamed fish, senbei crackers and many fruits; I consider it to be a feast. Taro and I are still sitting at the table when we hear the sound of a motorcar approaching. Taro runs to a front window and carefully looks through a slot in the curtains. He turns to us and smiles.

"Our friends have arrived. Remain here while I go meet them."

I watch Taro disappear through the front door. Soon I hear the 'clunk-clunk' of car doors closing, followed by a conversation in Japanese. While I cannot hear the conversation clearly enough to understand the words, I do know the tone of the conversation is light and friendly. Umeko sets a pot of hot tea on the table along with several cups and saucers.

I notice the tea pot, along with the cups and saucers are all of a design and pattern similar to that which my own mother has. I pick up one of the cups and examine the hand painted characters and it is if I am home again. I suffer a moment of home sickness, but my melancholy is quickly extinguished as Taro leads three men into the house. Two of them are clearly Japanese and are dressed in suits. The third man appears to be part Japanese and part, perhaps,

Portuguese, maybe five foot seven inches tall and is dressed in overalls. The first of the Japanese to come through the door is quite tall, perhaps as tall as five foot ten inches. The second is my height. I stand to greet them.

The taller man waives his hand indicating I should remain seated. "Please, no formalities today. For that matter, no names either. It is best you do not know who we are for our own protection as well as yours. Does this meet with your approval?"

"Yes, of course." I return to my seat as Taro takes the chair to my left. The taller man, who appears to be in charge, sits himself at the head of the table. The part-Portuguese appearing man takes a seat directly across from me while the third man has positioned himself alongside the front window and serves as a lookout. Umeko quietly slips out of the house.

The tall man places a small suitcase on the table, opens it and retrieves a file. He closes the suitcase, sets it on the floor, pours himself a cup of tea and takes a sip. The Portuguese man and Taro also pour themselves tea. I am anxious to get to business and forgo the tea.

The leader pushes the file across the table to me. "Let's review these documents one at a time." His tone lacks emotion and his demeanor is all business. I examine the first document which is a birth certificate for a person by the name of Kenneth M. Kida. I notice he was born within months of my own birth date.

"This is your birth certificate and is your best evidence to prove you are Nisei. With great difficulty we have managed to create death records for each of the parents listed on that certificate. Your father passed away when you were six and your mother passed away a number of years ago. You are an only child with no relatives on the island. It could not be any simpler. Should any of the authorities review your history, it will be very real, yet very brief. A nice, neat package!"

"Understand me so far?"

"Yes Sir, it is simple enough."

"It becomes more difficult. You will find additional papers in the file. One is a graduation certificate from a grade school that conveniently burned to the ground about seven years ago. All records prior to that time were lost. However, we have several pictures of the school so you can sufficiently describe it, should you be asked. You will also find the names of three teachers you must memorize along with the classes they taught. Two of them returned to Japan and the third is deceased. Again, enough background information for you to get by, without leaving a source to dispute you."

I review several photos depicting a single story, frame school house and a list of the teachers he mentioned and the classes they taught. Photos of the teachers are included.

"You will find photos and brief biographies of several people you would have grown up with. The persons who are deceased are noted. Two of them returned to Japan with their parents and the month and year of their departures are noted. The remaining person you might recognize as the man at the doorway." He points in the direction of the man posted as their lookout, who, in response, turns and smiles at me.

"The balance of the file is primarily brief news stories of island events. I urge you to spend all of your time these next few days to commit every detail to your memory. And, *this is critical*, be in a position to immediately destroy these records should the authorities appear unexpectedly! Destroy all of them, *except* the certificate of birth. Always keep that with you as it may save your life! As you know we are under martial law and everyone is under suspicion. Any questions?"

My mind is spinning as I try to digest so much information. "Yes, Sir. Is there no way you can arrange transport to take me to Nihau? I can make contact with my fleet there and escape." All three men laugh out loud.

"Nihau? You could offer one million yen and nobody would dare sail you there. Nihau? Who thought of that island as a rendezvous? It is almost deserted and inhabited only by natives, only a handful of them Japanese, at most, and a very long distance from here. Anyone sailing there would be questioned without a doubt!" The United States Navy has patrol boats circling all of the islands. He shakes his head back and forth and finishes his cup of tea, still laughing.

"Sir, clearly our intelligence felt it would be a suitable location. That not being the case, I can only wait for an invasion." I do my best to sound slightly offended without being belligerent.

The leader looks me over, glances at Taro and then back at me. "You made it this far, which speaks well for your future chances. We would all welcome an invasion, but certainly that is an event upon which we cannot plan. What we can plan, however, is to assimilate you into life on this plantation and provide for you here as long as it takes for us to finish this war. My best advice to you is simple: Memorize each word and every detail in this file and do so without delay. Treat these documents as the life savers they will likely prove to be and when you are comfortable enough with them, burn them."

"Yes, Sir, I will do that." Without saying a word the leader suddenly stands and we follow suit.

"We must go for the longer we delay, the more likely we raise suspicion. Our stated purpose for driving out here today was to agree upon the delivery of a truckload of pineapples." He reaches into his suit jacket pocket, withdraws a purchase order form and hands it to Taro.

"Please, if this is sufficient, then sign and date this order. I will have it with me in the event we are searched on our return trip." Taro takes the form from him and walks over to a nearby desk. He removes a pencil from one of the drawers and executes the purchase order. Accomplishing that, he returns and hands the tall man the executed pineapple order.

"Signed and dated, as requested."

"Good, then our business is complete. Thank you for the tea." All three men proceed through the front door without saying another word. I watch from the window as they drive away in their black, two door Ford coupe. I am wondering if I could reach them should a need arise when Taro touches my left shoulder.

"Come, sit down and begin your studies, Ken. I will start introducing you tomorrow when you accompany me on my daily rounds of the plantation." Taro leaves and I find myself alone, with much to learn and an uncertain amount of time during which I must become completely comfortable with every detail. I take the folder into my room and begin my studies, for now I must create myself anew, as Ken Kida of Kamooloa town. I consider the sound of it and am pleased as it has a good ring to it.

· · · · ·

A few weeks have passed since my arrival. I work on the payroll and make the morning rounds with Taro. I find life on the plantation to be relatively simple and straightforward. There is not a great deal of compensation paid to the workers, but they appear to be quite happy. In addition to Japanese language periodicals which have been allowed to resume publication, two or three times a week Taro obtains a copy of one of the Honolulu newspapers and I read them to him and Umeko, aloud. I do this to practice my English, which is getting better each day. They seem to enjoy listening to me and are keen to help.

The news of the war carries with it tales of massive Japanese conquests in remote regions of the South and Southwest Pacific, even in the Indian Ocean, but only an occasional reference to any possibility that Japan will invade Hawaii. In my opinion the Americans apparently believe we intend to invade the West Coast. I think to myself how terribly far away the West Coast of the United States is. Our fleet must be even greater than I know it to be if we can be launching the dramatic effort required to invade the United States mainland! If only they would first invade Oahu so I could rejoin the fleet. I resolve to bide my time and take each day on its own merit.

●　　●　　●　　●　　●

More weeks pass, life on the plantation is becoming quite routine and I find myself growing very comfortable in my new surroundings. One morning I am in one of the small supply huts taking an inventory when I notice the distinctive sound of many truck engines coming up the road to the main house. I know we are not expecting any deliveries and certainly no delivery would require more than one truck. My senses alert me something is wrong. As the sound of the engines grows closer I drop my clipboard and run to the main house.

A column of six Army transports, green canvas stretched across the cargo areas, led by two jeeps is slowly coming to a halt in front of Taro and Umeko's residence. I watch a Captain exit the first jeep and rapidly walk to the front door. Three soldiers carrying rifles are following behind. Taro opens the door just as I am rushing up in time to hear the Captain: "Are you the owner of this plantation?"

"Yes, I am the owner," responds Taro, just as kimono-clad Umeko arrives at his side.

"By order of the military governor, Lieutenant General Delos Emmons, I'm under orders to take *you*" he pokes Taro on the chest with his right index finger, "and every person of Jap ancestry under your so-called employment into protective custody until such time as the FBI or the United States Army deems otherwise!" He barks out the words very loudly, clearly intimidating Taro and Umeko. From the self-satisfied look on the Captain's face, it is clear he intends to frighten the old couple.

I cautiously approach the Captain, who is backed by another officer, as well as the soldiers, each with his rifle at the ready. Taking a deep breath, I seek to intervene. "Captain, Sir, do you intend to remove everyone right now?"

The Captain turns to face me. We are about the same height, though he is clearly at least ten years my elder and there is an unsettling fury in his eyes.

Instinctively, I place my hands to my sides so as not to present an aggressive stance.

"Who the fuck are you?" He shouts. "And why should I care?" He pushes me backwards with a hard shove. I am careful not to react as the soldiers have lowered their rifles and have them pointed directly at me.

"Sir, I work for this couple. This is just a simple pineapple plantation."

"I don't care what the hell you say this place is. These folks have been subscribin' to every Jap language publication they can get their yellow hands on and only God knows what they've been plotting. So them, and ya'll, and everyone else who supposedly *works* here is under our protection as of this moment. I'm giving everyone thirty minutes to gather their possessions and report back here. After that I'll send my men to drag ya'll in. Do I make myself clear?"

I vigorously shake my head in the affirmative. Taro and Umeko disappear quickly into the house and I follow. I feel badly for them as they are, rightfully, very upset. Taro, in particular, appears to be more than a little disoriented. I have already burned the materials I had been provided for my new identity, save the birth certificate and it is a good thing I did so as two soldiers have followed us into the house, one staying with me and the other with Taro and Umeko.

As quickly as possible I gather a few items of clothing, my certificate of birth, some canned goods and a bag of rice. I help Umeko pack two suitcases, mostly with food and the three of us slowly walk out to the waiting army trucks. The accompanying soldiers are pointing their rifles at us the entire time.

A sergeant has managed to obtain a copy of our payroll records and is crossing names off the payroll roster, one by one, as we are loaded into the trucks. Clearly the Americans appear to be efficient. There are more than forty of us and we are not told where we are going which causes me to be all the more nervous. I consider the likelihood I am in more danger at this moment than when I was being depth charged. Patience, clear thinking and my faith in an all knowing Buddha shall be my guide.

The convoy makes several more stops at individual homes where I witness entire families being quickly and roughly rounded together in the process. Age and gender are of no consequence to the American soldiers; what we all have in common is our Japanese ancestry. I learn at least four of the men in my truck are Nisei so I realize the Americans do not seem to care where we might have been born. At least not at this point.

We spend most of the day in the truck before we finally arrive at our destination, which is a makeshift encampment surrounded by fences with barbed wire and armed guards. We are immediately split into separate areas of the camp with no more than three or four persons from a given truck allowed to stay together. Time will prove that I will never see either Taro or Umeko again.

•　•　•　•　•

By July 1942, I find myself in a newly built camp somewhere near a city by the name of Oakland in the state of California. I am much more comfortable reading and speaking English and seldom slip into conversations in Japanese. I prefer to keep to myself as much as possible and avoid situations where the fact I lack a depth of knowledge regarding Oahu, let alone the United States, could be exposed. My larger problem is time; I have too much time on my hands. But the leaders amongst us have taken it upon themselves to construct numerous improvements and I join in the construction process.

Few people complain about the conditions or the confinement, at least not openly, and just about everyone participates with much more enthusiasm than I ever imagined would be possible under such conditions. I find the attitude of my fellow prisoners difficult to understand, especially after enduring sub-human conditions on the ocean crossing. We are constantly being watched over by soldiers who, in my opinion, if provided the opportunity would gladly shoot us all.

School teachers have formed classes so the children and many adults can continue with their primary education. Various religious groups from around the United States provide us with books and learning materials. While there is large-spread distrust, if not outright hatred, of us among the military I discover not all Americans are ready to condemn every person of Japanese ancestry. I find this interesting as the differences in attitude between the guards and the Caucasian volunteers are opposite one another. The volunteers understand the internees could not have had anything to do with the attack on the American fleet and appear to treat us as individuals, with what they refer to as "inherent rights."

What is also taking me time to understand is the general lack of rebellion among my compatriots for our confinement. If we are being protected, as we are told, then why do the guns in the guard towers point inwards? Why did my fellow prisoners not join in my plan to mutiny against the crew during our ocean voyage and let me then navigate us into Japanese controlled waters? I simply do not understand the mind-set of people I have come to admire and befriend.

• • • • •

I have one close friend, Fumio, or at least as close as I can dare. We have worked together on numerous construction projects throughout the first year, or so, of my imprisonment. He is quite philosophical and was born in a town near the city of San Francisco. Today he has brought me a flyer published by the United States Army.

"Look at this Ken, here's an opportunity for us to really do something!" Fumio hands me the flyer.

"This can be our ticket out of here and into the war fighting the Germans where we can definitively prove our allegiance to the United States!" He is very excited and has my complete attention. I am aware the majority of my fellow prisoners believe that polite submission to the confinement eventually will result in the American Army trusting us. Personally, I am not so sure.

Fumio's flyer states the American Army is seeking volunteers for a second Nisei regiment and all Nisei in good health may request to join. This is very interesting as it means I can escape this camp and fight again. Of course, not against my country, but instead, against the Germans.

My only personal encounter with Germans came while I was at Eta Jima where a contingent from the German Navy spent some time with us reviewing our methods and facilities. They struck me as extremely arrogant. I could not understand such an attitude for clearly the German Navy was not even large enough to patrol the Japanese Inland Sea let alone the Indian and Pacific Oceans as our own Navy would patrol. In fact, the German navy was no more than a thorn in the side to the navy of Great Britain. So now, just maybe, I could fight against the Germans, a proposition I find intriguing.

Despite my status of being in protective custody, I have been learning much about democracy and the United States and very much like it. I do not harbor any hatred against America, but I am not so sure I can trust Americans. Yet, this proposition is interesting. I know I can never return to Japan as I am aware I have been declared a deceased war hero so I will need to consider this option, but Fumio expects a decision from me right away.

"This looks good Fumio and appears to be a worthwhile endeavor. What do we need to do?"

"I'll come and get you tomorrow morning at ten and we'll go together to submit our applications. You can keep this flyer as I have another for myself. Right now I need to go ask a couple more men I know about whether they'd be interested. Remember, ten o'clock!" Fumio turns around and jogs off.

I stand still for a moment as I re-read the flyer titled, "An Opportunity to Fight the Germans and Italians." Obviously there is no way I can ever rejoin the war fighting for Japan. And with the disasters at Midway and Guadalcanal it is also apparent to me that there will be no invasion of the United States. Even my Commander-in-Chief, Admiral Yamamoto is dead. I decide to meditate and consider what the great Admiral Togo would do.

After hours of meditation I reach a decision. As a Samurai no longer with a fight of my own I decide I should do as any proper Samurai would do and 'borrow the battlefield' by joining the Nisei regiment. Tomorrow I will go with Fumio and seek to offer my services to what, by default, is becoming my adopted country. Finally I feel as if my life may be taking on a purpose again, something that has been lacking since my early days on Oahu.

● ● ● ● ●

Days pass and no word on my application when suddenly Fumio comes bursting in. "Ken! The Army's posting a list of names." He pauses as he gasps for air. "Everyone who's been accepted is on the list so let's get going!"

I jump from my chair and shout: "Let's waste no time!"

Fumio starts running, with me just behind him. It is perhaps four hundred yards to the large announcement board where all notices are posted and as it draws into sight I see many men are crowded around it. Fumio is a bit shorter than average and successfully wiggles his way through the crowd of what must be one hundred men, all vying for position. After a few moments Fumio emerges and runs up to me.

"Ken," he pants, "both of us have been accepted and must report to the Army's special recruiting tent at eight tomorrow morning!" Fumio is grinning ear to ear.

I, on the other hand, am subdued. I realize I am one step closer to a new battlefield and a new country, a step which will permanently place Japan into another lifetime. I also wonder if I should accept the position and risk discovery, but I cannot tolerate the inactivity any longer. I reason if I can fight against a new enemy and for a country I have not found to be anything like the Japanese government propaganda claimed it to be then why not? Clearly my destiny includes this new endeavor or why else would the opportunity present itself to me? I must trust that Buddha's wisdom will light my path and has, in fact, opened this door through which I must pass.

"Ken, let's take a long walk and talk about army training and Europe!" Fumio smiles. "I have read a great deal about Europe and would like to share my knowledge with you."

I return Fumio's smile. "Of course, my friend. What better way to spend the day?"

. . . . .

Fumio and I are standing in a long line of men, all anxious to learn of our new assignments. There are eight sergeants sitting, left to right, at a series of tables set up end-to-end. Eight corresponding lines of Nisei Japanese men are slowly working their way to the tables. There is a red line drawn on the ground to keep the next person in line just far enough from the table so they cannot over-hear the conversation.

The sergeant at the head of my line appears to be about fifty years old. Though he is sitting I can ascertain he is a tall man. He has many stripes on his arm and decorations on his uniform. I wonder why the American Army does not post him in Europe where his experience would be the most beneficial and consider the possibility he is recovering from wounds. Following a thirty minute delay it is my turn to approach the sergeant who does not even look up at me.

"Name?"

"Kenneth Kida, Sir." I respond. Now he does look at me.

"Don't ever call me Sir! Call me Sergeant. I'm not an officer." He pauses and stares at me, which causes me to feel in danger of being exposed. "I presume ya'll know the difference between a non-com and an officer, right?" His voice is dripping with sarcasm.

I stiffen and respond. "Yes Sergeant. No offense intended, Sergeant." My training suddenly snaps in and I feel as if I am a cadet once again.

The Sergeant looks me over from head to toe and removes his hat just long enough to wipe his brow with a green handkerchief.

"Good, I'll be with ya'll at Camp McCoy which's where we're sendin' ya'll for training. Return here at sixteen hundred hours for the swearing in ceremony and after that ya'll get your travel orders and by this time tomorrow ya'll be on a train. Any questions, soldier?"

"Yes, Sergeant, just one."

"Well, what the hell ya'll waiting for? Ask your question!"

"Sergeant, where is Camp McCoy?"

The Sergeant laughs, "Wisconsin! Y'all's goin' to love it there! Now take your damn orders and move on!"

I quickly exit the tent and find Fumio waiting.

"Fumio, where is Wisconsin?" I ask.

"Let's go to the library and learn all we can about it!" Fumio always seems to have an answer and as we walk to the library I think about the fact the Sergeant referred to me as "soldier." I realize I must readjust my mindset to that of a "soldier" and not that of a naval officer. "Soldier." I must make myself comfortable with this new role and dread the thought of being a soldier for I have seen how the soldiers in my own army are treated and it is not nearly on the level of a naval lieutenant.

●　　●　　●　　●　　●

About a week later our train pulls into our final stop, Camp McCoy, Wisconsin. Fumio and I exit our rail car and line up with the rest of the men, each of us with our respective squad. There are Sergeants and Lieutenants yelling orders up and down the line. There must be a thousand of us! In less than half an hour we are marching, four across, to Camp Mc Coy. Upon arriving I notice a few buildings and what appear to be acres of tents. I do not see many manned guard towers, such as what stood over us in California which is encouraging. It more closely resembles a military installation than a prison. The next morning we are to begin what we are told is a six month training period.

Our Sergeant is a man by the name of Yates, who only somewhat disguises his dislike for this assignment and of us. He is about six foot tall, one hundred eighty pounds, bald and wears what seems to be a perpetual scowl on his heavily scarred face. Our corporal is Nisei, a member of the Hawaii National Guard and much more approachable. The corporal enters our tent and announces we are taking a five mile "stroll" before chow and we are to fall out immediately.

Sergeant Yates is silently watching as we form up for the march. He slowly walks up and down our squad without saying a word. He mumbles something to the corporal, who quickly turns to face us and yells out: "Double time!" We are off for a five mile 'stroll' before chow. Given that we have been on a train for days, I don't mind at all.

Adjusting to Army food is more difficult than the physical training. However, today I discover they have included boiled rice with our dinner though I have grown to enjoy potatoes and to tolerate overcooked vegetables that are completely absent of flavor. Most of the time I am not familiar with the meats served and long for some nice fish. Any kind of fish.

As we begin the second month of training we have spent no time actually firing our rifles. It is a very impressive weapon and is quite unlike any I experienced in Japan. Today, however, we finally find ourselves on the rifle range where Sergeant Yates is yelling derogatory comments at us. It is obvious that just about every one of my fellow volunteers is unfamiliar with firing a rifle. However, Sergeant Yates remains very quiet when I am firing. I do not understand if he stays quiet because I am such an excellent shot or because he is waiting for me to miss so he can belittle me. Either way, I much prefer when he is not yelling as I do not understand half the words that come from his mouth.

The countryside around the camp features rolling hills, thick forests and numerous dairy farms. We routinely embark on hikes of up to fifty miles, carrying huge amounts of equipment. I do not recall ever seeing soldiers in the Japanese army carrying so much equipment. Some of the local civilians stop and stare as we march past while others do not appear to notice us. We have not had any opportunities to venture into the local town and I wonder how the locals feel about us.

After more than two months living in tents the new barracks are ready. Just in time too, as the nights have been growing cold. We immediately begin setting up our bunks and footlockers. Of course, now that we are in a barracks, there are daily inspections which are even more thorough than when we were living in tents and we soon discover Sergeant Yates can create many more opportunities to hand out punishments. One of his favorites is to order the performance of one hundred push-ups, especially if it is raining. Sometimes he has another soldier sit on the back of the unfortunate private performing push-ups.

•　•　•　•　•

Today marks the end of five months of training and results in our first serious accident. While practicing on the mortar range our corporal was demonstrating the method of dropping the mortar into the tube, but failed to pull his hand out in time. The mortar fired and cut off his thumb. We find ourselves without a corporal and with only a month of training to go, it is unlikely he will return in time to ship off with us, if ever.

"Kida!" I jump off my bunk and stand at attention as Sergeant Yates stands in the doorway. "Here, Sergeant!"

"Meet me in my office!" Sergeant Yates does not wait for me to respond and immediately leaves. I grab my hat and run after him. When I reach his office I discover he is already seated and I automatically stand at attention.

"Relax Kida and grab a seat." I sit on the wood bench he has set in front of his desk.

"As ya know, Corporal Sasaki isn't likely to be rejoinin' us for some time." He pauses as he lights a cigarette. "I've been watchin' you Kida." He leans forward as he looks me directly in the eyes. "Now let me make one thing very clear here." He takes three puffs, while staring at me the entire time.

"I'm no big backer of handin' rifles to ya Nips and sendin' ya'll off to fight alongside the rest of us. Nope. After Pearl Harbor it makes me downright antsy knowin' ya folks have guns and that we're bustin' our butts teachin' ya'll how to use 'em. But I can't control what them big shots in Washington tell me to do. All I can do is train ya'll as best I can and trust in the good Lord and General Marshall that they know what the hell they're doin'." He finishes his cigarette and puts it out in a tin ashtray on his desk.

"But I gotta say this," he lights another cigarette and leans back in the chair, "last month when those compadres of yours dived themselves into that half frozen lake and pulled out them drownin' local kids, that told me all I really need to know about y'all's loyalty, and bravery for that matter." I realize he is referring to an incident where three of my fellow soldiers dove into a near-frozen pond and saved the lives of two young locals.

"I'll fight them Nazis with your kind and have a little more piece of mind 'bout it. Mind ya now, I'm not sayin' I'd like it, but I'll do it without complainin' to nobody. Yep, yankin' them young folks from that pond tells me y'all's eyes might be slanted, but your'e a straight shoot'n bunch of American Nips." He returns his cigarette to his mouth and takes a huge puff, blowing smoke rings directly into my face. I really don't understand everything he just said, but shake my head in agreement.

"So, as of right now, Kida, y'all's the squad's new corporal and my new right hand man. Got anything to say?"

I am completely taken by surprise. So many thoughts are running through my mind as I attempt to digest everything he just said. I am going to be the right-hand man to someone who might sooner see me confined for the entire war? At least he is being up front with me, which does provide me some comfort. I know where he stands and I know he is going to follow the rules without regard to his personal opinions. I admire him for being man enough to recognize that he can't ignore bravery. Finally, I muster an answer.

"Thank you Sergeant. You will receive only my best efforts."

A smile actually crosses his face. He lights another cigarette. "Cigarette?" He says as he offers me one.

"No thank you Sergeant, I prefer not to smoke, if you don't mind." Again, he smiles.

"That's fine Kida. After some combat experience ya'll might just rethink that." I hold back an answer as I have been in combat and never felt a need to smoke. Of course, he cannot know so I remain quiet.

"That's settled so meet me back here at eighteen hundred thirty hours. I need to begin reviewin' company procedures with ya as there's a shitload of stuff to learn. Now get along to the Quartermaster and pick up some new stripes and get 'em sewn on pronto!" I rise and fight back the instinct to salute him.

"Thanks Sergeant. I will return at eighteen hundred thirty hours!"

•　•　•　•　•

I quickly adapt to my new responsibilities as the final month of training proves to be a whirlwind. Forced marches, rifle range, hand-to-hand combat drills, live fire drills and a great deal more. There is also time for baseball which I played as a youth and enjoy very much. Rumors abound as we near the end of our training; some say we are headed to the Mediterranean where we will join in the invasion of Italy while others say we are to invade Greece, and still others speculate we will be sent to England. Fumio, as usual, seems particularly well informed. We discuss the situation as we sit under a tree near the baseball fields.

"I hear we'll be sent to Camp Shelby in Mississippi." Fumio sounds depressed.

"Mississippi? That makes no sense."

"That's what I hear, and we're going to be informed tomorrow. Mark my words, Ken, the big brass doesn't trust us. I think it's as simple as that, my friend." We both grow quiet as we contemplate still more training.

"Hey, that was a good play you made at third yesterday." Fumio nudges me and smiles. "If only you could hit!"

"If only I could hit?" I pretend to be offended. "My uncle taught me to play when I was only eight. He even took me to see an American League All-Star team. I see no dishonor in two doubles which are more impressive than the two infield singles you managed my friend! I think the Americans call your hits 'bloopers'" We both laugh and the change of topic helps me relax. I know Fumio has proven to be correct most of the time when it comes to what the Army plans for us. But there is nothing I can do, save to wait for my orders. My evening meditation will be more important to me than most as I expect my new assignment in the morning. Meditation is important for my soul and I recall the words of Buddha: "Just as a candle cannot burn without fire, men cannot live without a spiritual life."

•   •   •   •   •

I awake to the chirping of many varieties of birds. The sky is revealing the first signs of daylight and I am anxious for the day to commence. Before anyone else in my platoon is awake I am dressed and ready for roll call. Surely, just once, Fumio could be wrong. Reveille, roll call, chow, all come and go. Still no word. Finally, Sergeant Yates makes his appearance.

"Corporal Kida!" "Yes, Sergeant!" I jump to my feet as I shout my response.

"Corporal, get over to Captain Sterling's office, Hut B, and make it snappy!" His usual gruff voice seems to me to be softened slightly as he is wearing just a hint of a smile. That little smile troubles me as it is out of character for him.

"Yes, Sergeant, I am on my way!" Without making direct eye contact, I trot from the hut and, as soon as I am out of sight of the Sergeant, break into a full run. I slow down and compose myself as I reach Hut B. The front door is wedged open and I walk in to find a pair of Japanese/American lieutenants sitting on a desk. Surprised, I stop, go to attention and salute. They appear a bit amused as they return my salute.

"Something we can do for you corporal?" Asks one of the Lieutenants.

"Yes Sirs, Corporal Kida reporting to Captain Sterling as requested." I remain at attention, awaiting a reply.

"Oh, so *you* are Corporal Kida." Just as I am about to reply he raises his right hand and says "No need to answer that." He is eyeing me very closely while the other lieutenant walks over to a closed door and knocks. From behind the door comes a response.

"Yes?" The voice sounds annoyed and I fear that must be Captain Sterling.

"Lieutenant Fuchida here, Sir. Corporal Kida has arrived."

"That's fine, Lieutenant, send him in."

Lieutenant Fuchida opens the door and motions for me to enter. The door is quietly closed behind me.

Sitting behind a wood desk that must be left over from a turn of the century school room is Captain Sterling. He looks to be in his late twenties, blonde hair, neatly cropped, a bronze star on his shirt, along with what I believe are engagement ribbons. I am not familiar with the patch on his shoulder which is in the shape of a shield. The upper portion depicts a gold Sun on the left side and a gold star on the right, over a blue background. There are five vertical stripes starting with red then gold, then red, then gold, then red. I have no idea what it signifies.

I stand at attention and salute. "Corporal Kida, as requested Sir." The Captain returns my salute.

"Sit down, Corporal. Like some coffee?" He motions to a steaming pot sitting on a field stove next to an open window. "Thank you Sir, but I have already had my share today."

"Well, I seldom take a pass on a cup of joe. Bad habit, I guess." His voice is calm and helps me relax. I watch as he walks over and pours some coffee into a large ceramic mug with the relief of a cow painted on it. He returns to his chair and opens a file lying on his desk. He sips at his coffee as he sifts through the file. Finally, he pushes it away and looks me directly in the eyes.

"Corporal, I've been watching you for the last four weeks after your sergeant sent us a report about you which piqued our interest. To be clear, I am referring to Army Intelligence."

With that statement, my heart drops into my feet. My God, I have been found out! Sitting still at this moment is tantamount to punishment. I feel my blood pressure rising and focus on the image of a cherry tree in full blossom. This image calms me, but just barely.

"Ever see a patch like this one?" He points to the odd patch on his left shoulder.

"No Sir, I have not." I can barely get the words out. Sterling notices I am nervous.

"Well, no need to worry because you're not in any kind of trouble. For your information this patch refers to the China-Burma-India theatre where I've been serving for the last eighteen months."

I breathe a sigh of relief. "I see. So that is the Chinese insignia. Now I recognize it." I reply, for in truth, I do recognize it now.

"Well, Sergeant, oh, excuse me, as I almost forgot, you've been promoted to Sergeant. We've had a great deal of difficulty coordinating air support, artillery support and the like due to a lack of interpreters over there. That's where you come in." Sterling finishes his coffee, walks to the coffee pot and refills his mug. He now leans against the window frame before continuing.

"I've put together five other Nisei soldiers with similar skills to your own from your class and they will form the basis of your squad. You can pick up the rest of your squad in Honolulu. In fact, you arrive there in about five weeks. From that point you and your squad will sail to Australia and eventually arrive in Burma. That will give you a good eight to ten weeks, perhaps longer, to get familiar with your men, study the field reports and prepare for your assignment in Burma." Sterling gulps down the last of his coffee, places the cup on the window ledge and returns to his chair.

"You see, once there we plan to fly you and your squad over the 'hump' to join the Chinese. We'll be starting a major campaign to connect our lines with the Chinese Nationals so we can carve an overland supply route from India which is critical to our success."

"There's going to be a critical push we're coordinating with the Chinese and the interpretive skills for both Japanese and Chinese of you and your men may prove be critical. And that's not to mention your superior training and discipline. In my opinion, and this is between you and me, the Chinese soldiers are brave, but poorly trained and their officer corps definitely lacks discipline."

"You previously indicated, and we have quietly tested, you have a reasonably good command of Chinese. I see from your records you also have a decent command of Korean. You never know, that could come into play before it's all over too. So, Sergeant, any questions?"

"Where do I meet my squad and when do we ship out? I want to get to work!"

"Good attitude. Your squad's gathered outside the mess tent as we speak. Pick up your stripes and sew 'em on before you meet them. First impressions Sergeant, always remember you only get one chance to make a first impression. So get your stripes on first because the men will wait. In fact, the longer they wait, the more scuttlebutt they'll indulge in. It'll afford you a great opportunity to go in there and set them all straight." Sterling pauses, a smile on his face.

"Oh, I suggest you don't choose your corporal until you have your entire squad together in Honolulu. You don't want those fellas out there thinking they got short-changed at the promotion ladder simply because they're in Hawaii. Got that?"

"Yes Sir. Anything else?"

Sterling stands, pulls out a sealed envelope from his center desk drawer and hands it to me. "Here's your formal orders. Good chance I'll see you in China sometime in the next year."

I rise and accept the envelope. "Kida, read your orders carefully. You'll find I have also included a brief rundown of your squad members. Unless you have any questions, that's it. Good luck!"

I salute and just before I turn to leave, I say: "Thank you Sir. I trust I will see you in China!"

I exit and very quickly walk to the quartermaster and pick up a few sets of stripes for my shirts, jackets and helmet. The quartermaster anticipated my arrival and had everything I need including a new helmet with netting. He proves more than happy to help as he is Nisei as well. I consider the fact my father died while fighting in China and now I will be journeying there myself. Is it an omen of my own death? Tonight's meditation cannot come too soon.

CHAPTER TWENTY NINE
FIRST IMPRESSIONS

It is March 1944, and my squad is assigned to the 150th Chinese Regiment. We are joining with the First Marauder Regiment of the famous 'Merrill's Marauders" and plan to attack a small village by the name of Lazu. The conditions are terrible and disease is rampant. All of us have, by now, contracted Malaria, but the Chinese are particularly short of medical supplies and it seems to me that untreated malaria is the accepted fate for the Chinese soldier. We are faring better as we are supplied with quantities of Atabrine. Though we are attached to the Chinese most of our supplies originate with our own army or the British. I cannot understand why the Chinese soldiers are so much worse off than we are and suspect some of the Chinese officers may be selling medical supplies on the black market.

The Japanese soldiers we manage to capture are surprisingly talkative. One young sergeant tells me that they have absolutely no medical supplies, no fuel and no reliable supply lines. By feeding him a hot meal of steamed vegetables and rice, he, in turn, outlines the locations of several machine gun positions in the area. The result is we save quite a few lives. After some brief but fierce resistance we capture Lazu and I am summoned to headquarters for de-briefing.

We are taking a short break as I watch an Army DC-3 coming in for a landing on a piece of ground that only weeks earlier was dense jungle. I have been ordered to attend a briefing at eleven hundred hours and am to serve as the interpreter for a Chinese General by the name of Weili. I have worked with him once before and recognize him as he disembarks from the DC-3. If he is here then something big must be brewing. I make my way over to the command Quonset hut a little before the briefing is scheduled to commence.

The hut is crowded with at least sixty officers as well as some non-commissioned officers. I immediately notice General Joseph Stillwell, standing on the stage, is engaged in a quiet discussion with Chinese General Huang Weili. Stillwell, I understand, is about sixty four years old, but his skin is ashen and his uniform, which is drenched in sweat, hangs on his almost skeleton-like body. I assume he is fighting one of the various jungle diseases we all must cope with at one time or another.

There is a large map of the area on an easel and the city of Myitkyina is circled with red ink. To the north and east of it is a black star. Our location is about twenty nine miles of jungle and difficult terrain to the south and east of Myitkyina and is also marked with a black star.

General Stillwell finishes his conversation with General Weili and turns to address us. The room quickly grows silent. I can almost hear the beads of sweat hitting the floor at my feet.

Stillwell gulps down a few mouthfuls of water, picks up a pointer and begins his address.

"Gentlemen, if you look at this map you can see the location of our new forward airfield." He points to the black star representing our present position. "From this new airfield we can better supply the front lines of our ally, Generalissimo Chiang Kia-shek, who will be commencing a major new offensive momentarily. The objective is the critically important river and rail port city of Myitkyina, which lies in the direct path of the critical overland supply road we are constructing, the Ledo Road. Once Ledo Road is open we can more completely supply and more effectively support our Chinese allies. This new land route should eliminate the need to fly supplies over the 'hump' and it will accelerate the defeat of Japan in China." Stillwell pauses as he takes a long drink of water.

"We're bringing together units of several different armies for this assault. Colonel Hunter will be leading 'Merrill's Marauders,' along with British, Australian and Indian Gurkas."

He points to a spot on the map above the objective. "The main Chinese assault will commence at this point about forty-eight hours from now. We will delay by roughly two days in the expectation that General Honda will commit most of his reserves to repel the Chinese assault. At that point we will launch our own effort through the back door and catch Honda in the middle."

"This operation will require an unprecedented level of co-operation between the various units and nationalities in the field." Stillwell points to a British Major.

"Lovell, I understand you'll be coordinating the Gurkas personally. We cannot afford any of the communication breakdowns we have occasionally experienced in the past."

Lovell stands in response. His neatly pressed shirt is drenched in sweat. Perched underneath his left arm is a baton. Of course, he is wearing shorts along with socks pulled up to his knees. It looks like a bad idea to me, as shorts in the jungle are an open invitation to insect bites and the diseases they bring.

"No Sir, I have seen to it that we have appropriate translators where they are needed and they are all very adequately rehearsed in battlefield procedures."

"Excellent, Major." Lovell returns to his seat as Stillwell resumes the briefing.

"General Weili," he looks in the direction of General Weili, who in responds with a smile, "will be acting as the field commander of the Chinese assault."

Stillwell hands the pointer to a nearby lieutenant and walks to the center of the stage.

"So gentlemen, if there are no further questions, you all have your sealed orders to review. Good luck!"

A sergeant off to the right side of the stage suddenly barks out: "Dismissed!"

That's my cue to get over to Stillwell's office. My squad is assigned to General Weili, which means we are going to be very close to, if not in, the front lines. Not something I cherish as I was never supposed to be going face to face with any Japanese, at any time.

When I arrive at General Stillwell's office I find General Weili, a pair of Chinese Colonels who I recognize and several of Stillwell's staff. After reporting in, I slip into a corner to observe.

"General Weili, I understand you have some concerns with respect to the interaction between our interpreters and your own troops," says Stillwell.

Weili is a very broad-chested man who appears particularly imposing due to the incredible number of medals and ribbons that adorn his uniform jacket. He is unusually tall for a Chinese and must weigh a good two hundred twenty pounds. Weili rises from his seat and straightens his uniform jacket.

"General I realize we need interpreters to coordinate between our front-line positions and your artillery and air cover. And let me make clear the fact we all admire the brave Japanese/Americans who fight alongside us in this war against oppression." Weili dips his head in my direction, which makes me uncomfortable in this room full of officers.

"The fact remains, General, that many of my men are unlikely to take orders from a non-officer. It is of no matter that your men are Japanese by heritage. We recognize they are Americans and our friends. However, what my men understand best is rank."

"Though I personally like and admire your Sergeant Kida, he is, after all, only a sergeant. I would find it highly regretful should there be an incident that could have been avoided if he were, instead, an officer? After all, it is completely within the realm of possibility that he may find the need to give instruction at times when delay could mean defeat. I am particularly concerned of the need to quickly and effectively communicate with your Army Air Force when in the field."

General Stillwell appears genuinely relieved to learn Weili's's concern is so simple.

"General Weili, it is my distinct pleasure to advise you that Sergeant Kida has just received a field commission to the rank of lieutenant.'

Weili raises his right eyebrow and replies: "That would be First Lieutenant Kida?"

Stillwell smiles. "Yes, of course, General." He turns and looks directly at me.

"Lieutenant Kida?"

I snap to attention. "Yes General?"

"You have just been awarded a field commission to first lieutenant. Congratulations! Now get yourself over to supply and pick up your lieutenant's bars. You and your squad are flying out of here with General Weili within the hour. Better tell your corporal he's just moved up the ladder. Oh, and you need to pick yourself a new corporal."

"Yes, Sir. Thank you!" I hold my salute.

"Good luck, Lieutenant." He acknowledges my salute and turns to continue his discussion with General Weili

I find my heart is racing as I quickly slip out and make for the Quartermaster. Apparently I impressed Weili somewhere along the way. Captain Sterling's words regarding first impressions come to mind.

•　•　•　•　•

A week later I am in the forward command post behind a major Chinese push to take Myitkyina. The Chinese ranks are spread pretty thin and my orders direct me to remain in the command post and coordinate the U. S. Army Air Corps support. I am observing a formation of four P-38's flying overhead when I hear the unmistakable sound of incoming artillery fire just as a Chinese soldier is working his way up the hill to me, bicycle in tow, no doubt recovered from the Japanese. Out of breath he approaches me, his breathing so heavy it makes understanding him a little more difficult.

"Sir," he says, "I have an urgent message for you from Battalion." He hands me an envelope the contents of which are written in Chinese so it takes me more time to digest.

"Thank you. Please wait while I write a response for you to take back. Why not go get yourself something to drink." I speak in Chinese, of course.

"Yes Sir, thank you." He slowly turns and leaves our little dugout, but is instantly thrown back, right on top of me, by the force of an exploding shell. I find myself covered in his blood and reach over to pick up the field phone.

"This is Lieutenant Kida. Can you hear me? I need to speak with General Weili. Can you hear me?" I duck under an adjacent table as another round of shells begin landing nearby. Just as the shelling moves on, another messenger arrives.

"Sir! A message from General Weili! The phone lines have been cut and the General was fearful you had been overrun."

I realize I am still holding the phone, drop it and take the message. I interpret the message and conclude Weili is feeling some hesitation as the Japanese have counter-attacked with more success than anticipated. The message also states tanks with infantry support following behind are driving towards my position.

I decide to contact the flight of P-38's that are still in the area and grab a walkie-talkie.

"P-38's, P-38's, this is Lieutenant Kida. I am right below you. Do you read me? Over."

Buddha is obviously smiling on me as they respond to my call.

"Lieutenant, this is Red Sky. We read you, over."

"Red Sky, this is Lieutenant Kida. Can you observe any Japanese activity ahead of our position? We are marking ourselves with yellow smoke as I speak, over."

"Lieutenant, I see your position. Give me a couple of minutes, Sir, over."

"Roger, Red Sky. Will wait, out."

The squadron makes a sharp left turn and flies over our positions revealing they have expended all their bombs and rockets. In less than a minute, I have my reply.

"Lieutenant, this is Red Sky. There's about a dozen Nip tanks bee-lining for your position. They're not more than three miles out. About a mile behind 'em must be four, maybe five hundred infantry. We're plum out of the heavy stuff, but we still have plenty of ammo left for our fifty cals and enough fuel to hang around maybe twenty more minutes. What's your pleasure?"

"Red Sky, I understand your situation. I would like you to take a couple runs at the tanks, then circle as if expecting more air support. This might make them stop and wait for their infantry to catch up. Or at least put a little fear in them. Maybe give them something to think about. I just need to buy some time, over."

"Roger, Lieutenant. We're goin' to buy you some time. Out."

Through my binoculars I watch the P-38's swoop down on the tanks. They begin to swerve left and right in evasive maneuvers, obviously fearful of being bombed. I take the opportunity to pen a response to General Weili, grab the nearest soldier and hand him the message.

"Take this back to our division reserves and give it to General Weili. Be quick as we are in danger of being overrun!" The mention of Weili gets the response I need. The soldier grabs the message and runs out.

While I am observing the P-38s as they aggressively dive towards targets that are now partially obscured by smoke and dust a Chinese Colonel leading about seventy soldiers comes running towards me from the rear. I salute, though he is more pre-occupied with the approaching tanks to respond.

"Colonel, it appears a column of tanks has penetrated our right flank and is less than three miles away. Significant infantry is somewhere behind them." I intentionally keep my voice calm as I speak to him in Chinese.

The Colonel is a bit winded and takes a long drink from his canteen. I find myself wondering if it is only water. He quickly climbs the three steps to our makeshift observation platform and motions for me to join him. Once alongside him he points to the P-38s, which are circling in the distance.

"Lieutenant, are those planes attacking the tanks?" His voice is shaky, at best.

"Yes, I directed them to strafe the tanks and remain above them as long as their fuel holds out. I think this may distract the Japanese long enough for us to regroup. Since the tanks have outrun their supporting infantry, there is a reasonable likelihood they will stop and wait, which will buy us some time." My intention is to calm him down and decide on a defensive plan for repelling the tank assault.

The colonel scans the horizon with his binoculars. "The tanks have stopped!

203

I cannot see their infantry from this vantage point, but the fact is your ploy has worked, so far. Good job Lieutenant!" The Colonel wipes the sweat from around his eyes and returns the binoculars to a case he has strung across his left shoulder. We climb down from the observation post and return to the relative safety of our dug-out.

"Since you say significant infantry is behind those tanks, let's use this time to fall back while we still can. General Weili is committing our full division reserves to support us, but they cannot arrive in time if those tanks and infantry continue their assault."

The Colonel starts to give the orders to withdraw but before he can get the words out of his mouth the sound of incoming artillery instinctively sends me diving to the ground. Exploding shells land all around us when I see the Colonel blown, literally, into pieces. At the same moment searing pain rips through my head knocking off my helmet. I pick it up and realize it is full of holes. I am confused, everything seems to be happening in slow motion and I feel something warm dripping across my eyes. I pass out before I can even bring a hand to my face.

•   •   •   •   •

I awaken to discover I am in a field hospital with bandages wrapped around my entire head, save for my eyes, nose and mouth. I try to lift myself so I can determine if my arms and legs are still there, but the pain forces me backwards.

"Easy Lieutenant." It is a female voice with a decidedly British accent. "You took some nasty shrapnel to your head. You'd better not move too quickly or you could give yourself vertigo!"

"You're British?"

"Yes Sir, but you need your rest now."

"Please, tell me where I am. Is this a POW hospital?"

The nurse laughs and responds "No, Lieutenant, this is a field hospital in Myitkyina. We captured the town a few days ago."

She pulls the blanket up to my chin before continuing. "You've been unconscious for about a week. I must say we've been very concerned about you. The Doctors removed quite a bit of shrapnel from your head and I'm afraid it will be some time in recovery before you will get your balance back." She pauses to take my temperature. Once accomplished, she looks at the thermometer and smiles her approval.

"In a week or two they are going to place you onto a plane and eventually you will be loaded onto a hospital ship bound for Pearl Harbor. The war is over for you, Lieutenant. At least for the foreseeable future. Now close your eyes and get some rest. I will have a hot meal brought around for you in a short while." My worst fears are alleviated as I can lift my arms and legs. Sleep comes easily.

•　　•　　•　　•　　•

I have been in the field hospital nine days since I first woke up and tomorrow I have a plane ticket out of here. A hospital ship will be my next stop and will sail me to Pearl Harbor for continuing rest and rehabilitation. I am concerned how my head will react to flying as the relentless headache I have is barely touched by the medications. I am also having some problems with hallucinations, so when I see General Weili walk up to my bed, I am dubious that it truly is him.

"Good evening Lieutenant," he says in English.

I blink a couple of times as I try to focus on him. Realizing it really is Weili, I attempt to sit up, but the convulsing rush of vertigo violently flings me back into the bed.

"Now, now, Lieutenant. Do not get up. They tell me you have a serious head injury." Weili reaches into his pocket and pulls out a small bottle of sake and slips it under my pillow.

"We captured this," he points to the bottle of sake, "when we took the city. I thought you might appreciate it." Weili is smiling.

"I have something else for you too." He reaches into another pocket and pulls out a medal with a large blue ribbon attached to it. He bends down and pins it to my blanket.

"I am awarding you the Chinese equivalent to the Bronze Star. Your quick thinking with those P-38's saved the day. The tanks did stop and by the time they realized they were not coming under a full air assault our reserves, along with our reserve artillery, were in position and we destroyed the entire tank column and most of the supporting infantry. Thanks to your quick thinking we did not lose any ground and dealt the enemy a blow from which they could not recover."

Weili, who had been leaning over me while speaking, stands upright, straightens his jacket and salutes me.

"Perhaps we will meet again when this conflict is over. That would please me very much."

Without saying another word he walks out of the tent. I will never see him again.

• • • • •

Ken suddenly sits forward and turns to face Gary.

"So, Gary, the Army sent me to Honolulu to recover. That battle ended in August 1944, and by the time I arrived here it was nearly Christmas. As it turned out, I would not be sent back as the war would be over before I fully recovered."

When I was discharged I had a pretty nice bankroll. I never spent much money, had no family to support and after about a year in various hospitals, I had a pretty good amount of cash available. I bought an air conditioning company that was for sale. As part of the transaction the owner, a Japanese/American, stayed on for almost a year teaching me everything. I quickly found I had a knack for engineering and spent two long training periods at the equipment manufacturer's New York factory. That experience made me decide I would always rotate my employees through the factory training program. And speaking of employees, I inherited two Koreans who were excellent technicians. My knowledge of the language grew rapidly with our interaction."

"Hah! A funny story about the name I chose. Originally I was going to name the company 'Ken's Klimate Kontrol.' I had seen many American companies spell words like that. But one of my staff advised me about an organization by the name of the Ku Klux Klan and that people might look at my company's name and draw an improper conclusion. So I chose Ken's Climate Control. Later I added the words, 'All Islands.' That is the story of our family business in a nutshell!"

"Gary, your grandfather is looking very tired. Why not join us for breakfast and he can finish his first life story in the morning. There is still a little more, you know, such as how we came to meet." Sun smiles at the sight of the two men enjoying each other's company.

"No problem, I will be here bright and early."

"Excellent, I shall make your favorite breakfast; eggs, rice, spam, Portuguese sausage and taro rolls!"

Gary smiles broadly as he can almost taste it.

CHAPTER THIRTY
LANI GALE'S PLAN

Lani Gale looks to be very smug as she politely sips a cappuccino while sitting across the desk from her editor, James Mori. Mori is sitting back in his leather chair while enjoying his own cappuccino. He insists they only use Hawaiian grown coffee and currently a small grower on Kauai has caught his attention and is supplying all the coffee consumed at the newspaper, including espresso roast. Today he is splurging and making use of his new espresso maker, though Jimmy did have some difficulty getting it to work.

"Chief, I must admit that reward idea of yours was a no-questions-asked stroke of genius! I have at least a thousand tips already. They're arriving by phone, fax, and internet and there's a line of people down in the lobby waiting to offer information. And it's only eight in the morning! Hell, I have tips from as far away as South Africa and Chile! It looks to me as if everyone in the world has seen this Yokoyama fellow at one time or another."

"Alright then. I'm going to add six more temps to work on tip follow-up. You organize them and make sure we are the first to find Yokoyama. I have a hunch he's still alive." Mori picks up the newspaper and points to a computer enhanced photo of what Yokoyama might look like today.

"Get this printed on posters and have them prominently displayed at every newsstand in the islands. Someone must know who he was and where he went. By God, Lani, we're going to find this man, or at the very least, we're going to find his tombstone."

Gale smiles, finishes her coffee and picks up her purse.

"Chief, we have the whole world helping us so it's only a matter of time now. Somewhere along the way he either told someone his story, or someone who helped him will step forward. And let's face it, one hundred thousand dollars speaks volumes!"

Gale rises from her chair and says, "On that note, I'm outta here!"

Mori smiles as he watches her leave. "It's a great day to be in the newspaper business." He thinks to himself.

CHAPTER THIRTY ONE
NURSE SUN JIN-HO

Ken and Sun are enjoying the view of the cherry blossoms from the backyard lanai. Sun is waiting for Gary to arrive so she can finish preparing breakfast when the sound of Gary pulling into the driveway draws their attention and the sight of him running hard for the lanai brings smiles to their faces.

"Grandpa! Kapuna! You scare me when I don't see you right away!"

Sun smiles at his excitement and quickly returns to the kitchen to finish cooking breakfast. Ken raises both his hands, palms up, motioning Gary to calm down.

"My dear grandson, do not be so worried. Obviously nobody has claimed the reward yet. If it is deemed I am to be discovered then what is there for me to do? We are not going to suddenly disappear so my advice for you is to not allow yourself be so easily alarmed." Ken's voice is barely above a whisper as he attempts to allay Gary's nerves.

"Please sit down and make yourself comfortable. Your grandmother is finishing a wonderful breakfast for us, just as she promised."

"Grandfather, isn't there something you can do to keep from being found?"

"Gary, I am over ninety years old and have enjoyed much luck and many blessings to have lived so long and to remain reasonably healthy. No, there is nothing for me to do except to continue as I always have. I recall no teachings of Buddha that would suggest I change my path at this point in life, a path that has served me so well for so long."

Sun carries out two plates, one overfilled with rice, poached eggs, Portuguese sausage and spam, and places it before Gary. The second plate is much more modestly filled with the same variety of food, which she hands to Ken. Sun disappears and quickly returns with her own plate, which, instead of spam and sausage, has a nice piece of ever-so-slightly seared ahi.

"Gary, please eat while your food is hot," Sun urges.

As they begin to enjoy their breakfast Ken finds himself watching Gary very closely, enjoying the moment. He knows time may be running out on him and that knowledge fuels his desire to finish the story of his first life.

"Gary, I imagine you still want to learn the balance of my story, especially since so many people are interested in discovering who I am!" Ken smiles at the reference to the one hundred-thousand-dollar prize offered for him by the newspaper.

"Of course, Grandfather." Gary talks through a mouthful of spam and Portuguese sausage.

"As you are aware I discovered I had an innate skill for understanding the principals of how an air conditioning unit operates. When an army reserve unit was authorized here in Oahu, I immediately joined. The extra pay, at a lieutenant's rank no less, truly helped me to more quickly grow the business, around which my life revolved. I had come to grips with the fact I could never return to Japan, so I only looked to the future and that meant I was only looking forward with respect to making my company as busy as possible and employing as many people as I could afford. My employees were mostly of Asian descent, but my marketing people consisted of a married couple from Dallas, Texas. You know them, Tracy and Nannette. You are friends with all five of their grandchildren!"

Gary smiles as he recalls the various adventures he shared with the two youngest siblings, both boys. "Yes, grandfather, of course I know them."

Ken and Sun finish their breakfast and wait for Gary to complete his. Once finished, Sun gathers all their plates, cups and glasses and takes them into the house. She returns with a large pitcher of iced tea and fresh glasses, pours each of them a glass and takes a seat to the left of Ken which allows her a clear view of her grandson.

Ken sits back in his chair, stroking his beard much as he has done before, and prepares to continue. Gary observes his facial features as decades appear to drop away, making him look much younger than he is.

"It was early in May 1950 and I was at my desk typing a proposal to install air conditioning into the showroom of a large Ford Motors dealership in Honolulu. It was a very exciting prospect and our biggest project ever, should our bid prove decisive. I recall it was lunch hour when the phone rang. I was the only person in the office and as I picked up the phone there was no hint my life was about to be turned upside down, yet again."

"Hello, Ken's Climate Control. What may I do for you?"

"Good morning, I'm looking to speak with Lieutenant Kida." The voice on the other end of the line is very formal.

"This is Lieutenant Kida. Who is calling?" I cannot disguise my surprise at being referred to as 'Lieutenant Kida.'

"This is Captain Lewis over at Hickam. Sorry to bother you, but I do have a couple of questions."

I cannot imagine what he might need to know. It does occur to me someone might have uncovered my background and I find myself suddenly quite nervous.

"Certainly, Captain. What would you like to know?"

"Well, first, I know you had a nasty head wound in Burma and spent more than a year in recovery. So tell me, are you suffering any lingering problems from that?"

"Thank you for asking Sir. I have experienced no ill effects for about three years now."

"That's good news. Glad to hear it. So tell me, your personnel file indicates you can both speak and read Korean. Is that true?"

I am surprised to be asked about my Korean language skills and think he might be wondering how I obtained them. But why would anyone be interested? I keep myself calm by thinking of the Ford contract. "Actually Captain, two of my employees are Korean so I practice my skills every day."

"That's great! Just what I was hoping to hear. Lieutenant, the Army needs your services again. You're being activated for a twenty-four-month tour effective as of next week!"

"Twenty-four-month tour? Where am I going?"

"Seoul."

"Korea?" I cannot disguise my total surprise.

"Yes, Lieutenant, Korea. Glad you know where that is. Get yourself to my office one week from today and in the meantime I'll be sending you written orders by courier as soon as I can sign them. Naturally, bring only the bare minimum. I hope this gives you enough time to manage your affairs, I understand you have a business to operate." The tone of his voice tells me I have no leverage on the issue.

"I imagine it would do me no good if I were to tell you I required more notice."

"Lieutenant, I would not go so far as to say it would do you 'no good,' but I would say that such a request would make no difference as to the final outcome.

So don't waste any time." My mind is racing and I want to hang up, but the Captain has not yet finished with me.

"Listen Kida, and keep this information quiet, we are really strapped for interpreters over there, especially interpreters with combat experience. Something seems to be brewing and we don't know what it is. But you are going to be part of our effort to discover just what in hell is going on and let me tell you that time is not on our side. So, Lieutenant, I'll see you next week. Any more questions?"

"No, Captain. I will await your written orders and look forward to meeting you."

"Great! Till then, waste no time!" He hangs up the phone leaving me staring at the receiver, in shock.

My first thought is I must finish this proposal and get it delivered today. However, I know I won't be here to oversee the project, if it is accepted. So I must immediately begin to make interim management arrangements. I put the phone down for a moment and think about who I need to call. After a few moments I decide Sammy will run the business in my absence and immediately dial his number over in the warehouse. Fortunately for me, Sammy answers right away.

"Sammy! This is Ken. Something major has just happened. Can you come over to the office?"

"Of course. I have no appointments until later this afternoon and can be there in ten minutes."

"Good, because it appears I am going to need you to run the company for the next two years so waste no time." I hang up and think to myself: Two years! What if I am killed? Then what? I decide to make an appointment with my attorney and shall direct him to create a document that will turn ownership of the company over to my top employees so they can continue the business and preserve their jobs in the event of my death. I have been given only one week during which I must accomplish a great deal!

On the day before I am to report we learn we have been awarded the big Ford dealership contract. I can relax knowing that contract assures a source of work and income for my staff over the next several months and it will certainly help smooth over the transition while I am thousands of miles away.

• • • • •

A month quickly passes and I am sitting behind a desk in Seoul, South Korea. I am typing a translation of recently captured documents taken from a North Korean patrol that had penetrated across the border and been captured. As I translate them it appears to me this patrol was a recon for a larger assault across the border. But how large would the assault be? I must also consider the possibility the information was intentionally planted to create a pretense for an incursion. My thoughts are interrupted by the loud ringing of my field phone. I pick it up as fast as I can as the racket it makes is most unsettling.

"Lieutenant Kida speaking." My mouth drops open as I listen to somebody identifying himself as 'Major Robinson' who is screaming the North Koreans have charged across the border by the thousands and I would get the hell out of Seoul if I had any sense at all. When he pauses to get his breath I respond:

"Yes Sir, I will do that right away." Without indicating if he was finished, he hangs up. I think he heard my response, but it does not matter as time is not on my side.

I notice Corporal Kane is typing reports and calmly walk to the door, trying my best to appear calm and collected.

"Corporal?"

"Yes Lieutenant?"

"Corporal, I have some very bad news. The North Koreans have swarmed across the border and apparently have routed the South Korean Army. Scores of thousands of North Koreans are heading directly for us and they are coming fast. We must pack up everything we can and burn the rest. ASAP!" There is an unfamiliar edginess in my voice as my concern over the situation has overcome my normal ability to exert complete control over my emotions.

"Sir, are we instituting General Evacuation Plan A?"

"No, corporal. That plan assumes we have time. If we are not out of here in a couple of hours we may not be going anywhere ever again. Pack up what you can, burn the rest. We need to get ourselves to Taejan. I am going to requisition a truck and you get us a good road map, then start packing everything you can. But first, call in the rest of the platoon and get them over here. I want to pull out fast!"

"Sir, you can count on me! Oh, and Sir, I have set aside about six dozen cases of emergency food supplies, just for such an occasion, along with a few choice weapons. Sergeant Toyoda was quite instrumental in helping me on my little rainy day emergency project."

I smile at the good news. "You two men are the kind of self-starters I like to have in my unit. Great work! Now get going while I find us a truck."

•   •   •   •   •

The retreat South is infested with fear and disorganization. The fleeing units of the South Korean Army are disheartened as well as undisciplined. I see defeat in the eyes of most of them which I find to be very unsettling. After two hectic days we stop retreating and are situated in a newly constructed defensive line near Taejon.

I have orders to attend a muster of all officers for a situational briefing. There must be over one hundred of us crammed into a very old warehouse and it is stifling hot. A make-shift stage has been quickly erected and someone has managed to find the flags, and flag stands, representing all of the countries present. A huge map of Korea is on a rickety easel to the right of the podium and the air is clogged with cigarette smoke, a habit I have yet to saddle myself with.

We come to attention upon the arrival of Major General Dean who briskly enters the stage from the left, picks up a large pointer and walks to the podium.

From the rear of the audience, responding to a hand gesture from the General, a Sergeant calls out: "At ease" and we return to our seats. General Dean waits as the room quickly grows silent.

"Gentlemen, as you are keenly aware the situation is critical. Supplies, replacements, reinforcements are all critical. Air support from the Navy has been the difference between slowing the North's advance and total capitulation. But it takes time to bring more aircraft carriers, more supplies, more troops, more of literally everything we need."

Dean walks over to the map and points to a location.

"We must hold the North Koreans right here at Taejon. It is absolutely imperative we hold this position for as long as possible and buy the time required to mount a full-scale counter offensive. I am requesting each and every one of you to help buy us that time."

He walks over to a table and pours himself a cup of hot coffee. I notice steam rising from the cup and wonder how does he drink hot coffee when his uniform is soaking through with sweat? Perhaps, like me, he has not been able to sleep.

"Intelligence has interrogated the small handful of prisoners we have managed to capture and it appears the North Koreans have likely committed all of their reserves as they seek to deal us a death blow. Clearly they have decided this is an all or nothing proposition and are betting they will win. Gentlemen, let's take them up on that bet and stop 'em in their tracks right here, right now." He is interrupted by scattered cheers.

An Army Major stands, seeking his attention.

"Yes, Major, you have a question?"

"Pardon me, sorry to butt in Sir." The Major has a Texas drawl, which brings a smile to Dean's face.

"Well, General Sir, it just seems to me that what them North Korean folks have on our doorstep is more like a stampede that's doggone running out of control. That's got nothing to do with gambling Sir. Again, beggin' your pardon, but from where I sit it just don't look to me as if they need any reserves." The Major returns to his seat and we all await the Dean's reply. Unfortunately, I have to agree with the Major. As an intelligence officer I often have critical information before Dean and 'stampede that's doggone running out of control' is a description I agree with.

Dean moves behind the podium and grips it with both hands. I can see his knuckles turning red.

"That is a valid point you make, Major. But the fact remains we must buy time. Anyone who can carry a rifle, anyone who can walk or crawl and pull a trigger; all of them are being pressed into the lines. Only doctors, nurses and necessary medical staff are exempted. Just as the North Koreans have pulled out all the stops, so must we!"

He returns to the map and points to an area to the south of where we are presently digging in.

"We have a pretty good fallback position here, near Pusan. Korean laborers and what few engineers we have available to us are busy building a series of redoubts. In the event we cannot, in fact, hold here at Taejon we will make Pusan our final stand before we turn this around and take the offensive."

Dean pauses as he drains his cup and takes a few moments to review his audience. We are all silent as we contemplate the coming day.

"Gentlemen! After Pusan there is only the Ocean and I absolutely disdain swimming in salt water so I urge you not to allow that happen!"

His comment results in a wave of somewhat nervous laughter.

"Godspeed to all of you!" He begins to walk off the stage as everyone stands, but pauses, turns to the gathering and salutes. He disappears through the same side doorway through which he entered. His speech does not convey anything to me other than the Army is planning on a further withdrawal to Pusan. In my mind this means I am part of a rear guard action, buying the General the time he needs. Unfortunately for General Dean, he will find himself a prisoner of the North Koreans in the near future.

•　　•　　•　　•　　•

It is about forty-eight hours since General Dean's briefing and I find myself commanding three very tired squads, spread across too much ground with too few machine guns. In fact, we have only one machine gun per squad and limited ammo and are lucky to have what we have. From what I can gather, after interrogating a prisoner we captured the night before, our sector is about to be the focal point of the next main North Korean assault. I have relayed this information to command without as much as a word in response. Their silence is haunting me and I fear we are being abandoned.

I have called my three sergeants together while there are still a few hours of daylight remaining.

Sergeant Toyoda has first squad which is stretched out across our left flank. He was part of the famous 442nd Nisei Division in World War II and survived the bloody and costly assault on Monte Cassini in Italy. As I recall his platoon suffered in the neighborhood of eighty percent casualties and he is my only combat-hardened sergeant. Sergeant Robert Mathias joined the Army in 1944 when he was seventeen. By the time he reached the European theatre the Battle of the Bulge had been fully rebuked. He has confided that he only had one occasion to fire his rifle in combat. Sergeant Yoon and his South Korean Squad were just called up from the reserves. They have not seen any action yet, so tonight will be their baptism. I am spreading them across the front of my command post and to the right.

I have managed one extra machine gun, along with a gunner and feeder which I have placed ahead of our command post which we have dug into the side of a hill. Corporal Kane, a couple of runners and I will be in the command post. Our advantage is we are sitting atop a hill. The North Koreans will need to charge uphill while we can fire down on them before they can even see our positions. I have their full attention as I begin my briefing.

"We can expect the North Korean assault to start around twenty two hundred hours. I want lights out at nineteen hundred and that includes no smoking. I do not want to give any indication of our positions until we open fire. Make certain your men know this." I pause as Kane and Toyoda light cigarettes.

"Might as well smoke as much as you can, while you still can." I pause to take a drink of water. The summer heat has been grinding us down. Relentless sun, spotty rations of hot food and seemingly endless withdrawals has been taking a toll on all of us. Cigarette smoking is the sole indulgence these days.

"Extra ammo is being passed out while I speak and it will have to be enough. Don't count on additional replacements, reinforcements or resupply. Assume we are on our own, save for Captain Lami's rovers and the handful of replacements who are working their way up here.

One thing we do have a surplus of are star shells and flares. Keep the sky lit up as often as you need to." Just then we all instinctively duck at the sound of an incoming round. Fortunately, it lands well behind our position.

"Guess they are just letting us know they have not forgotten about us." Nobody laughs at my joke. I know I am not particularly good when it comes to humor, but I do work at it.

"Captain Lami is with our reserves about two hundred yards to the rear. He can quickly disperse to either flank as needed. Any Questions?"

"Yes Sir." Sergeant Yoon speaks very broken English. I nod for him to proceed.

"I have only one of your interpreters in my squad. Unfortunately, I am the only other person who can speak English. We are spread out in four foxholes and I placed the interpreter into the second from the edge of our right flank. Do you think that is the best location for him?"

I look over the Sergeant for a few moments. His uniform still has the pressed ridges from the factory. It is likely he never expected to find himself in active service, let alone in the desperate situation in which he now finds himself and he certainly appears to be nervous.

"Sergeant, I believe that is perfect." He noticeably relaxes which is good as I don't want him so wound-up he freezes once the action starts.

"I think it best you camp yourself at the innermost position."

"Yes Sir. I will do that." Sergeant Yoon replies.

"Any other questions?"

"Yes Sir. If they break through are we to fall back?" Sergeant Mathias put his cigarette out before rising to speak.

"Fall back to where? In any event we cannot fall back without orders. The only position we might be able to reach is the reserve dugouts, roughly two hundred yards behind us. If we are ordered to pull back that is where we will regroup and I will send runners to advise everyone."

"Do we have any artillery support Sir?" The dour expression on Mathias's face tells me he already knows the answer.

"We have mortar support. The artillery needed to be repositioned, what was left of them that is, after they were targeted by North Korean artillery. But cheer up! I have personally delivered a map with our coordinates to the mortar group and marked each of our positions. They can quickly react and with excellent accuracy. We can count on that and I am certain we will be having breakfast together in the morning!"

"I like your confidence and determination," says Mathias.

"Let me tell you a short story about me to give you an idea of my determination." As I rarely talk about myself, everyone's ears seem to perk up.

"My father was killed when I was eight, leaving my mom to run the household and raise me and my siblings. I took it upon myself to help her in every way, but one day I did a stupid thing. I climbed a tall tree with a friend; a tree my mother had warned me never to climb as the branches were very brittle. Sure enough, I fell out of the tree, landed on my left arm and broke it. My friend wanted me to go straight home, but I was determined not to bother my mom so I walked myself to the doctor's office. He fixed me up, but also sent one of his nurses to my home ahead of me to advise my mom of my desire to minimize her inconvenience."

"So what did she say?" Mathias asks.

"She said she admired my will, but preferred I go to her first in the future and I should stay away from tree climbing."

Everyone has a brief laugh before returning to the business at hand.

Sergeant Toyoda has been silently puffing a cigarette, taking everything in. "Well, I guess this is apparently, as they say, 'it.' My squad's about as ready as they can be."

"Unless I see you sooner, I will see you all in the morning. Now get back to your squads and keep your ears open." I put as much confidence in my voice as I can muster.

•　•　•　•　•

217

The few hours between my briefing and the onset of complete darkness pass very slowly. It is a moonless night, precisely what I did not want. Much like the night we buried Kamita, what seems like decades ago.

Suddenly I hear shouting in the distance quickly followed by the sound of rifles then joined by the staccato sound of machine guns. Star shells burst overhead, one to the left, another off to the right. I climb the three stairs to my observation point and bring the binoculars to my eyes. Hundreds of North Koreans are rushing up the hill screaming as they fire their weapons. I call for Corporal Kane to bring in a mortar strike.

Just as Kane hangs up the field phone, the sound of incoming artillery instinctively sends me diving into the command dugout. A series of roughly eight shells explode all around us. The explosions then proceed along our left flank, reigning down as if they had placed a spotter behind us and knew exactly where my squads were dug in.

The machine gun position a few yards outside our post opens up. I decide to take a look, but just as I get up from my previously prone position back-to-back artillery shells land. The first shell explodes alongside the machine gun sending the gunner's headless body directly into my chest and forcing me backwards. The second shell lands behind us resulting in many screams.

I cannot imagine why there would be anyone behind us and I am immediately concerned that we have been flanked. Before I can react I see Captain Lami accompanied by nine soldiers. Simultaneously I hear the comforting sound of our own mortar rounds streaking outbound and into the approaching enemy.

"Corporal, take over the machine gun." Kane takes hold of the machine gun and begins firing as Captain Lami, blood smeared across his face, makes his way to me.

"Lieutenant, what's your situation?"

Just then several flares again illuminate the night. The gunshots cease, though the mortars continue.

"Let's take a look." My voice is calm, while my heart is racing.

The Captain and I move to either side of the machine gun. Scores of dead bodies litter the hillside. The mortar barrage is acting as a meat grinder at this point as the assault failed.

"Corporal, get on the horn and tell the mortars to cease firing and thank them for a great job."

"Yes Sir," replies Kane, who slips from behind the machine gun and makes his way back into the wreckage of the command dug-out. In a few moments the mortar barrage lifts and Kane returns.

"To answer your question, we are holding. I expect my squads to report in and then we will have a better idea of how we have fared thus far. But you Sir, you are wounded."

Captain Lami looks puzzled for when he swipes his right hand across his face he discovers he is covered in blood, except it is not his blood.

"I'm okay," he says. "We took a couple of rounds on our way in and lost most of my command." Lami looks over at the nine men who made it. "There were nineteen of us when we left."

We again hit the ground at the sound of incoming artillery. I dive to the right and Lami dives left. It proves to be a bad choice for a shell bursts just ahead of Lami, literally cutting him in half and killing four more of his men. I am lucky as I have some shrapnel in my left forearm, but nothing serious. Kane is brushing himself off and resuming his position at the machine gun.

A runner from first squad arrives, excited and out of breath.

"Lieutenant, Sergeant Toyoda reports first and second squads are each down four men. Also, Sir, first squad's machine gun is out of commission." He breaks out his canteen and takes a long drink. I look over at the five remaining reserves and spy one corporal among them.

"Corporal!" He looks over at me in surprise, then straightens himself up and responds.

"Yes Sir?"

"Are you wounded?"

"No, Sir, not at all."

"Excellent, take your four men and go with this private. Leave two of the replacements with second squad and send the balance, along with yourself and the private here, up to Sergeant Toyoda's positions. Got that?"

"Yes, Sir, we're on our way." I watch them disappear into the night.

"I imagine we can expect another assault as soon as the North Koreans can regroup. How's the ammo for the machine gun?"

"We have plenty Lieutenant." Kane's voice is calm and collected. It is amazing to me how quickly a person can become accustomed to battle conditions. Not so long ago he was in a near panic while we evacuated Seoul and now he is calmly manning a machine gun in the middle of the night in some place we never knew existed.

The silence proves temporary as a new wave of war cries penetrate the night.

Gunfire erupts up and down our lines. Flares turn the night into day revealing hundreds of North Koreans packed so tightly they are fighting each other for their respective footholds as they rush up the hill. They are recklessly charging forward without regard to the bullets and grenades penetrating their massed bodies.

"Corporal, call in a mortar strike for Coordinate Bravo-one, fire for effect!" I trust he can hear me over the cacophony of screams, gunfire and artillery bursts.

In a few minutes Sergeant Toyoda's runner returns, holding his left arm as blood oozes through his shirt sleeve. However, he is still grasping his rifle and wearing his helmet, both are good indications that panic has not set in.

"Lieutenant." He is panting, nearly out of breath.

"Take your time private." I use a firm, but calm voice. His breathing quickly returns to something resembling normal.

"Sir, First Squad was overrun and Sergeant Toyoda is dead. Just three of us made it out and are with Second Squad, but they've been hit pretty bad themselves and are following right behind me."

I hand the private my canteen. "Take a sit-down private." Kane is standing by at the field phone as he knows I am going to need him.

"Kane, call the mortars again and give them the reference points for first and second squads. Tell them to commence firing now." I point to Sergeant Mathias, who is leading the five surviving soldiers of the two squads and motion him to join me. I notice Kane is in contact with the mortar crews.

"Hold on a minute Corporal. Tell them to start walking their fire right down onto our position in five minutes. Let them know we will re-establish contact with them once we have reached the reserve command area and I will have further orders at that time."

"Roger." Kane calmly conveys the additional information.

I look around at the soldiers who just came in with Mathias and spot a lone corporal. I point to him. "Corporal, you have a mission." He quickly walks up to me. He is young, maybe nineteen years old and he looks a little scared, but still in control of himself.

"Corporal, go out to Sergeant Yoon and tell him to fall back immediately to the reserve command area. Understood?" I am looking him straight in the eyes and feel pretty confident the young man is understanding me. "Take this note with you." I quickly scratch out my orders in Korean as it occurs to me Sergeant Yoon and his lone interpreter might be dead and I know better than to make assumptions.

"A mortar barrage is going to be coming down on us soon, so it is imperative you get to Yoon and have him withdraw. Any questions?"

"No Sir. I'm outta here!" He immediately disappears in the direction of Sergeant Yoon's position.

"Sergeant Mathias, take over the machine gun position and keep an eye out for any stragglers." "Got it!' Mathias taps one of his men on the shoulder and they immediately man the machine gun.

Finally, the field phone rings. I am hoping for good news as Corporal Kane answers. "Lieutenant, I have Colonel Wolf on the line and he's asking for Captain Lami." Kane offers me the phone.

"Lieutenant Kida here."

"Colonel Wolf here, Lieutenant. I was under the impression Captain Lami brought the reserves up to your position. Where is he?"

"Dead Sir and barely a handful of the reserves made it here."

"What's your situation?"

"Not very good. First and Second Squads are overrun. Sergeant Toyoda is dead and what is left of them are with me. The mortars are firing on their old positions right now and in about four minutes they are going to start walking onto my own position. I have Sergeant Yoon pulling back to the reserve command area, which is where we are going now. We plan to hold that position with the two remaining machine guns."

There is a pause on the other end of the line. Finally, Colonel Wolf responds.

"Lieutenant, get the hell out of there as you plan. I promise I will have a platoon to support you within the hour. Just hold on 'til then. Now get moving Lieutenant. I expect to see you in the morning!"

"Yes Sir, I would like that myself." I crouch and firmly press my helmet to my head with both of my hands as an artillery shell bursts only a few yards away. As soon as the dust settles I quickly stand and call out:

"Grab your guns and as much ammo as you can and get the hell out of here!"

The men require no further encouragement and we fall back just in time. The explosions of mortar rounds are drawing near, precisely as I requested.

Our withdrawal a couple hundred yards to the rear command post proves successful and we lose no additional men. The mortars apparently caused the North Koreans to stop advancing, perhaps to regroup in the face of the mortar assault. We have been reinforced and the eastern sky is finally turning light. I am jarred from my semi-conscious state by the clattering sound of a field phone, soon answered by Kane, who had been using it to prop his head while napping.

"Lieutenant, its Colonel Wolf." He holds the phone out for me.

"Kida here."

"Good to hear you're still alive, Captain Kida." The Colonel's voice conveys his sense of relief.

"Sir?"

"Field promotion Kida, we're running out of officers. Congratulations."

I am a bit surprised and don't know what to say, so I keep it simple. "Thank you Sir."

"Listen up Captain, we're pulling back to Pusan immediately. The fly boys will keep our North Korean friends out there busy during the withdrawal. We've managed to get hold of a few 105's and even a 155 howitzer to provide additional cover for our re-positioning to Pusan."

"That's good news Sir. I trust it is a harbinger of better things to come."

I glance at the sky as four carrier based F9F Panthers, their wings fully laden with rockets scream past. In a few moments I hear the reassuring sounds of rockets exploding, followed by a very large secondary explosion and smile as it sounds to me as if they hit an ammo dump.

"Let's hope so, Captain. Now get your men and equipment together! A column of transports should be pulling up as we speak. I'll see you in Pusan. Out." The Colonel cuts off before I can respond. The sound of trucks is now clearly audible as it is time to get packing.

● ● ● ● ●

It only takes less than an hour to load the trucks with everything we can take with us. We burn or blow up anything we can't bring along and I make certain to be the final person to get aboard the last of the trucks. I disdain sitting up front in the cab and make it a habit to sit in the rear with my men. Today is no different. But today, my habit saves my life.

Just as my truck begins to move forward we receive a direct artillery hit to the cab. Our now driverless truck, cab on fire, careens down the embankment along the side of the road. The sensation of rolling over is the last thing I recall, along with burning sensations in my arms.

•   •   •   •   •

When I wake up, I find myself lying in a hospital bed. There is a bottle of liquid hanging to my left with a tube that runs into my left wrist. I am glad to see I still have a left wrist.

My head is bandaged, my right arm and leg are in casts. I tell myself to lift my left foot and relax when I see the blanket, where my left foot should be, lift from the bed. It hurts to breathe so I surmise I must have a broken rib. A very pretty Korean nurse, thermometer in hand, smiles as she addresses me in Korean accented English.

"Please open mouth Captain. I check your temperature, ok?" Korean Lieutenant-Nurse Sun Jin-Ho gently places the thermometer into my mouth.

Despite the pain from my wounds I am completely mesmerized by her. I can only describe what I feel as what it must be like when two long-lost lovers bump into each other in the dark, and upon recognizing each other it suddenly becomes day. I am at a loss for words and am embarrassed as I hear the first words I speak to her.

"Am I in Heaven?" I ask in Korean.

She smiles broadly as she removes the thermometer and replies in English;

"No Captain, you are in army field hospital outside Pusan and I am most pleased to report we have put stop to the invasion from the north. You still have slight fever so it be best if you rest." She tightens up the covers around me and checks the bandages on my head.

"Lieutenant, I don't recall how I got here. Last thing I knew I was in the back of a truck and we were rolling down a hill." I continue to speak in Korean.

She checks the pitcher of water next to my bed, fills a glass and hands it to me.

"Here, sip slowly." I do as requested.

"You arrived by ambulance truck two days ago. There were five men with you and they tell me no others survive. Corporal Kane and Sergeant Mathias have been inquiring about you. They each have broken leg, but are otherwise good and say they dragged you from burning truck." She walks around to the end of my bed, makes notations into a chart.

"They can visit tomorrow but today you rest, you drink plenty water and you eat. You have three broken ribs so do not move much. Understand, Captain?"

As I seek to establish a dialogue with her I do my best to continue my side of the conversation in Korean. "Yes, I have figured out that much already. Can you tell me what time is it?"

She pulls a watch from her skirt pocket. "It is fourteen hundred hours, Tuesday. I will get you "Stars and Stripes" if you like."

"Yes, that would be very nice, thank you, but how long is your shift?" I attempt to keep the inflection in my voice calm so as not to give away the fact my heart has been racing. I fear it only renders my Korean a little less polished. "I work to twenty one hundred hours so I will be here some time still. You be hungry?"

I want to tell her I am hungry, but not the manner of hunger that is fed by food. "Just a little. What time is chow?"

"Dinner is in three hour, but if you hungry now, I can make arrangement."

She stands alongside my bed, an image of beauty, awaiting my answer.

"Three hours is fine, thank you. I am sure you have other patients who need your attention more than I do." I watch the expression on her face. Perhaps, just perhaps, she harbors a small interest in me.

"I will return to check you later."

She walks towards a small desk at the end of the ward and converses briefly with another nurse. In a little while she leaves the wardroom so I close my eyes and return to sleep.

•   •   •   •   •

Suddenly Ken leans towards Sun and gives her a gentle kiss. They spend a few moments simply looking at each other before Ken turns to Gary.

"You certainly know the rest of my life! You must have asked me to relate the story of how we met a thousand times. When you were very young almost every time you came over to visit you would ask one of us to tell you that story."

Gary smiles. "I still get a kick out of hearing it."

"Gary, help me refill the iced tea and put together some cookies." Sun smiles, stands and takes the empty pitcher with her. She and Gary disappear through the French doors.

"I will wait here." Ken raises his voice to make certain they hear him.

CHAPTER THIRTY TWO
CONFRONTATION

Sun is carefully arranging three hand-blown glasses on a beautifully hand-painted china platter she bought at an estate sale on Maui thirty years earlier. She was taken by the craftsmanship of the set and when she realized it had been made in Japan, it was a done deal. There was no doubt in her mind Ken would appreciate that fact and they have made a great deal of use of the entire set over the years.

The glass pitcher is also hand-blown and skillfully painted by Sun herself. When she turned forty five, she found herself needing something additional to do with her life, as her youngest child was old enough to take care of himself. She took a series of classes and learned to make glassware. Over the next twenty or so years she made many sets of glasses, cups, saucers and pitchers, giving them as presents to relatives and friends. But this pitcher is special to her. It is the first one she ever made and though it has its small flaws it remains her favorite.

She has also set out a modest collection of cookies which are the efforts of three of her granddaughters. It is rare that at least one grandchild does not spend a weekend with them. Most of their children live within a few blocks of their home so it's very easy for them to visit. Family has always been of utmost important to Sun and Ken.

As for Ken, the term 'family' always extended to include the employees of Ken's Climate Control and their families. Frequent picnics at various state parks and beaches have been one of the hallmarks of Ken's Climate Control for more than sixty years. Though Ken is no longer active in the business his sons and daughters continue the traditions.

Gary is patiently watching Sun as she goes about putting together little snacks. He enjoys watching her and thinks it's unlikely his Kapuna even realizes she has been humming to herself the entire time. Finally, she appears satisfied, then frowns and adds a few napkins to the cookie tray. Smiling, she looks at

Gary.

"Please carry this tray with the iced tea and glasses. It is just too heavy for me. I will bring the cookies. Oh, I almost forgot the plates and napkins!"

Sun stops in her tracks, reverses direction and walks to a glass-fronted cabinet. From there she chooses the style of plate she desires and counts out three of them. She places them on the tray with the cookies, looks it over and smiles.

"That's better." Gary follows her out of the kitchen and into Ken's study. Just as she is placing her tray on the table alongside Ken, the doorbell rings.

"That's strange," she says, "I am not expecting anyone. Gary, go ahead and pour the iced tea for us and I will answer the door."

"Of course Kapuna." Gary proceeds to pour a glass for his grandfather, one for his Kapuna and one for himself. They can hear Sun talking to someone at the door as a man's voice is just barely audible.

Momentarily she returns, her face drawn into a tight frown. Her voice is shaky.

"Gary, please go to the kitchen and bring us two additional plates and glasses for our unexpected guests."

"Sure, Kapuna. Who's here?"

"Two representatives of the United States Navy." Her voice trembles.

Ken doesn't even flinch at the news.

Gary, however, is in an immediate panic. "What!" His voice is a loud whisper as he doesn't want to be heard by the visitors. "What are we going to do?"

"Gary, right now you are going to do as your Kapuna requests." Ken's voice is calm, too calm to suit Gary, but he dare not defy his grandfather.

"When you return, I will introduce you to our guests. You can then take your iced tea and wait for us in the hall. At present your Kapuna will proceed to escort them in and should we need anything we will summon you. And, Gary, please, stay calm. There is nothing any of us can do."

"I prefer not to be here at all and will wait in the hall." Gary slips out into the hallway, careful to stay out of sight, but not beyond earshot. He overhears Sun at the front door:

"Commander, Lieutenant, please follow me. My husband is in the den where we were just sitting down to some homemade cherry iced tea and cookies." Sun bows and motions for Pastwa and Yamura to follow her.

As they enter the den, Pastwa and Yamura, hats in hand, find Ken sitting in his over-stuffed arm chair. Pastwa is a bit taken aback at how small, and old, he looks. Ken appears to him as if he were a Buddhist monk, not a retired war hero.

There are three chairs arranged in a semi-circle around a small table upon which sits the pitcher of iced tea, a tray of cookies and three small dishes.

"Ken, these people have come to see you." She turns to face Pastwa. "I apologize, but could you repeat your names?"

Pastwa and Yamura smile. "Of course, Mrs. Kida. I am Lieutenant Commander Chris Pastwa and this is Lieutenant Karen Yamura. We're assigned to Rear Admiral Roman Reardon at Pearl Harbor." When Pastwa mentions 'Pearl Harbor' he looks directly into Ken's eyes, seeking a response." Not discerning any change in Ken's demeanor he briefly glances around the room, noting the orderly, almost military manner in which it is maintained.

"Captain Kida, please pardon our intrusion, but we would very much like to have a conversation with you, that is, if you don't mind." Pastwa is doing his best to keep his voice calm and friendly. He can well imagine the fear that is likely running through Sun and wants to defuse any situation before it develops. It's his intention to confirm what his gut has been telling him about Ken and desires to keep the meeting on a friendly basis.

"Captain, we shouldn't be too long." Yamura flashes a reassuring smile.

"Please sit down. Do you mind if Sun joins us?" Ken's voice does not convey any of the intense anxiety he is experiencing.

"Of course not, we'd would very much like to include her in the conversation." Pastwa thinks to himself that this couple appear very loyal to each other, a trait he admires.

As they take their seats they can't help but notice Ken's framed medals on the wall which are flanked by dozens of photographs of family and friends. Pastwa finds himself feeling a bit anxious, not unlike being in front of Reardon when there's bad news. Ken appears to be so small and harmless, yet he knows the heroics this man has accomplished both against and on behalf of the United States.

Gary cautiously enters the den holding two glasses and a pair of plates. He stops just inside the doorway, unsure as to whether he should enter.

"I have the extra glasses and plates." Gary walks over to the table and sets them down. He's about to begin pouring iced tea when Ken interrupts.

"Gary, first let me introduce you."

Gary pauses and turns to face Pastwa and Yamura. He has the look of a school boy in the principal's office.

"Gary, this is Lieutenant Commander Pastwa." Pastwa stands and extends his right hand. Gary reaches out and exchanges a firm handshake.

"Good strong grip, Gary. I appreciate a man who knows how to shake hands." Pastwa smiles and returns to his chair.

Pointing to Lieutenant Yamura, Ken continues, "This is Lieutenant Yamura. From her name I would gather she is likely Japanese/American?"

Yamura rises and extends her right hand. "Your grandfather is correct, I am third generation. Pleased to meet you."

"Nice to meet you both." Gary's voice is barely above a whisper.

"Gary has been accepted into your 'Annapolis' for the fall semester, so naturally we are quite proud of him." Ken is beaming and his pride is obvious.

"That's quite the accomplishment, congratulations!" Pastwa replies.

"That's right, you should be quite pleased with yourself," adds Yamura.

"Gary, please, if you don't mind I would like you to wait for us in the living room," says Ken.

"Yes grandfather. If you need anything just call." Gary turns to leave, but pauses when Yamura interrupts.

"Gary, perhaps we'll run into each other in the future. You never know, you could find yourself assigned to Pearl in a few years." Yamura smiles, her voice and demeanor clearly friendly, which does help him calm down a little.

"Yes, Lieutenant, you never know what might happen." Gary leaves the room, quietly closing the doors behind him resulting in a few moments of uncomfortable silence. Yamura takes a sip of the tea and breaks the ice.

"Why, Mrs. Kida, this is absolutely excellent. Do you grow your own cherries?" Yamura smiles as she looks directly into Sun's eyes.

"Thank you Lieutenant," replies a blushing Sun. "We have several cherry trees. In fact, my husband has always insisted we have cherry trees. They create particularly beautiful blossoms and they happen to be in full bloom right now."

Pastwa clears his throat and turns to Sun. "I agree with Lieutenant Yamura. This is the best cherry iced tea I have experienced, thank you."

Pastwa turns to face Ken. "Captain, Sir, can I assume you have been following the lead story of the Honolulu newspaper these last few days?"

Ken doesn't flinch. "Ah, yes, a most interesting story indeed. Quite remarkable and if true I think it would make a great script for a Hollywood movie." Ken answers in a matter of fact manner, providing no clue as to how nervous he is.

Pastwa attempts to convey the appearance he is comfortable and calm when he is actually quite the opposite. Since discovering Ken's complete background he's been seriously torn over what to do; his duty to the Navy or what he believes to be his moral duty.

"Sir, Lieutenant Yamura and I have been engaged in a great deal of research based upon the contents of a ship's logbook we recovered from the grave. The log I refer to is the same one being reprinted in the paper."

Ken appears interested, but not surprised.

"Really? I fail to understand what any of that would have to do with me."

Yamura and Pastwa quickly exchange uncomfortable glances as Ken is not making this any easier.

"Sir, forgive me, but I really must be blunt." Pastwa's voice is firm, but calm.

"Commander, please proceed. Tell us what it is that has brought you so far from Pearl Harbor tonight." Ken's voice is equally calm.

"Lieutenant Yamura and I have reason to believe, in fact we have very good reason to believe you are Lieutenant Commander Masaharu Yokoyama, a Japanese national, a 1939 graduate of the Imperial Japanese Naval Academy at Eta Jima and commander of the Imperial Japanese Navy midget submarine, *I-16-tou.*"

Pastwa and Yamura glance, alternately, first at Ken then at Sun, neither of whom flinches. If this were a poker game nobody would guess the elderly couple is holding a losing hand. After a few moments of silence Ken takes a deep breath. Instinctively Sun offers him a hand which he firmly clasps.

"Commander, Lieutenant, I have great respect for your research and congratulate you both on your thoroughness." Ken pauses as he gathers his thoughts. While on the one hand, Ken knew this moment was coming, on the other hand, he had been praying he would be proven wrong.

"You are correct, of course. I am that man. I assume you likely have many questions for me, but am I correct in thinking you must first place me under arrest and take me to your headquarters?"

Pastwa and Yamura appear genuinely surprised.

"Sir, we do have questions, but please, rest assured we have seen your service records with the United States Army. We are keenly, if not outright painfully aware you have served this country very well and without reservation. Sir, we have not come here this evening to place you under arrest, so please place yourself at ease." Pastwa turns to face Sun.

"And you, Mrs. Kida, we did not come here to take advantage of your gracious hospitality only to arrest your husband."

"That's correct, we have no intention of arresting anyone here," adds Yamura. "But Captain, we are very curious about how you could transform yourself from foe to friend in a relatively short period of time. After all, it is well known that when Kazuo Sakamaki was captured on December 8th and became Prisoner of War Number One he was quite fanatical and appeared intent on committing suicide, yet you volunteered to enter the Nisei brigade."

"Yes, we have both conjectured about that," says Pastwa. "We don't seek to take anything away from your service record, but to gain a better understanding of you is our goal. So please, provide us with your thoughts."

Ken sits a little further back in his chair as Sun adjusts herself so she can continue to hold at least one of Ken's hands.

"When I was first here, and by here I mean on Oahu, I heard rumors to the effect Hawaii was to be invaded. As you can imagine I had very little knowledge with respect to the overall scope of the planned attack on Pearl Harbor so I considered the rumors to be plausible. My initial thinking was that failing to obtain transport to the *I-16*, I would need to stay undercover for only a short period after which my then-countrymen would storm ashore and I would be reunited with my fleet." Ken pauses to gather his thoughts. "Of course that never came to pass." Ken pauses yet again as he struggles to maintain his composure.

"After I buried my engineer, it was arranged for me to live on a small pineapple plantation owned by an elderly Japanese couple. Life on the plantation was very simple and straight-forward. The work I was assigned was mostly office in nature, but I had the opportunity to interact with the field workers when I made the daily rounds with the plantation's owner. In that manner I witnessed, first hand, all the effort expended in running the plantation. I learned the names of all the employees, and, yes, they were all either Japanese Nationals or Nisei. Japanese was the language of first choice on the plantation so my practice of English was limited to private discussions with the owner and his wife, but I digress. If Gary was here he would confirm my tendency to carry my thoughts out on tangents, so please forgive me."

"Of course Captain." Pastwa finds himself unconsciously leaning forward, keenly interested in what Ken has to say.

"I was describing plantation life. It was a simple life and wages were low, but I was impressed by how well everyone conducted themselves and the extent of their happiness and contentment, even though they did not have an Emperor for guidance. I was, quite frankly, perplexed and bewildered."

Ken leans a little forward, as if for emphasis.

"Then one day the United States Army appeared with rifles and trucks and they took us all to an internment camp. They said they were protecting us, but all the machine guns and guard towers faced inwards, not out. It was clear that we were prisoners." Ken pauses as he lets out a soft sigh.

"At first I thought surely everyone would rebel, but it soon became clear that almost everyone understood the reason why they were not being trusted by the American Army. Oh my goodness! Some of the people I met in the first internment camp had even been in the Hawaii National Guard and there they were; prisoners. Everyone had been forced to abandon their homes and businesses without notice so I felt the situation would be ripe to foster a rebellion, but I did not yet understand the strength of the backbone my fellow captives possessed. Nor would I risk exposing myself when I was of the belief nobody would follow me."

"We were not being treated all that unkindly, but we could not leave the compound. There were some guards who were openly hostile and prejudiced, but they never exhibited that behavior if an officer was around. I took that to mean prejudicial treatment was not actively sanctioned. All in all, it was not a completely terrible life in the camp, but it was most certainly a *prison* camp."

Ken pauses long enough to release Sun's hand and take a long drink of tea. He retakes her hand and gets himself ready to continue.

"After a little time passed, they moved us to California. The boat ride was extremely uncomfortable, to say the least. The conditions on board were near-barbaric; the food was scarce and barely edible and medical attention was non-existent. Some people died and after about three days at sea I calculated a manner in which we could take over the ship so I could sail all of us to Japanese waters. However, each time I carefully attempted to open the topic of mutiny, I was met with stiff resistance. I was consistently advised to be patient and eventually things would get better."

"The conditions in California were much better, though the facilities were basically makeshift and temporary in nature. There were classes and various educational and social activities and I was learning the history of the United States, only it was not under the color of Japanese National dictum. And there were missionaries present who allowed me to familiarize myself with the concept of Christianity which seemed to convey a belief in love for man by his fellow man, not unlike Buddhism. Slowly my views softened and I came to formulate both an understanding and an appreciation for my fellow internees. And, of course, I was expecting to spend the rest of the war, perhaps even beyond, in captivity. However, one day the Army passed out questionnaires directed at all Nisei men of a certain age. After significant meditation and calling upon my ancestors for guidance, I completed the form and returned it."

"To win admission to the Naval Academy I had to beat out ninety five percent of the candidates, so it was my opinion there was no way the United States Army would reject me." Ken pauses as he looks from Pastwa to Yamura. "I can see from the expressions on your faces that you are perplexed at my application." Ken resituates himself, smiles at Sun and continues.

"I considered myself a Samurai and, of course, had studied the way of the Samurai and conducted my life accordingly. My Father, his father and his father before that, and so on, were Samurai. Here I was, thousands of miles removed from the war in which I had been engaged and had no cause of my own for which to fight any longer. I was a Samurai relieved of his Master, so I acted as a proper Samurai and 'borrowed the battlefield.' Literally, I borrowed the cause of the United States and was under the impression that Germany and Italy would be my new enemies. Except, to my great shock and not without some dismay, the army chose not to send me to Europe."

Ken pauses as he again looks at Pastwa and Yamura, both of whom are clearly taking in all he has to say and neither of whom, in Ken's opinion, appears to be experiencing disbelief.

"As you probably know it was my language skills that caught the attention of Army Intelligence. In particular, I was noticed by an officer in the India-Burma-China theatre. So I found myself taking a very long trip to a very difficult arena in which to fight a war." Ken pauses long enough to indulge in another sip of his tea.

"There were very bad living conditions in Burma. Infestations of biting insects and the diseases they brought with them were common among all of us. In fact I still carry the Malaria bug within my body. However, I felt very useful. Sometimes I would interrogate Japanese prisoners of war, but most of the time I was translating conversations between English speaking officers and Chinese officers. I was quite happy in my role with the United States Army and for the most part had been stationed to the rear of the front lines."

"I am sure you are aware that in the United States Army the officers treat the rank-and-file as if they are human beings which is very unlike the Japanese army at the time. So, yes, I felt good to be with them and was proud to have been made a Sergeant. I was becoming 'Americanized,' as they say; perhaps you might call me an American Samurai." Ken allows himself a small smile at his self-description.

"Despite papers that state I am Nisei and my service in two wars, I have never cast a vote in any election here. It is one thing to put my life on the line for this country, my adopted homeland, but I do not have the right to pretend I could vote, so I have never done so."

"Following the Korean War I was able to bring Sun to Oahu and we were married without delay. We have been blessed with eight wonderful children, all of them born here. When Sun passed her citizenship examination and was sworn in at the Honolulu Courthouse we celebrated with a large luau, complete with traditional American fireworks. It was a great moment for both of us."

Ken laughs and clasps both of Sun's hands into his own.

"It was as if it were the fourth of July that night!" Ken pauses and turns more serious.

"I always knew that one day the body of my friend would be found. He was an excellent engineer, sailor, loyal friend and I still miss him. As you know, it was a torpedo I fired that sank your *Oklahoma* and to this day I am haunted by the memory of watching sailors desperately scrambling for their lives as they sought to stay above water while she rolled over." An uncomfortable silence momentarily fills the room.

"Oh, forgive me." Sun, noticing Ken's fighting back tears suddenly releases his hand and seeks to lighten the tone. "Can I offer you some of these delicious cookies, or perhaps some cake?" Yamura smiles in response to the offer.

"Why that's very kind of you, but it's not necessary. We really need to be leaving soon, Mrs. Kida."

"Yes, Karen's quite right. We have an appointment with an Admiral and we very well can't leave an Admiral waiting, can we Captain?" Pastwa smiles as he looks towards Ken.

"Of course not, Commander. It is bad form to make your commanding officer wait."

"There is one other thing," injects Yamura, "speaking of Admirals, did you ever have occasion to meet Admiral Yamamoto?"

At the mention of Admiral Yamamoto, Ken perks up and smiles broadly.

"Yes, indeed. Admiral Yamamoto summoned us to his flagship, the *Nagato*. He gave a speech and then invited us all to dinner where he made many toasts and honored us with his story telling. He was very interested in each of us and knew our names, which very much impressed me and made it very clear he expected to host us again after completing our mission. I was humbled and proud to have met such a great naval officer. Indeed, in my opinion he was also a modest and most compassionate man."

Meeting someone who actually spoke with Admiral Yamamoto is quite a thrill for her, in part because she had made Yamamoto the subject of one of her theory papers back at the Academy.

"Thank you for that Sir. I've read a great deal about him and am of the opinion it was lucky for us Japan only had one like him."

Pastwa stands, followed by Yamura.

"Sir, we thank you very much for your hospitality but we really must be going." Pastwa turns to face Sun. "And Mrs. Kida I apologize for not having the time to sample what I am certain is your excellent baking."

Sun smiles, but doesn't say a word. She's not quite sure what's happening and believes it's probably best to simply say nothing.

"Perhaps I will be seeing you again soon?" Ken asks.

"No Sir, that's not very likely." Pastwa retrieves his hat from a side table, picks up Yamura's and hands it to her. "We must be off now. Again, Mrs. Kida, thank you for your generous hospitality."

Pastwa, followed by Yamura, offer their salute to Ken. Surprised, he returns the salutes and looks towards the French doors where Gary is lingering.

"Gary, please escort our honorable guests to the front door."

"Yes grandfather, no problem."

Ken and Sun smile as they watch Gary escort them towards the front entry. In a few moments they overhear Gary bidding them goodbye, followed by the 'clunk' of the front door being pushed closed. Gary comes running into the study, appearing confused and scared.

"What the heck just happened here? Are they coming back? Are you under arrest?"

"Calm down. I don't know the answers to your questions. However, they appear to be very honorable officers and they did state it is unlikely I will see them again." Ken takes a deep breath, pulls Sun's hands into his own and says, "We shall see what we shall see."

CHAPTER THIRTY THREE
A RETRACTION

Seated at three chairs lined left to right and directly facing Editor-in-Chief James Mori's very large teakwood desk are Pastwa, Reardon and Yamura. Standing behind Pastwa is Clarke, who notices Mori's wall clock is slow as it indicates it's only 8 a.m., while Clarke's watch clearly indicates it is actually five minutes later. He resists the instinct to adjust the clock. Two Shore Patrol Sergeants are blocking the doorway from any potential intruders.

Mori is sitting rather uncomfortably in his leather chair and Lani Gale is sitting on a folding chair next to him. She's suspicious of the reason for calling such an early meeting and is of the opinion the Navy is about to try and muscle them into backing down from their search for Yokoyama. Gale is braced for a fight.

Reardon, wearing every medal and ribbon ever accorded him is dressed to impress. He also made certain Pastwa, Yamura, and even Clarke, are similarly attired. He pulls his chair slightly closer to the desk and leans towards Mori.

"Now Jim, I have known you a long time, but stealing classified documents and printing them along with the results of what was, at the time, an *incomplete* investigation is some mighty serious business!"

"Roman, let me…" Mori starts to speak, but Reardon cuts him off.

"Don't even think about playing the friendship card with me Jim. If you'd simply taken a moment to call me and seek confirmation I would have made it clear you were toying with the commission of felonious and traitorous acts; I think the more accurate term may be sedition. To make matters worse, our tests results weren't even conclusive yet." Reardon pauses to let the words sink in. He glances at Gale, who's beginning to appear a little uneasy.

"Guess what Jim? The lab results are in now!" He tosses a large manila envelope at Mori who catches it and lays it on his desk without opening it.

"This whole thing is a hoax and if I learn you've been a part of it, may heaven help you! I promise all hell and a whole lot more will come down upon your head and you'll be shoveling wet shit for the next ten years!" Reardon's veins are starting to protrude along either temple and his face is turning deep red as he motions to Yamura, who takes his cue:

"When my tests came back it was apparent the materials used in making the so-called 'ship's log' were not available before 1972 and there was a chemical present on the metal case that would have the effect of speeding along the decaying process. In short, somebody put this together to look as if it had been buried there since 1941."

"Thank you Lieutenant. And Jim, there's still the matter of the body we recovered." Reardon's tone is menacing.

"Obviously some poor soul was murdered. We don't know who, but since the body was not discovered on U. S. Government property we are obliged to turn the entire matter over to the local homicide squad."

Reardon leans forward in his chair for additional emphasis.

"So you should be expecting a visit from Honolulu homicide soon."

Reardon adjusts himself to face Gale. "And that brings me to the matter of charges against you and your newspaper." Reardon angles himself so he can stare directly at a very pale-faced Gale. Mori looks to be on the brink of losing his composure, along with last night's dinner.

"Wait a minute, please, Roman," implores Mori, "we had no idea it was all a big fake."

"Just how does that mitigate anything Jim? You and Gale pilfered 'Top Secret' documents and then you finished off your illegal, seditious and immoral activities by publishing them!"

"Roman, wait, what if we were to publish a complete retraction tomorrow? Full front page! We admit we were fooled and that we were set up by some clever people who intended to perpetrate a hoax." Mori is pleading to the best of his ability.

Reardon sits back as he considers Mori's proposition. Pastwa, Yamura and Clarke remain silent and without facial expression. Reardon, a hint of a glimmer in his eyes, leans forward ever so slightly and lowers his voice.

"I assume 'Lois Lane' here would write the retraction, with a by-line of course."

Mori is obviously relieved.

"Of course, Admiral." Mori turns to Gale. "Get on it! I want a draft in one hour! Oh, and you'll be getting assigned to a nice cozy inner cubicle later this afternoon, so pack your stuff! Any questions Lani?"

"No Sir." Gale mumbles her reply and squeezes herself between the two SP's on her way out.

Reardon stands, followed by Pastwa and Yamura.

"Well that should do it. And listen Jim, don't let this happen again."

•　•　•　•　•

The four of them leave together and are in an elevator on their way to the first floor.

"Lieutenant Yamura." Yamura's body goes stiff. "I did some probing and discovered you placed an order to copy and bind your translation. The work order was pretty clear, you requested one copy be made and that both sets, the original and the photocopy be bound and marked as 'Top Secret-Eyes Only, One of Two and Two of Two.' However, it fell into the hands of a seaman who took it upon himself to make an extra copy, which, I assume, he proceeded to sell to Miss Gale."

"We have suspected as much, Sir." She quietly replies, expecting to be chastised, or worse.

"Well, you won't be seeing him around the base anytime soon. He's been posted to one of our weather stations in the Arctic Circle for a six month tour and that's just his warm-up. Afterwards he gets eight months down at McMurdo Station, Antarctica." Reardon startles the three of them as he suddenly laughs out loud.

"I visited one of those bases once upon a time. Miserable, simply miserable! Much worse than the brig could ever be." The bell rings signaling their arrival on the first floor and Reardon leads the procession through the front doors and onto the broad sidewalk outside. At the same moment detectives Kane and Ooha are exiting their patrol car parked nearby. They notice the uniformed naval officers and pause before Kane chides Ooha, "Don't not waste any time. Let's just get in and get out."

Pastwa, Yamura and Clarke pause outside the entry to salute, assuming the Admiral is leaving. He returns the salute and just as they are about to turn to leave themselves, he calls out to them.

"Oh, almost forgot." The three of them freeze. Thoughts run through their minds of working in the Arctic themselves for misrepresenting their findings to him. They each wonder how Reardon could have learned they faked the results.

"I just want to say I like the way you managed to tie up all the loose ends and clean up that mess. All three of you have twenty one day passes sitting on your desks, so I'll see you then." Reardon turns and walks over to a black Lincoln Town Car waiting for him. His driver is already pulling the rear door open as the three of them quickly make their way up the street.

"Damn Karen, I thought he was about to come down on us. Clarke, you didn't need to run that risk, but we do appreciate your help," says Pastwa.

"Thank you Sir. If you two don't need me, I'd like to get myself on a plane to Maui." Clarke's smile is so big it's as if he was walking into a donut shop.

"Have fun!" Yamura calls out as they watch him jump on "The Bus" bound for Pearl Harbor.

"Well Karen, we have twenty one days and my parent's beach house over in Princeville is just sitting there empty." She discerns a twinkle in his eye and knows he has a plan. "My boat's moored in Honolulu Harbor so how about we sail over to Kauai today?"

Yamura smiles and nuzzles up a little closer.

"Sounds perfect to me. How about giving me an hour or so before picking me up?"

"Done deal. I'll see you then." He gives her a gentle kiss on the lips and watches as she hails a cab and disappears into traffic.

CHAPTER THIRTY FOUR
COLONEL NAT'S

Reardon settles himself into the back seat of his Town Car and adjusts one of the cold air vents. He pulls out a bottle of water from the built in chiller, opens it and drinks nearly half the bottle in a series of large gulps. Smitty, his driver, has been watching in the rear view mirror.

"Back to the base, Admiral?"

"No Smitty, we have a few stops to make first. You know where 'Nat's Wholesale Sporting Goods' store is located?"

"Of course! He gives all military and police fifty percent off on range time and another twenty percent off on anything we buy. I'm on the range there at least twice a month!" He executes a U-turn while speaking. "I'll have you there in no time at all."

"Excellent, you can browse around the shop while I conduct some business with Nat." The Admiral settles back in his seat and pulls out the daily edition of the other Honolulu daily newspaper as he calculates it will be about a twenty minute drive.

Nat's Wholesale Sporting Goods, Army-Navy Surplus & Pawn store is owned and operated by Colonel Nha^t Nghien, who is commonly known as 'Nat,' or 'Colonel Nat.' Nat was a well-known and respected colonel in the South Vietnamese Army, renowned for executing lightening raids across the border into Laos and Cambodia where he would hit the enemy by surprise with a ferocity that earned him a price on his head. The North Vietnamese called him the "Black Death," a reference to the trademark black beret he wore, and still wears.

About six weeks before the South Vietnamese Army collapsed he suffered serious injuries while on a raid in far northwest South Vietnam. Ultimately he lost his left kidney and his left leg, below the knee. Thanks to his reputation within the U.S. Army he was flown to the hospital at Pearl for follow up surgeries. He was recovering in the Naval Hospital there when the North

Vietnamese rolled into Saigon. His application for political asylum was a slam dunk and Nat has since become a United States citizen.

While recovering from his wounds he was approached by the Central Intelligence Agency with a job proposal. With almost no money, crippled and out of work, he accepted the CIA's offer to join their Southeast Asia desk. In 1990 he retired and bought a vacant warehouse in a very tired part of Honolulu. The building features sixteen thousand square feet on the ground floor which he divided into a ten thousand square foot display room with four thousand square feet of warehouse in back with a pair of recessed loading docks. The remaining two thousand square feet serve as his offices.

On the second floor there is an additional ten thousand square feet set back from the front of the building. The pistol and archery ranges are upstairs, along with additional display space for guns, bows and ammo. He allows local gun and archery groups to use any of the three small conference rooms without charge. His twenty-four seven, three hundred sixty two day a year operation employs over sixty people, many of whom are refugees from Southeast Asia.

For anyone in the military, former military, law enforcement and fire fighters he offers large discounts on top of his already wholesale-style pricing. Nat's is also the place to go for the hard to find. If it's in any way related to firearms, outdoor sports, or Army/Navy surplus, including from the former USSR, he can get it, in the unlikely event if he doesn't already have it on hand.

Reardon has known Nat since the mid-eighties when he met him while on a special assignment in Singapore. They took an instant liking to each other and when Nat told Reardon of his plans to open a rather unique store, Reardon strongly encouraged him to do so. Since opening, Nat counts thousands of Navy personnel among his customers.

"Here we are Sir and we're in luck too, there's a parking space right outside the front door!"

"Well done, Smitty. I'll look you up when I'm finished so have some fun poking around in there. I may be an hour or so." Reardon exits the Town Car and walks into the showroom. Glancing around he spies Nat and one of his sales representatives behind a counter featuring binoculars and telescopic lenses. It looks as if Nat is explaining the operation of what appears to be night vision field glasses to a pair of customers. As Reardon walks over, Nat notices him and immediately stops what he's doing.

"Roman! It has been too long! Please, come over!" Nat motions to Reardon.

Nat's two customers turn around and give Reardon the once-over. One man, holding the night vision field glasses, is about five foot, ten inches tall, perhaps one hundred ninety pounds. He has short, curly, black hair, a deep tan and piercing deep blue eyes. He's clean shaven and is wearing a short sleeved brightly colored Hawaiian shirt which reveals no tattoos on either arm. His face is completely absent of expression.

The man standing to his right is about five foot, six inches tall and is very slender. Though he appears to be in his later twenties, his hair completely lacks any color pigmentation and hangs in straight, limp, uneven strands down to his neck. His jet black eyes sit deep in his face, which is pale as a full moon. His brightly colored shirt hangs on his bony frame and his shorts bring too much attention to his scrawny knees. Reardon isn't certain if the man is smiling or snarling.

They are one of the more oddly paired men Reardon has seen in some time. In fact, as they turn to look at him, he comes to a complete stop as the twitch in his right eye strikes him with a vengeance. Reardon momentarily closes his eye and lightly presses his right index and forefingers against the twitch which allows it to subside. Recovering from his built-in alarm system he puts on a broad smile.

"My dear friend, accept my apologies for being absent so long."

Reardon walks over to the counter where the four men are gathered. The two customers back off a little, creating some breathing space between themselves and Reardon.

"I see you are busy my friend. I can browse for a while and wait for you to finish."

"No, no, Roman." Nat motions towards his employee. "Jim can finish up. But forgive me, introductions are in order." Nat steps around the counter and takes position alongside Reardon and points to the dark-haired man.

"Admiral, these men have a sporting equipment store in Hilo. This is Cy, who runs the operation." Cy extends his right hand as he and Reardon exchange a particularly firm hand shake. Reardon finds himself fighting off the eye twitch the entire time.

"Pleased to meet you." Reardon says.

"My pleasure Sir. Never expected to bump into American royalty here. But then, this is Nat's so I shouldn't be all that surprised." His voice inflection is borderline sarcastic, but not enough to outright offend. While he strongly detests the American military Cy is aware he needs to keep good relations with Nat.

Nat nervously laughs in response. "That's a good one, 'American Royalty;' I shall remember that."

Nat points in the direction of the white haired man. "And Admiral, this is the Aussie."

Reardon accepts his hand shake. "The Aussie? That's your name?"

The Aussie doesn't release Reardon's grip and instead grips a little harder.

"Guess nick names can stick, but pardon me, I had a dingo's breakfast and I'd like to rack off so if you don't mind too much we'll just finish our business." The Aussie releases his grip and smiles, or sneers; Reardon's not sure which.

Nat interrupts before Reardon can respond. "Let's retire to my office. Coffee, Roman?"

"Why yes, that would be perfect."

Reardon and Nat walk through a nearby doorway leaving Cy and the Aussie with Nat's associate. They settle into Nat's office where a coffee machine dominates one of the countertops.

"Still drinking pure Kona, Roman?" Nat sifts through his supply of coffee packets.

"Sure, but tell me Nat, who are those two guys?"

Nat loads the coffee packet into the machine and presses a button. Blazing hot water forces itself downwards and, as if by magic, a blue mug with the Admiral's name on it is filling with the wonderful liquid that is pure Kona coffee. Nat removes the cup, hands it to Reardon, then picks out a packet of Kauai coffee and makes a cup for himself. When he has his own mug filled with his personal favorite he takes a seat behind his desk while Reardon chooses a comfortable armchair opposite him.

"I first met those two about three years ago. They run a first class sporting supply and guide operation out of downtown Hilo, over on the Big Island. The wild pig hunting industry over there has been growing and I've been selling them surplus Russian night vision goggles. The wild pig hunters go nuts over them and they are a very high profit margin item." He takes a small sip of his steaming hot coffee.

"So you really don't know much about their backgrounds?"

"Well, Cy claims to have been born in Georgetown, Virginia. Says he has a degree in engineering from MIT where he had won himself a scholarship. I have no reason to doubt him for when it comes to understanding technical issues, he is right on."

Reardon finishes his cup in a couple of large gulps, his mind racing as the energy exuded by the odd pair of customers has set off internal alarms.

"Well that covers him, but what of this 'Aussie' fellow?"

"You noticed he's a bit testy? Strikes me as someone who prefers his own company and usually doesn't talk much, which is a good thing. He seemed to not like you very much. Are you sure you never met before?" Nat takes a sip of his brew.

"How could I forget someone with pure white hair like that, black eyes, skin more pale than milk and what looks to be a perpetual snicker? No, no way I would forget that face." Reardon shakes off the memory and resettles himself deeper into his chair.

"Nat, I'm here because I need something that I am certain you can help me with."

"Excellent!" Nat grins widely. "I am always happy to be of help to you. What do you need, Roman? Anything! Just tell me what you need."

"Thanks, Nat. I knew you'd be the man. What I need is a sword, and not just any sword. And it can't be a replica either."

"Roman, if I have one sword here, I have two hundred. So can you narrow down the type of sword you are seeking?"

"Of course. It must be a sword befitting an officer of the Imperial Japanese Navy and therefore must date back to at least World War II. I prefer it be in as perfect condition as possible and if it has a suitable sheath, all the better, but that's not a requirement."

"Hhmm," Nat appears to be staring into space as he considers the request. "This wouldn't have anything to do with the story I have been reading about in the newspaper, would it?"

Reardon laughs out loud, taking Nat slightly aback.

"I just came from Jim Mori's office. You should have seen his face! I think he was going to vomit all over his desk when I told him the whole thing was an elaborate hoax and he was facing criminal prosecution. You can read all about it tomorrow and get a good laugh. In fact, next time you see Jim you might ask him about my visit with him this morning. Might be worth a grin to see him turn pale at the memory."

Nat laughs at the thought. "Wish I could have been there."

"So, can you fix me up?"

Nat contemplates for a few moments while finishing his coffee.

"You have time for another cup, if you like. I need to go out back to my private storage where I think I'll find exactly what you need."

243

"I can make it myself, my friend, so go ahead." Roman walks over to the coffee maker.

Nat smiles and quickly shuffles out the door. Reardon notices there is almost no limp in his gait today. Apparently Nat got himself a more up-to-date peg leg, he thinks to himself. Reardon picks through the collection of coffees and finds a packet of pure Kona. He loads it into the machine and watches as the black liquid, to which he has been addicted since Nat introduced him to good coffee, fills his mug.

About ten minutes pass when Nat returns carrying a sheathed sword and a file folder. He lays the sword on his desk.

"Roman, this ought to do the trick. This was taken from a Japanese Admiral by the name of Harada who committed suicide down in Cebu rather than surrender in the closing days of the war. This folder is the record confirming its authenticity."

Reardon smiles broadly as he carefully pulls the sword from its sheath. The non-cutting edge is beautifully engraved from the handle all the way to the tip. What appears to be genuine ivory is inlaid in the handle itself, as well as in the sheath. All in all it is a remarkable piece of craftsmanship.

"Nat, you have outdone yourself this time. How much do I owe you?"

Nat shakes his head from side to side. "Roman, I've had this a long time. In fact I took it as partial trade on some German World War II equipment I sold at a substantial profit. Apparently you have a good use for it so just take it and consider you owe me one somewhere down the line."

"Nat, you're truly a good man!" Reardon takes the folder and the sheathed sword.

"But do me a favor, if you could."

"What would that be?"

"Those two customers of yours, Cy and that Aussie fellow; drop me a list of their purchases over the last few years and ongoing. So long as it's not too much trouble, of course."

"I see, maybe you think something is not quite Kosher with them? Consider it done my friend."

"Thanks Nat, I'll be going now. I have a couple more stops to make."

Reardon returns to his Town Car, where Smitty awaits him. He slips into the back seat, reaches into an inside jacket pocket, pulls out a slip of paper and hands it to Smitty.

"Take me to this address, it's up in Kailua." Smitty looks at the paper and enters it into the navigation unit. Moments later the route, along with an estimated arrival time pop up.

"Be there in twenty seven minutes Sir."

Reardon smiles, looks out the window but cannot get those two men out of his mind. He has a really bad feeling about them and makes a mental note to follow up with Nat if he doesn't receive the purchase records within a week. Reardon is lost in thought when Smitty announces their arrival.

"This is it Sir."

Reardon glances at the house, picks up the sword and exits.

"I won't be long Smitty. You can leave it running." Reardon quickly walks to the front door and rings the bell. In a few moments the door slowly opens and the diminutive form of Auntie Lee appears from the shadows of her living room. She sees Reardon's uniform and is a little alarmed, which Reardon notices.

"Would you be Auntie Lee?" Reardon seeks to calm her and puts on his best smile.

"Why yes, I am. Do I know you?"

"No Auntie, but you have met some of my staff. You might remember a female lieutenant who came to excavate that skeleton from your yard?" Auntie Lee smiles and steps back as she opens the door.

"Oh yes, you must be her big boss! Please come in." She beckons him into her living room. "Can I bring you some nice iced tea and maybe some senbei? I made the senbei just an hour ago."

Reardon enters carrying the sword and folder and chooses to sit in one of her cozy armchairs. "Auntie, I would love to, but today I am pressed for time so I can't accept your generous offer." He motions to an empty chair across from where he is seated.

"Please, Auntie, take a seat. I have come here to propose a trade."

"Oh, ok." Auntie Lee sits down as directed, her attention more focused on the sheathed sword than on Reardon.

"Auntie I saw the picture of you in the newspaper holding the sword you found in your back yard. It looked to be pretty tarnished."

"Yes it is. I have been working on it, but I do not have the strength in my fingers that I once had."

"I can relate to that which is why I've brought with me a beautiful sword that once belonged to an Admiral of the Imperial Japanese Navy. He's long since dead so he has no use for it, obviously. I was thinking, however, you might prefer to trade that old sword you dug up for this beautiful one." He gives her a wink. "And this doesn't need any cleaning."

Reardon unsheathes the sword and offers it to her, handle first.

"Here, take a look for yourself. I think this would make a pretty good trade."

A huge smile sweeps across her face as she carefully takes it into her hands.

"Oh my! Look at this engraving! And this, is this ivory?"

Reardon laughs gently. "Yes, Auntie, it does appear to be genuine ivory. So what do you say, is it a deal?"

Auntie Lee carefully lays the sword onto a coffee table and quickly disappears towards the kitchen. In a few moments she returns holding the heavily tarnished sword and offers it to Reardon.

"Here, Sir! And thank you so much! You have made me so happy! Are you certain you do not have time for some nice iced tea and senbei?"

Reardon, still smiling, stands and accepts the tarnished sword from her.

"Thank you Auntie, but as I said, I'm on a tight schedule and must be going. I can see my way out, so why don't you sit down and take a good look at your new sword?"

Reardon returns to his Town Car and pulls out another piece of paper from his inside jacket pocket. Smitty is wondering to himself why the Admiral went in with a beautiful sword and returned with a tarnished one. But he knows better than to say anything.

"Here, Smitty, this is up on the North Shore somewhere."

Smitty peruses the address, enters it into the navigation system and drives away.

•　•　•　•　•

About forty minutes later they pull up to the address. Reardon takes the sword and strides to the front door where a covered lanai offers him shade from the mid-day Sun. Before he can knock, the door opens and Sun Kida is standing before him.

"Can I help you, Sir?" Reardon recognizes she is obviously nervous.

"Why yes, you can. Are you Mrs. Kida?"

Sun is surprised Reardon knows who she is, though she thinks to herself she should not be so surprised.

"Yes I am. I apologize, but I do not know who you are?"

"Well, let me introduce myself. My name is Roman Reardon, Rear Admiral Roman Reardon if you were wondering about my rank. I was hoping to have a minute of Captain Kida's time, if at all possible, ma'am."

It is only now that Sun realizes Reardon is holding a sword at his side, an old sword at that. She opens the door and gestures for him to enter.

"Please come in, Admiral; my husband's in his study."

Reardon follows her through the French doors, both of which are open and finds Ken is sitting behind his massive desk, causing him to appear even more diminutive than he is.

"Ken, this is Rear Admiral Roman Reardon." Ken begins to rise from his chair.

"No need to get up Sir, I only need a minute of your time."

"Thank you Admiral. At my age if I appreciate every opportunity to conserve my energy."

Reardon laughs. "That's a good philosophy, Captain."

He walks to Ken's desk and places the sword across the center, directly in front of Ken.

"Sir, I understand this belongs to you. I really couldn't live with myself if I failed to retrieve it for you." Reardon takes a step back from the desk.

Ken immediately recognizes the sword and his mouth drops open. Tears begin to fall down his cheeks.

"I really must be off now, Mrs. Kida so if you don't mind I'll show myself out." Reardon motions in the direction of Ken. "I think the Captain might prefer you remain here."

Neither Ken nor Sun find themselves capable of forming an answer as Reardon turns and leaves. Sun quickly moves to place her hands on the shoulders of her husband. Ken picks up the sword, but is unable to speak as he discovers he cannot repress the desire to cry.

CHAPTER THIRTY FIVE
NO LOOSE ENDS

The following morning Ken and Sun are enjoying a light breakfast on the rear lanai. The early morning calm is interrupted by the sound of Gary's car pulling into the driveway at what sounds to them to be an unusually great rate of speed. They both look towards the walkway in anticipation of Gary's appearance and in a few moments he comes running around the corner at break-neck speed, the morning newspaper in his left hand.

"Grandpa! Kapuna!" He's slightly out of breath, more from excitement than from the run.

"Gary, are you alright my boy?" Ken's voice, as is his custom, is low and calm.

"Haven't you seen this morning's paper yet?" Just then he notices the front page is spread out across the table. *"MIDGET SUB LOGBOOK A HOAX! HONOLULU POLICE OPEN INVESTIGATION OVER MYSTERY BODY. $100,000 REWARD OFFERED TO FIND PERPETRATORS!"*

CHAPTER THIRTY SIX
DR. JOHANSSON'S OFFICE

Gale enters Johansson's office and casually walks to the sofa. She kicks off her sandals, fluffs two pillows and assumes her usual position.

Yokoyama is fourth, clockwise, from lower left corner.

Yokoyama is far left, top row.

An "I" class Japanese submarine carrying a midget submarine.

Captured *I-24-tou*, sister to the *I-16-tou*, on display at the National Museum of the Pacific War in Fredericksburg, TX.

The *U.S.S. Oklahoma* after rolling over.

Note the 3 "rooster" tails and two torpedo wakes; one directed at
the *West Virginia* and one at the *Oklahoma*.

Note the stacked torpedoes and the jagged anti-submarine net cutter.

Captured *I-24-tou*.

Interior view of sister ship to *I-16-tou*.

Yokoyama's likely fatal torpedo strike against the *U.S.S. Oklahoma.* Note the significantly taller fountain rising from the port side of the *West Virginia*, anchored to the left of *Oklahoma* which is typical of the five hundred pound aerial torpedo strikes. The torpedo hit on the *Oklahoma* is much denser as the one thousand pound "Long Lance" torpedo throws significantly more water into the air, but at a lesser height due to the sheer weight of the water.

Rescue efforts to save crew trapped within the overturned *U.S.S. Oklahoma.*

Dual propeller assembly of a Japanese midget submarine. The Achille's heel of the *I-16-tou*.

***I-24-tou* lies beached and abandoned on Oahu, December 8, 1941.**

Captain of *IJN Chiyoda*, Kaku Harada

Admiral Isoroku Yamamoto

Imperial Japanese Navy submarine *I-16*. Early on December 7, 1941, she released the midget submarine, *I-16-tou*, near the entrance to Pearl Harbor.

Three Japanese destroyers docked side-by-side in Pearl Harbor, July, 2005.

WESTERN DEFENSE COMMAND AND FOURTH ARMY
WARTIME CIVIL CONTROL ADMINISTRATION
Presidio of San Francisco, California
May 23, 1942

INSTRUCTIONS
TO ALL PERSONS OF
JAPANESE
ANCESTRY
Living in the Following Area:

All of that portion of the County of Santa Clara, State of California, lying generally north and northwest of the following boundary: Beginning at the point on the Santa Cruz-Santa Clara County line, due west of a line drawn through the peak of Loma Prieta; thence due east along said line through said peak to its intersection with Llagas Creek; thence downstream along said creek toward Madrone to the point where it is crossed by Llagas Avenue; thence northeasterly on Llagas Avenue to U.S. Highway No. 101; thence northerly on said Highway No. 101 to Cochran Road; thence northeasterly on Cochran Road to its junction with Steeley Road; thence easterly on Steeley Road to Madrone Springs; thence along a line projected due east from Madrone Springs to its intersection with the Santa Clara-Stanislaus County line; together with all portions of Santa Clara County not previously covered by Exclusion Orders of this Headquarters.

Pursuant to the provisions of Civilian Exclusion Order No. 96, this Headquarters, dated May 23, 1942, all persons of Japanese ancestry, both alien and non-alien, will be evacuated from the above area by 12 o'clock noon, P. W. T., Saturday, May 30, 1942.

No Japanese person will be permitted to move into, or out of, the above area after 12 o'clock noon, P. W. T., Saturday, May 23, 1942, without obtaining special permission from the representative of the Commanding General, Northern California Sector, at the Civil Control Station located at:

Men's Gymnasium,
San Jose State College,
4th and San Carlos Streets,
San Jose, California.

Such permits will only be granted for the purpose of uniting members of a family, or in cases of grave emergency.

The Civil Control Station is equipped to assist the Japanese population affected by this evacuation in the following ways:

1. Give advice and instructions on the evacuation.
2. Provide services with respect to the management, leasing, sale, storage or other disposition of most kinds of property, such as real estate, business and professional equipment, household goods, boats, automobiles and livestock.
3. Provide temporary residence elsewhere for all Japanese in family groups.
4. Transport persons and a limited amount of clothing and equipment to their new residence.

The Following Instructions Must Be Observed:

1. A responsible member of each family, preferably the head of the family, or the person in whose name most of the property is held, and each individual living alone, will report to the Civil Control Station to receive further instructions. This must be done between 8:00 A. M. and 5:00 P. M. on Sunday, May 24, 1942, or between 8:00 A. M. and 5:00 P. M. on Monday, May 25, 1942.
2. Evacuees must carry with them on departure for the Assembly Center, the following property:
   (a) Bedding and linens (no mattress) for each member of the family;
   (b) Toilet articles for each member of the family;
   (c) Extra clothing for each member of the family;
   (d) Essential personal effects for each member of the family.

All items carried will be securely packaged, tied and plainly marked with the name of the owner and numbered in accordance with instructions obtained at the Civil Control Station. The size and number of packages is limited to that which can be carried by the individual or family group.

3. No pets of any kind will be permitted.
4. No personal items and no household goods will be shipped to the Assembly Center.
5. The United States Government through its agencies will provide for the storage, at the sole risk of the owner, of the more substantial household items, such as iceboxes, washing machines, pianos and other heavy furniture. Cooking utensils and other small items will be accepted for storage if crated, packed and plainly marked with the name and address of the owner. Only one name and address will be used by a given family.
6. Each family, and individual living alone, will be furnished transportation to the Assembly Center. Private means of transportation will not be utilized. All instructions pertaining to the movement will be obtained at the Civil Control Station.

Go to the Civil Control Station between the hours of 8:00 A. M. and 5:00 P. M.,
Sunday, May 24, 1942, or between the hours of 8:00 A. M. and 5:00 P. M.,
Monday, May 25, 1942, to receive further instructions.

J. L. DeWITT
Lieutenant General, U. S. Army
Commanding

SEE CIVILIAN EXCLUSION ORDER NO. 96

Marcus A. Nannini

Marcus Nannini began his journalistic career when he published his own newspaper in the sixth grade, charging twenty five cents for the privilege of reading the only printed copy of each edition. During his undergraduate years Nannini was a paid reporter and worked three semesters as the research assistant for journalism professor and published author Richard Stocks Carlson, Ph.D.

Nannini is a life-long history buff with a particular interest in World War II and the Pearl Harbor attack. His continuing curiosity over several Japanese aerial photographs and the turtling of the *U.S.S. Oklahoma* lead him to write *Chameleons*, first as a screenplay and now as a full-length novel.

Many months of research were devoted to *Chameleons*, underscoring Nannini's efforts to painstakingly recreate the experiences of his protagonist, "Ken Kida," both prior to, and following the Japanese attack on that fateful Sunday morning, December 7, 1941.

Nannini has six World War II non-fiction magazine articles appearing in *World at War* and *Strategy and Tactics* magazines in the near future. His next novels in the series, *Geographic Treachery* and *Vigorous Brutality*, will soon be available. Look for the Big Screen version of his non-fiction magazine story, Left for Dead at Nijmegen, which will be titled *Dinner with Himmler*.

ADDITIONAL NOVELS:

GEOGRAPHIC TREACHERY

Commander Pastwa and his team find themselves in a desperate battle with terrorists hell-bent on high-jacking three heavily armed Army helicopters and attacking the supercarrier *U. S. S. Abraham Lincoln* while she participates in the December 7th Memorial Ceremonies in Pearl Harbor.

VIGOROUS BRUTALITY

Reeling from a series of brutal murders, Commander Pastwa and his team struggle to learn the underlying motive of the terrorists. Perhaps too late, they discover a North Korean submarine is about to execute a midnight torpedo attack against a luxury cruise liner while she's still over one hundred miles away from the Big Island.

View other Black Rose Writing titles at www.blackrosewriting.com/books and
use promo code **PRINT** to receive a **20% discount** when purchasing.

BLACK ROSE
writing™

Made in the USA
Middletown, DE
28 November 2017